THE LIAR'S LULLABY

Meg Gardiner

LARGE PRINT

Oxford

First published in Great Britain 2010
by
Blue Door
an imprint of HarperCollins Publishers

Published in Large Print 2011 by ISIS Publishing Ltd.,
7 Centremead, Osney Mead, Oxford OX2 0ES
by arrangement with
HarperCollins Publishers

British Library Cataloguing in Publication Data
Gardiner, Meg.
    The liar's lullaby.
    1. Beckett, Jo (Fictitious character) - - Fiction.
    2. Forensic psychiatrists - - California - - San
    Francisco - - Fiction.
    3. Stalking victims - - Fiction.
    4. Singers - - Crimes against - - Fiction.
    5. Presidents - - United States - - Fiction.
    6. Suspense fiction.
    7. Large type books.
    I. Title
    823.9'2–dc22

ISBN 978–0–7531–8848–4 (hb)
ISBN 978–0–7531–8849–1 (pb)

THE LIAR'S LULLABY

21 MAR 2014

9.4 14

SOH 2/15

BOR
FICY

CHI
DEC '12

Get **more** out of libraries

Please return or renew this item by the last date shown.
You can renew online at www.hants.gov.uk/library
Or by phoning Hampshire Libraries
Tel: 0300 555 1387

Hampshire
County Council

C014971961

For Eleanor

CHAPTER
ONE

Hack Shirazi braced himself in the open door of the helicopter and gazed across San Francisco Bay at the crowded ballpark. Wind and engine noise buffeted him. The evening sun bisected his field of vision. The check had cleared, so he was going to deliver the Rambo. But they were running late, which put the failing gold light square in his eyes.

He shoved the banana clip into the Kalashnikov. "On my mark."

In the helicopter flying alongside them, the second team positioned themselves in the doorway. They swept over the bay toward the city. Whitecaps foamed on the surface of the water, five hundred feet below. In the pilot's seat, Andreyev held tight to the controls.

The Giants' ballpark was filled to capacity. People jammed the stands and covered the field from home plate to the centerfield stage. The two Bell 212 choppers would fly beyond it, circle back, and make their run at the target from out of the sun.

Andreyev radioed their man on the ground. "Rock and roll."

★ ★ ★

In the stands below, Rez Shirazi put a hand to his radio earpiece. "I hear you."

Rock and roll was just about all he could hear. It echoed from the bleachers along the foul line, where beer-marinated rednecks whooped to the beat. From the teeming field, where sunburned college girls sang along with the saccharine lyrics. From the corporate hospitality suites on either side of him, where venture capitalists sipped mojitos and dipped five-dollar tortilla chips in mango chutney salsa.

Shirazi shook his head. Ersatz rock and roll — drowned in country-western cheese sauce. Tasteless, drippy American cheese.

Through his earpiece, he heard his brother Hack. "Four minutes. Mark."

Rez clicked the timer on his watch. "Mark."

On the stage, near towering speakers that amplified their cornpone accent, a choir of backup patriots was woo-wooing, while a singer in two-thousand-dollar cowboy boots wailed about the trials of the common man.

You can take my work, you can take my cash . . .
but if you won't shake my hand, I'll light a fire up
your —

"Ass," Shirazi said.

The surrounding suites were jammed. People crowded the interiors and filled rows of seats on the balcony. But Rez's suite was empty: no food, absolutely no drink, no loiterers. He stepped onto the balcony and checked their gear. The CO^2 canisters were in place. The zip line was secure. It was a stainless steel aircraft cable, clamped through a forged eyebolt and anchored to the girders that supported the upper deck of the stadium. He glanced at the video camera, then over the edge of the balcony. The drop was substantial.

Andreyev's voice crackled through the radio. "I can't see her on video. Is she there?"

On cue, the door to the suite opened. Noise flowed in from the hallway outside. Tasia McFarland stormed in.

"Rez, they're following me. Get rid of them. I can't do this with all these people harassing me."

His nerves fired at the sight of her. "She's here." For a millisecond his skin itched and his ears thundered. "Oh, brother."

In his ear, Hack sounded sharp. "What's wrong?"

Tasia already had the climbing harness cinched around her hips. That was no mean feat. She was wearing a magenta corset, which trailed back into ruffles that dragged on the floor. Beneath it she wore ripped jeans and turquoise cowboy boots. The top half of her looked like Scarlett O'Hara halfway through a striptease. The bottom half looked like she'd escaped a cage fight with a rabid badger.

Behind her, people streamed through the door. Stadium security men. A make-up artist. A wardrobe assistant. The soundman.

She spun on them. "Stop hounding me. You're turning my head into a beehive. I can't think. Get out. Rez, get them *out*."

3

Rez put up his hands. "Okay. Chill."

Her eyes gleamed, jade bright. "Chill? This is an event. This is a supernova. I'm at the shore of the Rubicon. And these" — she waved at the entourage — "these vampires are filling my head with static. They're filling the score with noise and I won't be able to hear what I need to hear to protect myself out there. Get them *out*."

In his ear, Rez heard the director in the control booth. "Crap. Is she melting down?"

"You got it." Rez gestured the entourage back. "You heard the lady. Everybody out."

The make-up girl pointed at Tasia in dismay. "Look at her. She's been playing in the crayon box."

Rez pushed the girl toward the door.

The security men glowered. "This breaches protocol."

"It's not a problem," Rez said. "We've done the stunt a dozen times."

The soundman shook his head. "Her radio mike, she —"

"I got this." Rez ushered the last of the crowd from the suite.

The soundman shouted over his shoulder. "It's on your head, man."

"I'm the stunt coordinator. It's always on my head." Rez shut the door.

"Lock it," Tasia said.

Rez flipped the bolt. Tasia stalked around the room, glancing at corners and the ceiling, examining the shadows. Her ruffles trailed behind her like a peacock's plumage.

4

"I used to think fame was a shield. But it won't protect me. It's only made me a target," she said.

Rez glanced at his watch. "Celebrity's tough."

"Tough? It's a life sentence. And life's a bitch, and I'm a bitch, and then you die. Like Princess Di."

Over the radio, Andreyev said, "Three minutes. We are inbound, beginning our run."

"Roger," Rez said.

In three minutes a computer program would set the special effects sequence in motion, and Tasia would make her grand entrance as the helicopters overflew the ballpark. And she was blowing a damned cylinder.

"And I'm not camera shy. But there's an eye in the sky, watching me. Satellites, NSA, paparazzi. On TV, online, whenever I turn my back. I'm in their sights. Fawn in the headlights. Doe in the brights. Do, re, mi, fa, so long, suckers."

She stalked out the plate-glass doors onto the balcony and stared down at the forty thousand people who filled the ballpark. The music bounced off the glass, distorted echoes of the Star-Spangled chorus.

Rez followed her outside. "Let's get you rigged. It's going to be fine. It's just a stunt."

The breeze off the bay lifted her hair from her neck like swirls of caramel smoke. "It was a stunt in the movie. But in the movie, the star didn't do this. You know why?"

Because she's sane. "Because she's not you."

Because the star wasn't as ravenous for stage time as Tasia McFarland. Because the star wasn't brave or wild enough to hook herself to a zip line and fly forty feet over the heads of the crowd as fireworks went off from the scoreboard, singing the title song from the movie.

Bull's-eye was the latest in a series of action films that featured guns and slinky women. *Long Barrel. Pump Action.* The stuntmen had their own names for these movies. *Handguns and Hand Jobs. Planes, Trains, and Blown Brains.*

But the flick was a hit, and so was "Bull's-eye," the song. Tasia McFarland was top of the charts. And she wanted to stay there.

"Movie stars don't do their own stunts because they don't know jack about life and death," she said.

Her eyes shone. Her make-up looked like an over-stimulated six-year-old had applied it after peeping at *Maxim*.

"Stop staring at me like that," she said. "I'm sober. I'm clean."

Too clean? Rez thought, and his face must have shown it, because Tasia shook her head.

"And I'm not off my meds. I'm just wound up. Let's go."

"Great." Rez forced encouragement into his voice. "It'll be a breeze. Like Denver. Like Washington."

"You're a lousy liar." She smiled. It looked unhappy. "I like that, Rez. It's the good liars who get you."

In his ear, Andreyev's voice rose in pitch. "Two minutes."

Tasia's gaze veered from the empty suite to the heaving field. She squirmed against the tight fit of her jeans.

6

"The harness feels wrong." She pulled on it. "I have to adjust it."

A carabiner was already clipped to the harness. Rez reached for it. She slapped his hand. "Go inside and turn around. Don't look."

He glared, but she pushed him back. "I can't sing if my crotch is pinched by this damned chastity belt. Go."

And she thought that adjusting her panties in full view of a stadium crowd was the modest option? But he remembered rule number one: Humor the talent. Reluctantly he went inside and turned his back.

Behind him the plate-glass doors slammed shut. He spun and saw Tasia lock the doors.

"Hey." Rez shook the door handles. "What are you doing?"

She grabbed a chair and jammed it under the handles.

"This isn't a stunt, Rez. He's after me. This is life and death."

On the field, sunburned, thirsty, crammed on a plastic chair surrounded by thousands of happy people, Jo Beckett sank lower in her seat.

The band was blasting out enough decibels to blow up the sonar on submarines in the Pacific. The song, "Banner of Fire," was hard on the downbeat and on folks who didn't love buckshot, monster trucks, and freedom. The singer, Searle Lecroix, was a pulsing figure: guitar slung low, lips nearly kissing the mike. A black Stetson tipped down across his forehead, putting his eyes in shadow. The guitar in his hands was painted in stars and stripes, and probably tuned to the key of U.S.A.

The young woman beside Jo climbed on her chair, shot her fists in the air, and cried, "*Woo!*"

Jo grabbed the hem of the woman's T-shirt. "Tina, save it for the Second Coming."

Tina laughed and flicked Jo's fingers away. "Snob."

Jo rolled her eyes. When she'd offered her little sister concert tickets for her birthday, she figured Tina would pick death metal or *Aida*, not Searle Lecroix and the *Bad Dogs and Bullets* tour.

Despite her taste in music, Tina looked like a junior version of Jo: long brown curls, lively eyes, compact, athletic physique. But Jo wore her combats and Doc Martens and had her UCSF Medical Center ID in her backpack and her seen-it-all, early thirties attitude in her hip pocket. Tina wore a straw cowboy hat, a nose ring, and enough silver bangles to stock the U.S. Mint. She was the human version of caffeine.

Jo couldn't help but smile at her. "You're a pawn of the Military-Nashville complex."

"Sicko. Next you'll say you don't love puppies, or the baby Jesus."

Jo stood up. "I'm going to the snack bar. Want anything?"

Tina pointed at Lecroix. "Him. Hot and buttered."

Jo laughed. "Be right back."

She worked her way to the aisle and headed for the stands. Overhead, sunlight glinted off metal. She looked up and saw a steel cable, running from a luxury suite to the stage. It looked like a zip line. She slowed,

8

estimating the distance from the balcony to the touchdown point. It was a long way.

A second later, she heard helicopters.

Andreyev put the Bell 212 through a banking turn and lined up for the pass above the ballpark. The second helicopter flanked him. The sunset flared against his visor.

"Ninety seconds," he said. "Rez, is Tasia ready to go?"

He got no reply. "Rez?"

He glanced at the video monitor. It showed the balcony of the luxury suite.

He did a double take. The doors to the suite were jammed shut with a chair. Rez was inside, rattling the doorknob.

On the balcony Tasia stood with her back to him. She reached around to her back pocket, beneath the extravagant ruffles that trailed from her corset.

"Shit. Shit. *Shit*," Andreyev said.

From the door of the chopper, Hack Shirazi shouted, "What's going on?"

Andreyev yelled into the radio. "Rez, she's got a gun."

CHAPTER
TWO

Rez pounded on the plate-glass door. "Tasia, open it. For God's sake, nobody's after you."

In his ear Andreyev shouted at him. ". . . a gun. Rez, stop her."

Rez put his hand over his earpiece. Tasia turned around. In her right hand she held a pistol.

"What are you doing with that?" he said.

The gun was a big mutha. It was a goddamned Colt .45 automatic.

"Is that from Props?"

"It's from the department of authenticity," she said. "With a grand finale, it always comes down to a gun."

"On-screen, not in real life. Put it down."

"You keep thinking this is a show. So call this a solo with high-caliber backup."

"That thing drops on somebody's head and we're sued up the wazoo. Don't get me fired." He rattled the door again. "You can't take a weapon out there."

She smiled angrily. "Everybody else involved in this stunt has a gun."

"But theirs are fake."

"Exactly." She held up the pistol. "Fame can't protect me. Just Samuel Colt. And my music, 'cause the voice is mightier than the sword. Melody, harmony, counterpoint, lyrics. Remember that — if they get me, remember. The truth is in my music. Number one with a bullet, glory, halle-*lu*-jah."

"Nothing's going to happen, Tasia." Rez raised his hands placatingly. "Please put it down."

"Do you think I'm an asshole? I won't drop it." Her eyes swam with a feverish heat. "God, you actually think it's loaded."

For a moment her swirling hair took on the look of snakes. But the snakes were only in her head.

From the chopper, Andreyev said, "Is the gun a prop? Rez?"

"I don't know."

Tasia's voice hit him low and sharp, like a blade. "No, you don't. You have no idea what's out there. What's waiting. I'm talking about violence. I'm talking about propaganda of the deed. I'm talkin' 'bout a revolution — yeah, you know, we all want to change the world."

In his ear, Rez heard the director. "What's happening? Shirazi, for the love of Christ, what's she doing?"

"Tasia, put down the weapon."

She shook her head. "I put it down, and he gets me. Then it's open season. Car bombs in cities. Death squads cutting down women and children." She held the gun up, and turned it, seemingly checking that it had all its working pieces. "I used to think they wouldn't dare. But I was naïve. I was a child. A freaking child, playing around. Round, round, get around."

"What are you talking about?"

"Martyrdom."

Rez felt faint.

"It ain't always religious. Sometimes it's ungodly, and sometimes it's at the hands of the angels, not the devil. And this gun is from the source, the alpha and omega."

She grabbed her carabiner and clipped it to the trolley cable that hung from the zip line.

Into his radio, Rez said, "Get security. Send them through the luxury suites on either side of us and grab her."

Tasia turned abruptly and stared at him. "I told him. Warned him. So he's heard me. But he's going to hear me again, right now, a whole lot louder."

Jesus. "Come on, T—"

She waved the gun haphazardly in his direction. He flinched. She turned back to the crowd.

"Secret Service would have scoped it out beforehand."

Oh, crap.

"But they won't protect me. *Au contraire.* Loose cannon, loose lips, loose woman. I am on my own and in their sights. So it's just me and my music and the peacemaker here."

Onstage, the band segued into the intro to "Bull's-eye." On cue, the CO_2 canisters rigged around the balcony began discharging. Clouds of white smoke swirled around Tasia.

Shirazi stared at the barrel of the Colt. He had no way to determine whether the gun was loaded.

"Tasia, if there's a problem, come inside and let security handle it. You can't take a gun onstage. You'll terrify the crowd."

"No, I won't." She smiled again, darkly. "Watch me."

The director shouted in his ear. "Grab her."

"I'm trying. Did you call security?" Rez shook the plate-glass door one last time. He ran across the suite, opened the main door, and leaned into the hall. The corridor was crowded. A guard was loitering nearby.

Rez waved at him. "Tasia's locked on the balcony, freaking out. Go through the suite next door and grab her."

Behind him, she called, "Rez, you idiot. He'll get in."

The security guard hustled to the adjoining suite and pounded on the door. Rez ran back to the plate-glass windows. Tasia looked manic and distraught, her face blurred by the swirling CO_2.

"I can't let this happen." She turned on her headset mike and began gesturing to the people sitting along the balcony in the adjoining suites. "Hey, everybody. Join the party."

People looked up, surprised. As if she were hosting a street party, she waved everybody toward her. They held back, unsure.

"Come on!"

"What the hell?" the director said.

First one person, then another, stood up and climbed over the low barriers from the balconies of adjoining boxes. Then they all came. They swarmed over the barriers and mobbed her.

"Damn," Rez shouted into his radio. "She's surrounding herself with people so the security guards can't get to her."

More CO^2 canisters lit off. Dozens of fans, hundreds, crowded around Tasia before they were lost in the white mist of carbon dioxide.

And understanding swept through Shirazi. "Tasia, no."

He grabbed a chair and swung it into the plate glass. It bounced off. The pane was ultra-thick safety glass, and the blow left barely a mark.

The first round of fireworks ignited. Tasia faced the stage and raised the Colt.

CHAPTER
THREE

Standing center stage, guitar in his hands, Searle Lecroix hit the high note at the end of the verse. The crowd reached toward him, swept up in his performance like wheat pulled forward by a prairie wind. He grinned and pushed the cowboy hat down on his forehead.

In the stands behind home plate, carbon dioxide swirled around Tasia. Lecroix hit the downbeat. On cue, she began to sing.

"*Give me a shot of whiskey with a chaser of tears . . .*"

Her soprano filled the air like silver. The crowd cheered. Lecroix felt a rush.

He hit the chord change to G major. Tasia's voice gained power.

"*Give me a shot of courage, blow away all my fears . . .*"

Her magenta corset swam in and out of view through the smoke. The crowd was spilling onto the balcony around her. What on earth? And she had something in her hand. It caught the light.

A gun.

He lost the beat. The bass player glanced at him.

Theatrically, like she was a gunfighter practicing a quick draw, she swung the gun up, aimed at the stage, and pretended to pull the trigger. The second round of fireworks whizzed into the air from the stage scaffolding. Tasia jerked her hand up, miming recoil. The fireworks burst with a crackle and poured red light on the crowd.

It looked like Tasia had set them off. She raised the gun to her lips and blew on the barrel.

Wow. The girl wanted to tie the crowd in knots. Indulging herself in some fake gunplay — *Drive the guys crazy, why don't you?*

More fireworks lit off, green and white. Again Tasia raised the gun, fake-fired, and blew on the barrel.

"*Fire away, hit me straight in the heart . . .*"

Lecroix's own heart beat in double time. Above the stadium, two helicopters flew into view. The third round of fireworks burst, red, white, and blue. Tasia's voice rocketed above them.

"*Baby, give me a shot.*"

She raised the gun again. Smoke obscured her.

A sound cracked through the ballpark like cannon fire.

Below the Bell 212, the ballpark swept into view. Andreyev heard Rez yelling at him over the radio.

"The weapon's not a prop and —"

A colossal *bang* cracked through Andreyev's headphones.

"Christ." Ears ringing, he called to the pilot of the other helicopter. "Break off."

16

Was Tasia Goddamned McFarland firing at him? The second chopper veered right. Andreyev banked sharply, following it.

Hack shouted, "Too close!"

He'd banked too hard. He jerked the controls, but it was too late. His tail rotor hit the second chopper's skids.

The noise was sudden, loud, everywhere. The chopper shook like it had been hit with a wrecking ball. The tail rotor sheared off.

Hack yelled, "Andreyev —"

The chopper instantly spun, losing height. Andreyev fought with the controls. "Hang on."

The engines screamed. The view spun past Andreyev. Bay Bridge, downtown, sunset, scoreboard. *God, clear the scoreboard, get past it and ditch in the bay and don't auger into the crowd —*

"Hang, on, Hack."

The bay swelled in his windshield.

Onstage, Lecroix heard metal shearing. He glanced up. In the sky above the stadium, debris spewed from one of the stunt helicopters. The crowd gasped. The chopper spun in circles, engine whining. It keeled at a sharp angle and dropped behind the scoreboard toward the bay.

The security guards waved at the band. "Get down. Look out."

A slice of rotor blade buried itself in the stage like a hatchet.

The drummer leaped up, knocked over his kit, and hit the stage with his hands over his head. Lecroix threw down his guitar and jumped into the crowd.

A chunk of the chopper's tail plunged like a meteor into the front row seats. Screaming, the crowd fled. Lecroix fought against the tide, aiming for the stands where CO^2 canisters continued to spew white smoke.

Lightning seemed to run through him. He knew where the first God-awful banging noise had come from. And why it was deafening, infinitely louder than the pyrotechnics or guitar solo.

The gun had fired, next to Tasia's headset mike.

A gearbox slammed into the field. The flight of the crowd became a stampede. Lecroix struggled to stay upright. And from out of the smoke Tasia came sliding toward the stage on the zip line. She twirled, slow as a lariat, hanging by the harness around her hips. Her head was back, arms flung wide, as if offering herself to heaven. Blood saturated her hair. It dripped like fat tears onto the fleeing crowd. Lecroix tried to scream, but his voice was gone.

Jo ran from the snack bar toward the shouts and wailing. She heard metal slicing metal. She rounded a corner and saw mayhem.

People were racing away from the stage. Debris was raining from the sky like bright metallic confetti. Beyond the right field wall, smoke rose from the bay.

"Oh Jesus."

18

A chopper had gone down. Nausea spiked her stomach. She dropped her popcorn and ran toward the field.

"Tina," she said.

A chunk of debris smashed into the stanchion at the back of the stage that anchored the zip line. With a twanging sound, the steel cable snapped loose. It dropped like a heavy whip into the crowd.

"Dear God."

A woman was on the zip line. Jo saw her plunge helplessly into the crowd.

People poured toward her. They pushed, stumbled, fell, piled on top of one another. She tried to fight her way through them. Then, like a top note, she heard her name being called.

"Jo, here."

Tina was running in her direction. Jo pushed through the surging crowd and grabbed her.

"The helicopters collided," Tina said.

Jo pulled Tina against a pillar and watched, eyes stinging. The stampede flowed toward the right field stands. People poured over the railings and fell into the dugout.

A stadium official took the microphone and begged for calm. The screams turned into wailing and an eerie quiet in the upper reaches of the ballpark.

"What just happened?" Tina said.

"The worst stunt catastrophe in entertainment history," Jo said.

She wasn't even close.

CHAPTER
FOUR

Twilight veiled the sky, blue and starry, when Jo and Tina walked from the ballpark onto Willie Mays Plaza. But the stadium lights blazed. Police cruisers lined the street. On the bay, searchlights on a salvage barge illuminated the rough waters where the helicopter had crashed. Third Street was lit by television spotlights. The night was whiter than a starlet's red-carpet smile.

Jo hung her arm across Tina's shoulder. Exhausted and numb, they headed toward her truck.

Ahead, leaning against an unmarked SFPD car, was Amy Tang.

The young police lieutenant had a phone to her ear and a cigarette pinched between her thumb and forefinger. A uniformed officer stood before her, getting instructions. Her coal-colored suit matched her hair, her glasses, and, it seemed, her mood. Barely five feet tall, she was tiny against the Crown Vic. She looked like a disgruntled hood ornament.

Jo veered toward her. Tang looked up. Surprise brushed her face. She ended her call and dismissed the uniformed officer.

"You were at the concert?" Tang said.

"Tina was on the field."

20

Tang's mouth thinned. She glanced at her watch. Two hours had passed since the stunt disaster.

"Fire Department and paramedics were swamped. We stuck around," Jo said.

Tang nodded slowly. "Lucky thing you love country rock so much."

Tina pulled off her straw cowboy hat. Her curls were lank. "Yeah, every stadium should have a barista and a shrink on emergency standby."

"Brewing coffee and listening to people's problems — I'm sure that's what you did, and well," Tang said.

Jo and Tina had helped ferry supplies and comfort distraught concertgoers. But Jo didn't want to talk about that.

"Congratulations on your transfer to the Homicide Detail, Amy. Why are you here?"

Tang's sea-urchin hair spiked in the breeze. She didn't answer.

Jo stepped closer. "A body's lying on the field, covered by a tarp. And tonight came close to being a remake of the *Twilight Zone* disaster, starring my sister as Woman Hit by Crashing Chopper. I want to know what happened."

"It's Tasia McFarland." Tang's face turned pensive. "And I want you to know what happened. I think I want your professional opinion on it."

Jo felt a frisson. "Her death is equivocal?"

"Fifty points for the deadshrinker."

Jo was a forensic psychiatrist who consulted for the SFPD. She performed psychological autopsies in cases of equivocal death — cases in which the authorities couldn't establish whether a death was natural, accidental, suicide, or homicide.

She analyzed victims' lives to discover why they had died. She shrank the souls of the departed.

But the cops normally requested Jo's expertise only when a death remained indecipherable even after a long investigation. If the SFPD already considered the death of Tasia McFarland — notorious, splashy, icon-of-Americana Tasia McFarland — to be equivocal, this case was going to be tricky, as well as inconceivably high profile. Jo had a brief image of her professional life igniting like a matchstick.

And she saw her sister beside her: tired, lovely, lucky to be breathing.

She handed Tina the keys to her truck. "I'll catch up with you."

Tina kissed her cheek and whispered, "I'm fine. There was no instant replay. Don't dwell on it."

Jo blinked. Tina squeezed her hand and headed off.

Tang flicked her cigarette away. "Come on."

They headed back into the ballpark. Tang said, "Pilot of the first helicopter's missing, presumed dead. Stuntman who was in the back of the chopper survived, barely."

Jo ran her fingers across her forehead. Her face was stinging. Tang glanced at her, and hesitated.

"Sorry, Beckett. This must hit close to home."

"That score's already on the board. I can't take it down."

Her husband had been killed in the crash of a medevac helicopter. But she couldn't avoid discussing aircraft accidents, any more than she could rewind her life three years and get a second swing at the day Daniel died.

"Keep talking," she said. But as they walked, she sent a text message to Gabriel Quintana. *Am OK. With Tang, will call.*

"The second chopper managed to crash-land at McCovey Point with no fatalities," Tang said.

They passed through a tunnel and emerged onto the bottom deck of the stands. The ballpark's jeweled views, of San Francisco and the bay, were the greatest in Major League Baseball, and Jo usually met her parents at the stadium for a Giants game at least once a summer. Now forensic teams, photographers, and the medical examiner were working the scene. The yellow tarp stood out, as bright as a warning sign.

"I saw her drop," Jo said. "Debris hit the stanchion where the zip line was anchored. It collapsed and she fell like . . ." A ribbon of nausea slid through her. "She fell."

"The fall didn't kill her," Tang said. "She had a gunshot wound to the head."

Jo turned, lips parting. "Somebody shot her? She shot herself? What's confusing about her death?"

Tang walked down the aisle toward the field. "Aside from the fact that she slid down the zip line with half her throat blown away?"

"Aside from that."

"And that at least seventy-five people in the crowd were hit by falling debris or trampled in the stampede?"

"And that."

"And the fact that Fawn Tasia McFarland, age forty-two, born and bred in San Francisco, was the ex-wife of the president of the United States?"

Jo slowed to a stop. "No, that, without a doubt, most definitely covers it."

CHAPTER
FIVE

Tang turned to Jo. "Tasia's death could be an accident. Could be suicide."

"Could be murder?" Jo said. "Somebody may have just shot the president's ex to death?"

Tang nodded.

Jo felt an electric tremor of excitement. "You want me to perform a psychological autopsy on Ms. McFarland?"

"This is going to be an alphabet soup investigation. SFPD, NTSB, DA's office. Join the line-up. I want you to turn on your radar and cut through the clutter. Will you?"

Jo thought of reasons a fast-rising lieutenant might want the assistance of a forensic psychiatrist: ass covering, running up the score on the opposition, positioning a scapegoat to take the arrows. But Amy Tang had always played straight with her.

The cops called Jo when they could identify *how* a person had died — a fall, an overdose, a collision — but could not determine *why*. Jo investigated a victim's state of mind, and retraced his final hours, to pinpoint whether he had tripped from the roof or jumped;

overdosed on barbiturates accidentally or deliberately; stepped carelessly in front of the bus, or been pushed.

Some police officers dealt reluctantly with Jo, seeing her as a sorceress who cast bones to divine a victim's fate. Some, like Tang, treated her as an investigative team-mate who could uncover the emotional and psychological factors that led to victims' deaths. Working with Tang was like holding a cactus-covered live grenade. But Tang cared about putting the good guys first, and bad guys behind bars. She didn't play games.

"My sister could have been sliced in two by a helicopter blade. I will," Jo said. "But I don't want to end up in a meat slicer myself."

"I want your perspective and insight. This will be a backstage role, not a star turn."

"Did you know that when you lie, your cheek twitches?"

Tang huffed. "All right. This case has enough celebrity, politics, and carnage to feed the world. But you'll be a consultant, not the lead investigator."

"Great. Tell me about the case."

"Tasia McFarland apparently bled to death when her carotid artery was severed at the jaw line by a forty-five caliber bullet."

"Did she pull the trigger?"

"I don't know."

"That's a hell of an admission."

"It certainly is." Tang's shoulders tightened, as though somebody had turned a knob. "We need to slam the door on this case. You saw the media outside. The networks, cable, the BBC, Al Jazeera, Russia Today, and some camera crew from, I swear, the Garden Gnome Channel. And they all want to eat us for lunch."

"Again, I refer you to the image of the meat slicer."

"As thrill rides go, this'll be cheaper than Disneyland." Tang gazed at the field. "Fawn Tasia McFarland died in front of forty-one thousand witnesses. Cameras caught it from three angles. And we can't see the shooting on any of them."

The breeze swirled through the ballpark, blowing Jo's curls around her face. "Who claims Tasia was murdered?"

Tang nodded at the shiny yellow tarp. "Tasia does."

"Tasia left a message," Tang said.

"But not a suicide note. What did she say?" Jo said.

"I'll get to that, but first let me explain how we got to *this*." Tang nodded grimly at the yellow tarp on the baseball field. "She was supposed to slide down the zip line, singing the song from that action movie. Guns 'n' poses. All butch-and-big-hair, patriotism and sexual innuendo. She turned up with a real gun. A Colt forty-five."

Jo raised an eyebrow. "Classic weapon. And a hell of a choice."

"She liked big statements."

"Was she known to carry?"

Tang shook her head. "No. I've spoken to her agent and manager, plus the tour manager and the concert promoter. Nobody had ever seen her with firearms. But she wasn't the most reliable person — which we'll also get to."

High above the stands the American flag snapped in the wind, vivid under the stadium lights. Jo brushed her hair from her eyes.

"Ballistics?" she said.

"Don't count on it. The shot was through and through. We haven't found the round or the brass. We're bringing in metal detectors, but I'm not hopeful."

The field was churned to bits. The scene was hopelessly contaminated.

"How many cartridges were loaded?" Jo said.

"That's part of the problem. After the fatal shot, the weapon fell into the crowd and a bunch of idiots fought for possession of it."

Jo almost guffawed. It seemed preposterous, yet unsurprising.

"They grappled like bridesmaids fighting for the bouquet at a wedding. One guy finally got it and ran off, then had second thoughts about selling it online. He turned it over. Unloaded — says that's the way he got it."

"You're sure it's the weapon?" Jo said.

"There's DNA on it. Of types I have no doubt will prove to come from the victim."

Tang didn't need to say *blood, bone, brain matter.* Her face said it for her.

"Tasia told the stunt coordinator the weapon was unloaded," she said. "But he didn't know if she was lying, teasing him, or serious. And the Colt's capacity is seven-plus-one."

Seven rounds in the cylinder plus one in the chamber. "You think she checked the cylinder but not the chamber — and actually believed the weapon was empty?"

"It's possible. The gun's twenty years old. The round that killed her could have been in there for decades. But without the bullet and the casing, we can't tell."

"You think it was an accident?" Jo said.

"You think it wasn't?"

Jo stated it as clearly as she could. "Self-inflicted, contact gunshot wounds to the head are presumptive evidence of suicide."

Tang grumbled. It was as close as she came to sighing.

But Jo knew the statistics. The majority of gunshot deaths in the United States were suicide. Almost as many were homicide. Only a small percentage were accidental.

"If a victim has a history of depression, the presumption of suicide is even stronger," she said. "Did Tasia?"

"Yes."

"But you think it was a prank? Stupidity?"

"It's been known to happen. Brandon Lee died filming *The Crow*."

"That was an accident. Unequivocally. Fatal error on the movie set. Nobody noticed that a bullet had jammed in the barrel of the gun. When the weapon was reloaded with blanks and fired again, the jammed round discharged and hit Lee in the chest."

"That actor on a Hollywood TV set shot himself with blanks."

"Jon-Erik Hexum. Also unequivocally an accident. Hexum didn't realize that blanks can discharge with enough force to kill. He put a stunt gun to his temple, apparently as a joke, and pulled the trigger." Jo stuck her hands in her pockets. "On the other hand, there've been televised suicides. A reporter in Florida sat down at the news desk, made a crack about bringing viewers blood and guts in living color, put a revolver to her head, and fired."

Tang's mouth pursed. "Never challenge a forensic shrink on death trivia."

"I'll take Onstage Fatalities for two thousand, Alex."

Tang looked like she had a burr under her shirt. "We're checking whether Tasia purchased ammunition recently."

"What's gnawing at you?"

"The wing nuts are out there, the political banshees, and you can bet they're getting ready to fly. I need to shut down any talk that dark forces are at work here."

My superiors want me to shut it down was the undertone.

"You're talking about murder," Jo said.

"If somebody killed Tasia, I need to know it. And to know if her death is a fuse that's been lit."

Jo's hair blew across her face. "You'd better tell me about the message she left."

"It's a recording. It's her playing two songs she wrote last night. Plus a rambling statement, saying, 'Publish this in the event of my assassination.'"

30

"She used that word?"

"Hear for yourself."

Tang took an audio player from her pocket. "The tracks are called 'After Me' and 'The Liar's Lullaby.' She left it for her boyfriend."

They each put in an earbud and Tang pushed *Play*. Jo heard a piano, spare and melancholy, and Tasia McFarland's shimmering soprano.

"After me, what'll you do?"

The melody was mournful, Tasia's voice bright and riven with cracks. She hit a hard minor chord and let it fade. Then she spoke.

"I'm in danger of being silenced. If that happens, I won't be the last."

Her speaking voice was bold, ringing, and rushed. "Searle, my love, my baby boy, Mister Blue Eyes with the silver tongue, listen close. Turn your ear, turn your heart, turn your head. Because I might not make it."

Jo glanced at Tang. "Lecroix?"

Tang nodded.

"Things have gone haywire," Tasia said. "I can't tell you more than that. Telling you more would kill me. But if I die, it means the countdown's on."

A chill inched up Jo's neck. She glanced at the tarp on the field.

"It means time's running out like a train headed for a wreck. My death will be the evidence." Tasia inhaled, like a swimmer coming up for air before plowing on. "I was confused, but not anymore. I thought I got away without being followed. But they're after me. Robert

31

McFarland makes that inevitable." She paused.
"Publish this in the event of my assassination."

She played a heavy chord on the piano, and began to
sing.

You say you love our land, you liar
Who dreams its end in blood and fire
Said you wanted me to be your choir
Help you build the funeral pyre.

The chill crept across Jo's shoulders.

But Robby T is not the One
All that's needed is the gun
Load the weapon, call his name
Unlock the door, he dies in shame.

The melody changed up and went into the refrain.

Look and see the way it ends
Who's the liar, where's the game
Love and death, it's all the same
Liar's words all end in pain.

Tang stopped the playback. "There's another verse,
but you get the gist."

"That's the creepiest song I've ever heard."

They stood above the field, silent under the harsh
lights and the wind.

"'They,'" Jo said.

"Unfortunately. And no, I don't know whether it was just a paranoid rant."

"Did she have a psych history?"

"Manic-depression. But that's not my point."

"She was bipolar? That's huge. It's —"

Tang raised a hand. "It's not my point."

Jo thought about it. "If she genuinely feared for her life and brought the gun for self-protection, it argues against an intent to commit suicide."

"The stuntman claims she said, 'He's out there,' and 'It's life or death.' Maybe she was acting. Maybe she was delusional. But maybe not."

"Are you suggesting somebody really wanted her dead? Why — because she was once married to Robert McFarland?"

Tang turned to her. "Will you perform the psychological autopsy? Are you in?"

"You bet I'm in."

"Good. I need you to find out why Tasia McFarland was carrying a pistol that, according to California firearms records, is registered to the commander in chief of the United States."

CHAPTER
SIX

You can take my cash, but if you won't shake my hand, I'll light a fire up your ass . . .

The music raged through the parked truck. Ivory turned it up. "You tell it, Searle."

The man sang about the hardest life around, Ivory thought — being a white American. Work yourself into the grave, while the government confiscates your wages and an ungrateful world demands handouts or tries to blow you up.

She stared across the street at the ballpark. "It's time to launch a rocket up somebody's crack."

Behind the wheel, Keyes chewed on a toothpick. "Unbunch your panties."

"Searle Lecroix's woman just got shot down like a dog. Two choppers got taken out — you think that wasn't to cover the shooter escaping? You should put on a pair of tighty-whiteys yourself, and bunch them so tight you squeal."

"Like you know how to fire a rocket launcher?" he said.

"You'll teach me."

That finally earned her a look from him.

"Tasia dying wasn't any accident. It was a government hit, no joke." *Government* came out "gubmint." "Government brought down the twin towers, Keyes — they wouldn't think twice about killing McFarland's first wife."

Keyes looked away again. He watched the police and media spectacle outside the ballpark with a cool eye. People took that look for boredom, Ivory thought, when really he was scanning the scene for threats, soft targets, weak points in the police cordon. Years of experience, it came as a reflex to him.

"Question isn't what the government does. It's what we do about the government." He turned off Lecroix's music. "And entertainers don't have the answer."

He took out his phone and went online. His face, pale and pocked, looked vivid. His anger didn't run hot; it was reptile anger — cold and submerged and liable to erupt in ruthless bursts. Being near it made Ivory feel confident. She was in the vanguard, with a man who would be the teeth and claws of the fightback.

She leaned close and saw him load the Tree of Liberty home page. On-screen was a message to the faithful.

Government, even in its best state, is but a necessary evil; in its worst state, an intolerable one.
— Thomas Paine

"When did this post?" she said.
"Ten minutes ago."
Tree of Liberty was the cyberdomain of True America. It was the online outpost of people like Keyes and Ivory, who saw the nightmare of government

tyranny darkening the horizon. Tom Paine was their voice crying in the wilderness.

His post began, like all his essays, with a quote from the original Thomas Paine, the American revolutionary. Then it launched.

And so it begins.

Today, in front of a stadium crowd, the Enemy and his legions struck down Fawn Tasia McFarland. And they murdered her in such an audacious fashion because they knew what they'd pull off: a charade.

The circus monkeys of the mainstream media are already spinning Tasia's death to suit Robert McFarland. "It was an accident. Stunt calamity. Boo hoo".

Bullshit. The White House killed her because of what she knew, which was plenty.

The traitor who has seized the Oval Office is a smooth-talking jackal, but he can't put the rumors to rest. Because, despite his lies, the truth is the truth: He *was* born in Cuba. Castro *did* finance his education. Despite the cover story concocted by the Pentagon, *he* called in the air strike that killed seven men in his platoon, and he did so because they were about to blow the whistle on his sexual deviancy and treason.

Nobody was better positioned than Tasia to know Robert McFarland's lies. She was once his consort. And she was a patriot. Read her interviews. She didn't shrink from speaking truth to power.

Now power has shut her up.

Before tyrants launch a crackdown, they assassinate their most dangerous foes: the people who could expose or stop them. Tasia's murder is like a flare fired into the sky. It's a signal that McFarland's troops are moving into position. Time is short.

Robert Titus McFarland must be stopped. Who will do that? The dumb populace, grown soporific on junk food and reality TV? Never. When the government opens its internment camps, they'll slouch through the gates without complaint, like cattle.

Patriots must stop McFarland. And it's pucker time, because he has us in his sights. But we refuse to shrink from the coming fight.

His name is Legion, people. Stand up. Rip off his mask.

Rise.

Keyes and Ivory stared at the screen. Nobody knew who Tom Paine was. Tree of Liberty skipped around the Net, changing host sites to prevent the feds from tracing it. Paine was a specter.

"Fuckin' A," Keyes said.

Ivory drew a breath. She had chills. "We're at ground zero. We need to send him photos."

Nobody had met Paine, but Keyes and Ivory volunteered as his scouts. Keyes got out of the truck and crossed the street toward the ballpark. Ivory put on a ball cap and followed.

The cap said BLUE EAGLE SECURITY. She was clocked in for work, so she covered her hair, which she dyed as snowy as a swan's wing. She covered her tattoos with long sleeves. And at the depot, she kept her opinions to herself. She worked in San Fran-freak-show, where whack jobs could parade bare-butt naked, chanting about diversity, but an Aryan woman had to hide her Valkyrie Sisterhood tattoos and apologize for the crime of being born white.

Outside the ballpark, it was a scene. News trucks, reporters with microphones. And police cars lined up for a hundred yards, lights shrill, a bigfoot presence that made her skin creep.

Keyes tapped his watch. "Sixty seconds, max."

They were on a late run, one of Blue Eagle's night pick-ups in the city. The truck's onboard computer automatically tracked their route. It had logged them taking a detour to the ballpark, and if they loitered there too long, their jobs would be toast.

"Do you care?" Ivory said. "When the fightback comes, these jobs won't matter."

"When the fightback comes, I want access to the truck and everything in it. So I stay on the payroll until shots are fired."

The Blue Eagle uniform shirt stretched across his sloping shoulders. Years in the army, Ivory thought; a decade spent working as a security contractor on behalf of the government, earning three hundred thousand dollars a year, and for what? To get fired. To end up sitting on his butt behind the wheel of a courier truck, wearing that cheap-ass shirt. The "gubmint" had reduced a warrior to a delivery boy.

Ahead, barricades were set up. Behind them people huddled, lighting candles, laying flowers, crying. A TV crew was interviewing a Mexican woman and her little girl. The woman wiped her eyes. "Tasia grew up here — it's like losing a member of our family. How could an accident like this happen?"

Ivory kept her voice low. "The lie's taking root."

Keyes's face flattened, like a club. "Soon enough we'll give her something to cry over."

They kept moving. Being near so many cops gave Ivory the willies. She had a record. She'd been caught patrolling the border. Illegals infested America like lice, but hunt them, take their drugs, and you got called a criminal.

Keyes snapped photos with his phone. "Didn't I tell you, Frisco is at the heart of the government's plans?"

Ivory nodded. He certainly had told her San Francisco would be a staging center during the government crackdown.

"Killing Tasia here proves it," he said.

He sent his photos to Tree of Liberty. Nearby, the little Mexican girl laid a spray of white carnations by the barricade.

"God have mercy on their souls," Ivory said.

"Mercy, on *lice*?"

Keyes eyed her with what felt like disgust. True America, the realm of freedom and power where they lived — in their hearts — was a hard-core place.

"Don't hurt my feelings. I meant God better, 'cause we won't."

He should know how serious she took it. She risked everything for True America. This job, her whole life in San Francisco, was a front. And if the cops found out, she'd take a hard fall.

Then Keyes put a hand on her shoulder. "The rocket launcher rests right here. I'll teach you."

She lifted her chin, thrilled. Around them, gawkers and weepers continued to gather. Cops came out of the ballpark, and a few stragglers who had been at the concert. Some wore bloody clothing. One, silhouetted by the white light of television cameras, was a lumbering figure in fatigues, a — *no motherloving way* — a Goliath holding a chunk of the turf from the field as a souvenir.

Ivory turned and pulled Keyes toward the truck. "Freak alert. The night crawlers are coming out."

Keyes didn't linger. When you drove an armored car for a living, you couldn't afford to be late to the bank.

CHAPTER
SEVEN

"Robert McFarland owns the Colt forty-five?" Jo's heart rate kicked up. "I'd better see the footage of the shooting."

"You should. But don't expect it to clarify anything," Tang said.

Tang led her to a control room on an upper deck of the ballpark, overlooking the field. One wall was lined with television monitors. Cops and stadium officials filled the room. Below, under the bleached stadium lighting, forensics techs in white bodysuits searched the scene. The medical examiner was preparing to move Tasia's body to the morgue. A gurney had been brought in and the yellow tarp pulled aside. Against grass churned to dust, Tasia's clothing stood out, sharp swipes of magenta and black. She looked small, delicate, torn.

Tang asked a tech to run a video. Jo braced herself.

She had seen people die — as a physician, an investigator, and a wife. Death, that radical moment, was a desperately intimate thing to watch. Being of Coptic descent, with a basting of Japanese Buddhism and a thick shellac of Irish Catholic education, Jo believed that death didn't equate to annihilation. Still, as the video started, she knew she was going to feel like she'd had her bell rung. She slipped her emotional chain mail into place.

The footage began with Searle Lecroix and the band playing the introduction to "Bull's-eye." Then the camera swiveled to reveal Tasia on the balcony of the hospitality suite.

Her outfit was a western twist on the Madonna-whore dichotomy: like a barrel-racing champion had taken control of the Mustang Ranch. *Yee-haw, by Victoria's Secret.* Her waist harness was clipped on to the zip line. Knowing that the cable was going to collapse gave Jo, as a rock climber, a visceral feeling of dread.

Beneath the thundering music, Jo heard muffled shouting. Tasia was wearing a headset mike. Jo couldn't make out her words, just a rising tone of indignation — or fear. Inside the suite, the stuntman rattled the doors.

Tasia turned and beckoned to the crowd. The gun flashed in the sunlight. As people surged onto the balcony and surrounded her, stage smoke erupted. She broke into song and aimed the pistol at the stage.

"Holy crap, she's blowing on the barrel," Jo said.

She watched, aghast. The music soared. The crowd swarmed around Tasia. CO^2 obscured the view.

The roar of the gunshot was sharp and shocking.

Tasia emerged from the roiling smoke, hanging limp from the climbing harness, and slid down the zip line. The gunshot wound was plainly visible, a gory rose blooming on her neck and head.

The camera swerved. The scene turned to panic, falling helicopter debris, collapsing stage scaffolding, people screaming.

Then, amid the chaos, the camera zoomed in on the field. In front of the stage Tasia's broken form lay on the grass. Beside her knelt Searle Lecroix. Her headset mike amplified his voice above the torrent of noise.

"For the love of God, somebody help her," he cried.

Jo exhaled. "Stop the video."

The air seemed to smell of smoke and salt water and the wretched, oily stink of wrecked aircraft. She stared at the screen.

It was impossible to see who had fired the gun.

"Somebody could have taken the pistol from her, or grabbed her hand and squeezed the trigger. Still, three seconds before the shot, Tasia had possession of the weapon," she said.

She thought about Tasia acting out a high-risk, sexualized game with the Colt .45. Blowing on the barrel was showy, attention-grabbing behavior. Not playful, exactly — more like shtick. And suicides, in the moments before death, tended not to goof around.

"Can I talk to the stunt coordinator?" she said.

"Sure. Guy's name is Rez Shirazi. Fifteen years experience on feature films."

Tang led her to one of the corporate hospitality suites. As they walked, she summed up what Shirazi had already told the police.

"He tried to talk Tasia into putting down the weapon — the only thing she was supposed to take onstage was her bad, Botoxed self. She refused, but didn't threaten him or the crowd or herself. Wasn't angry. She was frazzled and terrified."

Tang knocked on the door and entered the hospitality suite. It was filled with cops and stadium officials. A television was tuned to a news channel. Shirazi was pacing, phone to his ear. When Tang introduced Jo, he ended the call and shook her hand.

"I've been talking to detectives and lawyers for two hours," he said. "Please, read my written statement, or else ask me something new."

He had warm eyes in a rough face, and bounced on his toes as he talked, like a welterweight boxer. In film credits, Jo thought, he'd get stuck as "Thug" or "Crazed Bomber."

"I'm assessing Tasia's state of mind. Can you describe her mood tonight?" she said.

"She was wired."

"Can you be specific? Wired meaning happy? Coked up?"

"Not coked up. At least, she said she was clean. And not happy. I've seen her ecstatic, zooming a million miles an hour, and she had a smile, man . . . but tonight she was agitated." He circled his hands, seeking the right description. "Once she started talking, I couldn't get her to stop. It was like her mind was a popcorn machine."

He shook his head. "I heard she was bipolar. Tonight she seemed manic *and* depressed. She was energized but dismal. Saying things like, 'Life's a bitch and then you die. Like Princess Di.' And making musical . . .

44

jokes, kind of, but bummers. 'Do, re, mi, fa, so long, suckers.'"

"She mentioned death, more than once?"

"She said tonight was all *about* life and death. She mentioned martyrdom. Car bombs, death squads, holy war." He tilted his head. "Then she mentioned the Secret Service. And said, 'He's out there.'"

"You think she was referring to the president?" Jo said.

"Maybe. But I thought tonight's main event was supposed to be a concert, so what do I know?"

"Anything else you noticed about her attitude tonight?"

"Yeah. Everything was exaggerated. She came in with the corset undone more than usual, the jeans slung lower, and her make-up was just extreme." He looked weary. "She acted like she was the center of the universe. All performers do, but tonight she really believed it was all about her. She seemed — on a mission."

"And this was a change from her mood recently?"

Shirazi rubbed his chest as though it ached. "Yeah. At the start of the national tour, couple months back, she was really up. Bubbly. Then she went flat. Moody, withdrawn — I mean, it was a noticeable swing. But over the past few weeks, everything's been building up. Her energy and her . . . discontent."

"Wired but miserable."

"You got it."

His phone rang. He took the call, said, "On my way," and hung up. "My brother was in the helicopter that hit the bay. He just came out of surgery. I need to get to the hospital."

"All right," Tang said. "Anything else you can tell us before you go?"

"I got a terrible feeling she was going play with the gun like a toy. It was a recipe for disaster. And I wish I could tell you what happened. When I couldn't break the plate-glass windows, I ran for the suite next door, to see if I could get to her on the balcony. But I heard the gunshot." His voice ebbed. "I ran out of time."

Tang gave him her card, and said she'd be in touch. He headed out the door.

"Initial assessment?" Tang said.

"Besides the fact that Shirazi feels guilty that she died?" Jo said. "Get a tox screen on Tasia. If she wasn't on cocaine or amphetamines, she was having some kind of manic episode."

"You don't sound convinced about that."

"Manic episodes are characterized by euphoria, and Tasia sounds far from euphoric. But other things fit," she said. "With mania, people can't stop talking. Their speech becomes pressured. And they're showy. They wear bright-colored clothes and tons of inappropriate make-up. It looks . . . off."

Tang nodded. " 'Playing in the crayon box' is the phrase the make-up woman used."

Jo thought again about the game Tasia had acted out with the Colt .45. "They can also be hypersexual. And they can have grandiose delusions."

"Like they're the target of an assassination plot?"

"When people with bipolar disorder become paranoid, they think massive forces are threatening them. Not merely the neighbors and the mother-in-law and their shrink."

"Such as the president of the United States?"

"There's the rub," Jo said.

Behind them, conversation bubbled above the noise from the television. Jo mulled what she'd seen and heard.

"Three possibilities. One, the pistol was defective. It just went off," she said.

"Unlikely. But we'll tear it apart and find out."

"Two, Tasia McFarland put the gun to her head and pulled the trigger."

"You believe that less than you did ten minutes ago."

"Three —"

On the TV, a news anchor said, "Now we go to the White House, where President McFarland is about to speak about the death of his ex-wife."

CHAPTER
EIGHT

Jo and Tang crowded around the television with the cops and stadium officials in the suite. On-screen, the White House press secretary stood at a podium, pudgy and diffident. The pressroom was a forest of jutting hands, all raised to ask about the death of Robert McFarland's first wife, the lovely, tragic, maybe crazy Fawn Tasia.

A reporter asked, "Did the president know that she was in possession of the Colt forty-five?"

"The president isn't going to comment on matters that might fall within the scope of the investigation into Ms. McFarland's death. Obviously he wants to avoid any remarks that could compromise the investigation."

"But did he deliberately leave the gun with her when they divorced?"

The press secretary adjusted his glasses. His forehead looked shiny. "The president will issue a statement momentarily. If I could —"

"Tasia McFarland was a diagnosed manic-depressive. Did the president know of that diagnosis at the time he left a large caliber semiautomatic pistol in her possession?"

Jo said, "Wow."

There was a stir in the pressroom. The press secretary said, "Ladies and gentlemen, the president."

The camera swiveled. Robert Titus McFarland strode toward the podium, grave and purposeful.

He had the ascetic build and weightless gait of a cross-country runner. His hair, black as a priest's cassock, was shorn unfashionably short, a legacy of his army years. His temples were salted with gray.

He gripped the edges of the podium. He looked drawn. He didn't have the aw-shucks charm of Bill Clinton, didn't have Kennedy's élan or Reagan's disarming ability to project whimsy. He had a craggy dignity and laconic style that pundits called "western" and attributed to his Montana roots.

He peered into the lights. "The news tonight from San Francisco has come as a shock, and has saddened me, deeply."

He let that last word fall heavily. He let it roll across the press corps until it pinned them to their seats and smothered all noise in the room.

"My thoughts are with the family of the pilot who lost his life, and with all those who were injured."

McFarland was an outlier: a working-class liberal, a warrior turned antiwar. He had grown up in a double-wide trailer on a cattle ranch outside Billings, son of the ranch foreman and his Salvadoran wife. He won the state cross-country championship, received a commission to West Point, and served as an army officer in hot zones across the globe before — famously — resigning his commission in protest over a friendly fire incident for which junior officers took the blame while higher-ups escaped censure. He returned to Montana, went to law school, practiced environmental law, and went into politics. His rise was swift. He won the presidency after serving five years in the Senate.

He had a reputation as a quick-thinking, hard-driving politician, a man who held everything in his head like a mental battlefield map and maintained rapport with underlings and rivals. In other words, a commander.

Along the way he'd married and divorced Fawn Tasia Hicks. And for two decades he had carefully avoided talking about her. He'd been remarried, to the calming, outdoorsy First Lady, for seventeen years. They had twin sons and a golden retriever, and kept roan quarter horses on their spread outside Missoula. As a political liability, Tasia had been no cause for alarm, not even a wisp of smoke on the horizon. She'd been a curiosity.

Not anymore. Jo watched him, thinking: *Let's really see who I voted for here.*

McFarland gazed around the pressroom. "Tasia's death is a tragedy. Sandy and I extend our sympathies to her family, and join her friends and all those around the country who are tonight mourning this . . ." He slowed, and his voice deepened. ". . . loss."

He looked down and shifted his weight. Still gripping the podium, he shook his head. Then he seemed to throw a switch.

"Prepared remarks don't cut it at a time like this." He looked up. "This news is a kick in the gut. Tasia was too young to die."

Behind him, at the edge of the screen, stood presidential aides and the White House chief of staff. McFarland glanced their way. Their presence seemed to bolster him. He straightened.

"Tasia was a force of nature. Plain and simple, she had more personality than anybody I've ever met. She could have moved mountains with a stare if she wanted. And for all her singing talent, and her fame, what marked her out was her generosity of spirit. She had a heart as big as the sky."

He paused. "Learning that she was shot to death with a pistol I bought is shattering. There's no other word for it."

A buzz ran through the pressroom. McFarland took time to consider his next remark.

"I didn't intend to take questions this evening, but on my way in, I heard somebody asking if I knew Tasia had bipolar disorder when I left the gun with her."

In the background, the White House chief of staff stiffened. K. T. Lewicki had the bullet head of an English bull terrier, and he looked like he wanted to tackle McFarland. The president didn't see it, or deliberately ignored it.

"The answer is no," he said. "Tasia and I were married for two years. She was twenty-three when we divorced. As I understand it, she was diagnosed with bipolar disorder in her early thirties."

He scanned the room, making eye contact. "I bought the pistol before I deployed for duty overseas. She was going to be home on her own. I wanted her to have a reliable means of defending herself." His tone sharpened. "And before you ask — it never crossed my mind to take it from her when we divorced. That pistol was supposed to protect —"

His expression fissured.

". . . protect her." A glaring light seemed to shear across his face. "Offer a prayer for her. Thank you."

He turned and left the podium. He couldn't have left faster if the room had been burning. A reporter said, "Mr. President, had you spoken to her recently?"

McFarland raised a hand as he walked away. "No."

Another reporter called, "Do you know why she brought your gun to the concert? Mr. President, did she ever speak about suicide?"

He shook his head and strode out the door.

In the hospitality suite, people wandered away from the television. Behind Jo, a man said, "Conscience has him by the throat."

Tang turned. "Mr. Lecroix."

Searle Lecroix stood at the back of the room, hands shoved into the pockets of his jeans, staring at the TV from under the brim of his black Stetson. "That man's just one more person who let her down. But at least he seems to know it."

His smoky drawl sounded hoarse. His face was drained. Tasia's baby boy, her Mister Blue Eyes with the silver tongue, looked like he'd had the stuffing pounded out of him.

Tang walked over. "I didn't know you were still here."

"I couldn't leave while Tasia's out there," he said. "Leave her lying on the field with people picking her over — I couldn't. She deserves to have somebody nearby who cares." His timbre dropped. "What happened to her?"

"We don't know yet," Tang said. She motioned Jo over. "This is Dr. Beckett."

Tang explained what Jo did, and asked Lecroix to let Jo interview him.

"You want to talk about Tasia from a psychological perspective? Now?"

Jo shook her head. "Tomorrow or the day after."

He agreed, and gave her his cell phone number. "You going to find out who let this happen?"

"Maybe you can help us figure that out."

He nodded. "They're taking her to the morgue. I need to go." He touched a finger to the brim of his hat. "Lieutenant. Doctor."

They watched him walk down the hall, shoulders slumped. After a moment, Jo said, "I was going to tell you Possibility Number Three."

"Please."

"Tasia planned to shoot somebody besides herself. But an unknown person in that swarm of fans got hold of the trigger and shot her first."

"Now you believe somebody was out to get her?"

"Now you don't?" Jo said.

"I don't know. I mean, you heard her. 'Liar's words all end in pain.'"

CHAPTER
NINE

Tang dropped Jo at her house on Russian Hill. She handed over a thick manila envelope.

"The concert video, photos of the scene, witness statements from the stuntman and stage crew. And Tasia's 'in the event of my assassination' recording."

Jo paused. "Using her ex-husband's gun is a huge statement."

"No kidding, Sigmund." Tang pointed at the envelope. "Figure out what she was saying."

The car grumbled away.

The night air was cool. The cable car tracks hummed with the sound of gears and cables ringing beneath the road. Jo climbed her front steps.

Her small house sat across from a park, surrounded by grander, brighter homes painted building-block colors. Hers was a fine San Francisco Victorian with iron-red gables. The front yard was a spot of grass the size of a paperback book, bordered by gardenias and white lilacs. Inside, her Doc Martens sounded heavy on the hardwood floor. Her keys echoed when she dropped them on the hallway table.

Jo never would have chosen the house for herself. She would have struggled to afford it. But her husband had inherited the home from his grandparents. He and Jo had redone the place. Knocked out walls, sanded the floors, installed skylights.

When Daniel died, his absence from the house had been excruciating. Early on, Jo had moments when she was overcome with an urge to shatter the windows and shout, *Come back to me*. Daniel's parents would have loved for her to sell it to them. But she'd made it her home, and now couldn't bear the thought of giving it up.

She went to the kitchen and fixed coffee. The magnolia in the backyard was laden with flowers. Under the moon they shone like white fists. Music from a neighbor's house floated to her, a Latin tune with sinuous horns. She felt jacked up, like she'd spent the evening strapped to a rocket sled.

She heard a sharp knock on the front door.

She answered it to find Gabe Quintana standing on the porch, hands in the pockets of his jeans. One look at her and his eyes turned wary.

"Maybe I should have called first," he said.

"The concert ended with the star and a stunt pilot dead, fans trampled, and me signing up for a case from one of the more exotic rings of hell."

"Want me to come back another time?"

His black hair was close-cropped. His eyes had a low-burning glow. *Right*, Jo thought. He didn't believe for a second that she'd kick him out.

"Some day I'll actually say yes. Just to keep your self-confidence under control," she said.

His smile was offhanded. "No, you won't."

Laugh lines etched his bronze skin. He leaned against the door frame, his gaze rakish.

Jo grabbed him by the collar of his Bay to Breakers T-shirt and yanked him through the doorway. She kicked the door closed and thrust him against the wall.

"Watch it. I can push your buttons and bring you to your knees" — she snapped her fingers — "like that."

"Promise?"

She held him to the wall. "I haven't seen you for twenty-four hours, and it's your fault that twenty-four hours feels like a long time."

He wrapped his arms around her waist. "My buttons. Yeah, I'm the one whose control panel is blowing up here."

He kissed her.

Sometimes he seemed as still as a pool of water. Sometimes he seemed reserved to the point of invisibility. She knew that the surface reflected little of the turbulence beneath, that it hid his intensity and resolve. He was an illusionist, a master of emotional sleight of hand.

His cool served him perfectly as a PJ, a search and rescue expert for the Air National Guard. He came off as affable and reassuring. But sometimes, when he was challenged or threatened, his attitude changed, and Jo glimpsed the warrior he had been.

And was about to be again.

One day gone, eighty-seven left. Gabe had been called up to active duty. At the end of the summer, he and others from the 129th Rescue Wing had orders for a four-month deployment to Djibouti, to provide combat search and rescue support for the U.S. military's Combined Joint Task Force-Horn of Africa. He'd be back at the end of January. After that he'd remain on active duty for another eight months, but thought it possible he would serve much of that time at the Wing's headquarters, Moffett Field in Mountain View.

But as always when reservists were called up, Gabe's life was getting blown to the wind. He wasn't just a pararescueman; thanks to the G.I. Bill, he was also a graduate student at the University of San Francisco. Deployment was going to tear up his academic schedule. But his first priority was his ten-year-old daughter, Sophie. He was a single dad. His ex-girlfriend lived in the city but on the fringes of competence, and saw Sophie only twice a month. Gabe had gone to painful time and expense to modify his custody arrangement so that Sophie would live in San Francisco with his sister and her husband while he was deployed. Sophie wasn't happy that he was going. But she knew it was his job. She'd been through it before.

Jo hadn't. But, holding him, she set that aside. She tried to stop the ticking in her head.

He brushed her curls from her face. "You okay?"

"Once I saw Tina, I was great."

His face looked sober. "It was only a close call. But I know that's too close."

She suppressed thoughts about any dangers involved in his deploying to the Horn of Africa. And she knew she was far more head over heels for this man than she could ever have imagined.

"What part of hell does your new case come from?" he said.

"I'm going to perform a psychological autopsy on Tasia McFarland. It seems I'm going to ride the tiger."

His eyes widened. "Excited?"

She had to think about it a moment. "Yes."

"Ready for the predators to come at you out of the tall grass?"

"Undoubtedly not."

"You really are a thrill seeker, aren't you?"

Sharp guy, Gabe Quintana. She put her hands on his shoulders. "I am. How long can you stay?"

He smiled and pulled her against him. And his cell phone rang.

Jo leaned back. He answered the call.

"Dave Rabin, what's up?" he said, and within five seconds she knew that thrill seeking of a radically different kind was on his agenda.

"Sixty minutes. I'll be there." He flipped his phone off. "Merchant tanker five hundred miles off the coast, reports a fire in the engine room. They're adrift and down at the stern. Multiple casualties."

Jo reluctantly let him loose. A buzz seemed to radiate from him. He put a hand on her hip and kissed her again.

"Bring 'em back," she said. "Be safe."

He ran down the steps toward his truck. She hung in the doorway and watched him go. She didn't want to close the door, to turn back to Tasia McFarland and the unblinking certainties of death. She watched him go until he was out of sight.

58

CHAPTER
TEN

Noel Michael Petty thudded up the hotel stairs, sweaty and winded, cradling the artifact inside the fatigue jacket. The hallway was dank but empty. Petty rushed inside the hotel room, slammed the door, and leaned back against it, breathless. Nobody had followed. Nobody had even noticed. Not at the ballpark or anyplace along the route to the Tenderloin.

That's because, when you hover like an angel, you become invisible.

Quick, latch the chain. Clear a space on the table. Shove aside the scissors and the news cuttings. Let the tabloid articles and glossy magazine photos flutter to the floor. Take a breath.

Carefully, ceremoniously, Petty pulled open the fatigue jacket and removed the artifact. It was a piece of turf from the baseball field, a lump of grass and earth about the diameter of a compact disc. Petty set it on the table and ran a hand across it, stroking the grass like a baby's soft hair.

Victory is mine.

Stepping back, Petty pulled off the green watch cap and turned on the television. Tonight's events were historic. It was vital not to miss a moment, not one beautiful second.

There — news. Images sparkled on the screen, familiar and thrilling. The smoke so black, the blood so messy, Tasia's hair so thick, fanning around her head in a gold comet's tail. People screaming, fleeing from her body. Tasia had terrified the crowd, dying like that. What a cow.

Bursting through the crowd came Searle Lecroix. Petty grimaced.

Too late, Searle. She's gone. She can no longer suck the love from a man's bones. We're free.

Free. Petty glanced at the artifact. It was a memento of deliverance, like a chunk of the Berlin Wall.

Lecroix shoved his way past the ravenous onlookers on the field, gawky strangers who wanted a piece of Tasia McFarland, who wanted a chance to say, *I was there.* But they were only about celebrity and sentiment. They would never understand. Tasia's death was not an accident. It was a triumph.

On-screen, Lecroix dropped to his knees beside Tasia's body. Petty cringed.

"Searle, you fool."

The death of a cow should not affect a man so. It was a painful sight. It diminished the victory.

If you believed the gossip, Tasia had lured Searle Lecroix into her bed. But he couldn't have known her. He couldn't have given himself to her and received back in turn. Not from an unhinged, half-lunatic fame-whore who had fucked the president to get where she was.

60

Lecroix gripped Tasia's hand. He begged, "Help her."

Smarting, Petty turned away. But Tasia's face followed. She stared down from the walls of the hotel room. Hundreds of photos, her beautiful face, her filthy gaze, her dark inner light, staring, *knowing*.

Petty stared back. "But you didn't know what was coming. You refused to listen."

Tasia had snubbed NMP. Then ignored NMP. She'd had the *gall* to rebuke and disregard NMP.

A smile squeezed Petty's lips, full of pain.

Stop that. You are not a fat, weak-kneed fan. You are a righteous guardian and protector of the truth and the Good Ones. Petty scratched an armpit.

The hotel room smelled stale and fuggy, like a cheap costume for a stage play. But that's what this Tenderloin dive was — a disguise. Nobody would look here for a hovering angel.

The news switched to a White House press conference. Robert McFarland was praising Tasia. He was waxing melodic about her talent.

The thrill of victory subsided. Petty sloughed off the fatigue jacket and sat heavily on the bed. *Generosity of spirit* . . . was McFarland joking? The president of the United States was beatifying Saint Tasia, the Holy Cow.

Slut, thief, liar.

A heart as big as the sky. Letting out a moan, Petty thundered to the table, grabbed the artifact, and threw it at the television.

This was insane. It was . . . a spell. The vixen had bewitched even the leader of the free world.

All Petty's work had been in vain. The king rat of politicians, a man of the smoothest tongue, a hypnotist, was spreading the lie. People would buy it. *Heart as big as the sky* would become conventional wisdom. It would twist people's minds, turn them into Tasia-lovers. It would burrow under the skin of people who needed protection. Tasia, thief of hearts, would steal yet again, just as she'd stolen from NMP, but this time from beyond the grave.

Her death hadn't ended the battle. It had only intensified it.

Petty heard a voice, a whisper, a promise. *Don't tell. You're my eternal love. Shh.*

Deep breath. It was time to slough off Noel Michael Petty. Time to put on the camouflage that kept the Protector safe and anonymous. It worked on the Net, where nobody knows you're a dog. Now, offline, Petty needed to assume the guise. Full-time, with no slip-ups.

Going into the bathroom, Petty faced the dingy mirror. *From now on, you're not Noel.* You're not a sweaty fan who follows the tour around the country. You're *him*. NMP.

Tasia hadn't seen the end coming. Neither had Searle Lecroix, though he'd been onstage, staring at her. And judging from the news footage, Lecroix still didn't see. Tasia still held him in her thrall. And now the president was hypnotizing the public into believing the same thing. Somebody had to stop it.

62

Somebody needed to expose Tasia once and for all. End the love affair with her. Get proof, and make noise, and shut the liars up for good.

You are NMP, the archangel, the big bad bastard. You are the sword of truth.

You're the man.

CHAPTER
ELEVEN

In the morning Jo woke to the radio. ". . . investigation into the death of Tasia McFarland. A police source tells us that a psychiatrist has been hired to evaluate Tasia's mental state."

She sat up.

"Our source believes that the police are working on the theory that Tasia committed suicide, and want a psychological opinion to back it up."

She reached for the phone. Saw the clock: six twenty. Too early to harangue Lieutenant Tang about departmental leaks.

She heard the foghorn. She kicked off the covers, pulled on a kimono, stumbled to the window, and opened the shutters. Fog skated across the bay and clung to the Golden Gate Bridge. But uphill, the sun was tingling through the clouds. The magnolia in the backyard looked slick in the early light.

The news continued. Not a word about a merchant ship on fire and down by the stern five hundred miles off shore. Not a word about the 129th Rescue Wing. Accidents at sea could entangle rescuers in disaster, and she listened, shoulders tight, for the words *Air National Guard*. Nothing.

She grabbed her climbing gear and drove to Mission Cliffs. She found a belay partner and spent forty-five minutes on the gym's head wall. It soothed her. Hanging fifty feet off the ground, with nothing but a void between her and a broken neck, always cleared her head.

She was at her desk by eight. She'd finally cleared out Daniel's mountain bike and *Outside* magazines, and turned the front room into her office. She kept gold orchids on the bookcase and her favorite *New Yorker* cartoon framed on the wall — where a drowning man yells, "Lassie! Get help!" And Lassie goes to a psychiatrist.

Normally she began a psychological autopsy by reading the police report and the victim's medical and psychiatric records. But those weren't yet available. To determine NASH — whether a death was natural, accidental, suicide, or homicide — she needed to assess not only the victim's physical and psychological history but also his or her background and relationships. Jo interviewed family, friends, and colleagues, and looked for warning signs of suicide or evidence that anyone might have intended the victim harm. She built a timeline of events leading up to the day of the victim's death.

Since she didn't have records, she read press accounts of Tasia McFarland's psychiatric history. It was sad and brutal. And Tasia hadn't hesitated to talk about it.

Tasia had been diagnosed with bipolar disorder at thirty-two. But she'd whipped between mania and depression for years before that. Volcanic highs and hideous lows had played out in public — tantrums, car wrecks, drug binges, and flights of creativity — as she veered from teen singing sensation to washed-up party animal to comeback queen. In short, as analyzed by *Rolling Stone, Mother Jones,* and *People* magazine: sex, drugs, and rock 'n' roll.

But bipolar disorder was a devastating diagnosis. The DSM-IV, the *Diagnostic and Statistical Manual of Mental Disorders,* defined Bipolar I Disorder as the occurrence of one or more "Manic Episodes or Mixed Episodes," though people often had major depressive episodes as well.

During a manic episode, people didn't need sleep and didn't feel tired — for a week, a month, two months. They felt on top of the world. They might learn new languages or take up a new instrument. Their extraordinary energy and sense of power came on spontaneously, without being triggered by any outside event, such as graduating from college or winning an Oscar, that could generate euphoria.

Jo wondered about Tasia, revved into the red zone on the night she sang a hit song to a stadium crowd in her hometown.

Manic people could be gregarious and entertaining. In fact, physicians training in psychiatry were told: If you're highly entertained by a patient, consider mania as a possible diagnosis. But while manic people could be lovable, they could also be exhausting.

HLS 25/9 19708

Sones, M
Collect By 19 Aug 2023
Yateley

Reserved Item

Branch: Yateley
Date: 5/08/2023   **Time:**   12.58 PM
Name: Sones, Margaret

Item: The liar's lullaby [text (large print)]
C014971961

Expires: 19 Aug 2023

And when patients dropped into depression, they crashed. Guilt and hopelessness overwhelmed them. Suicide was common.

And mixed episodes were the roughest of all: A person's mood disturbance met the criteria for manic and major depressive episodes simultaneously. Mixed episodes were difficult to diagnose. Jo believed they were the state in which people were most likely to commit suicide.

She thought about the way Rez Shirazi, the stuntman, had described Tasia: hyper but dismal.

She got herself a cup of coffee. She needed Tasia's prescription records and toxicology results. When well medicated, people with bipolar disorder could be accomplished and creative. They became physicists, computer scientists, artists. A number of famous classical composers had been bipolar.

But people often went off their meds because they loved feeling manic. They loved the explosion of creativity brought on by mania.

"Art and madness" was a cliché. But Jo had attended a med school lecture series on the mind and music. Strong evidence existed that Schumann had bipolar disorder. Gershwin may have had ADHD. And composers' mental states influenced their compositions. Bipolar composers, she recalled, loved repetitive melodic motifs and sometimes became obsessed with particular sounds or tempos.

Jo listened again to "The Liar's Lullaby." Her musical ear wasn't sharp enough to pick out clues buried in the melody, but the lyrics were disturbing enough. *You say you love our land, you liar / Who dreams its end in blood and fire.* The third verse was less eerie, but nonetheless sad.

I fell into your embrace
Felt tears streaming down my face
Fought the fight, ran the race
Faltered, finally fell from grace.

She tapped her fingers on the desk, wondering if the verse referred to Tasia's marriage.

Few photos existed of Tasia and Robert McFarland together. But online she found an old, and vivid, magazine photo essay. Tasia had met McFarland while performing for the troops, and several photos showed her mingling with soldiers. McFarland was prominent among them. He looked young, handsome, and sure of himself. In one lighthearted shot, McFarland and a bullet-headed officer Jo recognized as K. T. Lewicki, now White House chief of staff, had hoisted Tasia onto their shoulders. In another, taken soon after the McFarlands' marriage, they brimmed with energy — seemingly from being in each other's presence. Tasia looked like a saucy cheerleader, ready to single-handedly rouse the army to victory. McFarland looked like he believed himself the luckiest man alive: confident, swimming in love, and unselfishly proud of his talented young wife. They were laughing as though the world had revealed its secrets, and was beautiful.

At nine, Amy Tang phoned. "Tasia's autopsy is this morning. Medical and psychiatric records might be with you this afternoon, but full tox and blood work will take days. Her next of kin will meet with you at 10a.m. — her sister, Vienna Hicks."

Jo wrote down Hicks's phone number. "Did you know that police sources are talking to the press about me?"

"As I told you, this is a *cheap* thrill ride, not the Pirates of the Caribbean. But I'll remind people to keep their mouths shut."

Jo looked again at the photo of Tasia and Robert McFarland, young and in love. She didn't know how Tasia had gotten from there to writing, *But Robby T is not the One / All that's needed is the gun.* She wondered if Tasia's sister could tell her.

CHAPTER
TWELVE

Shortly before ten, Jo drove downtown. The streets of the Financial District were packed with cars and delivery trucks. The sidewalks bustled. The sun flashed from skyscraper windows, and wind funneled between the buildings. Jo pushed through a door into a coffeehouse where silverware clattered and the staff wore facial piercings and protest buttons pinned to berets. Vienna Hicks waved from a table against the windows.

Jo worked her way through the crowded room. Hicks stood and clasped her hand. "Dr. Beckett. I'm Vienna."

Vienna Hicks stood six feet tall and weighed two hundred pounds. Her ash-blue suit was impeccable. Her red hair looked like a runaway fire.

"Thanks for meeting me," Jo said.

"I was downtown on business. I'm a paralegal at Waymire and Fong. They're handling Tasia's estate, and they'll tackle any lawsuits that get filed against it."

She sat again, solidly. Her physique looked too grand for the tiny table. She had the forceful gaze of a grizzly bear. She eyed Jo up and down, and didn't look dazzled.

"Psychiatrist. Guess I shouldn't be surprised. They're running on empty, aren't they?" she said.

"The police?"

"They don't know how to label Tasia's death."

"The police are searching for an explanation. I'm here to help them find it."

Vienna tapped manicured nails on the table, patently skeptical. "This place is stifling. Let's walk."

She stood and headed for the door, parting the crowd around the counter like an ocean liner. Jo hustled after her. Outside, Vienna threw a crimson scarf around her neck and strode along the sidewalk toward the Embarcadero Center. The scarf whipped in the wind like a crusader's banner.

"You want a label? The media gave Tasia enough of them to carpet the streets at a ticker-tape parade." She put on a pair of oversize sunglasses. They barely contained the force of her gaze.

"Starlet. Mouseketeer. Pop tart," she said. "Loser, reality show contestant, drug addict."

She headed toward the waterfront. "A-list dropout. Fame whore. Presidential reject." She glanced at Jo. "Manic-depressive."

"Was that officially diagnosed?"

"By a board-certified psychiatrist. Rapid-cycling Type One bipolar disorder."

Vienna's cat's-cream skin was nearly luminous in the sunlight. Her red hair flew about her head in the wind.

"You want to know if she killed herself? Fully possible. Her major depressive episodes were deeper than a bomb crater."

"When did she begin showing signs of the disorder?" Jo said.

"Her teens. It became obvious in her early twenties. During her marriage."

"Was it a factor in her divorce?"

Vienna's jaw cranked down. "You'd have to ask him."

Him being the man who got 67 million votes in the most recent election, whose face graced the cover of every news magazine on the rack, and whose voice echoed from the television every ten minutes, day and night. Piece of cake.

"You don't speak to Robert McFarland, I take it," Jo said.

"I don't even speak *of* him. And I never speak *out* about him. Tasia did that enough when she was off her medication."

Jo nodded. Ahead, she saw the clock tower at the ferry building, the bay, and Alcatraz.

"Besides," Vienna said, "you don't need to hear my opinion on Rob. There's plenty to go around. Read the *Vanity Fair* profile, the one that described Tasia as a hopped-up, bebop Bunny wannabe with her gleaming eyes on the prize."

Jo kept her mouth closed. If Vienna wanted to talk, she wanted to hear it.

"I presume you've got the whole IMDb-of-crazy database that lists Tasia's greatest hits of conspiracy theory," Vienna said.

"I've seen a few clips."

"Fox News?"

"Talking about the Second Amendment. Assault rifles for all. Homeland Security putting tranquilizers in the water supply," Jo said. "The YouTube rant against the Federal Reserve."

Vienna's mouth pursed. "The vitriol was clinical paranoia, and yeah, it was embarrassing as well as frightening. But in her defense, she was off her meds then. In recent years she got much better treatment and good med management. The political rants stopped."

They paused at a corner. Palm trees stood sturdy against the breeze, fronds cutting the air. A tram rolled past, orange and yellow, one of the mid-twentieth-century electric trolleys recently resurrected by the city. When it stopped, Jo half-expected to see Humphrey Bogart climb off, fedora rakishly cocked.

"Being Tasia's sister must have been difficult —"

"Eight years of medical training for that insight? You went to public schools, didn't you?"

"— but you must have felt both angry and protective of her."

Vienna's Afrika-Corps-size sunglasses hid her eyes, but she radiated heat. The light changed. Vienna plowed across the street toward the waterfront.

"And helpless," Jo said. "As if she was being taken from you by a host of banshees, and you were powerless to stop it."

Vienna walked on for a few seconds. Then she turned to Jo and pulled off the shades. She let out a slow, barely controlled breath.

"People feasted on her like vultures. And she enabled it," Vienna said. "She was so passionate about

performing — so talented, so needy for an audience, so
. . . *panicked* about the idea that all the attention might
go away. She practically staked herself out on the
ground and called them down to tear chunks from her
flesh."

"I'm sorry for your loss," Jo said.

"Thank you. Tell me it was an accident. Please."

"That's why I'm talking to you."

The wind blew Vienna's scarf skyward. "I know."

"Did you know she had the gun?"

"It always worried me."

Jo surmised how Vienna felt: In a perverse way, the
fait accompli was a relief. The dread she had lived with
for years, the fear that her sister would suffer harm, had
come to pass, and brought with it release from the
awful pressure and anxiety. None of that lessened
Vienna's grief. But the grinding worry that never went
away . . . had now gone away.

"Did she ever threaten to shoot herself?" Jo said.

"Not in so many words. 'What's the point?' she'd say.
'Who'd miss me? Would people treat me like Kurt
Cobain if I played his final verse?'"

"That must have been awful for you. Did she ever
attempt suicide?"

Vienna's lips parted, words seemingly on the tip of
her tongue. Tart words. Then she checked herself.
"Maybe *he* can tell you. Or at least supply her medical
records from the army hospital."

Superb. Intra-family feuds, with a guy who had
round-the-clock Secret Service protection.

"Any attempts you personally can tell me about?" Jo said.

"Half-hearted, twelve years ago. Southern Comfort and a dozen ibuprofen."

Vienna glanced at the bay. A windsurfer scudded along atop the whitecaps, his lime-green sail a shark's fin.

"She also said she pictured herself going out like fireworks on the Fourth of July," Vienna said. "Did you know she was writing an autobiography?"

"No. Did she leave notes? A draft?"

"Notes, photos, lots of recorded ramblings. She wasn't writing it herself."

"Ghostwriter?"

"Man named Ace Chennault."

Jo took out a notebook and wrote it down. "Know how I can reach him?"

"He's around. He's a music journalist, was on the road with her for the last few months, gathering material." She smiled briefly, a flash of teeth. "There's family, and then there's entourage."

"When was the last time you spoke to your sister?"

"Yesterday morning. She called to make sure I'd gotten the tickets she sent."

Jo stopped writing. "I'm sorry, I should have known you were at the concert."

"Yeah."

The clipped syllable sounded like pain itself.

"How did she sound?" Jo said.

"Soaring, but agitated. Sort of . . ." She tilted her hand side to side. *Comme ci, comme ça.* "Disconcerted. Fizzing like peroxide."

"How long had she sounded that way?"

"A few weeks. But she could swing from mania to depression within days."

Rapid cycling indicated a deteriorating psychological condition. It meant the bipolar disorder wasn't under control. Rapid cycling could result from the disorder's progression over many years, or from poor medicating, self-medicating, or a patient going off her meds.

"Did she ever have mixed episodes?" Jo said.

Vienna frowned. "Not as far as I know."

"What was she like when she was hypomanic?"

"Like a Saturn rocket. Full throttle, roaring straight for the sky. Incredibly creative. She'd write songs and record all night. Funny and outgoing."

"And when she experienced full-blown mania?" Jo said.

"*Challenger.* Blast off, screaming for outer space, *ka-blooey.*"

"Did she engage in dangerous behavior?"

"She'd hit the sack with every man in arm's reach. Snort cocaine, even out the coke with vodka-and-OxyContin smoothies, cool off by driving the Pacific Coast Highway, headlights off, hundred miles an hour. Surely you've seen her mug shot online," she said. "I posted her bail."

She stared at the whitecaps on the bay. "Listen, I'm venting here. But the last few years, Tasia worked at managing her life. She quit the drugs and the booze binges. Stopped being promiscuous. She didn't crash into the dark, dark holes like in the old days. She didn't have week-long sleepless jags where she rewrote the

Ring Cycle as an epic about stock car racing. She was stable."

"Did you see her often?"

"No. She has a house near Twin Peaks, but she's been touring."

"Did she talk to you recently about ending her life?" Jo said.

"No."

"Did she seem to be making any preparations — had she given away any of her possessions? Made a will?"

"Wrote a will ten years ago. Otherwise, no."

"Did she have any enemies?"

Vienna turned her head slowly, and gave Jo the remorseless grizzly bear gaze. "The police played her 'I'm going to be assassinated' recording for me. It was . . . shocking. But I have seen no evidence that anybody killed her. If you have any, tell me. I mean now, Doctor." The gaze didn't relent. "I want the truth."

Jo knew that Vienna didn't simply want the truth; she needed it. Without it she would live like a wounded animal, bleeding and painstricken, burdened with doubts and guilt her entire life.

Jo hoped she could help provide her with it. That's why she did the job.

"I don't yet know what happened, but I'm trying my best to find out. Could anybody have wished your sister harm?"

Vienna fought her emotions. "Real harm, not conspiracy theory bullshit? People are saying she took a bullet meant for Searle Lecroix, or that the stuntman shot her — he has a Muslim name, Shirazi, so it's a jihadist plot to destroy country music. Or she was given hallucinogenic drugs that made her shoot herself."

That, Jo thought, was actually an interesting possibility.

"She made enemies right and left. She was a diva. Ninety per cent were showbiz rivals or family members she antagonized. But did people hate her enough to what, secretly load bullets in a gun she thought was unloaded? How preposterous is that? How many people had access to that gun? Not many."

Vienna looked at the windsurfers on the bay, their sails iridescent in the salt spray and sunshine. "The medical examiner's expediting the autopsy. They'll be releasing her body, and I have to plan the memorial service. I need to bury my sister. You understand that, Dr. Beckett?"

"Perfectly."

She looked at Jo. "Did somebody kill her? I have no idea."

CHAPTER
THIRTEEN

These are the times that try men's souls.
— *Thomas Paine*

The cursor blinked on the screen. His fingertips tingled. He typed the words that transformed him.

Call me Paine.

His thoughts pulsed. When he spoke aloud, people found him clumsy. An awkward white guy, soft around the middle — human mayonnaise. But when he sat before the glowing computer screen and reached into the minds beyond it, he became fluent and convincing. Power surged through his fingers.

The jackal in the Oval Office is playing games with us. Legion is plying us with lies. He thinks we can't see his ass hanging out.

Beyond the rooftops, downtown San Francisco gleamed in the morning sun. The Transamerica pyramid was a lustrous white edifice, the waters of the bay deceptively smooth. The postcard view disguised the degenerate reality. Whores, addicts, gays. And everywhere, coming out of drainpipes and cracks in the sidewalk, illegals. The ROW — the Rest of the World — a seething mass infecting the nation with their leprosy and laziness.

The city was a magnificent arena. What exquisite irony that the end game should play out here.

Watch the video footage from last night's concert. Not the film shot by the official camera crew — that footage has already been altered to depict the story the gubmint wants sheeple to believe. Watch videos shot by concertgoers. Raw footage of Tasia's death. It reveals the shocking truth.

He wiped his palms on his jeans. He was logged on through an anonymizer, a tool that stripped out identifying information about his computer and made his activities on the Net untraceable. Supposedly.

The discussion boards at Tree of Liberty were heaving. Thousands of comments. Battle cries. Pledges to fight to the death. The passion was unbelievable. His people, the online rant-'n'-ravers, loved Paine. They needed him. They *bought* him. The stock he owned in ammunition manufacturers was going to shoot through the roof. And some commenters were more than mere armchair insurgents. Tom Paine had real volunteers out there.

But these were nerve-racking days. Tasia was gone, and time was desperately short. To save himself from a full-blown attack, he had to act now. Fear touched the back of his neck with a dry heat.

The truth, despite what the more excitable members of our community believe, is that the shooter did not execute Tasia from the stunt helicopter.

I know what some of you think — *Look at the stuntmen's names*. Shirazi. Andreyev. And yes, Shirazi is a Muslim name. Andreyev is Russian. These men come from enemy stock, but the facts are indisputable: Neither shot Tasia. The angle of fire is wrong.

In the hall beyond the door, people passed by, laughing and chatting. Paine pulled his hands from the keyboard. His heart was racing.

He was a jack of many trades, but he was a master of persuasion — written, emotional, and political. He hated the word *prankster*. *Intimidator* suited him better. He was the rock in the gears, the sugar in the gas tank. He stopped things. Or kicked them off. Politicians talked; Paine turned propaganda into deeds.

He picked up a matchbook and flipped it between his fingers. He needed to stoke the fire.

Analyze the videos. They're blurred and shaky, but look. Her murderer fired a single shot from a high-powered rifle from the stage rigging in centerfield.

The gubmint will use Tasia's murder as an excuse to confiscate our firearms. Expect the second amendment to be suspended within the week. National Guard checkpoints will be erected after that. We'll be stopped, arrested, and interned. Be ready, people.

Yeah, that was good. He was getting warmed up now. His blood heated his hands.

The police investigation into Tasia's death is puppet theater. The SFPD will never produce the bullet that ended Tasia's life. Doing so would prove, incontrovertibly, that she was killed by a round fired from a military-issue sniper rifle, not a Colt .45.

And now the authorities have thrown another curve ball. They can't silence the outcry over Tasia's assassination, so they've decided to smother us with psychobabble. They've hired a psychiatrist to analyze Tasia's death.

This is not a joke.

Tasia's murder had been bold, incredibly so. She was a fire, and she'd been put out. But much worse was coming, straight at him, unless he took action immediately. Government minions — Legion's legions — would descend on him like demons. Robert McFarland could cry for the TV cameras, but his people certainly weren't. They were thinking *Finish the job*. They would come for Tom Paine.

Authority always did. He had to strike first.

We'll get "insights" into Tasia's "tortured" mind. This psychiatrist will give us a sad, *I'm-so-sorry* face, and blame Tasia's mother and American society for her "tragic suicide." You know she will — she's from San Francisco. She's a gubmint lackey, a useful idiot.

This is how tyrants plant their boot on our faces. Not always with a midnight knock on the door, but through the comforting lies of a quack.

A chill curled down his arms. He would put out the call. Keyes, the ex-merc who now drove for Blue Eagle Security, would answer, and that atavistic white power groupie he worked with, Ivory.

Tasia warned us. She came to the concert armed with the jackal's gun. She raised it high. She could not have shouted a louder message: True Americans will not go quietly.

To quote Thomas Paine: Lead, follow, or get out of the way. Who's with me?

Yes, Keyes and Ivory would be dying to ride to the rescue. The question was how many people could they take with them when they rode off the cliff?

After Jo said goodbye to Vienna Hicks, she walked back to her truck along crowded streets. Businessmen's ties writhed like snakes in the wind. Above skyscrapers, clouds fled across the blue sky. When she turned on her phone it beeped with multiple messages from Tang.

But the message she wanted, one from Gabe saying he was safe on dry land, wasn't there. Her breath snagged. Her emotions caught on a bramble, fear glinting in a corner of her mind.

She shook loose from the feeling. He would call. She wouldn't. She would wait, because that was the unspoken rule. Instead she called Tang, who sounded like she'd been chewing on sandpaper.

"Give me joy, Beckett. I need progress."

"Tasia's sister thinks it's fully possible she committed suicide."

"'Fully possible' doesn't work. I need concrete results."

"You sound like you're sitting on a sharp rock."

"You been watching the news? 'Still no information on the bizarre death of Tasia McFarland, and with each passing hour speculation grows that the police are incompetent, in on the conspiracy,' blah blah repeat until nauseated. The sharp rock's sitting on me."

Jo stopped at a corner for a red light. Taxis and delivery trucks jostled for space at two miles an hour, horns quacking.

"I need Tasia's medical and psychiatric records. All of them, including files from the years when she was married to Robert McFarland," she said.

"Army records, yeah. Getting paperwork from the military is going to be like pulling teeth from a chicken."

"You expect them to drag their feet?" The light changed and Jo crossed the street, dodging oncoming pedestrians. "Who's got their thumb on your neck, Amy?"

"You want the list alphabetically, or in order of political throw-weight? The White House wants this to go away. K. T. Lewicki called the mayor to express the administration's support for our investigation. In other words, the president's chief of staff wants us to turn off

84

the gas and snuff this story *out*. Get me something we can use, or we're going to get squashed."

"Still nothing on the search for the bullet?" Jo said.

"The Tooth Fairy is more likely to put it under your pillow than I and the department are to find it."

"The Warren Commission found a magic bullet on a hospital stretcher in Dallas after JFK was assassinated."

"*Beckett*." Tang's next words were barked at her in sharply inflected Mandarin. "Don't you dare inflict that conspiracy garbage on me."

"Political paranoia is as American as apple pie and obesity. We dine on it as a nation."

"The departmental powers want me to clear the case by the end of the week. Get me something solid, Jo. I need progress by tomorrow so I'll at least have dog chow to feed to the brass."

"On it."

"Have you gone to Tasia's house yet?"

"Next stop."

"Step lively, chickie."

NMP — *You are not Noel Michael Petty, you are NMP, the big bad bastard, the sword of truth* — gazed down the hillside. He was invisible in the thick brush, hovering like an angel.

A man was inside the house below. A man in a shiny blue blazer who had parked in the driveway and jogged to the door, sorting keys in his hand.

Hours of surveillance were about to pay off. Hours of silent hovering, of waiting for the chance to get inside the house without breaking in, because break-ins brought the police, or left forensic evidence, and — *Don't tell, precious love, promise me* — NMP was no fool. And now, finally, the property manager had shown up.

To Tasia's house. The battle was about to be joined.

Blue Blazer Man, quick and skinny, scurried inside the house and shut off a beeping alarm. He opened a window to let in fresh air. He came to the sliding glass patio door and opened it a crack, thank you very much. Then he disappeared.

NMP waited. Inside that house lay proof, and the truth, and NMP was going to get it, because the truth will set you free.

A minute later, the front door slammed. Blue Blazer Man got back in his car and sat there, making phone calls.

NMP slipped down the hillside and ran across the backyard. Noel Michael Petty might have lumbered, or tripped and fallen, but not NMP. He glided inside through the sliding glass door.

He stood there, dizzy.

It looked like Tasia. It *smelled* like Tasia. Slowly he turned his bulk to take in the panorama. In the living room was a grand piano. Sheet music lay on top of it. He balled his fists and pressed them to his mouth.

Don't squeal. Don't gasp. He saw the photos on the walls. Oh, the photos! So many famous people, all lined up to get their picture taken with Tasia.

He crept along the wall and examined each in detail. He recognized many of them from TV and magazines. Red carpet shots. Awards ceremonies. Tasia singing the national anthem at the Indianapolis 500, wind blowing her hair across her face like a shroud — a portentous shot. To finally see those famous photos first-hand felt like coming home.

See, Tasia: I know you. I've been this close to you, from the beginning.

This hallway, this house, validated everything. All the hours, the days, the *year* NMP had spent gaining familiarity with Tasia's background. Learning about her early life, her school days, her early forays into entertainment; they all showed here. The weekends NMP had spent at the library, the online all-nighters tracing her life through articles and links, images and videos, music downloads, chat room discussion threads about her, snarky comments by know-nothings . . . he had followed her lifeblood, from her beating heart to her fingertips. That's how well Petty knew her.

Petty.

Stop calling yourself by your last name. You're NMP. Out on the streets, you're three letters, no more. No ID, no driver's license or wallet, no way to identify you. You're NMP, big bad bastard of the Tenderloin.

NMP knocked a fist against the side of his head as a reminder to be careful.

Then he fought down a giddy giggle. He was inside Tasia's house. It was like exploring the heretofore-undiscovered tomb of an ancient ruler. And, oh, goodness — in the living room were photos that weren't to be found on the Net. Private snapshots, albums showing Tasia with friends and family. Photos from the *Bad Dogs and Bullets* tour.

NMP's stomach soured. Who were those people? Entourage. Stage crew. Groupies, managers, hangers-on, bandmates, stuntmen. Why did they get backstage passes? NMP was the tour's most fervent follower. Where was his backstage pass?

Not fair. Not motherloving fair.

He was seeing her soul, at last, and it was corrupt.

Disgusted, NMP crept into the kitchen — and saw signs of Searle. The empty box of KFC in the trash. Searle Lecroix was an extra-crispy man; it was in *US Weekly* magazine. Up the stairs, creeping on tiptoe, big bad dude moving like Papa Bear sneaking up on Goldilocks, finding himself outside her bedroom door, her fantasyland, her center . . .

Her clothes were draped across the bed, the nightstand, the chair, the floor — as if she had performed some debauched striptease. Guitar leaning against the chair. Boots by the bed.

Petty gasped, a hard involuntary moan of pain.

Outside, a car door slammed. Petty lurched to the window and peeked through the blinds. Somebody was here. Petty fled the bedroom.

CHAPTER
FOURTEEN

Tasia McFarland hadn't been solely a singer. She had written songs from the time she was a child. The melodies seemed to spin inside her head, growing louder and more insistent until they woke her at night and demanded that she play them on the piano. The music seemed to jump from her hands like sparks, and she would play until her fingers stung. By the time she finished high school she had written two hundred songs and a fully orchestrated rock cantata.

Jo drove up winding streets through the Twin Peaks neighborhood where Tasia and Vienna Hicks had grown up. The city tumbled around her in all directions, houses and apartments stacked on ridges and crammed into valleys like dice. The view was one that sold the place to the world. The bay glittered. The Golden Gate anchored the city to the wild Marin Headlands to the north. Along the western edge of the city, the fog curled against the beach, cold and thick.

As the hill rose higher and grew ridiculously steep, the streets became rustic. Eucalyptus groves grew in ravines, filling the depths with shadow. Manicured lawns bordered the snaking road. Neat homes boasted groomed gardens and rustling, well-tended pines. She followed the road past Sutro Tower. The radio mast rose almost a thousand feet above the peak. No matter how aggressive the fog became, Sutro Tower's three gigantic prongs protruded above it. The mast was like a science fiction monster, awaiting the signal to awake and rampage through the city below. Or so Jo had imagined when she was nine.

Tasia's house was an Italian-style villa tucked against the hillside, gazing down on the Financial District and the bay. Jo got out of the Tacoma and a biting wind stung her cheeks. The driveway was so steep she nearly needed crampons.

Behind her on the street a car door slammed. "Hang on, there."

Jo turned and saw a man walking toward her. "Are you the property manager?"

He climbed the drive, shaking his head. He was in his mid-thirties, with a guileless face and boyish blond hair, dressed in jeans and a *Bad Dogs and Bullets* T-shirt. His hands were stuffed in his pockets but the nonchalant façade didn't hide the red flush in his neck. He was out of shape.

"You the psychiatrist I heard about?"

"I'm Dr. Beckett. And you?"

He stopped beside her. "Ace Chennault."

"Tasia's autobiographer."

"The author is gone but the ghost remains."

He tried to sound jocular, but only managed forced. Belatedly he extended his hand.

Jo shook it. "I'd like to interview you. I'm —"

"Performing a psychological autopsy. I know. News travels fast."

"Apparently."

"Perhaps we can help each other out."

His cloudless smile and baby-fat cheeks must have gotten him interviews with kindly grandmothers and with rock singers who were needy for a big brother's attention. His voice had a hint of jollity. But Jo sensed a practiced stratagem behind the sad clown's eyes. Journalists, one had once told her, needed to connect instantly and deeply with people they interviewed. They needed the illusion of intimacy, of being a person's best friend for a day or an hour, to get the really juicy quotes.

And Ace Chennault was a journalist who'd just lost his biggest source — and source of income.

"Can we set up a time later today?" Jo said.

"I thought we could do some horse trading. You want to poke through my notes and listen to the stream-of-consciousness narration Tasia recorded?" He smiled again. "I'm willing to share it all with you. But be fair. Give me something in return."

"Such as?"

"Your unique insights into her mind."

A mental warning light blinked red. "If my report becomes part of the public record, you'll have access to it."

"That's not what I was hoping."

"I figured not. But I'm working for the SFPD. They have dibs on my work."

The smile broadened. "No tit, no tattle?"

She put on a practiced face of her own: neutral. "Can't play it that way."

Behind her the front door opened. A man in a blue blazer extended his hand. "Dr. Beckett? I'm the property manager."

Jo stepped into the front hall. Chennault followed.

"Excuse me?" she said.

He shrugged, gesturing *no biggie*. "I've been here before. Stayed in the guest room half a dozen times."

"Okay, but right now I'm the one with permission from the police to come inside. Sorry, Mr. Chennault."

He raised his hands. "Wouldn't want to muddle the pack order, Alpha girl. Mr. Manager and I'll wait while you take your tour."

Jo smiled firmly, neutrally, at him. "How about we grab coffee after this?"

Hands still up, he retreated. When he reached the door, he put his hands together and bowed, like a Thai offering a *wai*.

She watched him walk down the steps toward his car. To the property manager she said, "Have you seen him here before?"

"No, but I'm not here very often."

"I'm going to survey the house. I may be a while."

"I'll be in the car. Got calls to make."

Jo took out her digital camera and walked deeper into the house. It was compact and elegantly appointed. Food in the kitchen: organic arugula, an empty KFC bucket in the trash. Vitamins, herbal supplements, and a bottle of Stolichnaya on the counter.

92

She wandered into the living room. The plate-glass windows overlooked a small backyard that rose steeply into bottlebrush trees and rhododendrons on the hillside.

The police had been through the house already, and apparently hadn't found any evidence of a crime. So Jo was looking for the contours of Tasia's emotional landscape. And she was looking for traces of her final day.

Two big bookcases were haphazardly piled with paranormal romance novels, old copies of *Entertainment Weekly*, and a country music Listeners' Choice award.

Mixed in with the spicy books about hot girl-on-werewolf love was a copy of Gerald Posner's *Case Closed*. Jo picked it up, perplexed. The book was an anti-conspiracy text, considered an authoritative tome debunking conspiracy theories about the Kennedy assassination.

Why was Tasia interested in JFK? Or presidential assassination?

She snapped a photo of the bookshelf.

The grand piano was covered with slumping piles of music manuscript paper. Jo was certain that the police had shuffled through them looking for a suicide note. They hadn't found one. The manuscript paper was covered with Tasia's compositions. Musical notes crowded the treble staff. The lyrics rushed across the page, as if Tasia had been gasping to keep up with the music that poured from her head.

Propped on the music stand was "The Liar's Lullaby." Tasia had scored a complete arrangement for piano. At the top she'd scribbled *Allegro. Counterpoint/ Round.* Dense chords packed the bass clef.

Said you wanted me to be your choir
Help you build the funeral pyre.

Jo picked out the piece on the keyboard. The melody was minor key, droning, repetitive, sad. It sounded almost compulsive. From the evidence heaped on top of the Steinway, Tasia had been filled with desperation and obsession.

Jo carefully photographed each sheet. Then she went upstairs.

In Tasia's bedroom she found disorder. The bed was unmade and clothes were strewn on the floor.

Jo's own wardrobe was functional. She wore tailored blouses and well-fitting pants that allowed her to simultaneously look professional and run for her life. No pencil skirts, no scarves that wrapped around her neck. Nothing that would prevent her from leaping out a window if a schizophrenic gangbanger heard voices telling him the bitch needed cutting, or a psychopathic convict decided, on a whim, to strangle her. She had combats for the weekend, sweats and shorts for climbing, and a black suit for testifying in court. If she wanted to go high fashion, she'd put on her paisley Doc Martens.

The thought that Tasia McFarland, or anybody, would treat designer clothing — clothing that cost enough to put a teenager through college — like dishrags dropped on the floor to mop up spilled coffee, boggled her. Either Tasia had been inured to the privileges of fame, or she was so depressed that she couldn't even pick up a . . . she looked at a label . . . Dolce & Gabbana dress from the bathroom floor.

She took more photos. Then she turned to the bed. The covers were turned down on both sides. Two pillows had distinct impressions. A set of men's boots sat beside it. Worn, well-loved red cowboy boots.

On an easy chair, beneath a gauzy pile of women's blouses, she found a man's shirt that still smelled of aftershave. She checked inside the collar. A cleaner's mark read *SL*. Leaning against the chair was an acoustic guitar.

Searle Lecroix had, it seemed, been serenading Tasia shortly before her fateful trip to the concert.

She headed into the bathroom. The wind sliced through the open window. Half a dozen prescription bottles sat on the counter.

Tasia's pharmaceutical cornucopia looked as colorful as confetti. Antianxiety drugs. Vicodin and Tylenol with codeine. Sleeping pills. Diet pills, aka amphetamines. Prozac.

Lithium. From the scrip label, the prescription had been filled two months earlier, but the bottle was full.

Off her meds.

Jo lined up the bottles and took photos, making sure she got the labels and the prescribing physicians' names. All these bottles would be checked by the medical examiner and cross-referenced for tox screening in connection with Tasia's autopsy. But Jo wanted to verify their contents for herself.

The wind whistled through the open window. She heard a car drive past the house. Men's voices batted about on the wind.

The floor creaked behind her. She turned.

The bedroom looked exactly as she'd seen it moments earlier. The floor creaked again, in the hallway beyond it.

Chennault.

Damn, the nosy bastard had snuck back inside the house. She strode out of the bathroom toward the bedroom door. "Excuse me."

Again the creak. She stepped into the hall. Nobody was on the landing.

"Mr. Chennault?"

She told herself she hadn't imagined it. Again she heard men's voices outside. She walked to the landing, where a picture window overlooked the street. The hairs on her arms prickled.

Beside his car, Chennault stood talking to the property manager.

Slowly she turned. Behind her, outside a hallway closet, stood a figure in fatigues and a balaclava.

Five foot eight, probably two-fifty, and breathing hard. Jo's gaze went to his hands. Gardening gloves.

She ran for the stairs.

She sprinted, two steps, three, and heard him coming. His feet thumped on the carpet. *Run*, she thought. She leaped down the stairs two at a time.

A hand grabbed her hair. Her head snapped back.

She swung an elbow and hit padded flesh, heard his thick breathing, felt his meaty presence. His hand twisted her hair. She lost her balance, missed a step, and fell.

She threw out her hands and hit hard, knees to stomach to her face. The masked man grunted and toppled with her. They slid down the stairs and thudded against the hardwood floor.

He landed on top of her. His weight, his smell, were crushing. She squirmed, fingernails out. His flesh was soft and red around the collar. She clawed at his neck.

He lumbered to his feet and careened into the living room, hitting the wall as he ran. He threw open the plate-glass patio door.

Jo clambered to her feet and stumbled for the front door. Looking back, she saw the intruder flee across the backyard.

She threw open the front door. "Help."

Chennault and the property manager looked up, startled, and rushed toward her.

Jo found her phone. Fingers shaking, she punched 911. She pointed at the back of the house. "Man in a balaclava. Ran out and into the trees."

The property manager gaped at her, and at the open patio door, with seeming confusion. Chennault took the same long second, then put a hand on Jo's shoulder.

"Are you hurt?" he said.

She had the phone to her ear. Her ribs were killing her. Her face had rug burns. She couldn't swallow because her throat was bone-dry.

"I'm okay."

Through the patio door, she saw movement. The bottlebrush trees were heavy with red blooms, and they swung as the man in the balaclava ran past. Chennault saw it too. He hesitated only a second before running out the patio door.

"Nine-one-one. What is the nature of your emergency?"

"An intruder just assaulted me."

Jo ran after Chennault. He was already across the yard and running for the trees. Up the steep hillside, the rhododendrons rustled like a black bear was tearing through them.

She gave the 911 dispatcher the address. "I'm in pursuit on foot, with another civilian."

Part of her thinking, what the hell was she doing? Another part thinking, *Look around. Make sure there's not another one. And what the hell am I doing?*

"Stay on the line, Dr. Beckett," the dispatcher said. "A unit is on the way."

"Wouldn't hang up for a million bucks," Jo said.

She aimed for the trees.

CHAPTER
FIFTEEN

Jo ran up the hill behind Tasia's house, phone pressed to her ear. Her heart beat like a snare drum. Branches swung past her face. The hillside smelled of damp earth and the musk of the attacker's clothing. Above her, the bushes swayed violently as the attacker bowled through them.

"He's a hundred yards ahead of me, heading for the top of Twin Peaks," she told the emergency dispatcher. "The other civilian is closer to him."

Rhododendrons were dense on the hillside. Sunlight gashed through the leaves, looking unnaturally bright. Damn it. How had the guy gotten into the house?

Ahead, Ace Chennault muscled through the brush. Ungainly but purposeful, he closed the distance on the attacker.

"Chennault," she hollered, "watch out for weapons."

She put the phone back to her ear. "We're heading toward Sutro Tower. How long for the unit to respond?"

"They're on the way," the dispatcher said.

The damp ground gave way beneath her feet. She pitched forward and her hand hit the slope. The attacker disappeared from sight, followed by Chennault.

She heard them threshing the bushes. She put her arm up to shield herself from branches and plowed after them.

The hillside flattened and she came out onto a dusty field. Ahead lay eucalyptus groves, then a chain-link fence. Sutro Tower stood beyond it, a fulsome red and white in the sunshine, rising mightily three hundred yards overhead.

The attacker was following the fence line into the distance. He had a smooth stride and was surprisingly light on his feet, motoring toward freedom. Chennault sprinted raggedly behind him.

"He's headed west. If he gets past Sutro Tower . . ." She tried to picture what lay beyond the antenna. Glades, more eucalyptus, steep ravines. ". . . he could lose us."

She ran, beginning to blow hard. On the far side of the hilltop the attacker darted into a eucalyptus grove and dropped from sight over the lip of the hill. Five seconds later so did Chennault.

Jo passed Sutro Tower. "They're in heavy woods, heading downhill."

At the lip of the hill she slowed. The ground pitched harshly into trees and tangled undergrowth. The vine-covered ground was a morass of eroded gullies. A fallen eucalyptus, at least a hundred feet tall, spanned a ravine like a bridge.

Chennault was eighty yards ahead, pummeling downhill like he couldn't stop. She didn't see the attacker. In Chennault's wake branches snapped and leaves crunched, but nowhere else. A black wire of warning spun around her chest.

She scanned the terrain. She had a rule: Listen to the whisper on the wind. Hear the still small voice that says, *Watch out*.

She cupped her hands in front of her mouth. "Chennault, be careful."

He barreled onward, seemingly certain that he was still on the attacker's trail — or maybe just out of control. He put a hand against a tree trunk to slow himself.

Behind him the attacker rose from a thicket. In his hand he had a rock the size of a softball. He whipped his arm overhead and smashed it against Chennault's head.

Chennault staggered, crashed into another tree trunk, and toppled like an upended floor lamp into the ravine.

The wind snapped through Jo's hair. She clutched the phone, horrified. "He attacked the man who was chasing him. Get the cops here. Hurry."

"They're coming, Doctor."

The attacker stared into the blank space where Chennault had fallen. His shoulders heaved. The rock looked sharp and bloody.

"Get them to come faster."

The attacker continued to stare into the ravine. *Shit.* How far had Chennault fallen? The attacker weighed the rock in his hand. Eyes downslope, he inched over the edge of the ravine. *Dammit. Damn.*

"A man's down and the attacker's moving on him again," she said. "And I don't have a weapon."

Deep in the distance, a siren cried. Jo cupped her hands in front of her mouth and yelled down the ravine. "That's the cops."

The attacker turned. His dark eyes peered at her from beneath the balaclava.

Her voice sounded dry. She told the dispatcher, "He's watching me."

Fear whispered, *Run*. But if she fled, the attacker would have free range to finish off Chennault. She forced her legs not to bolt. The siren grew louder.

She gritted her teeth and shouted, "Hear that?"

For another moment the attacker stared at her. Then, without a sound, he turned and disappeared into the trees.

The siren grew shrill. A police cruiser heaved into view. Jo pointed at the trees and yelled, "Assailant ran that way." Then she scurried down the slope to the edge of the ravine. A trail of broken vegetation delineated Chennault's fall line.

She couldn't see him. "Chennault?"

From the depths of the ravine, beneath moss and fallen logs, came moaning. She sidestepped down the slope, hanging onto branches and crawling green vines. The shadows deepened. Above, the siren cut off and car doors slammed.

An officer called, "Are you all right?"

"Man's hurt. He needs rescue."

The moan came again, like the lowing of an animal. She followed the sound and found him half-buried in creepers and mucky earth.

102

God, scalp wounds were bloody. If she hadn't seen the rock smash against Chennault's head, Jo would have thought he'd been shot.

She crouched at his side. "Hold still. The police are calling the paramedics."

"Damn," he moaned. "Bastard brained me, didn't he?"

Wild vines had wrapped around him. Beneath the copious blood his face was white. He tried to sit up, and screamed. His left arm was fractured and his elbow dislocated.

Jo gently held him down. "Stay still."

"Make a great postscript for the book," he said, and passed out.

CHAPTER
SIXTEEN

When Jo got home the sun was high in the sky. She parked the Tacoma beyond the park and hiked toward her house, feeling spooked.

Chennault had been evacuated by the paramedics to UCSF Medical Center. He couldn't give the police much information about the attacker. Neither could she.

When her phone rang she grabbed it and peered at the display. A pang went through her, disappointment covering worry.

"So, have the police discovered how the guy got into Tasia's house?" she said.

"The property manager opened the back door before you came," said Amy Tang. "He snuck in while nobody was looking. Bigger question — who was he?"

"And what did he want?"

"Thief?"

"Ghoul? Somebody seeking relics to sell on eBay?"

The cool wind shook the Monterey pines in the park. A cable car clattered past, bulging with tourists. The gripman rang his bell.

"I have another question," Jo said. "Will he be back?"

"Watch yourself."

"You bet."

She hung up but clutched the phone in her palm as she walked. *Come on. Ring.*

How could it be that modern life was saturated with communications devices, that the information age spewed gossip and barking commentary night and day, that the entire electromagnetic spectrum was alight with phone calls and texts and breaking news about celebrity boob jobs — but when she wanted news that the PJs of the 129th had safely touched down at Moffett Field, she was utterly in the dark?

She tucked the phone in her back pocket. A second later she pulled it out again and called Vienna Hicks. When she told her about being attacked by the intruder at Tasia's home, Vienna said, "Holy crap, are you okay?"

"Aside from a rug burn on my face, I'm perfect. But Ace Chennault was taken away in an ambulance."

"Poor bastard. The guy never did look like he could duck."

Jo smiled. "Do you know anybody who might want to break into your sister's house?"

She tossed it out like chum on choppy water, not really expecting an answer. She checked for traffic and jogged across the street toward her house.

"Maybe," Vienna said.

Jo slowed. "Really?"

"Don't look a gift horse in the mouth, Dr. Beckett. Can you meet me at Waymire and Fong this evening?"

"Certainly."

"Bring your secret psychiatric decoder ring."

"Want to clarify that?"

"Six o'clock. I'll tell you when I see you."

Jo saw the green VW Bug drive past at the same moment the driver saw her. The woman's head swiveled sharply. She whipped a U-turn and double-parked in front of Jo's house. The VW's air-cooled engine squealed. Exhaust stank from its tailpipe. The driver climbed out.

The concrete beneath Jo's feet abruptly felt hot. She didn't move.

The woman marched toward her. "I thought you'd have a secretary, or an office at least, that would be open for normal business hours."

She was slight and colorful, with bangly red earrings that clicked in the sunlight. Her hair was dyed skidmark-black, with a magenta streak along her forehead. She wore silver rings on her fingers and toes. Her T-shirt said MARKHAM PRINTING. Ink was her thing. She had a Gothic tattoo on her left forearm. SOPHIE.

She approached, scowling. "You're Jo Beckett, aren't you?"

She looked like a butterfly whose wings had been pulled off and sewn back on. Beautiful and damaged, struggling to stay airborne, and angry about it. She was Dawn Parnell, Sophie Quintana's mother, Gabe's ex-girlfriend.

Jo couldn't conceive of a good reason for Dawn to know where she lived. Or to be there. Not a happy reason, not . . .

"Is it Gabe?"

"Yeah," Dawn said.

The sun all at once seemed to hum, a high-pitched tone that drilled through Jo's chest. "Did something happen?"

Dawn's eyes were the hazel of a kaleidoscope, too bright, spinning with emotion. *Not Gabe. Don't tell me. Please, Jesus.*

"Where is he?" Dawn said.

"Did they — didn't the Wing tell you . . ."

"I'm late for work. My shift started at noon, and it's his day."

"What?"

Dawn pointed up the street, perhaps toward the print shop where she worked. "Gabe has Sophie during the week. But she got sick at school and the nurse couldn't find him. So they had to call me. And now I'm late."

"Wait." Jo raised her hands. She heard the beseeching note in her voice. "Don't you know where Gabe is?"

"No. That's why I'm here." Dawn said it slowly, as if to a recalcitrant child.

"You haven't heard anything from his family, or the one-twenty-ninth?"

"No. And I can't afford to miss my shift. I do that, I get docked. And if I lose my job, I get in trouble with the custody people."

Jo's heart was banging like a kettledrum. She felt like she was trying to grab a handhold on a wall of cotton candy.

"Nothing's happened to Gabe?" she said.

Dawn looked at her crooked. "Except I can't find him. I had to pick Sophie up from the school nurse's office."

Jo's vision throbbed. Gabe was all right. She walked toward the idling VW. "Is Sophie okay?"

"Fever and vomiting. Stomach flu's going around the school."

Sophie wasn't in the car. Jo stopped and figured it out.

Dawn crossed her arms. "I can't take her to work."

"Did you bring her here?"

"Gabe spends time with you, right?"

Jo turned toward her front porch. "Where is she?"

"I have to book. I'm already in deep with the boss." Dawn marched back to the car. "You should tape a note to the door when you leave. Let people know where you are."

"Where's Sophie?" Jo said.

Dawn pointed next door at the redbrick mansion that dominated the street. "Your neighbor said she could stay with him until you got home."

She opened the car door, and paused. Her gaze slid over Jo. For a moment, she seemed ready to comment on what she was looking at. Then she got in and drove away in a film of gray exhaust.

This is your mom. This is your mom's brain on drugs.

Jo pressed her fingers to her eyes, trying to stop the hum and the heat and the acid pulse of the adrenaline that coursed through her veins. Be fair, she told herself. Dawn was monitored by the courts to make sure she was clean. To maintain her visitation rights with Sophie she had to submit to random drug testing, and she had to keep her job.

Dawn had been through rehab twice. She was eking it out, day by day, watched over by her parents. According to Gabe, they seemed at once broken and hopeful because their beautiful girl — who had enrolled at San Francisco State to study marine biology, dropped out when she got pregnant, and recovered from childbirth with a variety of self-chosen chemical pick-me-ups — was now living independently, and employed in a business that didn't get raided by the DEA.

Gabe's all right.

Maybe.

Jo walked next door to the mansion. From the balcony, plaster statues of Roman gods gazed down at her. As she climbed the steps, footsteps bundled along the hardwood hallway inside.

"Coming, Jo."

She pinched the bridge of her nose. Did he have an infrared Jo-cam that alerted him when she neared his porch? The deadbolt flipped and Ferd Bismuth opened the door. His eyes crinkled behind his glasses as he smiled.

"Of course you're here. I told Sophie's mom you'd come. I knew it."

"Thanks for stepping up to the plate," she said.

He ushered her in. "I couldn't let Sophie wait on your front porch, for Pete's sake."

"But please, take off the surgical mask."

He slumped. Reluctantly he unhooked the mask from his ears. "Come on."

He led her toward the living room. The mansion had high ceilings, huge windows, and a staircase with a heavy wooden banister. Jo envisioned Bette Davis at the top of the forbidding stairs, dressed as Baby Jane, ready to pitch Joan Crawford from her wheelchair. Ferd lived in the mansion as a long-term house sitter. The owners had taken a nine-month trip to Italy. They'd been gone sixteen. If the Spitzers stayed away much longer, Ferd could gain squatter's rights.

From the living room sofa, bundled under thermal blankets, Sophie gave Jo a finger wave. Pillows were piled around her like sandbags, perhaps in the event that she exploded. A can of 7UP sat on the coffee table beside packets of moistened towelettes and a box of latex gloves. Sophie's chocolate-chip hair curled against her forehead with sweat. Her eyes, bright with fever, looked like glazed marbles.

Perched on the arm of the sofa was Ferd's monkey, Mr. Peebles. He had a thermometer in his busy little hands.

"And I see that today we're playing *Outbreak*," Jo said.

Mr. Peebles shook the thermometer like a pro. He squinted at it, bared his teeth, and cooed in alarm. He must have seen Ferd do the same a hundred times. He stuck the wrong end in his mouth and posed like FDR smoking from his cigarette holder. He pulled it out again. Jo crossed the room and grabbed it before he could insert it anyplace else.

Welcome to Ferd's palace of hypochondria.

The little capuchin, officially Ferd's "emotional support companion," fixed her with an unnerving stare, like he was silently adding her to his shit list. And with a monkey, that term was literal.

"Don't get cocky," she said. "I can outwit you just by counting to three."

Mr. Peebles scampered across the sofa and jumped onto Ferd's shoulder. Jo sat on the edge of the sofa and rubbed Sophie's arm.

"Look like you hit rock bottom, champ. You hanging in?"

Sophie shrugged. Jo put the back of her hand to the girl's forehead.

Ferd approached. "Her temp was a hundred one point three when I checked ten minutes ago."

Sophie turned her shining eyes to Jo. "When's my dad going to get here?"

"As soon as he can after he gets back."

"Gets back? Where'd he go?"

Jo mentally slapped herself on the forehead. Don't *increase* the kid's anxiety, you dork. "He's out with the Wing. But I know he'll pick you up as soon as possible." She brushed Sophie's damp hair off her face. "Feel pretty lousy?"

"Hideous."

Jo raised her eyebrows. "Not merely disgusting?"

"H-i-d-e-o-u-s. It was on my vocabulary quiz today. I barfed on the test paper."

Jo smiled. Sophie's sense of humor always took her by surprise. "I'll vouch for your ability to use the word in conversation."

Jo's smile waned. Her day was packed to the gills and she felt like a heavy stick was prodding her between the shoulder blades.

"Think you can walk next door to my house? My guest room has a big warm bed. You can watch TV and sleep until your dad gets here."

Sophie nodded. Ferd got her backpack and Jo helped her on with her shoes. At the door Jo turned to thank Ferd, and saw the can of Lysol in his hand. She glared. He hid it behind his back.

"Feel better, Sophie," he said.

She replied without expression. "Wilco."

Jo paused on the top step. "I'm glad you were home. Really."

"It was fortunate."

Ferd's face, so often tangled with anxiety or dreamy with unrequited love for her, was sober. He didn't have to say anything else. They were both thinking it. Nobody could count on good fortune.

CHAPTER
SEVENTEEN

Jo tucked Sophie in bed, upstairs in her guest room. She pulled a down comforter over the little girl and turned the television to Nickelodeon.

"If you want, I can call your aunt Regina and see if she can pick you up."

"Aunt Regina's at traffic school."

"Then we'll wait for your dad." She handed Sophie the remote. "I'll be downstairs. Call if you need me."

"If I do, you'll come back?" Sophie sounded like she was on a rickety bridge, crossing a canyon alone.

"Of course I will. I know you'd rather be in your own bed, but look at this as a field trip to Dr. Jo's House of No School and all the TV you can sleep through."

Sophie nodded tightly. Her lips were pressed together, white. Jo told herself: Get the anxiety out of your voice, your face, your posture. She sat on the edge of the bed and smoothed the little girl's hair back from her face.

"Did you always know you wanted to be a doctor?" Sophie said.

"Actually, I started thinking about it when I was a little older than you."

"Really?" Sophie's eyes brightened. "Is it hard?"

Jo thought about her answer. "It's a challenge. But I think challenges are a good thing. Medicine is fascinating. And best of all, you get to help people. There's a lot to learn, but lucky for me, I liked school."

"I do, too."

"Tell you what. When you feel better, I'll tell you stories about medical school. Funny ones."

"And about gruesome diseases? Like flesh-eating bacteria." Sophie was smiling. She turned serious. "I wouldn't be afraid to talk about it. It would be fascinating."

Jo swallowed a smile, strangely touched. "Was that word also on your vocabulary test?"

"I would have got a star, except for the barf." She became thoughtful. "What's gorilla warfare?"

Jo went still. "I'm sorry?"

"Do monkeys fight people?"

"No. Where'd you get that idea?"

Sophie shrugged. "I heard the teachers talking about gorilla warfare."

"It's g-u-e-r-r-i-l-l-a. People — rebels. Don't worry about the monkeys."

Or about your dad, going away to battle.

Sophie nodded. Jo snugged the comforter around her and went downstairs.

In her office she sat down at the desk, leaned on her elbows, and rubbed her forehead. Anger served neither her nor Sophie. She told herself to let it go.

She told herself to watch out for Dawn Parnell.

Her cell phone rang. It seemed to ring all the way through her like a fire alarm.

She grabbed it. On the display, she saw *Tina*. "Yo."

"Try not to sound so thrilled to hear from me."

Jo cleared her throat. "Yo, my *sistah*."

"Be that way, then."

"Sorry. This day has exploded like a cherry bomb. The case is treacherous and Sophie's here, sick, and" — she got up and shut the office door — "Sophie's mother practically drop-kicked her out the door of her car, poor kid. And Gabe's been on a rescue since last night and if I don't hear from him soon I am going to have a psychotic break. I mean I'm going to crawl up the wall and across the ceiling."

"Jo, I'm sorry. What kind of rescue?"

"Sea rescue. A tanker's on fire five hundred miles offshore. That means mid-air refueling of the Pave Hawk."

"Sit down. Put your head between your knees. Don't eat the wallpaper."

"They should be back."

"They will be."

"It's been fourteen hours."

"Jo, listen to me. Gabe's a pro, and strong. And so are you. *Strong*. I mean it."

The conviction in Tina's voice brought her up short. She exhaled.

"Thanks. Sorry." She sat down and ran a hand through her hair. "Let's start again. Yo, my *sistah*, what's up?"

"Are you watching the news?"

Jo's landline rang. This time the buzz she felt was low and anxious. "No."

"You're on it."

"Hang on, my other phone's ringing."

"Of course it is," Tina said.

Jo picked up the landline. Amy Tang said, "If this crap goes viral we may not have till the end of the week to clear the case."

"What crap?" Jo told Tina goodbye, took the landline to the living room, and turned on the television.

"I tried to keep your name out of things, but some numb nuts leaked it."

The local news bulletin was on. A reporter was standing outside Tasia McFarland's house. Behind her, two police officers guarded the front door.

". . . have not confirmed the identity of the man attacked by the intruder, but our sources are telling us it's" — she glanced at her notes — "Ace Chennault, a music journalist who was traveling on assignment with Tasia's tour."

"I hear your TV. That's Triple A ball. Flip it to the majors," Tang said. "The Freakout News Network."

Jo changed to a national news channel. Behind a neon-blue desk, a blonde correspondent was interviewing a guest straight off the cliché shelf. Plump, disheveled, wearing a tweed jacket and bow tie — markers that saved the network the trouble of writing out a name tag saying PROF. JO wondered if they'd sent an intern on a scavenger hunt to the nearest college campus with a list that read, *Neanderthal skull from Anthropology Dept; Cheerleaders' spanky pants; Absent-minded professor.*

116

". . . no indication that she was so depressed that she was likely to commit suicide. I've analyzed videotape from the three performances preceding the concert in San Francisco, and the evidence is simply not there."

"What's this?" Jo said.

"This," Tang said, "is the clock starting on your fifteen minutes."

On-screen, the blonde correspondent nodded thoughtfully at the professor. "What warning signs would Tasia have given if she had in fact been suicidal?"

"Oh, boy," Jo said.

Tang said, "I'm guessing it takes ninety seconds before you scream for somebody to hand you a band saw, so you can slice either the television, the professor, or yourself in half."

The professor threaded his fingers together. "Let's examine what she didn't do. She didn't leave a suicide note. She didn't seem what in lay terms we call "blue." She was headlining a successful tour. She was in the limelight, receiving the accolades of adoring fans."

A bony finger seemed to scratch at Jo's stomach. "Who is this guy?"

"Read the screen," Tang said.

Jo's eyes twitched. *Gaspar Hellman, forensic psychiatrist.*

"So you're saying that Tasia didn't appear suicidal?" the blonde said.

"That's correct."

The blonde nodded ponderously. Her hair, elaborately windblown and lacquered, moved like a wig Jo had last seen on the singer from the B-52s. Her blue eyes gazed

117

from a heart-shaped face, kitten sweet, with neat white teeth. Her name was Edie Wilson.

"So you're saying the police psychiatrist has it wrong," she said.

"We know nothing about the qualifications of this 'psychiatrist,'" — air quotes — "if that is in fact what Dr. Beckett is. We know only that she has been retained by a police department that has a direct interest in shifting blame for Tasia's death away from those who might have profited from it."

Edie Wilson nodded vociferously. "Cui bono."

Professor Herr Forensic Psychiatrist Hellman lowered his face to peer at Wilson over his tortoiseshell frames. "You know your Latin. And what it implies."

"No," Jo said, "she knows what's on the teleprompter and she's spouting the crap the producers whisper in her earpiece. Gah. Jeez."

This was surreal. On the crawl at the bottom of the screen, she swore she saw *Russian mail-order brides win World Cup* and *Unicorns discovered, seek power-sharing deal with My Little Pony.*

Edie Wilson frowned. "Women don't shoot themselves. It's well-known." Thoughtful pause. "Could it be possible that she was playing Russian Roulette?"

"I can't . . . women do shoot themselves . . . this is . . . oh, crap," Jo said.

"That's it, Beckett. Let it all out," Tang said.

The bony finger spun around Jo's midsection again, and in her head she heard a spectral voice saying, *Neener-neener-neener.*

118

Tang wasn't laughing, however. She sounded deadly serious. "You may reach the same conclusion Dr. TV is pontificating about. Are you sure you want to contradict him?"

"He's mouthing off without any evidence. Spouting shallow, uninformed opinions about suicidality. About a woman he knows nothing about, hasn't examined . . . about *my* case."

Gaspar Hellman stroked his goatee. "You're exactly right, Edie. Cui bono. Who benefits? By claiming that Tasia ended her own life, who gains?"

"That's a frightening question, professor," the blonde said.

"Frightening? These people don't understand — or don't care — how uninformed speculation upsets the victim's family." Jo clawed a hand into her hair. "Tang, this can mess up my work."

Cui bono? — It benefited the bottom-feeders who preyed on public tragedy. Witnesses might begin to demand money from Jo before they talked, because the tabloids and E! were paying them. They might say, "I can't talk to you until next week . . . TMZ has an exclusive with me until then." By which time, they'd have shaped their story for maximum tabloid sensationalism and personal publicity.

She heard a sharp knock on her front door. Phone to her ear, she stalked down the hall to answer it. "They're playing Machiavelli for sport. Making me look like a tool, like this is a board game. They're in it for entertainment but it's not funny."

She grabbed the doorknob. "Hang on, somebody's here. If it's the Clownface News Network, they're going to get a jaw full of my fist."

"Beckett, you shock me."

"Metaphorically speaking. Bozos."

She opened the door. There stood Gabe.

CHAPTER
EIGHTEEN

He took in her ferocity and put up his hands. "What did I do?"

For a moment she stood motionless. Then she unwound and jumped into his arms. Threw herself against him, hugged him fiercely.

She held on to the phone. "Later, Tang."

Hanging up, she put her hand against Gabe's chest. She tried to calm down. Failed heroically. He swept her back inside.

"Welcome back to dry land, Sergeant." She was smiling. She fought the urge to jump up and down. She stood on tiptoe to kiss him.

He swept her down the hall. "Where's Sophie?"

"In bed in the guest room."

He glanced up the stairs. He had a baseball cap in his hand. He slapped it against his thigh. "I never told Dawn where you live. That's a promise."

"I never doubted that."

He slapped the ball cap against his leg again. "Maybe she got it out of Sophie somehow. I don't even want to think that she may have followed me here."

"It's moot now."

Jo wanted to grab him and bury her face in the warmth of his shirt. But he was stalking the hall like a hungry cat.

"Did she pester you?" he said.

"She was mostly concerned about getting to work on time. That's why she brought Sophie over."

"Dumped her." He stopped. "That's what she did. Dumped her little girl."

Hot patches washed his cheeks and neck, as if painted with a burning brush.

"Thank God you happened to be home. I hate to think what she would have done if you weren't here." He ran a hand roughly through his hair. Looked at her. "What?"

All Jo's training in psychology, her understanding of the dynamics of family splinter groups, whisked around her like moths. Cautioning her to keep her mouth shut. Warning: Don't insert yourself into a sharp and rickety relationship. But she had to tell him. And she had to keep her own anger out of it. Mouth off, feed his ire, and she'd only worsen the situation.

"I wasn't home," she said. "Ferd was."

She had occasionally seen Gabe look like he could kill a man barehanded. It was his stance, his expression, the unremitting fierceness of his gaze. The utter self-confidence that transmitted, silently and with complete conviction, *Do not fuck with me.*

She saw it then. Really saw it, for the first time. Her skin went cold. She resisted the compulsion to step back from him.

122

He opened his mouth, and closed it. His gaze distilled. For a long moment he held as still as a stone carving.

"Was she high?" he said.

"Not in any obvious way."

His gaze traveled the hallway, but Jo knew he wasn't seeing anything in front of him, least of all her.

"She's not going to do this again. I won't have it."

Jo lowered her voice to a murmur. "Gabe, I don't know if you can control it."

From upstairs came a girlish call. "Daddy?"

Gabe's gaze broke from Jo's. He took the stairs at a jog, gripping the banister like a neck he was wringing.

Jo stayed put. The black heat in Gabe's eyes had run through her, so hot she nearly shivered.

She had never truly seen him. She'd only thought she had. She had seen the veneer, the practiced glare that served as a warning to foes.

But a moment earlier, she had seen him exposed. She had seen a molten core. She had glimpsed him out of control. She had glimpsed real violence.

And she didn't want to follow him up the stairs.

She walked into the living room. The news had moved on from sticking pins in her to analyzing old photos of Tasia with Robert McFarland. The crawl at the bottom of the screen now read, *Controversy over police psychiatrist in Tasia McFarland case*.

She turned off the television. Stared out the bay window at shadows scrubbing the sidewalk in the breeze.

A minute later Gabe carried Sophie down the stairs. Her head lay against his shoulder, eyes sunk with fever.

"Feel better, girl," Jo said.

Sophie smiled.

Gabe headed straight for the door. "Let's get you home, cricket."

Jo opened the door. His expression was so fiercely protective, and openly pained, that Jo's breath caught.

And she saw for the first time the bruises that ran down his neck, and the black eye that was developing. And, with his sleeve ruched up from lifting Sophie, the bandage that was wound around his forearm. Betadine stretched out from beneath it. She saw his exhaustion, which was only being kept at bay by the heat of his anger.

He curled past her and out the door. "Thanks. I'll call you."

"Gabe." She followed him outside and down the steps. "Everybody . . ."

Something warned her to stop herself. Don't ask, not with Sophie listening. And he finally did turn, and gave her the raw, disintegrated stare of truth.

Things were not all right. Not everybody had come back to shore alive.

CHAPTER
NINETEEN

At 6p.m. Jo walked through the vaulting marble lobby of the Art Deco office building at the bottom of Sacramento Street in the Financial District. She climbed the fire stairs to the fifth floor and stepped into the plush lobby of Waymire & Fong LLP.

The receptionist stood behind her desk applying pearly pink lipstick, about to bolt the office for the evening. When the fire door closed behind Jo, she looked up like a startled hare. The lipstick swerved across her chin.

"I have an appointment with Vienna Hicks," Jo said.

The receptionist wiped off the lipstick. "Jesus, you came out of nowhere."

Nobody climbed the stairs around here, that was certain. But Jo bet half the attorneys spent an hour on the StairMaster at the gym.

The receptionist picked up the phone. Jo wandered the lobby. The building was old enough to have tall sash windows. Outside, sunlight hit the sides of surrounding buildings. It reflected orange, a hot note that seemed to touch each pane of glass like a twang, singing the city toward evening. Down Sacramento Street, between skyscrapers, a sliver of the bay scintillated blue.

The receptionist set down the phone. "Ms. Hicks will be right out."

Jo lingered by the windows. The building was built of excellent gray granite. The Art Deco design had copious edges and corners. It would make an elegant rock-climbing problem. For a moment Jo felt an urge to attack it.

"Dr. Beckett."

Vienna's swooping voice caught her like a lariat. Jo turned. Vienna loomed in the hallway, fists planted on her hips. The receptionist stood behind her desk gripping her purse. Vienna waved her toward the elevator.

"I'll escort Dr. Beckett out, Dana Jean. And I'll turn off the lights. And feed the lizards. Shoo."

Dana Jean scooted for the elevator. Vienna beckoned Jo down the hall.

Jo followed her toward her office. "I'm surprised you're still here."

"The day after my sister died, you mean? I'm listed in the phone book. The media's camped out on my driveway. The office is a sanctuary."

She turned a corner. Vienna didn't seem to walk down the hall so much as to fill it, like a gliding manta ray.

"That's why I asked you to come down here. Call me anal compulsive, or passive retentive, over-protective, but Tasia was my baby sister and I don't want the cops or the tabloids getting information that's irrelevant."

"If you thought it was irrelevant, I wouldn't be here."

Vienna's office was crowded with two desks, a dead potted cactus, and shelves of case binders. She thumped down into her chair like a depth charge, opened a desk drawer, and took out a phone.

"Tasia forgot this, a couple of months ago. It's an unlisted number and I haven't shown it to anybody else."

"So the police don't know about it?" Jo said.

"I see no point. A phone? Tasia had lots of phones. She had gewgaws and knickknacks all over the place. She picked them up like candy. At awards ceremonies, she got amazing goodie bags. I'm not talking potpourri and scented soap. I mean vintage Champagne and Xboxes and five-hundred-dollar shoes."

Jo had seen some of those on the floor in Tasia's bedroom. "That's all?"

"Maybe a Stinger missile at the Grammys, I don't remember."

Jo sat down across the desk. "Have you gone through the information on the phone?"

Vienna inhaled. Held it, like she was fighting hiccups, or her conscience. Finally exhaled. "I didn't. Until the police contacted me about the break-in."

Jo kept the heat out of her voice. "Why didn't you tell me this morning when I called?"

Vienna looked out the window. "You have a family? Siblings?"

"Yes."

"Any of them live their lives like a crystal vase? That's rolling across a firing range?"

Her voice was strong, even boisterous, but Jo heard a cracked note in it.

"Any of them live like a dove that's set free in a peace ceremony and flies straight into the eternal flame? And keeps flying, while you try to douse the fire or keep her aloft or avert your eyes?" she said. "Every time, I'd think I got the flames extinguished. And this beautiful creature would fly on, soaring in circles. And I ran around beneath her flight path with my hands out, begging God not to let her wings disintegrate, not to let her ignite again, not to let her fall."

Vienna pressed her lips closed, as though to keep her voice from quavering. "Thank God our folks aren't still alive to suffer through this."

Her eyes welled. Jo's own stomach tightened.

"I'm sorry," she said.

"She left a bunch of stuff around my place. But it's personal. I see no need to hand it to the police. That would be like pulling the covers off her in the morgue and inviting everybody to stare and point." Brusquely, she wiped her eyes. "But they are already."

She straightened. "How do you work? You hand everything straight to the cops? Or can you keep some information out of your report?"

"I'm not a police officer. I'm a civilian consultant, and I have the same obligation as any other citizen if I discover evidence of a crime. I'll report it. But I'm preparing a report for the police and it will become part of the public record. You should regard any information on that phone as available to the courts."

128

Vienna's expression tightened. The look in her eyes was brittle.

"That said," Jo added, "I'm not obligated to divulge every scrap of information I obtain."

Vienna covered the phone with her hand. "So you understand — context, I mean. I want to protect my sister."

"Understood."

"When Tasia's bipolar disorder was out of control a few years ago, she projected a lot of her feelings and fears on to others. Rob especially."

Rob, the commander in chief.

"Periodically she'd express a lot of anger about the things he was doing that she thought were 'evil.' Her word."

"Things relating to their married life?" Jo said.

"No. It had no connection to reality. She talked in grandiose terms about him being a threat."

"To her personally?"

"To the nation. This was when he was in the Senate. You're doing a great job of not shouting *paranoia*."

"I presume there's no record of abuse or assault in their marital history."

Vienna shook her head. "Never. Rob was a prince. Until he turned into a frog, anyhow. But that's just divorce, ain't it?"

Paranoid people blocked out psychic recognition of their own faults. They disavowed upsetting attitudes and traits in themselves — envy, hate, aggression — and instead projected those attitudes on to others. That's why paranoids saw threats all around them.

129

"Did Tasia think McFarland intended to harm her?" Jo said.

"Not him. The government. FBI. CIA. But I have to stress, her condition was out of control."

"What happened?"

"At first she wallpapered friends and family with manic manifestos. She issued 'communiqués' to me. But eventually she wrote to Rob's Senate office accusing the government of persecuting her. He called me."

"Robert McFarland phoned you, personally? About Tasia? What did he say?"

"I don't talk about Rob."

Jo spread her hands. "You're tantalizing me here. Please."

Vienna hesitated. "All I'll say is, he could have sent the letter to the FBI. Instead, he called me."

"Are you saying he wanted to be sure Tasia got help, and quietly?"

"She was off her meds. He understood that. I got her hospitalized."

"That must have been distressing."

"I used to weigh a hundred and ten pounds," Vienna said.

Jo kept her expression even.

Vienna laughed, brief and sharp. "You must clean up at the poker table, doctor. That's the deadest deadpan expression I've ever seen. I've always been a bountiful Botticelli gal."

Jo let one side of her mouth curl up.

Vienna leaned her elbows on the desk. She eyed Jo up and down, as she'd done that morning. This time, she seemed to decide that Jo passed muster.

"It was a turning point. After that, Tasia gradually got things under control. The paranoia diminished. The communiqués ended. She stopped ranting about politics, or about Rob, period. That was all in the past." She pushed the phone across the desk. "Or maybe not."

Jo picked it up. "What's on here?"

"Tasia used the phone's Web app to browse antigovernment extremist sites."

Jo turned it on. "Did she just browse? Or did she contribute?"

"She was offering pseudonymous comments on rabid right-winger sites. That could kill her reputation, forever. Do you see why I want to keep this confidential?"

"Pseudonymous. Do you think people knew who she really was? Think one of them broke in to her house today? Was somebody from an online forum threatening her?"

"They're nasty folks. I find that completely plausible."

Vienna spun her chair to face the window. The phone powered up. A colorful screen offered Jo a selection of programs.

"Any place you suggest I start?" she said.

"Web browser. Most recent."

Jo went online. The most recent Web site Tasia had accessed was treeofliberty.com.

She scrolled through the topics listed on the front page. "Not bedtime reading for the children, is it?"

"Maybe in places where they keep cyanide capsules in the medicine cabinet, so they can put down the wife and kiddies before the Red Army storms the bunker."

"The hot topic of discussion is Tasia's 'assassination.'"

"I didn't read any of those essays. I don't need to have a stroke today."

Jo was about to access one, but saw, at the top of the page: *You are logged in as Fawn01.*

"She really didn't tell them who she was?" Jo said.

"You want to go through months and months of that stuff? Be my guest. But who's going to hose you off afterward?"

The tenor of commentary on the site varied from smug to ravening to vicious. Jo skimmed Tasia's contributions. Though written in a tone of histrionic ennui, her comments seemed coherent — in contact with reality, as agreed upon by participants in the forum. They wouldn't have passed a history or citizenship exam. But neither would they have caused a psychiatrist to think Tasia was psychotic.

"Tasia writes under a pseudonym. Did she have to give an e-mail address to sign in?" Jo asked, more to herself than to Vienna.

"I limit my online forums to Cakelovers for Peace. I don't know." Vienna shrugged. "I presume she was hiding this activity from us, and trying to segregate it from her computer by using this phone."

132

Jo picked her way through the phone's screens and programs. Nothing obvious. She went back to the forum. Picking a topic, she decided to add a comment.

"Let's see how they like my opinions on the Supreme Court," she said.

As soon as she clicked the link to add a comment, the screen brought up a dialogue box. It showed Fawn01 logged in, with an accompanying e-mail address.

"Got you," Jo said.

The e-mail address was tied to the phone itself. It must have been set up automatically with Tasia's account. Jo showed it to Vienna.

"Recognize that address?"

Vienna shook her head. Jo went to the mail program. If it was password protected, she'd be in trouble. But Tasia's paranoid tendencies hadn't been thorough and well organized. She'd set the program to remember her password. Jo found herself directed straight to Tasia's account.

Inbox: 1427 messages.

"Whoa."

Vienna leaned over the desk. "Wait, how many messages?"

"Fourteen hundred." She checked the dates. "In the last three months."

She scrolled through the inbox. The hairs on her arms stood up. "Who's Archangel X?"

Ever done this?
   Would you like me to do this to you?
   Why won't you answer me?
   ANSWER ME

Jo opened that one. Involuntarily, she hissed through her teeth.

Nobody said you were allowed to be so rude. I have written to you many many times and you won't even dignify me with an answer. You are a full-on BITCH.

"What?" Vienna said.

Next one down. Like 99 per cent of the messages in the inbox, it was from Archangel X.

You have no right to ignore me. I'll see you, bitch. I'll see you onstage. I'll see you when you sleep. I'll see you in the hereafter.

Jo grabbed her own phone. She dialed Amy Tang. Vienna read the screen. "Oh God."

"Yeah," Jo said. "Your sister had a stalker."

CHAPTER
TWENTY

NMP got off the rattling Muni bus at Turk Street. The bus stop was scribbled with graffiti. The sun skimmed the rooftops to the west. It was gold and sharp, like an accusing finger, pointed straight at him. NMP glanced around.

No. Don't let them know you suspect they're after you. Walk.

He pulled the watch cap low on his forehead and rumbled down the street. The wind bitched between buildings. He squeezed his hands into knots, panicky. People could see him. Hovering like an angel had failed.

Keep it together. You are NMP, the big bad bastard. You are the sword of truth.

Show it. Walk the talk. You carry a deuce, deuce and a half — show the street every nasty ounce of it. Make 'em think if they screw with you they'll suffer. Then they'll keep their distance.

And if they don't, they'll get a rock to the head.

The Tenderloin wasn't a place to get caught alone as night fell. Garbage stank from rusting trash cans. On a vacant lot, behind a chain-link fence woven with weeds, three men leaned on the bumper of a car. They were as thin as oil dipsticks, laughing.

NMP had been riding the bus and walking alleys, staying on the move, since the encounter at Tasia's house. And everywhere, people had stared. The way people at school used to stare, or at the movies, or the library, at Noel Michael Petty, Wide Load. The way Noel's sister and her friends used to snicker on the school bus at Jesus-what-a-fat-ass.

And today's skirmish had been a sickening failure.

All NMP's surveillance, all that time spent hovering above Tasia's house. And finally, when NMP got the chance to slip inside, the music journalist showed up, and the stranger, the woman who was taking photos. The woman had been in *his* space. Looking. Stealing the private moment. NMP knew what they were up to. They were planning to turn Tasia's house into a shrine. The Basilica of the Fame Fucker. Where they could perpetuate the lie. Talking love love love.

NMP should have hit the man harder. More times. For good.

He neared a decrepit pick-up truck, parked at the curb. A dog was locked in the cab. The mutt leaped at the window, barking at him.

Tasia's bedroom. Guitar leaning against the chair. Boots by the bed . . .

He wanted to scream, but couldn't. *Shh. Don't tell, precious love.*

Striding up the grimy street, Petty groaned. Searle had watched Tasia perform her striptease. Searle had undressed by her bedside. She had taken him, debauched herself with him, left her smell, his smell, everywhere in the bedroom, like a rebuke. Like a slap in the face.

For months, NMP had refused to believe it. NMP had stayed *loyal*. Tabloid gossip, stage-managed lies, boiled up for publicity — that's what Tasia's alleged "affair" had to be. Had to. But it wasn't fiction. It was true.

A cry escaped his throat.

The dog kept barking. NMP tramped to the truck and barked back. The dog went berserk, claws scrabbling, slobber flecking the pick-up's window. NMP grabbed the truck's radio antenna. He sawed it back and forth until it broke off. He stuck it through the crack at the top of the window and jabbed it at the dog. Over and over again.

"Hey."

He rattled the glass and whipped the antenna and hit the mutt until it cowered.

"Hey, motherfucker, stop it."

The men by the trash can were shouting. NMP pulled the antenna out, turned, and slashed the air with it. The men stopped shouting. Like that.

NMP stepped back, panting. Holding on to the antenna, ready to whip anybody who approached him, he ran. At the corner, the lights of the hotel marquee fizzed, spastic red neon. THE BALMORAL. Three letters were out, so it looked like THE MORAL. Yeah, the moral of the story was, never trust Tasia McFarland. NMP shoved through the door, huge hands flat on the glass, face burning. The clerk looked up, barely, and back down at his lap. A TV on the desk showed the rictus grin of Robert McFarland, Tasia-humper. NMP rushed past and up the creaking stairs.

Tasia the slut. Tasia the crazy whore. Taking Searle Lecroix into her bed. Like she'd taken other men, like a trail of slime back to her teens. The greedy bitch. Having the president of the United States wasn't enough for her?

What kind of insatiable succubus nymphomaniac had to take the president, throw him aside, and then go after the rest of the men of America? What kind of empty hole had to take Searle Lecroix at the end?

When NMP was waiting?

The hotel room was stuffy and dispirited. Petty shut the door and pounded his head against it. No fair. No fair.

NMP was finished waiting. If he couldn't hover, he could strike.

Jo hiked up Parnassus Avenue toward the UC San Francisco Medical Center. The sun was casting a hallucinogenic red light across the Pacific. She hitched her satchel higher on her shoulder and leaned into the hill. Outside the med center entrance, men and women with cameras and microphones were clustered on the sidewalk. The press was waiting for news on Ace Chennault.

In the lobby Tang was pacing, phone to her ear. When Jo walked in, she waved her toward the elevator. "We have five minutes to talk to Chennault."

Jo accompanied her across the lobby. "How's he doing?"

"Good condition. They're keeping him overnight for observation. He's lucky." She pushed the elevator call button. "And don't even think of asking me to walk up the stairs. Clock's ticking."

Jo's claustrophobia hissed *tiny space*. They stepped into the elevator and Tang pushed the button like she was grinding out a cigarette butt. On somebody's face. The doors closed.

Jo's palms were sweating, but she gave Tang a sickly grin. "Let me guess. You just won the lottery."

"This case is holding together like a carnival ride that just broke loose from its moorings. Get ready to careen across the fairground."

Tang's phone bleated. She looked at the display, exhaled, and ignored it.

"Amy?"

"You first. What's got your back up?"

"Somebody may have been stalking Tasia."

Tang turned sharply. "How'd you find that out?"

"She had a cell phone we didn't know about."

She told Tang about the messages she'd found. "Cyberstalker at a minimum."

The elevator stopped and Tang marched out with Jo behind her.

"What's your news, Amy?"

"A new twist in the case. Unfortunately, it comes via tabloid television."

She headed for the nurses' station, badge out. Jo fished her UCSF ID from her satchel and slipped it around her neck.

At the desk Tang said, "Here to speak to Mr. Chennault. I called up."

Her phone beeped again. The nurse behind the desk pointed to it, but Tang raised a hand. "I'm turning it off."

The nurse directed them to Chennault's room, reiterating, "Five minutes."

They found Chennault propped up in bed, face sallow, eyes reflecting the light from the television. His left arm was encased in a blue cast and immobilized in a sling. A patch of his blond hair had been shaved. Stitches ran across his scalp, Frankenstein-style. He muted the television.

"Not quite the writer's normal day, was it?" he said.

Jo smiled. "Glad you're going to be all right. How do you feel?"

"As lousy as I look. The SS matrons at the nursing station won't give me anything stronger than Tylenol."

Tang crossed her arms and hunched into herself. "Can you can tell us anything about the person who attacked you?"

"Packed a punch like a rock. Actually, it was a rock, wasn't it?"

"Did he say anything?" Tang said.

"Not a word. And I didn't see his face, just his back. Big bugger. Hauled ass, and I mean that literally. He had a butt like a rhino."

He tried to look wry, but beneath the pudgy, boyish features, his smile seemed exhausted.

"Anything else?" Tang said. "Any logos on the clothes?"

Chennault shook his head.

"Anything unusual in the way he ran? His stride?"

Another shake of the head. He swiped at the thermal blanket that had slid off his leg. He had a tattoo running around his ankle. In italic script, Jo saw SEMPER T — Chennault pulled the blanket up.

Tang nodded. "What did he smell like?"

Fabric softener and Right Guard deodorant, Jo thought.

"Clean clothes. And — aftershave, maybe," Chennault said.

Tang said, "Did you go with the tour to Washington, D.C., last week?"

"No." The smile seemed ever more forced. "The publisher wouldn't spring for me to tag along."

"Did you talk to Tasia about the time she spent in D.C.?"

"A bit. Why, Lieutenant?"

The television flickered blue on the wall. Chennault glanced at it. His bonhomie fell away like a dropped towel. A banner headline read, NEW TASIA SHOCKER.

The door opened and a nurse bustled in. "Time's up."

Jo tried to watch the screen but the nurse hustled her toward the door.

Chennault said, "Wait." His smile seemed pathetic. "Can I give you a call tomorrow?"

"Of course." Jo gave him her card.

Back at the elevator, Tang turned on her phone. Within seconds it began beeping. She hissed like an angry cat.

"What's going on?" Jo said. "What's the New Tasia Shocker?"

The phone rang. Tang glared at it. "Sorry. Got to take this."

She answered, and spoke in monosyllables all the way down to the lobby. Outside, backlit by a crimson sunset, the press had clotted around a man in a suit the color of bone. The reporters, camera people, and sound-folk looked like iron filings pulled toward a magnet on an Etch A Sketch. The man raised his hands as if urging caution.

"What's this?" Jo said.

She and Tang went through the automatic doors.

". . . yet again remind you that the police department is doing everything in its power to bring this investigation to a conclusion."

Beneath her breath, Tang said, "We're screwed."

The speaker's dark hair and mustache were neatly clipped, as though by a gardener prepping the grass at Wimbledon. His aviator shades reflected the fiery sunset.

A reporter said, "Has the FBI been brought into the investigation?"

The man shook his head. "No. There's no indication that a federal investigation is warranted. The San Francisco Police Department is fully engaged in resolving the matter of Ms. McFarland's death."

Tang nudged Jo around the fringes of the press pack. "Donald Dart. Departmental spokesman. If he's here it means the brass is covering themselves with grease and

142

trying to slide out from inside this case as slick and fast as they can."

Another reporter said, "But what about the attack today?"

"That's suspected burglary and assault. We're searching for the assailant."

Behind Dart another man stood at parade rest, hands clasped behind his back. His bald skull was sunburned. He was chewing gum, trying to look intimidating.

His gaze lit on Tang. He walked toward her.

"Give me a minute," she said to Jo.

The bald man led her aside.

Jo didn't consider Lieutenant Amy Tang to be combative. She was dogged and unyielding, but didn't lash out in anger. When challenged or cornered, she drew in on herself, like a porcupine flashing its quills.

That's how she looked talking to Baldy.

He towered over her. Jo couldn't hear what he was saying, but he articulated each word with toothy care. Tang's face had emptied into blankness.

In front of the microphones, Dart wrapped up his remarks. "That's all for now. Thank you." He turned and walked away from the press. A few reporters shouted questions after him, but none followed. The lights shut down and microphones retreated. He strode toward Baldy and Tang.

Tang raised her voice. "Because it's an open investigation."

Baldy continued chewing his gum.

Tang shook her head and walked away from him. "I'll speak to my captain. Take it up with him."

"We already have," Baldy said. "Don't march off, Lieutenant."

Tang swept past Jo. "Let's go."

"Lieutenant. This is out of your hands," Baldy called.

Jo glanced at him. Baldy propped his hands on his hips. She could swear he looked pleased.

She jogged to catch up with Tang. "Amy."

Tang walked down the drive, face splashed with the dying sun. "Cowards."

"What's going on?"

"That's Captain Chuck Bohr, one of my superiors. He's taking charge."

Jo glanced back. Bohr and Dart were chatting. Dart stroked his mustache. He looked like an extra from *Reno 911!*

"I'm being sidelined," Tang said.

"You're off the case?"

"No, but I might as well be. They're taking official charge of it, because it needs massaging at a higher level. They think they can massage the case out of existence." She pulled out her cigarettes. "They can't."

"What's going on? What's the new Tasia shocker?"

"Last week, the *Bad Dogs and Bullets* tour played a concert in Washington," Tang said. "Tasia and the band stayed at the Four Seasons in downtown D.C. But the tabloids just published a cell phone photo somebody snapped in the bar at the Hyatt, in Reston, Virginia. Tasia's telling the bartender to hand her the entire bottle of Stolichnaya."

144

"That's not a shocker," Jo said.

"Shortly afterward, the same citizen snapped a man leaving the Hyatt via the loading dock."

They walked down the hill. Jo spread her hands. *And?*

"It was nighttime. But the tabloids enhanced the photo. There's no question. It's Robert McFarland." Tang lit her smoke. "Hail to the Chief."

CHAPTER
TWENTY-ONE

Can you prove they met?" Jo said.

"I was afraid you were going to ask."

"But you don't think Tasia and the president were both at the Hyatt for a quilting bee."

"No. They were having a private summit."

Jo's pulse beat like a conga. "Last night at the White House press conference, a reporter asked McFarland if he'd spoken to Tasia recently. He said no." She re-ran it in her head. "I'm sure he said no."

"He lied."

"That means —"

"Don't say it," Tang said. "I know what it means. It means you're going to stick your finger in an electric socket."

Tang was right. The implications washed over her like a wall of water. They filled her with trepidation and excitement.

"So do I call the White House switchboard, or can you get me the number for the president's private secretary?" she said.

When Jo had asked Searle Lecroix for an interview, it had been a piece of cake. It had been a piece of pecan pie. Reaching the president of the United States was another matter. Getting a chance to ask him, directly, about meeting his first wife three days before she was killed with his gun, would be like lassoing an ICBM in flight.

Tang left Jo outside UCSF Medical Center, with a list of names and phone numbers at the White House. Jo gazed across Parnassus and down the hill, past the pale stone of Saint Ignatius Church and the University of San Francisco, across the forested hills of The Presidio, to the Golden Gate Bridge. The Pacific and the bay shone in the sun like mercury.

She took out her phone. She couldn't Facebook McFarland, or leave a comment on the First Lady's Twitter feed, or crash through the White House Rose Garden and knock on the window of the Oval Office.

She cleared her throat. She was a professional. She had the duty and the authority to do this. She punched in the switchboard number.

"White House."

She stifled a whimper and the urge to squeal, *Omigod, omigod.* She asked to speak to Sylvia Obote, the president's secretary. When Obote answered, "Office of the president," Jo heard her own voice wobble like an unbalanced bicycle tire.

"This is Dr. Johanna Beckett calling from San Francisco."

"How may I help you?"

Just speak. The woman is not going to ban you from the White House tour for daring to call. "I'm conducting a psychological autopsy on Fawn Tasia McFarland for the San Francisco Police Department."

Silence.

"I'm reconstructing Ms. McFarland's final days. It's important that I speak to the president about his meeting with her."

Obote must have been expecting something like this call. "If you'll e-mail me your bona fides and attach a list of questions, I'll forward them to the White House counsel."

"Certainly. I'd be grateful for any information the president can give me, and I'm aware that his time is valuable." *Suck-up.* "But time is also of the essence to the investigation. Speaking to the president directly will be of even greater value than having an e-mail exchange."

Obote reeled off an e-mail address. "I'll forward your request to the appropriate people."

"Thank you, Ms. Obote."

Obote ended the call. Jo held the phone like it was glowing red.

She wondered whether Obote would go back to filing her nails and moving tiny armies around the board in the game of Risk she was playing on her desk, or whether black helicopters and parabolic microphones and men with tiny earpieces were even now being moved into position outside her house on Russian Hill.

Maybe this was how paranoia began.

When Jo pulled into Gabe's driveway, the evening star was skimming the western hills. His two-bedroom home in Noe Valley was tucked beneath a live oak on a quiet street, packed in among houses filled with young families. His 4Runner was in the drive. The leaves of the live oak rustled in the night wind. She rapped on the door.

When Gabe opened it, his face was shadowed. Even without seeing his eyes she knew he was exhausted.

She held back. "Bad time?"

He pulled her inside, wrapped her in his arms, and buried his face in her hair. "Never."

The lights were amber. The house smelled like strong coffee. His laptop was open on the living room coffee table.

"How's Sophie?" Jo said.

"Sleeping like a zombie. Moaning and puking."

Arm around her shoulder, he headed to the living room, dropped onto the sofa, and pulled her down beside him. On the wall hung prints of the Golden Gate Bridge and the Hindu Kush, beside watercolors Sophie had painted in bold greens and blues. Next to the computer, a marked-up chapter of his dissertation slumped across a copy of Kierkegaard's *Either/Or*. He stared at them vacantly.

Whenever Jo asked him why he'd chosen to study theology, he gave her facile reasons. "I was a good little altar boy" was his favorite.

But few air force enlisted men chose to study Catholic moral theology as a career plan. His courses provided a respite from the rough world where he worked. But she suspected that something personal underlay his quest to unpeel the universe. Perhaps it was a longing for connection, or an ache he wanted to soothe. He wasn't mystical. He didn't bow to doctrine, or pine for stigmata. At times he tunneled into his studies, attempting to connect with an eternity that surrounded the broken world of time and space he was stumbling through.

Sometimes she liked that. But sometimes she felt a grabbing sensation in her chest, and wished that, instead, he would bury himself in her life.

And Gabe's pensive side was at odds with his professional life as a pararescue jumper. At Moffett Field, the motto of pararescue was written on a hangar wall in letters six feet tall: SO THAT OTHERS MAY LIVE. On the back of those words, he threw himself bodily into the abyss, day after day.

His chief master sergeant had once joked to Jo that a PJ's job boils down to "recess with toys." In search and rescue work they skydived, drove snowmobiles and Jet Skis and ATVs — sometimes straight off the loading ramp of a transport plane. They scuba dived, and jumped out of helicopters and fixed-wing military aircraft. They didn't earn movie-star salaries. They weren't famous like Delta Force or the Navy SEALs. They ate adrenaline for breakfast, lunch, and dinner, and sometimes they got thrown onto the front lines in combat, performing rescues and surgery on the battlefield.

Sometimes they flew five hundred miles offshore to rescue sailors from a burning ship. She laced her hand with his. His face was drawn.

150

"The merchant tanker was sinking when we reached it. Fire started in the engine room but had spread out of control by the time we arrived on scene," he said. "Three crewmen were already dead. Fire, or drowned belowdecks. Eighteen others had gone into the water. Only half of them got into their survival suits beforehand. And three-quarters couldn't swim."

"Bad day at black rock," she said.

"We rescued four."

"Thank God."

He nodded. But Jo sensed that more was coming. She hung on to his hand. He leaned back and closed his eyes.

"Dave Rabin got hurt."

"Bad?"

"A bulkhead failed from the heat of the fire. It blew out and caught Dave in the back of the head."

"Where is he?"

"ICU at the General. In a coma."

Against her instincts, she didn't try to salve him. She simply held tight to his hand. Gabe didn't add anything to his brief report. He didn't want to talk about it. Like so much. Like his past, and his air force days.

She knew that he didn't want to show weakness in front of her. And he didn't want Jo to be afraid for him. He wanted her to stand behind him. And she was a physician — to speak reassuring words about Rabin's condition, about his chances of survival and recovery, would have rung false.

Gabe ran his hands roughly across his face. Finally he turned to her. The lights were warm. His eyes

151

seemed fraught and yearning. Without a word he stood and led her upstairs.

He shut the bedroom door. The lights were off, the window open. Beyond plum trees and crowded rooftops and the city's knitting yarn of phone and electrical wires, the western sky had deepened to indigo. Overhead, the stars poured down.

He picked her up and swung her onto the bed. He rolled on top of her, raked his fingers into her hair, and kissed her.

He hauled her sweater over her head. She fumbled his T-shirt off. He pressed her against the pillow and worked his way down her body, kissing her neck, her chest, her ribs. He unbuttoned her jeans and kissed her belly button.

In the half-light from the window she saw the bruises on his neck. They extended in an angry line down across his clavicle and along the right side of his chest. She saw the old scars by his hip, the ones he didn't talk about. The ones she was still waiting for him to explain.

Jo tried to slow him down but he seemed famished. He threw off the covers and wrangled her to the center of the bed.

He didn't look at her but put his head next to hers and wrapped himself around her. His heart pounded against her chest. A part of her wanted to speak, to pause, to savor his body against hers, to tell him what he meant to her, how she ached for what he was feeling. But in the dark, adrift on pain and regret, he wanted only to prove that he was still alive. They made love fiercely, clinging to each other, their bodies growing hot. At the end she reached overhead to grab the headboard and steady herself. He threw himself against her over and over, his eyes shut tight, and she bit his shoulder to stifle her own cry.

Afterward, he held tight for a minute, chest heaving. He rolled away and lay on his back, spent. Then he pulled her against his side and stroked her hair.

Finally, in her ear, he whispered, "Thank you."

She wanted to say, *Stay with me. Don't leave. Let me in. Be mine.* But as he stared at the ceiling, she shut her eyes and said, "Any time."

CHAPTER
TWENTY-TWO

The morning sun burned against the silvery sheet metal of trucks parked at Blue Eagle Security. At a desk in a corner of the garage, Ivory hunched over the computer, drinking a Mountain Dew. Her feet, planted wide beneath the desk in her black work boots, tapped in time to the jitters in her head. She read Tom Paine's latest message. *Tasia warned us. She came to the concert armed with the jackal's gun. She raised it high.*

Ivory whispered the rest: "'She could not have shouted a louder message: True Americans will not go quietly.'"

The desk area was grubby, a cubbyhole stuffed with paperwork and maintenance logs. Keyes loomed beside her. Saw she was logged on at Tree of Liberty. "You want to get your ass shit-canned?"

"I'll delete my browsing history. Don't treat me like an idiot."

But she glanced around. An armored car rumbled out of the parking lot, stinking with diesel exhaust. Keyes waved to the driver.

Ivory tapped the screen. "That break-in at Tasia's house yesterday, it was the government. The cops have beefed up street patrols, looking for this intruder. It's a perfect excuse to set up roadblocks. Then bring in the National Guard."

"You positive it was the cops that broke into Tasia's house, and not a night crawler fan?" Keyes said.

Ivory flushed. Why did he have to embarrass her? Her face felt red-hot. She covered her cheeks with her hands. She hated color. She was white from her snowy head to her polished toenails and bleached everywhere in between. She was pure.

Tasia had been pure too, a blonde, golden. "Tasia could have been a member of the Valkyrie Sisterhood. She should be avenged."

Keyes spun her around in the chair and put his hands on the arms. "This is not about your white trash prison gang. It's about stopping this city from becoming a prison. It's about keeping this country free."

She looked at the floor. Nodded. San Francisco sat, like the striking surface of a match, at the tip of a peninsula. Seven miles long by seven wide, it was surrounded by killer surf, frigid riptides, and vicious currents. Block the freeways heading south, blow the bridges, sink the ferries, and you cut it off. This place wasn't goddamned Malibu. It was a fortress. And right there in the bay was Alcatraz, the perfect concentration camp.

She saw that it worried him. She saw it in his strong face. He stared past her at the computer screen. *To quote Thomas Paine: Lead, follow, or get out of the way.*

Who's with me?

Ivory didn't know what had gone down when Keyes worked for the security contractor overseas. But Keyes had gotten fired after Robert McFarland was elected. Keyes thought McFarland might turn men like him into scapegoats for a repudiated foreign policy. Shoot ragheads, come home with booty — follow an honored tradition, and face prosecution. Meanwhile, McFarland bowed to foreign kings. Keyes carried millions of dollars in his truck, and who did it go to? Arabs and Jews. The ragheads sold America their oil, the Zionists pocketed the interest on the deal, and it all went through the Federal Reserve Bank here in San Francisco.

That's one reason he refused to pay taxes, which also had the government on his back. But he had that look in his eyes again, the anger.

"Move," he said.

She scooted out of the way and he took over the keyboard. He typed a message to Tom Paine at Tree of Liberty. "*To quote Thomas Paine: 'The strength and power of despotism consists wholly in the fear of resistance.'*

"*I resist. Contact me off the board.*"

Jo woke early, and alone. Outside the window, morning fog cloaked Noe Valley. She found Gabe downstairs in the kitchen, halfway through a pot of coffee. He was holding his cell phone. He tapped it against the butcher-block table, as if doing so would make it ring.

"Any news on Rabin?" she said.

He shook his head.

When she got home, she headed into her office and checked e-mail. She had no messages from the White House. But what was she expecting, a bouquet of helium balloons?

She sat down at her desk, powered up Tasia McFarland's cell phone, and waded deep into the frightening e-mails she had received from Archangel X.

The first one was sent in February. *Hi, Tasia. Huge fan here. I just read that you're going to be on the Bad Dogs and Bullets tour. Fantastic!! Is everything I read in the fan mags true? (Haha.) When will your new album be released?*

It was signed *NMP*.

Tasia took three weeks, but she replied. *Hi NMP — glad you're a fan. New album out March 30. Thanks, Tasia.*

Thirty minutes later NMP wrote back. *Wow, is that really you? I assumed a celebrity would have minions writing her e-mail. Thx re album. But what about the fan mags? All the gossip true? NMP.*

Tasia hadn't replied. And for six weeks, there were no messages. But on April 30 Archangel X wrote: *Holy cow, I just heard the new single. It's amazing. Your voice sounds so fresh. But what I really can't wait to hear are your duets. Kimber Holloway? Searle Lecroix? That's got to be some powerful music. Peace, NMP.*

Five days later Tasia responded: *Great, thanks!*

That two-word message, apparently, turned on the tap. Twenty minutes after Tasia sent it, NMP wrote back an epistle that Jo could only classify as a *cri de coeur*. The cry of a twitching, chilly, overheated heart.

Since my messages make you happy, I have to tell you, this tour is something I've been looking forward to for a long time.

NMP went on to elaborate about "*My long-time intricate love of music that germinated in childhood and flowered throughout a painful adolescence.*" The tone became increasingly intimate — as though NMP thought that Tasia's pro forma response to fan mail made them confidantes.

Tasia didn't reply.

NMP wrote: *Did you get my message? Just checking.*

That was followed by more silence on Tasia's end. Then by a string of six dozen messages from NMP, sending Tasia links to cute videos. But underneath the lighthearted facade lay a hunger for connection and a growing presumption of intimacy. The first dozen cutesy messages were hopeful — as if NMP were trying to lure a puppy to take a treat. Then for a while they settled into a rhythm: NMP would send aphorisms and humorous links morning, noon, and evening.

Jo rubbed her eyes. A low-key dread was building to a stronger suspicion.

Archangel X, or NMP, seemed to be an adult. Sounded literate. Used full sentences and standard grammar. If Jo had to guess, she'd say NMP was a native English speaker, probably had some college education, and — given that all the musicians mentioned in the e-mails were white-bread Nashville stars — there was a good chance he was Caucasian.

Eventually, when his puppy biscuits failed to elicit a response from Tasia, he wrote: *I go by the handle*

Archangel because I'm named after the Archangel Michael. And I'm like him — a protector. Think of me as a guardian angel. You can trust me.

Tasia didn't reply.

The next set of e-mails came in pulsing batches, twenty-five or thirty in a short time span. Their tone became intrusive and resentful. *I read online that you and Searle Lecroix hooked up. That's not true, is it?*

When, for the three hundredth time, Tasia didn't reply, NMP wrote: *Who said you could date Searle?*

Jo exhaled. Stalker, 100 per cent lock on that. *Do you love Searle? Why are you doing this?*

Until, finally: *Slut.*

At that point, Tasia finally responded. *From now on all your e-mails will be deleted.*

And Archangel's response took a turn. *Well, well. You finally worked up the nerve to answer me. Took you long enough, you coward. I thought you were my friend, that you understood me. But this is what you do? You tell me I'm "deleted." You slap me in the face. Are you ashamed? Are you embarrassed, you filthy SLUT?*

The next message consisted of a list, comparing Tasia to Pol Pot, Lucretia Borgia, Cruella De Vil, and four hundred other villains.

Jo checked Tasia's outbox. The *all your e-mails will be deleted* message was the last one she wrote. Jo wondered if she had paid the slightest bit of attention to the e-mail account after that, or even to the cell phone. She had eventually forgotten it at her sister's place.

Did she know that Archangel X was hounding her?

Jo called Tang. "Archangel X was undoubtedly stalking Tasia. Perhaps only cyberstalking, but the most recent messages are alarming."

"Any idea who it is?" Tang said.

"Not yet. No name. But this character says he's named after the archangel Michael. And NMP could be initials."

"Gender?"

"You mean, is Archangel really Irina Bendova, beautiful young girl from Novosibirsk, who wants to marry me?" Jo said.

"Can you run it through one of those programs that tells you whether it's a man's or woman's writing style?"

"Those are useless. I come out as more macho than Steven Seagal," Jo said. "I have Archangel X's e-mail address. Can you track it down and get me a name?"

There was a heavy pause. "Maybe. It'll take time."

Jo turned back to the e-mail stream. "I don't think Tasia saw some of these. Toward the end, long after she'd stopped replying, Archangel wrote, 'Do you think you're better than everybody else?' "

"Nice."

"Archangel becomes increasingly concerned about the gossip magazines and the rumor that Tasia was seeing Searle Lecroix."

"That was all over the entertainment news."

"Here's what worries me." She ran her finger down the messages in the queue. "Probably the last five hundred messages focus on how awful it is for NMP that Tasia's having an affair."

"What kind of stuff?" Tang said.

"Jealousy. Ownership. I wouldn't pin homicidal intent on Archangel based on these messages alone — they're not openly threatening, but they're aggressive and disturbing. Here's one. 'What are you doing to me? I can't take this.'"

"I could interpret that as a threat."

"Or as a plea. Here's another. 'It's wrong. Why are you doing this? You have to take Searle? There are others out there for you. I'm out here, waiting. Selfish cow.'"

"Sounds like a snotty teenager."

"Or a fan consumed with his idol. 'You're breaking my heart. You need to break up with Searle or NMP will do it for you.'"

Tang paused. "That's a threat. And "NMP"? He refers to himself in the third person?"

"Yes," Jo said. "NMP also sent photos. Porn. And they're disturbing."

All at once, Tang sounded weary. "Go on, tell me."

"The message says, 'Have you ever done this?' The photo shows a naked man having intercourse with a giant scorpion. The scorpion's tail is swinging up between the man's legs, and it's about to plunge its massive stinger into his back."

Tang was quiet a moment. "You drawing any psychological conclusions from that?"

"A whole host," Jo said. "Here's the big thing, Amy. After all the hysterics, NMP wrote, 'See you in San Fran. I already have my ticket.'"

"Beckett, that's a solid lead."

"Good."

"Forty thousand people bought tickets. But it's a thread."

"Archangel X may have been at the concert. He may have caught up with her. Can you get the name of the person who owns that account?"

"It'll probably take a subpoena. And before you say it, I'll get on it."

"How long?"

"No promises. Maybe days."

"Any evidence that a stalker had been following Tasia? Complaints to police, requests for a restraining order, vandalism, break-ins at her —"

"At Tasia's house?" Tang said.

"I'm way ahead of you. The man in the balaclava. The intruder."

Tang was silent. "That would put an entirely new spin on this case."

"Can you find out?"

"I'll get back to you."

"Amy, if this pans out, you'll be a star. You'll take the spotlight off the political machinations and put it on a straight-out stalker."

"Good God, woman, you're a Machiavellian. I didn't know you had it in you."

When Jo hung up, she felt pumped and antsy. She felt that, even after reading fourteen hundred messages from Archangel, she was missing something. Some inflection, some subtext, was eluding her. Something was burning beneath the surface of Archangel's words, like a fire in a coal seam belowground.

She didn't want to wait for more information about Archangel X. She grabbed her computer and went to find Ferd Bismuth.

CHAPTER
TWENTY-THREE

Paine shut the door and opened the curtains. Downtown San Francisco peered back, swathed in fog, dumb and unaware. Fatigued, pressed for time, he sat down at the computer and logged on to Tree of Liberty.

Disquiet vibrated like a wire along his arms. The government's security machine was circling him. An intruder had broken into Tasia's house. And he'd heard the news today, oh boy. Robert McFarland could not escape the consequences of Tasia's death any longer. Things were coming to a head.

Fightback began now. He wrote:

Today in the Usurped States of America, police officers haul citizens to jail if they resist the assertion of raw control over their liberty. Speak up, and the cuffs get slapped on. The message is, Lie down and take it.

Thank you, sir, may I have another?

Beneath it lies the relentless drive to power. The authorities want us defenseless and humiliated: sheeple, subject to whim and slaughter. That way, when the crackdown comes, we'll stand there and let them slit our throats.

A gray heat crisped the edges of his vision. The intruder's incursion at Tasia's house was, frankly, crazy. Camo and a balaclava, middle of the day? Bizarre. This was a dramatic escalation, a sign of imminent breakdown.

The gloves were coming off. And the Usurper's minions would go for broke. They were after him: Paine-killers.

It was nothing new. The authorities always came after him. In the army, the military police had surrounded him in the barracks. They stood there in their shining helmets, holsters unsnapped, and took his weapon away.

Humiliation heated his skin. He'd never found out who pinned the rifle mishap on him. Garcia? That was the logical conclusion, though by then, Garcia had been swathed in bandages in the hospital, on a morphine drip, a freak with one eye and three fingers. Everybody fussing over *him*. Ignoring the conspiracy against Paine.

The gray heat crept up his neck, seemed to uncurl down his throat. Paine pecked at the keys. He couldn't type fast enough.

The jackal wants to disarm his own citizenry, tell the world "we're sorry," and hand the keys to our country to the ROW.

Wake up. Resistance to unjust authority isn't simply a right; it's a duty. Spilling the blood of despots isn't a crime; it's self-defense.

165

Nobody had ever appreciated the threats against him. As a teenager, the jocks pushed him into the tiles in the shower. But when he shoved smaller kids into the nozzles and faucets, hard — did it when the jocks were watching, so they could see that he wasn't a wimp — he was the one who got hauled to the principal's office.

And then he heard the principal talking to his counselor, through the office door. "He complains of being bullied, but he's so sarcastic and vindictive that he eggs others into mistreating him."

The counselor claimed *he* was the bully. She taught him a lesson: People in authority want only to put their thumb on your neck.

Setting the counselor's station wagon on fire had brought him a deep, if temporary, satisfaction. Shame that her old border collie had been asleep in the back, but she should never have left the dog in the car. That was on her shoulders.

And that was the start of his real career.

A salt breeze blew through the open window. He set his fingers on the keys.

Yeah. His counselor. And the English professor who called him out for plagiarism. And the sadistic drill sergeant who stuck him in a barracks full of homosexuals. All the gays, pretending to be his buddies, Garcia wanting to have a beer, play pool, talk. And the drill sergeant doing nothing, waiting for him to buckle.

He'd had to take matters into his own hands.

166

To Quote Thomas Jefferson: The Tree Of Liberty Must Be Refreshed From Time To Time With The Blood Of Patriots And Tyrants.

He posted the essay. Words were ammunition, and he was a semantic magician, a Houdini with words. But guns alone brought about real change.

That's why he'd been kicked out of the army with a psychiatric tag on his file — because he knew about guns. He'd acted in his own defense, protected himself from the filthy threat. Nobody had been able to prove that he'd rigged Garcia's weapon to explode in his face. They had only suspected, and so they'd discharged him.

But Three-fingers Garcia had learned the power of a single person to wreak havoc. Paine had left a matchbook on his bunk as a message. *I smoked you.*

He had sent many matchbooks to others in the years since.

The goddamned army. And who was now commander in chief? A former army major. Another Hispanic, a greaseball in everything but name. McFarland, the wetback foreign enemy on domestic soil. Garcia all over again, writ worse. Because he'd destroyed Tasia.

On-screen, the page refreshed. *I resist. Contact me off the board.*

Paine smiled. Keyes had written to him.

Many people wanted to contact him off the board. Access to him boosted their egos. It should — he had spent fourteen months building Tree of Liberty into a digital war camp. He had fanned the winds of outrage like a maestro. And now Tom Paine was an icon. People tried to impress him. Some of them went beyond words into political stunt-jumping. They dumped truckloads of manure on their congressman's doorstep or wrote death threats to senators or turned up at town hall meetings with firearms strapped to their thighs.

But Keyes, he knew, was serious. Keyes was a big data point in his files. They'd exchanged background information over the months, though Paine's history was fictitious. Keyes had worked for an Xe-type contractor. He'd engaged in arms smuggling and money laundering — or as Keyes called it, "paperwork irregularities" — and gotten fired. He was an ideal operative.

Paine reviewed an early e-mail Keyes had sent him:

Live free or die is my motto. Experience with small arms, shotguns, rifles, explosives. U.S. army, private security contractor in Iraq. Fearless. Two years night work with the Freemen's Posse along the U.S. border with Mexic-ho, chasing greasers and confiscating contraband they tried to sneak into the USA. No criminal record. Never been caught. I'm clean.

The man was a thief and a vigilante. And he had no criminal record. Some people played up their criminal convictions, like scars, giving them credibility in the fight against the all-devouring Gub. But Keyes played up his clean slate.

Paine had been waiting for him to write. Still, he played hard-to-get. He wrote: *Words are cheap, friend.*

Four minutes later Keyes replied. *And blood is dear. It's time to fuck up the Gub.*

Paine went to a Web-based e-mail service and set up two new accounts. Using the first, he wrote to Keyes.

Talk is cheap, and vulgarity is cheapest. Clean up your mouth before you speak to me.

Keyes came back almost immediately. *Forgive me. I meant you no disrespect.*

Paine replied. *We need warfighters. We need patriots. Wait ten minutes and then log in to a Webmail address I will give you.* He provided login information — a user name and password. *Check the outbox for a draft message. I will write to you there from now on.*

Then he signed in to the second new e-mail account. He opened a new message and typed. He would not send the message. He would save it as a draft and log out.

As a way to keep communications secret, this technique worked for al Qaeda. It could work for the good guys too. There would be no record of messages sent, no packets of information flying around the Internet, just various additions to the draft, which he and Keyes would read in turn.

He wrote: *I have a new task for you.*

At the cubbyhole desk in the garage at Blue Eagle Security, Keyes read Paine's draft e-mail.

169

You have, I presume, heard the latest news about Robert McFarland. The fightback begins now.

We need intelligence. Get information on Tasia's family, friends, the police, and people "investigating" her death. We need to discover which of them McFarland's operatives are shadowing. And I need you to obtain it, because you're a clean skin.

I need photos.

Keyes read that phrase, *clean skin*. He'd told Paine only half the truth. He had a criminal record, but it had been sealed as a juvenile. However, both he and Ivory had something better than clean skins: multiple skins. Fresh identities, numerous passports. His came courtesy of his former employer, which had arrangements with the State Department and CIA. Officially, those identities had been deactivated when he got fired, but they still fooled most civilian agencies, not to mention your average business.

And Ivory was a *nom de guerre*. Her fresh skin, the fake name on her driver's license and employment records, came courtesy of her useless sister in Arizona, who had no clue her identity was being borrowed.

Every illegal from the ROW could shove him aside and get a job in the U.S.A. Well, fuck 'em. He and Ivory could use fake IDs too.

He read Paine's words on the screen and didn't have to think twice, because he knew that Tom Paine wasn't just a mouthpiece, not just a provocateur. He was a righteous subversive, a saboteur who used fire and violence to bully political cowards into doing what

170

needed to be done. Tom Paine would see things through.

He wrote back: *Will send photos this afternoon.*

He logged out. Wiped the computer's browser history clean. It was on. He was going to make a difference.

CHAPTER
TWENTY-FOUR

Patchy mist turned the air along Geary Boulevard brighter than white. This stretch of the boulevard ran straight and flat all the way to the beach. The buildings had a retro feel: old movie theaters, well-tended trees, appliance stores painted a mustardy green that looked leftover from a WWII Quonset hut. Down the street, the golden domes of a Russian Orthodox church gleamed in the sun and shop fronts had signs in Cyrillic script. Jo swung the pick-up into a parking slot outside Compurama.

Inside, the staff skittered around like nervous prairie dogs. Two of them huddled behind the cash register, comparing iPhones. Jo counted to five and, when they continued their avoidance behavior, knocked on the counter.

One looked up. He was about twenty, as thin as a baguette, with hair that swept over one eye.

"I'm looking for Ferd," she said.

The boy tossed his hair and pointed toward the back of the store.

Compurama was crammed with aisles of computers and peripherals and a gigantic rack of candy and beef jerky. She found Ferd in a corner with a colleague, a towering woman with a ponytail. Ferd had a remote control in his hands. She heard the whir of an electric motor. A little vehicle approached.

"Is that a robot?" Jo said.

Ferd turned. His face popped with surprise at seeing her, then split into a grin. For a second, she thought he was going to hop with excitement.

He rushed toward her. "This is Ahnuld."

Ahnuld was a foot tall and knobby with bits and protrusions. It ran on four fat tires, like a Tonka truck. It was covered with BIOHAZARD and RADIATION warning stickers. It looked like the spawn of WALL-E and a DVD player.

"Cute," Jo said.

"He's on loan from a friend in the robotics lab at Berkeley. This is the beta model for a competition later in the year."

"Road race, or robot cage battle?" Jo said.

The woman with the ponytail cracked a smile. "Self-guided urban navigation."

"Watch." Ferd pressed a switch. Then he set the remote on a shelf. "He'll negotiate a lap around the store on his own, using ultrasonic sensors. Okay, Ahnuld. Off you go."

The cobbled-together little thing whirred away, zigzagging worryingly. Ferd gazed at Jo, his face beatific. Like she was the Virgin of Guadalupe, or Barbarella.

She said, "Have a problem. I need to trace an e-mail address and find its owner."

He straightened and hitched up his pants. "At your service. What information do you have?"

"An address. Hotmail. Plus messages to and from."

Ferd ran his tongue across the inside of one cheek. "Bambi? Thoughts? Beyond whois" — the domain and database search function — "or an IP lookup?"

"Bambi?" Jo said.

The woman with the ponytail said, "Bambi Hess. We met at Ferd's Halloween party."

It took Jo a second to recognize her. "The Klingon."

"*QaStaH nuq!*"

She looked like she could tear a man in two by grabbing his ankles and pulling. Jo suspected a previous career in logging or, possibly, actual Klingon conquest.

"What's more important — finding out who this guy is, or *where* he is?" she said.

"Who." Jo thought about it. "But pinpointing the where could help narrow down the who. And it might help me track what this guy's been up to. Evidence. It would form a timeline, and maybe a map. "What can you do?"

"Depends. An e-mail handle is useless by itself. Anybody can sign up for a Hotmail account without providing their real name or contact information. Do you know someone who works for Hotmail? Someone who'd slip you a name?"

"No. And I don't know anybody I could bribe either, if that was going to be your next suggestion," Jo said.

"Fair enough," Bambi said. "If you had, say, admin privileges on a Web site or blog where he left comments, then you could look up the X-Originating header in the e-mail and trace his IP address to the source."

"I can ferret around online and see if this person has commented somewhere."

"Might help."

Ferd scratched his head. The Brylcreem had turned his hair into a misshapen attempt at punk sculpture, stiff and greasy.

"How much do you trust me?" he said.

Jo raised an eyebrow. "You asking me?"

"Forward me some e-mails from this guy. I can do a traceroute. Maybe capture the location where he's logging in from. And if that location changes . . ."

"You could track him, if he's on the move."

"Theoretically."

"How closely could you narrow it down?" she said. "Country? City?"

"If I get really lucky, the source address might tell me where it originated — even inside a particular building. At a mall, say, or on a campus."

Archangel X had asked Tasia about the *Bad Dogs and Bullets* tour. Jo wondered if tracing his e-mails might illuminate a trail, and show that he'd been following Tasia.

"That would be useful," she said. "Could you do it without tipping him off?"

Bambi smirked. "You mean, without e-mailing him directly and saying, 'Where are you, douche wad?'"

Jo turned to her with a flat stare. "Who said he's a douche wad?"

"Why else would you be after him? He ripped you off, or he's spamming you. Or broke up with you, right?"

Jo flattened the stare to a metallic sheen. "He's my opponent in an MMRWRPG."

Bambi's eyes widened. The question on her lips looked like, *Huh?*

"Massively multiplayer real-world role-playing game," Jo said. "First to track the other wins."

"Wow. Real world?"

"The realest."

She wasn't about to say anything else in front of Bambi. Around the corner, whirring happily, came Ahnuld. He was weaving and knocking into the shelves. Somebody had taped a Pepsi to him. Also a cigarette.

"Good luck," she said.

As Jo turned the key in the Tacoma's ignition, her phone rang.

"Dr. Beckett? Dr. Gerald Rhee Park."

Park was the physician who had prescribed Prozac to Tasia McFarland. "Thanks for returning my call."

"I doubt I can shed much light on Ms. Hicks-McFarland's demise. I only saw her twice."

Jo felt surprised. "You prescribed an antidepressant."

"She had symptoms of major depression. So, yes, I wrote her a scrip for Prozac."

"Can I ask why you wrote it out to Fawn Hicks?"

"To protect her privacy. And if you'll excuse me for stating the obvious, the brouhaha surrounding her death only confirms that she was right to be cautious. I

176

wrote the scrip using her first name and maiden name, both of which were on her driver's license."

"That also meant that a pharmacy wouldn't be able to cross-check the prescription against her other scrips for drug interactions."

"Miss Hicks was an adult, Dr. Beckett."

"Did she tell you that she'd been diagnosed as bipolar one?"

"She presented with frank symptoms of major depression. I prescribed accordingly."

"She was given Prozac without a mood stabilizer?" Jo pinched the bridge of her nose. "What sort of practice do you have?"

"I'm a primary care physician."

"You're not in psychiatric practice?"

"No. And to be frank, Dr. Beckett, your insinuations are quite without merit."

"I'm insinuating nothing," Jo said, knowing she was. Anger rising. "Prescribing an SSRI without a mood stabilizer onboard could have flipped Ms. McFarland into a manic or mixed state."

"I did everything possible to help Ms. McFarland to the best of my ability and the highest professional standards."

"Did you see her for any follow-up visits?"

"A phone consultation. She was experiencing a significant reduction in her symptoms. So if you'll excuse me, this conversation is at an end."

He broke off the call. Probably to phone his attorney, and prepare a malpractice defense and maybe a defamation lawsuit against Jo.

She shook her head. Park had prescribed Prozac, an SSRI — selective serotonin reuptake inhibitor — without knowing that Tasia was bipolar. That prescription had possibly sent her into a mixed state — hyperenergetic, agitated, and maybe even suicidal.

The phone rang again. It was the Psych Department receptionist from UCSF. "Heads up. We've been getting calls all morning. The media has your name."

She felt a spark of dismay. "Who called?"

"Fox, CNN, a wire service reporter, plus somebody was asking for you at the front desk. You have a bunch of messages. Would you like me to read them?"

"Sure. Thanks." She ran her hand through her hair in frustration.

Everybody wanted her to call back. She wrote down their names. She seemed to hear a rumbling sound in the distance. A freight train, bearing down on her.

"You going to return their calls?" the receptionist said.

"After I return from my trip to Mars."

She fired up the truck.

Back at the house, she felt an increasing uneasiness, like an itch. Archangel X had gotten under her skin.

She paced, ate a banana with peanut butter, and made a pot of coffee. While it brewed, she called Tang. "Anything new?"

"We have initial tox results from Tasia's autopsy. She was clean. No cocaine, no opiates, no illegal substances."

"Prescription meds?" Jo said.

"Prozac."

"Nothing else?"

"Nope."

After hanging up, Jo felt antsier than before. She found the business card belonging to the property manager for Tasia's house, and gave him a call.

"Vandalism. Interesting you should ask," he said. "I have a call in to Ms. McFarland's insurance company. There's some exterior damage that needs to be repaired."

The itchy feeling climbed Jo's arm, as if silverfish were running along her skin. "What kind of damage?"

"Graffiti."

She had run out the back door and across Tasia's backyard. She hadn't seen graffiti. "What and where?"

"On the back wall of the house. And on the fence, which is up in the trees."

"What does it say?" Jo said.

"I can send you photos."

Jo gave him her e-mail address. When the photos arrived, the crawly silverfish feeling intensified. "When did you discover this?"

"Yesterday, after you were there. After the break-in."

Jo couldn't believe she hadn't seen it. Of course, she hadn't had a chance to do an exterior tour of Tasia's house. And when she ran after the intruder, she hadn't looked back. If she had, she would have been shocked. On the back wall, in dripping black spray paint, somebody had written *tart, slag,* and *BURN.*

"Have the police seen this?"

"Yeah. I walked around the house with an officer yesterday after the incident."

The images didn't have the finesse of experienced gang tagging, or the *joie de vivre* and cynicism of street art. They were pure message, angry and sharp.

"Here's another one, from the fence at the top of the hill. It's on the back side, where nobody saw it until after the break-in," the property manager said.

These were worse. *You betrayed me, now you pay.*

Tasia BITCH SLUT opens her legs for anybody

"Don't paint anything over. It's evidence," she said.

When she finished the call, she phoned Tang. "Why didn't anybody tell me about the graffiti at Tasia's house?"

"It's pronounced 'sidelined,' Beckett. But forget that for the moment. I just talked to a rental car agency. Tasia and her posse rented three SUVs before the concert. Two were returned on time, but the third never made it back to the airport."

"Because Tasia drove it to the ballpark the night she died."

"It's still there. And guess what?"

"It's vandalized."

"Extra points for the deadshrinker. You advance to round two."

"What happened to it?"

"Keyed, tires slashed, superglue in the door locks."

"Graffiti?"

"Scratched into the driver's door. The C word. Not *conspiracy*."

180

Jo stared out the window. "This unequivocally went beyond cyberstalking."

"Think it's Archangel X?"

Jo looked at her computer. "I'm going to try to find out."

Tang was silent for a moment. "Do that. But be careful. This guy may already have attacked you once and put Chennault in the hospital. Watch your back."

CHAPTER
TWENTY-FIVE

Searle Lecroix was staying at the St. Francis. When Jo hopped off the cable car, a salsa band was playing in Union Square. The hotel doorman smiled and tipped his hat as she went through the doors.

Inside, conversations bounced off the high ceiling and dark wood paneling. She called Lecroix from a house phone in the lobby.

"Doctor, come on up," he said.

"I have a table in the bar."

Lecroix's drawl thickened. "The media knows I'm here. Take a look outside, see if you don't spot a ferret with a camera."

She glanced out the revolving door. Across the street on the square stood a man with a camera on a strap around his neck.

"Unless y'all want your face splashed across the tabloids, with 'Psychiatrist questions Searle about Tasia's death,' I suggest you come upstairs."

"I'll be right there."

Jo climbed the fire stairs to the sixth floor, where the stairwell door opened to a hush. The hallway walls featured gilded mirrors — *See yourself, framed in gold.*

When Lecroix answered her knock, she couldn't hide her surprise.

He smiled, slow and melancholy. "Thought my entourage would greet you?"

He was dressed as he had been at the concert: the full cowboy. The jeans were tourniquet tight, the boots worn down at the heels. He touched the brim of his black cowboy hat and welcomed her into the suite.

In the living room, an acoustic guitar was propped against the end of the sofa. Lecroix offered her a seat and took a chair across from her. Sunlight refracted from the chandeliers, cold and splintery. Sheet music was spread across the coffee table. Jo saw a half-written song, titled, "Angel, Flown."

"Has the memorial service been set?" she said.

"Tomorrow afternoon at Grace Cathedral." He gestured at the song-in-progress. "I'm writing a tune in her honor. I'm also gonna sing 'Amazing Grace.' " He set his hands on his knees and took a breath. "That song gets me every time."

Jo waited until he exhaled. "Can I ask about your relationship with Tasia?"

"That's why you're here," he said.

"How long had you been seeing each other?"

"Since February. We met to rehearse 'Bull's-eye.' " He eyed her from under the brim of the cowboy hat. His gaze was magnetic. "I really liked her. She was a terrific gal."

Jo couldn't tell whether his words were sincere, or a practiced line. "At her house, I saw a pair of boots and a guitar."

"Both mine."

"You spent the night before the concert with her?"

"Spent it at her house, but she worked all night, composing. She was buzzing like a hornet. She'd been up — gosh, by then she'd been up for five days."

"Can you tell me about her mood?" she said.

"Which one?" His smile was brief. When it vanished, it left an afterimage of sadness.

"Start from the beginning. What was she like when you met her?" she said.

"Ball of fire. Outgoing and fun. And creative, my God, the songs just poured out of her. And the girl could sing."

"When did that change?" Jo said.

He picked up the guitar. "Round . . . April. It was like she fell off a cliff. At first I thought something bad had happened, some family problem. But now I think it was a depressive episode."

"Can you describe the change?"

"Storm cloud swallowed her up. One time we found her inside a closet at the studio, sitting on the floor, cradling her head in her hands."

"In a closet?"

"She said that way none of them could ruin her life."

"Who?"

"Them. You know. The famous *them*."

Jo laced her hands together. "Was she specific?"

"She had a list, starting with the president. He was bringing the country down. He didn't believe in America. Didn't believe in the women and men who

184

love this country and would do anything to make it work."

He took off the cowboy hat. His skin was sun-weathered. "She never used his name. Said 'the president.' Isn't that strange? And don't you think she was projecting?"

"How so?"

"Saying he rejected the country, wanted to hurt it, didn't love it the way it deserves to be loved — don't you think she was talking about herself?"

Jo tried not to smile. "You ever study psychology, Mr. Lecroix?"

"It's Searle. I just understand human nature." He picked out a bluesy line on the guitar. "Also I have a B.A. in Economics from Texas A & M, with a minor in Psych."

Jo leaned back. "Did Tasia ever threaten to harm herself?"

"No."

"Did she ever mention the possibility that somebody might want to harm her?"

"The Secret Service, the White House chief of staff, and this guy who stands on Hollywood Boulevard with a religious placard, who she thought was planning to put her into a government concentration camp."

He paused, and read the question in Jo's eyes: Why did he stay with Tasia?

His face saddened. It reminded Jo of how he looked after the concert, and his blunt anguish at seeing Tasia dead.

"Hearing paranoid talk did make me wonder if I should break up with her. But I knew about her bipolar disorder. And about a month ago, things changed."

"Tell me about it."

"She got a whole lot more energy. I thought maybe she was snapping out of the blues, and getting back to her old self."

Jo didn't want to tell him, but *her old self* was a mirage. The up-and-down mood swings were intrinsic to Tasia McFarland's personality. The baseline was what had eluded her.

"What happened?" Jo said.

"Bubbly again. Just a hoot. She seemed so glad to see me. *Real, real* glad. That's why I was so awful tired the other night," he said.

Goodness, he was either tongue-tied, or being an old-fashioned gentleman. "She wore you out physically?"

"Day and night. Two, three times a day. At home, in the studio, on the tour bus." He shook his head, wide-eyed, almost amazed. "And one day I came home and found a brand-new Corvette sitting on my driveway, wrapped up with a fat red bow. She'd bought it for me."

"What did you think?"

"That maybe her contract with the label was a whole lot better than I'd imagined. Or she was thanking me for working as her" — he blushed — "stud horse."

Jo checked off two symptoms of uncontrolled mania: hypersexuality and extravagant spending.

"Did you ever see her take drugs? I mean both prescription and illegal drugs."

"She used to take a lot of pills but she quit them. She wanted to live clean."

And Jo knew that all her fears about Tasia's mental instability were true. "Did she explain which drugs she quit taking, and why?"

"Said she'd been prescribed medications to deal with a chemical imbalance. But they made her feel flat."

"Flat in what way?"

"Emotionally. They sucked away all her joy and energy and creativity," he said. "She'd decided to live holistically, focus on positive thinking. And she had a new doctor, got rid of the others who'd been doping her."

Jo wasn't surprised. Tasia had stopped taking her medication because she craved the buzz and sense of invincibility that came with being manic — and then she'd lurched into depression. But instead of talking to her psychiatrist, she had gone to Dr. Gerald Rhee Park and persuaded him to prescribe Prozac. The antidepressant had induced a mixed episode, making her agitated and depressed, and increasing the risk of a suicide attempt.

"Can we talk about the twenty-four hours before her death?" Jo said.

Lecroix ran his fingers up the neck of the guitar. "We ordered dinner in. She was too busy composing to go out."

"Just the two of you?"

"About 9p.m. her writing collaborator came by. The ghostwriter — Ace." He glanced up. "She had me shoo him off."

"She wouldn't see him?"

"She said, no interruptions. And believe you me, Ace didn't like that."

"I imagine not."

"She'd been ignoring him for the previous week. Ace was going crazy. He was on a deadline to produce the first draft of the memoir."

"Why wouldn't she talk to him?"

"I think Tasia had serious second thoughts about the whole project. Dredging up her past turned out to upset her in a major way."

"Her past, meaning her marriage?" Jo said.

"She never talked to me directly about those years." He twanged the strings of the guitar. "You think that's strange? Rhinoceros in the room and all?"

"I don't know. Did you know she met with Robert McFarland in Virginia —"

"No. Heard it on the news, like everybody else." He stopped playing. "I got no idea what they talked about. Tasia didn't take me into her confidence."

His face flushed a deeper red.

"What were her most recent opinions on President McFarland?" Jo said.

Lecroix's voice rose. "You heard that song she wrote about him. 'The Liar's Lullaby.' And she left that for me. What am I supposed to make of that?"

Jo let him cool off for a moment. "At her house I saw a copy of *Case Closed*. Was she interested in the Kennedy assassination?"

"Ace gave that to her."

"Why?"

Lecroix practically snorted. "To 'educate' her out of believing in conspiracy theories. Tasia read the book, but didn't really care about JFK — she cared about Jackie. Talked about what it must have been like being First Lady, living in a bubble, struggling with a marriage and young children." He paused. "Most of all, she talked about the babies Jackie lost, and how terrible that was."

"Babies?"

"Jackie had a miscarriage and a stillborn baby, and a preemie who died just a couple months before Dallas. Tasia identified with her." His shoulders sagged. "Tasia had lost more than one pregnancy herself. Even mentioning pregnancy made her sad and angry." He sighed. "She never elaborated on it. And I let it lay."

Jo parsed the expression on Lecroix's face, and tried to fit this information into her understanding of Tasia. Lecroix looked down and continued to pick out a melody on the guitar.

"Did she ever talk about contributing to discussions at an extremist Web site — Tree of Liberty?" Jo said.

"No. I'm no right-winger, and I didn't think she was, either." His face turned wry. "I perform with the flag hanging behind me onstage, but patriotism didn't draw her to me, or do it for her. In the long run, I don't think Tasia would ever have settled down with a singer. She'd kept much more important men than me in love with her, and that was her biggest buzz of all. Power."

Jo thought for a moment. "Was there any difference in her attitude before she saw McFarland in Virginia, and after?"

Lecroix's voice sank. "You asking if she went there to try and get him back?"

He seemed sad, confused, and proud, all at once.

"Is that what you think?" Jo said.

"I got no idea. How am I supposed to handle this news? My girlfriend goes to a hotel for a one-on-one with the president, and I have to hear about it on TV?"

He began picking at another blues line. The steel-stringed melody filled the room, bright and aching.

"The night before the concert, at Tasia's house," Jo prompted.

"Ace finally gave up and left. Tasia was racing a hundred miles an hour. I thought making love might calm her down, but she kept up a running commentary the whole time. Like she was announcing the Daytona Five Hundred, live and in High Definition."

Jo tried not to smile at the image.

"She seemed . . . you ever seen a horse with a burr under its saddle? It can't settle down. That was her. But overnight, the invincibility came back. When I got up in the morning she seemed like steel." He stopped playing. "I wish to hell I knew what was bothering her."

"Did she ever mention a stalker?" Jo said.

He frowned. "No. Was somebody following her?"

"Maybe. Did she ever talk about messages from fans?"

"She was warm and generous with the fans. Made a point of replying to every person who wrote to her. But she never mentioned a stalker, and I think she would have. She felt surrounded by threats. If somebody was after her, she would have been screaming about it. What's going on?"

"It may only have been cyberstalking, but it's possible that somebody followed her to San Francisco."

"You think a stalker shot her?"

"I don't know."

"Goddamn." He shook his head. "There's crazies out there. Are there ever. I have a security system at home, and on the road I carry all kinds of protection."

"Sounds wise."

He grew pensive. "You think some stalker was after Tasia for herself? Or because of who she used to be married to?"

"That's an excellent question."

Lecroix's sad eyes grew serious. "Who's more likely to have stalkers?"

"The president, no question. But I don't know whether somebody who's obsessed with him might also want to harm his former wife."

But she knew something Lecroix most likely did not. Stalkers fit no definable personality profile. But she'd met one in San Quentin, a man who had killed his estranged wife. He had a peculiar historical obsession that, Jo learned afterward, he shared with a strikingly large number of violent stalkers: He was fascinated with presidential assassins.

"Anything else you can tell me?" she said.

He hesitated. "Yeah. At the concert, I thought for a second Tasia was aiming the gun at me. That tells you everything. I didn't know her at all."

Jo nodded, and stood up. "Thanks."

"You going to go call the Secret Service now?"

"Among others."

"Best make it quick. The president's coming to the funeral. He's gonna be here tomorrow."

CHAPTER
TWENTY-SIX

As she trooped down the stairs at the St. Francis, Jo called and left a message for Amy Tang.

"I just interviewed Searle Lecroix, and I'm worried. Tasia may have been only part of the stalker's focus. I think the SFPD should alert the Secret Service." She explained, adding, "It's a stretch. But better safe than sorry."

Next she phoned Vienna Hicks. "Is what I'm hearing about the memorial service for your sister accurate?"

"Grace Cathedral, tomorrow afternoon. Searle's going to sing. Bless the guy, he's actually kind of sweet and awkward," Vienna said. "And it's true — *he* is coming."

"Robert McFarland."

"I spoke to him. I got it from the horse's mouth." Vienna sounded both snarky and amazed. "I'm sure his people vetted it. The idea of the president attending his ex-wife's funeral must have polled well."

"So he'll be in San Francisco tomorrow?" Jo said.

"What's that tone I hear in your voice?"

Jo reached the ground floor, opened the fire door, and headed for the lobby. "I need to talk to him."

Vienna guffawed, an honest-to-God barking laugh. "And I want to grow wings and fly like Tinkerbell, sprinkling pixie dust on the city."

"Do you have a direct number for him?"

"No." She laughed again, but let it fade. "I do have the direct number for his chief of staff." She paused. "Who sent me a condolence card, believe it or not."

Jo got out a pen. "K. T. Lewicki has a heart?"

"We know each other from the old days. He had a soft spot for Tasia. I think he understood, even before Rob did, how mentally fragile she was. After the divorce we stayed in touch, and he'd always check with me that she was doing all right." Her tone turned cautious. "What would you talk to Rob about?"

"His meeting with Tasia in Virginia. Why he lied about it. Tasia's mental state at the beginning, middle, and end of their marriage. Whether he knew of any threats to her."

"Did you get hit on the head when you were a kid, or are you just unaware that asking those kinds of questions can have consequences?"

"My sister says I'm an adrenaline junkie. Could you give me the number?"

Vienna gave her several numbers.

"Thanks," Jo said.

She walked into the lobby. The information she'd gathered was giving her the heebie-jeebies.

Tasia had received fourteen hundred e-mails from Archangel X. They indicated a pattern of increasing intensity, obsession, and threat — though never explicit. Yet Tasia had never responded to, or even

194

opened, most of those e-mails. As far as Jo could discern, she'd never mentioned them to her agent, manager, family, or boyfriend. She may not have been aware of the most recent spate.

The vandalism was highly disturbing, and a warning sign of a personality headed toward violence. And Tasia, according to Searle Lecroix, had been afraid. According to the stunt coordinator, Rez Shirazi, she had believed that an assassin lurked among the crowd at the concert. She had talked of sacrifice and martyrdom.

It may have been the ramblings of a woman gripped by grandiose paranoia. But there were too many pieces of information, rolling around like marbles, for Jo to dismiss it.

Her gaze fell on a newspaper. The front-page photo showed President McFarland and his staff huddled in conversation in the Oval Office.

She walked to a quiet corner, as far from the echoing noise of the lobby as she could get, and she phoned the White House.

The phone was answered briskly. "Sylvia Obote."

"Jo Beckett."

After a pause, Obote said, "Yes, Dr. Beckett. I've forwarded your questions. I'm sure the president will respond in due course."

Obote didn't sound impatient, but her smooth efficiency had an edge to it.

"Thank you. I hear that the president is coming to California for Tasia McFarland's memorial service. I —"

"The president is attending the memorial as a private citizen and friend of the family. I'm afraid he'll have no time in his schedule to speak to you."

"That's not what I was going to ask." Not anymore, at least. "I've received some disturbing information. Someone may have been stalking Ms. McFarland. I think the Secret Service should be aware of the situation."

This time Obote's pause was briefer. "Give me the information. And I'll put you through to the presidential protection detail."

Jo heard Obote typing notes as they talked, though she presumed their conversation was being recorded, and perhaps relayed to NSA headquarters in Fort Meade, Maryland, and from there to a polar-orbiting spy satellite that was even now turning its mirrored eyes toward Union Square in San Francisco.

"Thank you for the information, Doctor," Obote said. "I'll transfer you."

There was a series of clicks and silences and eventually the phone was picked up again. A brisk, southern male voice answered and took down all the information as Jo repeated it.

"This may be nothing, but I didn't want to let it lie," Jo said.

"And you were right to do so."

"Good. I presume you're part of the president's detail, Special Agent . . ."

"Zuniga. Yes, ma'am. And we appreciate the information."

She thanked him and said goodbye. And she looked again at the newspaper. Noise echoed in the vaulting lobby. She dialed a new number. She stared at the photo: a bullet-headed man conferring with President McFarland, leaning close, eyes intense.

"K. T. Lewicki's office."

If she couldn't talk to the president, she'd talk to his chief of staff.

Kelvin Tycho Lewicki was known as the Point Man. Gatekeeper and guard dog, he was tied to Robert McFarland by long-standing friendship. He controlled the president's schedule and controlled access to the Oval Office and the man himself.

Lewicki had gone to high school with Rob McFarland. At the University of Montana, he wrestled on the college's Division I NCAA squad. He was renowned for winning matches in which his opponents withdrew with dislocated joints. Later, as a lieutenant in the army, he served with McFarland overseas. After a decade in the House of Representatives, he'd been picked by McFarland as his right-hand man.

Whereas McFarland was as smooth and cool as Gary Cooper, Lewicki was blunt and funny, and known to go for an opponent's knees. He and McFarland had scrapped politically for years. His own aspirations for higher office had been bested by his friend, and then coopted when McFarland brought him into the White House as chief of staff — a move seen by pundits as a "team of rivals" tactic.

But Lewicki had been the best man at Rob and Tasia McFarland's wedding. He had devoted his entire adult life to public service. And he had shown enough humanity, and connection, even after all these years, to send Vienna Hicks a condolence card.

A minion answered Lewicki's office phone. Jo repeated her list of qualifications and requirements and alarming possibilities, intoning them like a spell. She gazed at Lewicki's photo on the front page of the newspaper. He was built like a coil of steel cable. Sinewy, gray-eyed, built to take the tension, or to whiplash an enemy.

"Connecting you," the minion said.

The connection clicked through. "K. T. Lewicki. How can I help you, Doctor Beckett?"

His voice was clipped and nasal. He spoke like a man used to attacking in powerful bursts — wrestling opponents, Taliban strongholds, the Speaker of the House.

Jo's intake of breath was involuntary. "Yes. Thank you for taking my call, Mr. Lewicki."

Just breathe. This is your opening. Go for it. Dynamic.

"I'm working with the SFPD to ascertain —"

"Tasia McFarland's cause of death. I know."

Ping, like a BB, hitting her in the side of the head. "I know it's bold of me to ask, but it's vital that I speak with President McFarland about his ex-wife's state of mind."

"Bold? No, it's ballsy. Obviously you've decided to go through me."

198

"You are the Point Man."

"So I'll point out that the SFPD's investigation into a tragic mishap at a concert is snuffling so exhaustively through minutiae that it's becoming neurotic."

"It's far from clear that Ms. McFarland's death was an accident."

"Even so, whatever the circumstances, the president was three thousand miles away when it happened."

"And she met with him three days before being shot to death with a pistol he owns."

Lewicki was quiet a beat. Jo heard papers rustling on his end. "I've heard you're tenacious, Doctor Beckett. But sometimes there's a fine line between tenacity and obsession."

Now it was Jo's turn to pause. "This is a matter of being thorough. This is due diligence, and it's what I owe the criminal justice system, Ms. McFarland, and her family. And given the media attention, reaching a dispositive conclusion is vital, to quash rumor and misinformation."

"You know there's no such thing as dispositive with the infortainment industry. And after a certain point, the investigation becomes less a thorough examination and more a fishing expedition with dynamite. That fine line? Sometimes it's between tenacity and recklessness."

"I don't want to harm the president. I want to determine the truth," Jo said.

There was another, longer pause, and she realized she'd stepped onto Lewicki's turf. She'd played straight into his hands, like a wrestling opponent maneuvered for a crushing fall.

"You do like to take chances, don't you?" he said. "You raced BMX and mountain bikes in high school, I hear. Won some — is this correct, 'bouldering' competitions? — as Johanna Tahari. There's a nice photo of you climbing in Yosemite, from *Outside* magazine. Glad you take advantage of our National Park system, Doctor."

The *ping* turned into a hail of BBs.

"And I know you've been willing to risk yourself in aid of others. I'm sorry about your unfortunate loss a few years ago," Lewicki said.

The lobby of the hotel seemed to fill with a sound like rain pounding a tin roof. "I need to speak to the president," she said. "If that's a risk, I'm shocked."

Unfortunate loss. The bastard, bringing Daniel into this. Risk? What was he implying?

"So convince me," Lewicki said.

"Before her death Tasia was being stalked."

Quiet on the line.

"It appears that an obsessed fan was cyberstalking her, at the least. Maybe in person. What worries me is that this person's messages occasionally mention the president."

"You need to speak to the police and the Secret Service."

"Done. I spoke to Agent Zuniga," Jo said. "This investigation is now working on two levels. One, to ascertain the manner of Ms. McFarland's death. To do that I need to reconstruct her last few weeks. And to determine her state of mind, I need to talk to the president."

200

"Why?"

"She left a recorded message. In it, she expresses a fear for her life. She mentions the president. It made no sense until the photos surfaced from the hotel in Reston. Now it makes only partial sense. The only person who can clarify and explain is Mr. McFarland."

Another long pause. "I'll get back to you."

"Thank you."

The click on Lewicki's end sounded final, like a nail being hammered into her chances.

The noisy echoes in the hotel lobby filled the silence. Jo put away the phone. She felt the marble floor shift beneath her feet. She had a strange feeling that she'd just undermined herself.

She walked to the door. The doorman opened it before she could touch the handle.

Outside, she put on her sunglasses. A brisk breeze lifted her hair. Strands of mist skirted across the blue sky. A cable car rolled by, crowded with office workers and tourists, brakeman pulling on the lever. When it had passed, she saw the photographer across the street in the square. His camera was lifted to his face, aimed at the door of the St. Francis, catching her.

After a second he lowered the camera. Stared. When she didn't look away, he took a pack of cigarettes from his shirt pocket and turned his back to light up.

People swept past Jo on the sidewalk. Traffic jangled and sunlight bounced off car windshields. Jo turned and walked south toward Market Street. She kept her eyes on the photographer. He glanced over his shoulder at the door of the St. Francis, took out his phone, and made a call.

She kept walking. The photographer looked up and down the street, as though searching to see where she'd gone.

Maybe paranoia was infectious.

At the corner she stopped and waited with the crowd for the light to change. The buildings around the square rose above her. The city was a buzzing hive. Within half a mile were Chinatown, Financial District skyscrapers, and the soup kitchens of the Tenderloin. Protecting the president in such a dense urban area had to be a nightmare.

K. T. Lewicki's creepy recital of her own history had caused her fingertips to tingle, like she'd stuck a pin in a wall socket. She couldn't call it a threat. Nothing was overt. But the warning had been in every syllable Lewicki spoke.

Back off. Declare Tasia's death an accident.

"Prick," she said.

The light changed. She strode with the crowd across the crowded intersection. Sunlight slanted between buildings and the wind shirred across her skin.

Tasia could no longer speak for herself. But perhaps somebody else could speak for her. She called Ace Chennault, Tasia's ghost.

In Union Square, Keyes held the phone to his ear and turned away to block out the noise from the salsa band.

Ivory answered. "News?"

"I just saw the police shrink come out of the Saint Francis and walk away."

"You sure?"

"I got her photo. E-mail Paine. Tell him she was there to talk to Searle Lecroix." He started walking. "I'll send him the photos within the next half hour."

He snapped the phone shut.

CHAPTER
TWENTY-SEVEN

Ace Chennault had been released from the hospital, and Jo arranged to meet him for coffee near the Civic Center. She took off at a brisk walk.

The straightest route between the swanky designer stores of Union Square and the grandeur of the Civic Center took Jo through the demimonde of the Tenderloin. The neighborhood began suddenly: Under blue skies, with ultramodern hotels and skyscrapers visible a block away, the streets seemed to empty of traffic. Men shambled along the sidewalk. They were skinny. They wore saggy jeans and beanies. They were white, they were black, they had few teeth. Among the few vehicles in sight were a decrepit parked pick-up and an electric wheelchair driven by a gent with a bushy white beard, whose bandanna was tied pirate-style over his ponytail.

Jo jogged across a street, holding tight to her satchel. On the far corner, a man in crooked aviator shades strutted by, hands fidgeting at his sides.

"Vicodin. Vicodin," he chanted.

She jogged past.

"Hey, baby. Vicodin."

No thanks. At the St. Anthony Dining Room, the kitchen must have been about to open. Outside its doors people stood in line behind ropes that ran around the block, as if the mission were a trendy club. Across the street the Islamic Center was open as well, but the sidewalk outside it was empty. The Catholics, it seemed, had more popular food.

She passed a low-rent hotel with a buzzing neon sign. Near the door, an employee was scrubbing the sidewalk with a bucket of soapy water and a broom. On the sign, several letters were out. THE MORAL flickered on and off. Jo didn't know whether that should be taken as a promise, or a warning.

After a few blocks she emerged onto the broad plaza that led to the Civic Center. The people of the Tenderloin thinned out, like eddies along a shore. The golden dome of City Hall shone in the distance. On the plaza, an antiques fair was set up, farmers'-market style. She walked toward the Federal Building, looking for the Starbucks, and heard a man call her name.

"Over here."

From a bench in the distance, Ace Chennault waved at her. When she approached, he held out a cup of coffee. "Didn't know how you take it, so it's black."

She sat down beside him. "Thanks. How are you feeling?"

He shrugged. His broken left arm hung in the sling. Blue cast, blue sling, blue mood. The black sutures crept along his scalp like a crusty centipede.

His boyish face looked haggard. "I was a micro-celeb for ninety seconds. But the reporters are gone and the painkillers have worn off."

Walk around the corner, Jo thought. *Mr. Vicodin will fix you right up.*

He looked at his feet. "Actually, I'm damned lucky. I just came from the funeral home. Paying my respects to Tasia. Pretty awful."

Jo gave him a moment. At the end of the plaza beyond the antiques market, City Hall was framed by the green boughs of trees that stood like a military honor guard.

She got her notebook. "Ready to talk?"

He took out a digital audio recorder. "Mind if I record this?"

"Not at all."

She was surprised, yet not. She'd never had an interviewee record a psychological autopsy interview. But then, she'd never interviewed a writer facing the collapse of his high-profile publishing deal.

Chennault fiddled with buttons, struggling because of the cast. "Journalists get quotes wrong all the time. You'd be amazed. Reporters write down stuff that never came out of people's mouths. Usually in demeaning ways."

"I need facts, and your impressions. I have no reason to want to demean you."

"Good. Excuse my suspicious nature, but I did just get attacked by a rock-wielding caveman."

He pressed *Play* and held the recorder up, staring at her intensely.

"For the record," Jo said, "is Ace your legal name?"

"You accusing me of using an alias?"

"Getting the quote right."

He smiled. "Sorry. Ace is a *nom de plume*." The smile turned charmingly rueful. "Anson isn't a great name for a rock 'n' roll journo."

"And Chennault?"

"All mine."

She wrote it down. "Did Tasia talk to you about her marriage?"

The smile mutated again. "You'll have to wait to read about it in the book."

She flattened her expression. "Please."

"Sorry, Doctor. Journalistic privilege. I will tell you two things. Tasia was off her rocker, and the revelations will be explosive."

"Would you like that phrase to go in my report?"

Now he flashed his teeth. "Please."

She guessed that this was a new form of viral marketing. She hated it.

"Did Tasia ever speak about a stalker?" she said.

He blinked sharply, as if he'd been poked in the eye with a stick. "Who was after her?" He pointed to his crusty sutures. "This guy?"

"I don't know. The police are trying to piece it together. Did she ever talk about somebody threatening her? Somebody, that is, within the realm of what we call consensus reality."

"Besides 'They,' you mean. No." He leaned back, pensive. "Wait. There was this one time."

A man approached them. "No sitting, folks."

He was a rent-a-cop dressed in black tactical gear. He waved them along like a couple of vagrants.

"It's a park bench in Federal Plaza," Jo said.

He looked away. "Not during the antiques market. Private event."

He had a buzz cut and a pierced eyebrow. His black flak jacket said MONDO SWAT. He was about eighteen years old.

Chennault pulled a face and gestured to his sling. "No mercy for the wounded?"

Still looking away, the kid waved again. "Everybody has to keep walking. Those are the rules."

Chennault spat a laugh. "*Jawohl*, Herr Himmler."

He stood up. "Doesn't matter I got these stitches from chasing down the intruder at Tasia McFarland's house, does it? That we're trying to get to the bottom of the biggest case in the United States? Gotta follow those orders."

The rent-a-cop looked at him with sharp surprise. Chennault ambled away from the bench toward City Hall. Jo followed him.

He shook his head. "See what public education hath wrought. Clueless about the irony of booting citizens out of a public place." He glanced over his shoulder. "Yeah, now he's regretting it. I gave him something to think about." He eyed Jo. "And if you think Tasia liked me because I'm not scared to speak up, you're right."

Touchy, touchy, Jo thought. And needy for attention. Also in physical pain.

"Is that why you gave her a copy of *Case Closed*?" she said.

"Tasia had the celebrity habit of believing every conspiracy theory she heard. I wanted to educate her about the Kennedy assassination. And the moon landing, and other fake 'conspiracies,' but she mostly cared about Jackie."

"You said somebody might have threatened her," she said.

"Concert in Tucson, last month. I was watching the show from the wings. Right after she made her entrance on the zip line, there was this guy in the front row. Just standing there, while everybody else was cheering and clapping. Staring at her. It was creepy."

That was less than nothing. "Just staring?"

"Yeah. Until he climbed the barrier and tried to rush the stage. Pulling off his clothes."

"Security stopped him?"

"Yeah. White guy, pudgy, maybe late twenties. They tossed him back, he melted into the crowd."

If that's all the incident amounted to, Jo doubted there would be any record of it. She also noticed that as Chennault answered questions, his memory for detail improved remarkably. She wondered if he was exaggerating. Overly helpful witnesses were an occupational hazard. She listened to everything people told her with a high index of suspicion.

"I hear that you stopped by Tasia's house the night before she died, and she refused to speak to you."

His poked-in-the-eye look returned. "It ever occur to you that Searle Lecroix might have an ulterior motive for saying that?"

"Such as?"

"Trying to scotch an autobiography that might not portray him in the most flattering light. Making me look bad to help his own cause."

"Is that what you think?"

"I think nobody's considered the possibility that Searle wanted out of his relationship with Tasia, but couldn't do it while they were on tour. I think nobody's figured out how convenient it was that Tasia died and Searle didn't have to break up with her. And that he played the heartbroken hero that night on the baseball field, begging people for help, but actually did nothing to save her."

Jo held her counsel. Chennault's eyes cut back and forth, avoiding her gaze. The light in his eyes was injured and sly.

"Maybe you ought to ask Lecroix about that fat fan who rushed the stage in Tucson. The answers he gives you might surprise you," he said.

A man shuffled past them, shirtless, white hair blowing in the wind like wild flames. His bare back was the canvas for a green tattoo.

Chennault gestured at him. "See that? *Semper Fidelis*. It means 'always faithful.'"

Jo ignored Chennault's condescension. As if a physician would be unfamiliar with Latin phrases, or most Americans with the motto of the United States Marine Corps.

"Your tattoo says something similar," she said.

He nodded, his sad eyes reddening. "Know how few people can abide by those words these days? Ask Lecroix about that. I think that's what Tasia's death is

210

about." He turned to go. "*Semper*. Think about that. *Always* is what counts."

In the musty hotel room, above red neon letters spitting THE MORAL, Noel Michael Petty put on a jean jacket and watch cap. Oakley sports sunglasses, like Major League Baseball players wore. Looked in the dingy mirror, made two fists and shook them.

You are NMP. Badass bastard. A man nobody wants to mess with.

But things were near catastrophe. *Shh. Tasia is bad. She's dangerous.* NMP stuck the computer in a backpack. He needed to get online, needed to see if there were any messages for him. *Hush, precious love, don't tell, they'll ruin you, they'll ruin everything.*

Mr. Don't-mess-with-me got the car antenna he'd torn from the old pick-up truck, telescoped it down, and put it in the pocket of the jean jacket. Looking at the walls of the hotel room, Tasia's beautiful hideous cow face, her kissing Searle, waving to the president, NMP inhaled and left to begin the hunt.

CHAPTER
TWENTY-EIGHT

The cable car clattered up Russian Hill. Jo stood on the outside steps and hung on against the steep angle. She drank from her ever-ready stainless steel coffee mug. Apartment buildings and struggling pedestrians slid past. The cable car crested the lip of the hill and stopped at the corner. She hopped down. Immediately a Japanese tour group swarmed aboard, eager, smiling, dressed spotlessly in Burberry. The gripman rang the bell. Jo crossed the street and saw another group, clustered on the sidewalk outside her house.

Cameras. Boom mikes. Make-up and cigarettes.

Her face heated. How the hell did the press get her address? And if she threw herself headfirst into the hedge, would they see?

She veered across the street, pulled out her phone, and hit speed dial. A second later she heard, "Tang."

"They found me. The press is parked outside my front door."

"Christ."

"How? Somebody from the police department?"

"I hope not."

Jo continued along the sidewalk beside the park across the street from her house. In the middle of the

212

press pack was a blonde mane. Jo thought her head might explode.

"Edie freakin' Wilson's here. What am I supposed to do, hide until dark, when they go in search of alcohol?"

"Beckett, I'm sorry. But you're going to have to soldier through it."

"I know. And dammit, I can't run from my own house." She hung up.

At the far end of the block an engine revved. She glanced up. In her head she heard a bugle, heralding the arrival of the cavalry. Gabe's 4Runner was waiting at the corner. Behind the wheel, he waved for her to hurry.

She picked up her pace. And a man in a wrinkled black shirt, who was sitting on her lawn, pointed.

"Hey," he called. "Jo Beckett."

The herd turned around. She kept going. *Shit.*

"Doctor."

"Jo, wait."

Gabe's truck was a hundred yards away.

"Jo, did Tasia kill herself?"

Edie Wilson's strident voice carried on the breeze. "Who killed Tasia McFarland, Dr. Beckett?"

They swarmed from the sidewalk between parked cars and streamed across the street. Ahead, Gabe pulled out and drove toward her. *My getaway driver,* she thought, with a surge of affection.

"Why are you running away? What are you trying to hide?" Wilson called.

Jo stopped.

She couldn't run away. Gathering herself, she turned and walked toward them. Microphones sprouted near her face like pinecones. Shutters clicked.

"Jo —"

"Tell us —"

Stick to the script. She raised a hand to quiet them. "I'm afraid I can't answer most of your questions, because my investigation is ongoing. Once I file my report, I'll be able to describe my findings."

"How many shots were fired from the Colt forty-five?" a man shouted.

"Is it true Tasia posted a suicide note on Twitter? Was the site hacked to delete it?"

"Is the intruder who attacked Tasia's biographer a staffer for the McFarland reelection campaign?"

The questions felt like spittle. "Sorry, I can't answer those" — *dumbass* — "questions."

Gabe pulled up behind them and stopped in the middle of the street.

Edie Wilson turned a shoulder edge-on to the pack and chipped her way to the front. She shoved a microphone in Jo's face like a spear. "Why didn't the Secret Service protect her?"

Jo blinked and her lips parted.

"Were they directed not to?" Wilson said.

The question was so mind-bogglingly inane that, momentarily, Jo simply stared. "Ms. McFarland didn't have a Secret Service protection detail."

"Why not? Were they pulled off the case?"

"No." Under the glare of the cameras, she tried to think. What, exactly, were the rules on Secret Service protection? "I believe that Secret Service protection is limited to the president's immediate family. If —"

"If Tasia wasn't immediate family, who is?" Wilson said.

Gabe gunned his engine. Over the tops of the reporters' heads Jo saw him through the 4Runner's window, waiting grimly.

"Excuse me, but that's my ride," Jo said. "As soon as I've finished my report the SFPD will issue a statement."

She dodged the pack like a broken field runner and headed for the 4Runner. Wilson dogged her.

"Why don't you want people to know the truth?" she said.

Don't rise to the bait. "I'm digging for the truth."

"What can psychiatry offer to this case other than fuzzy feelings and soft excuses?"

Jo grabbed the door handle and held on, tight, to keep from taking a swing at Wilson. She got in the 4Runner and through force of will, smiled pleasantly. Like a Miss America contestant. Who had a pit bull biting her ass.

Wilson blabbered about subjectivity and excuse-making. Jo heard the subtext. *What are you hiding? Don't you love America?*

Through gritted teeth, she said, "Drive."

Gabe put it in gear. "Over them?"

Jo pointed down the street. He pulled out.

She put on her seat belt and forced herself not to look back. She knew if she did, she'd see pitchforks and torches.

"Thanks for the rescue."

"Where to?" he said.

"Anyplace." She got her phone. "Except Lombard Street. They could catch us on the twisty part."

She phoned Vienna Hicks to warn her that national heavy hitters had joined the roving press pack. Vienna's laugh was bold and melancholy. "I don't talk to them. The head of the law firm issued a statement on behalf of 'the family.' That's it. No tears, no gossip, no hissy fits. Good luck, Jo. Welcome to the blender."

Gabe gunned the truck up the hill past Victorian apartment buildings with blue and gold gables. Behind his sunglasses, his face remained solemn.

"Great timing, dude," she said.

"I was in the neighborhood."

That wasn't it. "You just decided to drop by?"

He stopped at a stop sign. No traffic was coming, but he didn't pull out. He stared emptily up the cross street. Something was wrong.

"Did you go by the hospital to see Dave Rabin?" she said.

"Only family's allowed in the ICU. I didn't get to see him, just talked to his wife."

Jo put a hand on his knee.

"No change." Lowering his shoulders, almost physically snapping himself back, he pulled out. The sun fell in a stripe across his face. "He needs to wake up."

And wake up *now*. The longer Rabin stayed unconscious, the less likely it was that he would ever

216

come back. She kept her hand on Gabe's knee. His hands were tight on the steering wheel.

"What?" he said.

"I was about to ask you the same thing."

Apartment buildings streamed by as they headed down a steep hill. He pulled off his shades and pinched the bridge of his nose. The laugh lines around his eyes looked tired. He looked as if he couldn't bring himself to talk.

"What is it?"

"I've been driving for an hour. I . . ."

He wouldn't look at her. She tried to puzzle it out and couldn't.

"Sophie?" she said.

"She's improving. Stayed home from school today, but she's better. My sister came over to stay with her so I could go by the hospital."

"Gabe, what's wrong?"

He stared dead ahead. "I got new orders today."

It took her a second. "New military orders?"

"I report for duty in seventy-two hours."

All at once the sun felt hot and painfully bright. "You're serious."

"I report Friday morning. Fly to New York, transiting to Afghanistan next week."

The summer sun hardened into a yellow light that seemed to screech in her ears and fill the car with the noise of blowing sand.

"Next week. Next *week* — Afghanistan?"

"No joke."

She blinked. Jesus God, going active, straight into a war zone, and PJs didn't wear a red cross on their sleeve, they performed combat search and rescue. The yellow light jaundiced everything in the truck: her hands, the air, Gabe's rugged, beautiful face, which was set like stone. She couldn't cry. Had to keep it under control.

"What happened?" she said.

"It's the United States military. It's a vast, relentless bureaucratic machine. Somebody changed my orders. I say, *Yes, sir, I'll go where you point me, sir.*"

She was gripping his leg so hard that her hand was trembling. She pulled it back into her lap. *Maintain. Clear your head of that awful sound,* that rush like radio static, bright and harsh, that filled the car and pressed on her until she couldn't breathe.

There had to be a mistake. He could talk to his commanding officer and find out how the paperwork had gotten screwed up.

A cold fever swept through her, a moment of panic. The abyss yawned open and showed her a glimpse of its black depths, the eternity that swallowed people whole and snuffed out their breath, their hearts, their promise.

She dug her fingernails into her palms. For a hideous instant Daniel's face appeared before her, his eyes pinned on her in the seconds before the abyss drew him into the irrevocable realm of death.

She shut her eyes. *Stop it, Beckett.* "Have you told Sophie?"

"No. I got the call while I was at the hospital."

Gabe didn't need her mewling. He had sought her out. She had to stand up.

"Pull over," she said.

He looked at her. She nodded at the curb. He pulled over and stopped.

Jo got out. A moment later Gabe did as well. He walked around to the sidewalk.

She took his hands in hers, gripped them fiercely, and put them to her lips.

"Anything," she whispered. "Whatever you need. You say the word. You don't say the word, and it's still anything. I'm with you."

He nodded.

She swallowed, and opened her mouth to speak. He drew her close. Pulled her head onto his shoulder, held her, rested his head against hers.

Seventy-two hours. How could orders get changed so quickly, and so radically? She thought of everything he had worked painstakingly to arrange. Sophie, and the custody arrangement. *Dawn.* Would Dawn now try to take custody of Sophie?

He spoke into her ear. "It's going to be fine."

She nodded. Seventy-two hours. It was nowhere close to fine.

"I'll be back. We'll make things work. I love you, Jo."

She held on to him. The wind poured over her back.

CHAPTER
TWENTY-NINE

Paine tapped his keyboard, sorting through more of the photos Keyes had sent him. The television was tuned to a news channel, the constant, flickering background to his life. News channels offered hints about reality, distortions that barely touched the heaving, snarling, matted-fur actuality that lurked beneath, hidden from view. News wasn't effective mass communication; it was an opiate of the sheeple.

The only truly effective form of mass communication was political violence. And Paine was its messenger.

And though he was a superb writer, his biggest impact had been . . . call it performance art, rather than essays. A fire here, an electrical mishap there, a severed brake line someplace else. The key was, he never attacked the target directly. The people who hired him paid lots of money to make sure he didn't. All he had to do was get an assignment: Convince this state senator that his vote on the highway bill was ill informed. Show that community organizer that she shouldn't protest chemical dumping in protected wetlands.

And Paine, though that's not what he called himself during these — lobbying efforts — would do so. He'd persuade the state senator to vote intelligently. Maybe his granddaughter would show up for kindergarten to find that her school had burned down. That's all it took. That, and a matchbook that arrived in the mail at the senator's office the same day.

But now he had a major problem.

He was in San Francisco working on the biggest message of his career. This message was to be his legacy, his gift to the nation, and his retirement fund, wrapped up in one spectacular package. But his meticulously constructed scheme was close to collapse, thanks to traitors, vultures, and Legion's legions. Plan A had turned to dust, and Plan B was hanging by a thread.

The thing was, he had already been paid half his fee in advance. He couldn't fail. If he didn't finish the job, didn't get the message out, he wouldn't simply lose the second half of his payday. He'd get a bullet to the head.

The television screen flickered. Paine looked up. The report switched to a shot of a San Francisco neighborhood. Reporters jostled to intercept a young woman with long brown curls. A caption read *Jo Beckett, Forensic Psychiatrist*.

Edie Wilson shoved a microphone in Beckett's face. "Why didn't the Secret Service protect her? Were they directed not to?"

Paine stilled. A poisonous vine tangled itself around him.

They might go after Beckett next. And she would talk. He watched her on the screen, a slight woman with a calming voice, parrying the reporters' bombardment. Easy, when all that was at stake was her dignity and self-control. Impossible, when the Usurper's storm troopers tore through her life.

He looked at the photos Keyes had sent. Beckett, her hair blowing in the breeze as she stood outside the St. Francis. She knew too much. She needed to get the message. And he was the man to send it.

CHAPTER
THIRTY

Gabe drove Jo home, but first he did recon. He cruised past her street, just fast enough that he wouldn't look like a burglar casing the neighborhood. They saw no signs of a press presence, such as neighbors dragging themselves down the street with their legs gnawed off by ruthless questioning.

Jo's face felt hot. "I pride myself on my belief in free speech. But I want to jab those people with a cattle prod until they squeal like broken microphones."

"'And crown thy good with brotherhood, from sea to shining sea.'" Gabe glanced in the rear-view mirror. "Love of country is full of contradictions."

America, America, tearing him away — and he'd signed up for it. Her stomach clenched again.

When he stopped outside her house, he said, "Come over tonight. They'll be back, and you don't have to be here."

"I'll grab some things and clear out before they show up again."

His face was intense, his eyes poring over her, almost swallowing her up. She leaned across the cab and kissed him. Then she jumped out and ran up her front steps.

Inside she hurried upstairs and stuffed clothes in a backpack. In her office, she gathered her notes.

Don't think about Gabe's new orders, she told herself. But the rough hand of fear grabbed her by the throat. And in the depths of her mind, a worm of suspicion began to stir. Why Gabe? Why now?

"No." She shook her head. That kind of thinking was paranoid.

She picked up her files to put them in her satchel. On the top of the stack were e-mails Archangel X had sent Tasia.

Why did you do this to me? You could have any man on the planet. And you betrayed me.

I'm waiting for you.

Beneath that message were more in the same vein. Angry, rambling, ambiguous, self-absorbed messages, bemoaning Archangel's own sad sorry life and punctuated by sharp jabs at Tasia for *ruining things*. Once again Jo felt that she had missed some meaning in the messages. Maybe that was because Archangel was an out-of-whack personality, prone to whiny, recursive navel gazing. But Jo had the nagging sense that the messages could be deciphered, that she should be able to get inside Archangel's frame of reference, and find out what his reality was.

Her phone rang, loud and close. She jumped. Picked it up with her heart jitterbugging.

"Jo, I've found him," Ferd said. "I've found Archangel X."

NMP hunched over the table and stared at the computer screen. The place was annoyingly noisy. Nasal voices, businessmen laughing at some kind of

224

financial wizardry they'd performed, dishes and silverware clattering. It degraded NMP's ability to concentrate. The Big Bad Bastard needed some mental space in order to focus.

Tasia's official Web site had been updated. The front page read *In memory*, with a soft-focus photo in which she looked about seventeen and ready to recite the Pledge of Allegiance at a 4-H Club convention.

Appropriate. A cow, mooing to the cows.

Hush, precious love. Don't tell anybody. It's dangerous.

Almost two hundred thousand people had digitally signed the site's condolence book. The comments expressing sympathy ran into the thousands. And new information had just been added: The memorial service was confirmed for Grace Cathedral.

The Web site pretended the memorial service was the farewell performance to end them all. But it wasn't; just a pathetic encore to Tasia's exit from the stage at the ballpark. The site didn't list the celebrities who planned to attend, but a little window had links to the latest news — read that, screaming pop gossip and headlines about their dead heroine — and those headlines listed the famous and glittering and sickening people who were going to dress in designer black and grab hymnals and weep crocodile tears over the cow in the casket. The head of Tasia's record company. The mayor. The winners of twenty-five cumulative Grammys.

And the president of the United States.

Muffin crumbs stuck to the tabletop. NMP brushed them away.

The president was coming. And Searle Lecroix was confirmed to sing. "Confirmed" — like he was the headliner at this exclusive gig. He was going to perform "Amazing Grace" and a "very special song composed in Tasia's memory," titled "Angel, Flown."

Angel. As if *she* were one of the seraphim.

And the president was going to sit in the front row and listen to that garbage. NMP couldn't bear it.

He had hoped this expedition would prove to be reconnaissance — a foray to reassure him. *Precious love, hush, it's dangerous, believe me, I love you.* But NMP saw that it was, in fact, the final battle. All powers were arrayed against Archangel. He'd been betrayed, bayoneted in the gut. But he could still speak.

NMP brushed crumbs from the keyboard. Logged on, and began to type.

Jo ran up the porch steps at the red-brick mansion. Ferd was waiting at the front door.

"Where is he?" she said.

"Online. Right now."

In the living room Ferd's laptop was open on the coffee table. Afternoon sunlight fell through the tall windows. Jo stepped around an obstacle course, set up on the floor with books, boxes, and six-packs of root beer. The little robot, Ahnuld, had been stymied negotiating the course and crashed into a pile of World of Warcraft action figures.

"Where is Archangel X right now in physical space?" Jo said.

"Here in the city."

Ferd sat down on the sofa. His screen was covered with long columns of data.

"Those e-mails you sent me — I checked his X-Originating header and did a traceroute to find out where they came from."

"Are you sure about this?" she said.

"It's not like GPS, but it's a valid technique."

She peered at the impenetrable strings of data. "Where is he?"

"Financial District. A Starbucks. I —"

"You have the address?"

"On Kearny."

"Let's go. Bring the laptop."

"No need. I can get e-mail from my phone. But let me put Mr. Peebles in his crate."

He dodged the robot and ran down the hall. For a man who, as far as she could tell, had last gotten exercise in primary school, he was surprisingly quick on his feet.

Five seconds later he sprinted up the stairs, carrying the monkey under one arm like a football. "Can't leave him loose with Ahnuld. The ultrasonic navigation system drives him insane."

He dashed back down. "You think Archangel's really a dangerous stalker?"

She followed him down the front steps. "I'm worried enough that I think we should find him. We'll take my truck."

"What about the police?"

Jo pulled out her phone and dialed Amy Tang. "Already on it."

NMP typed furiously. A table of jabbering secretaries stood up, scraping chairs on the tile, and pushed past, purses and fat asses swinging.

"Watch it, Wide Load," NMP said.

One of the women turned, eyes round as saucers. "What did you say to me?"

"Watch where you're going, Double-wide. Some of us are working."

The woman's face reddened. But her eyes went even rounder, as if she couldn't match NMP's voice to the person she saw sitting in front of her. As though she couldn't absorb such brutally accurate, cutting wit coming from a Big Bad Bastard of the Tenderloin.

One of her friends moved her along. "Ignore it. It's just mindless bitching."

How *dare* she?

No. *Ignore it*. That's what everybody did. Ignored NMP. Everybody. The baristas here who wouldn't clean the crumbs off the fucking table. Tasia.

For a moment NMP's vision pulsed. The unmitigated *gall*. Then he slid his glance around the Starbucks. It was packed, but a few people at nearby tables were shooting surreptitious glances at him. He put his head back down. Focused on the screen. Focused his wrath back where it belonged.

Tasia had ignored NMP. So had people on the boards at all the Tasia fan sites, eventually. And people on the boards at Searle Lecroix fan sites too — they didn't want to hear about Tasia's treacheries, even though she had sunk her fat cow fangs into their hero.

Even the government had ignored NMP. The e-mails
— detailed, painstakingly documented messages — to
the White House had been swallowed up or ignored,
except for the first one: *Dear Mr. President, Your
ex-wife is a skank.*

Of course the messages had been sent anonymously,
as had the letters, with no return address — but
somebody should have replied publicly. It was only
decent.

And now there was all this cacophony online.

All this grief over Tasia, NMP wrote. *Everybody's
crying over a lie. So let me write the truth here.*

NMP refused to be ignored any longer.

*Let me tell you about the angel, flown. And about
martyrdom.*

CHAPTER
THIRTY-ONE

Jo revved the Tacoma through traffic in the Financial District, heading toward Kearny. She swerved around a garbage truck like Ahnuld the robot on its obstacle course. Ferd grabbed the dashboard to steady himself. She tossed him her phone.

"Call Tang again. If she's still out, ask for her boss."

She accelerated over the lip of a hill. They strained against the seat belts. Ferd pushed a series of numbers and spoke to at least three people before finally reaching the captain's office.

"Yes, I'm calling on behalf of Dr. Johanna Beckett. It's an emergency."

Jo shook her head at him. She couldn't claim this was an emergency — yet. "Urgent."

"No, sorry, this isn't an emergency, it's urgent." Ferd wiped his forehead. A moment later he straightened. "Yes, thanks, I'm calling for Dr. Johanna Beckett."

She swerved to the curb and stopped in a red zone. Took the phone. Chuck Bohr was on the line — the bald, bull-chested cop who had argued with Tang outside UCSF Medical Center.

"I have a lead on the person who was stalking Tasia McFarland."

230

"What kind of lead?" Bohr said.

She explained as fast as she could. "He may still be at the Starbucks. Can you send somebody to meet us there?"

Bohr paused only a second. "I'll send a plainclothes officer. We'll keep it quiet. What are you wearing?"

She told him, and he said, "Fifteen minutes. If the stalker's online, keep him talking."

"Thanks."

She pulled out again, and almost instantly braked to keep from rear-ending a Camry. She pointed at Ferd's phone. "Is Archangel X still online?"

"Can't tell. Connection's too slow." Ferd turned the phone over and over in his hands. "Are we being legal here?"

She glanced at him sharply. "If somebody online tells you where they are, no law against that. Unless there's something you aren't telling me."

He ran a hand across his hair. For once he hadn't bothered to slick it down with Brylcreem, and it flopped in his eyes.

"Ferd?" she said more pointedly. "How did you find Archangel X?"

"Don't be angry."

"What did you do?"

"I set out some candy, and he stopped by to pick it up."

"Tell me."

"I snooped around online for his footprints. He sent Tasia McFarland fourteen hundred e-mails — I figured maybe he sends messages to other people too, or maybe he comments online. You know, on blogs and news stories about her, on the boards at celebrity and music sites, or in chat rooms."

She cast him another glance. "And he does?"

He nodded vigorously and his glasses slid down his nose. He pushed them back up. "A few music discussion boards, and some of the political sites that have been delving into conspiracy theories about Tasia's death."

"You didn't hack into the sites, did you?"

"The term is cracking, not hacking, and what makes you think I know how to do that?"

"Sorry. Did you worm your way into some site and uncover information about Archangel X?"

"Sort of. I commented on a political site."

"How did that help you? Archangel X replied?"

"He engaged me in debate."

She looked at him. "Ferd. My God."

"Then I set up my own blog. About politics and conspiracy theories and music. And sure enough, he came over to leave his comments there, on a post about Tasia."

She looked at him with increased interest.

He raised his hands calmingly. "This is where it gets iffy. I wrote about twenty-five posts, and I altered the time stamps so it looked like I'd had the blog going for a couple of months. And I engaged in a bit of sock-puppetry in the comments section."

"You faked a bunch of comments?" Jo said.

"I wrote comments myself, using a couple of dozen commenter IDs. 'Mad as Hell,' 'John Galt,' 'Loverboy.'"

As *Loverboy* escaped his mouth he turned bright red, from his collar to his hairline.

"And Archangel X joined in the discussion?" Jo said.

"Indeed he did." He exhaled, trying to get over his embarrassment. "And because I'm the administrator of the site, I captured all kinds of details about his IP address. I set up the blog with a bit of extra software that displays all the raw information that routes the message from sender to recipient. So I could see who his ISP is, who all the intermediate hosts are, and it's apparent that he's been logging on through a Bay Area service provider."

"You sure he's not faking that?"

"No. But he doesn't seem interested in digital fakery. He's more interested in making his points and hiding personal information emotionally than technically."

Jo shot him a look of surprise. Ferd Bismuth, emotionally astute?

He reached over and turned on the air-conditioning. "Awfully hot in here. I think I'm getting a fever."

"Explain how you pinpointed him downtown," Jo said.

"I'll show you."

From the corner of her eye she watched his thumbs jump around his phone. Ahead, the skyscrapers of the Financial District were fading from sunlight into an engulfing wall of fog.

"Need to keep him engaged," Ferd said.

"You've been — what have you been doing?" she said.

His thumbs tapped the phone. "Provoking him into commenting at a memorial site for Tasia. I didn't want him to get up and leave the Starbucks."

"Sharp thinking. But back to how you know he's at this particular coffee place."

"I know how to read the runes. The raw source headers in the blog-Web interface. They show that he's sending from a site being run by the phone company, under contract to a local provider. That tells me it's at Starbucks — they use the phone company for their Wi-Fi network. And I have a friend with some oomph, who helped me read the interior marking data — it specifies the particular Starbucks Wi-Fi the customer is using. Useful little utility to have."

"Which gave you the one on Kearny."

"Hey." He squinted at the phone. "I just managed to get online. Archangel replied to one of my comments. Let me poke him some more."

He went back to the thumbs. "I'm telling him Tasia was too pure to stay in our world. She's gone to a higher plane, and she'll be watching over all of us. The president especially. Like a guardian angel. That'll rile him up."

"Not too much, I hope." Jo circled the block to wend her way through the one-way streets.

"So, are we legal here?" Ferd said.

"You bet we are. But I want law enforcement to back us up."

"How are we going to figure out what this stalker looks like?" he said.

"We're going to start with big men online in the Starbucks. I think Archangel is the man who broke into Tasia's house."

The Starbucks was a red-painted corner location, with big plate-glass windows, in an old brick building covered with fire escapes. Jo circled the block twice but found no parking spaces.

"Don't you have special dispensation to park here for emergencies?" Ferd said.

"Not even if you burst out with bubonic plague."

Ahead, a delivery truck pulled out from the curb. Jo floored it and snatched the spot. She and Ferd jumped out and strode across Kearny toward the Starbucks.

"Look for somebody who's online," she said.

They walked in, and stopped. It was one of the biggest, busiest Starbucks she'd ever seen — hot, noisy, and jammed with people.

All of them were online.

At tables, in corners, behind newspapers, from all angles, even waiting in line at the counter, everywhere she looked, people hunched over computers or had their eyes pinned on cell phones. At one table a mom peered at a laptop. In the stroller beside her, a baby waved a muffin in one hand and an iPhone in the other.

"Oh, dear," Ferd said.

"Get a table. I'll get coffee and try to narrow down the possibilities."

She got in the line. If Archangel X was the hefty intruder who had tackled her in Tasia's house, she'd have to extrapolate. Nobody in the Starbucks was wearing camo and a balaclava. Plenty of the men looked like they would shop at the Big 'n' Tall. Ferd found a table and sat down, clutching his phone like a phaser.

She took a longer look at the various people who were engaged with their computers and phones.

Most of them were reading while they drank their coffee. Every now and then, leisurely, they'd scroll down a page. A few others were flitting around the keyboard. At the counter a woman in a green hat held her laptop against her chest, screen open, typing with one finger while holding out her mug to the barista for a refill. Only a minority of people were typing furiously, as if engaged in an online flame war. But that still left around twenty people. Jo edged up to the counter and ordered two large coffees.

When she set Ferd's coffee on the table, he said, "Archangel X's last comment was ten minutes ago. If he's gone, I wouldn't know it yet. I've provoked him with a really snide reply to his last comment, so we'll see."

He looked around, blinking rapidly, and wiped his upper lip. He couldn't have looked shiftier if he'd had a bomb strapped to his chest. Jo took a swallow of her coffee and panned the place. This was San Francisco, supposedly the center of laid-back California. And 90 per cent of the people in sight had nervous tics and compulsive behavior.

Ferd sat up straight. "He just posted. Oh, dear."

He showed Jo the phone. "*Angel*"? *Tasia was a COW. She trampled everybody's dreams. She deserved to die.*

Oh, dear, indeed. "It's too hard to tell who's replying to you. There's a lag in the timing."

Ferd frowned and his eyes zigged back and forth, as though he was computing something. "I have an idea. Maybe I can kick him offline."

"How?"

He got his wallet and took out a Starbucks prepaid wireless access card. "Fire up your laptop."

She got it from her satchel. "What are you going to do?"

He took the laptop. "You sure this isn't illegal?"

"I don't know what you're going to do. And I'm a doctor, not a lawyer."

He brought up a browser. Using the wireless access card, he logged on to the Starbucks network from Jo's computer.

He took a theatrically deep breath. "I'm going to call Customer Service. Here goes."

He called the number on the back of the wireless card. After a moment he said, "Hope you can help me. I'm sitting in a Starbucks in San Francisco and I can't get online." He listened for a moment. "Tried that." Nodding. "And that. Ran through everything, did a self-diagnostic. I'm having no luck."

He flicked a look at Jo and nodded like a rabid beaver. "My e-mail address, sure. It's Archangel X, no space, at Hotmail," he said.

Jo smiled at his audacity. For the next minute she listened to him answer questions. Customer service was running him through a drill to find out what the problem was. Ferd, to her surprise, was charming and persistent.

Finally he looked up, bright-eyed. "Let me put you on speaker so I can type." He set the phone on the table. "Could you repeat that?"

A youngish voice echoed from the phone. "I'm accessing real-time information for your location. My information shows that you *are* online."

Bingo. Jo balled her hands and pressed them against her knees. Archangel X was there.

Ferd cleared his throat. "No, I'm not."

"You're on — I see you here on my screen. Your machine is transmitting data, and it's logged in under the Archangel X address."

Jo was amazed. AT&T and Starbucks were doing the dirty work for Ferd.

Ferd put a note of innocent desperation in his voice. "Please, could you help me? I know you say I'm online but I'm sitting here with an *access denied* message, wasting the money I paid for this wireless card, feeling my ulcer act up. Can you reset my connection?"

After a pause, the customer service voice said, "Okay. Hold on."

Jo was impressed. Ferd, by being ballsy and smart, was going to force customer service to break Archangel X's connection.

238

Ferd picked up the phone and covered the mouthpiece. "When Archangel X gets knocked off, look around to see who gets upset."

They waited. Ferd, still covering the mouthpiece, said, "How far do you want to take this? If I can get customer service to help "log me in again," I might be able to hijack Archangel X's connection with log-in info. He won't be able to get back on. That'll really tick him off."

Jo checked her watch. It had been six minutes since Bohr told her a plainclothes cop was on the way.

"Okay."

"But we have to be fast."

Customer service came back. "Sir, I'm now going to reset your connection. Wait sixty seconds and log in again."

"Thank you," Ferd said.

He hung up. They looked around, trying not to be obvious.

People continued to drink coffee and fiddle with their electronic toys. The baby in the stroller threw the iPhone to the floor.

Jo glanced back at her screen. "Did it work?"

Ferd looked at her computer. "We'll find out."

What was this?

NMP stopped typing. The wireless signal had dropped out. The page wouldn't load, wouldn't send the comment to the board.

"Stupid . . ." Pounding the keys. No joy. Tried logging in again — got an error message.

What was going on?

NMP leaned back. Were they watching? Somebody monitoring the boards?

Damn, was the government tracking NMP's digital warnings about Tasia?

NMP, Big Bad Bastard, Archangel X, felt his heart beat faster. He looked around with just his eyes. He felt his mask begin to slip. Noel Michael Petty peeped out for a second, mewling like a kitten.

Somebody had tattled. And with wrenching insight, like fat hands grabbing a rib cage and tearing it open, NMP knew who had told. It cut like a knife. Proof, the finale. The last betrayal.

Petty had been so careful, watching every word, taking on the disguise of NMP, moderating all comments behind the digital avatar of Archangel X. Protecting Noel Michael Petty. But also protecting Noel Michael Petty's idol.

For nothing. NMP closed the laptop. Felt the antenna, broken and sharp, waiting.

CHAPTER
THIRTY-TWO

Edie Wilson stopped pacing and pointed at the television screen. "That car. The SUV."

In the studio at the network's San Francisco affiliate, she and a news producer huddled in an editing suite, watching the video her cameraman had shot outside the police shrink's house. The producer paused the playback. It showed the black Toyota 4Runner, caught driving away from Edie and the rest of the press herd.

"And?" the producer said.

Edie waved at the screen. "The shrink went with this guy. If we find him, we're one step ahead of everybody else next time we want a quote from her."

"Did you try contacting her through the SFPD's media relations people? Set up an interview?"

"Tranh, the police department is never going to let us talk to her. And now she's had a warning. She'll guard herself from saying anything revealing."

"Isn't that her job?" the producer said. "Keeping things confidential?"

Edie sat down next to him. "She's trained not to spill things her patients tell her. But that's consciously. The trick will be to work on her unconscious. Get her to let down her guard. That's the fun of this job."

"And to what end?" Tranh said.

Edie threw her hands in the air. "You kidding? This is the story of a lifetime. We have to attack it." She pointed at the screen. "This psychiatrist knows what's going on. And she's hiding it from the public. It's our responsibility as journalists to bring it to light."

"The public has the right to know."

"Don't give me that little postmodern millennial sneer. They do." She scooted her chair closer to Tranh and lowered her voice. "Look at the SUV. Handsome young guy at the wheel — probably her boyfriend. She'll stick close to him." She nodded at the screen. "Advance a few frames."

When Tranh advanced the video, Edie tapped the screen with one of her bitten-down nails. "Stop. That. See?"

Tranh paused the video. Edie pointed to the SUV. In the back window was a sticker. She didn't need to ask him to zoom in.

"Isn't that interesting," she said.

"'My kid is an honor student at Saint Ignatius School'?"

"No, the other one. It's military."

He worked on the focus. "Air National Guard. Moffett Field."

"So maybe there's a connection with the government," Edie said.

This time, she didn't bother telling Tranh to wipe the sneer off his face. He knew he was in a losing game. She was a woman on the rise, and if she wanted to play the story from this angle, he couldn't stop her.

242

"Just make it worth our time," he said. "It needs to be good television."

She smiled. "Great. Zoom out. Get the tag number on the SUV."

Tranh did.

Smiling, Edie called her researcher. "I need you to find somebody in the California DMV who can run a license plate. I don't care who or how, but get me the name and address of the owner."

She hung up. "You won't regret this, Tranh."

"Be sure I don't."

CHAPTER
THIRTY-THREE

Ferd typed on Jo's laptop. He bit his cheek and glanced around the Starbucks.

On his phone, Jo read the running blog commentary between Ferd and his dozen sock puppets and Archangel X.

Talented, I grant you. Tasia could sing. But so can a humpback whale, or a factory siren. And those last two aren't sluts. Tasia spread her legs and swallowed half the men in the western United States. She was so greedy that she didn't leave anybody for the rest of the country's women.

Ferd had replied, *Is that your best imitation of a political statement?*

Archangel X: *Greed and rapacity ARE political statements. Possession is political. Hoarding is political. Exclusion is political. And Tasia collected trophies, hoarded them, created a barrier that was totally binary. In or out. Some of us were fooled for a while, and even thought of ourselves as fans. But she screwed us, figuratively if not literally.*

Then, farther down the page: *None of this shit matters. She ended everything for me. There's only one thing left to do.*

244

The air seemed to grow cooler. "Dear God. He's going to go out in a blaze of glory."

"What?" Ferd looked at Jo with deep worry, and then at her computer. His voice rose with excitement. "I'm on. I got it. I'm in as Archangel X. We've locked him out."

Jo gestured for him to quiet down, and called Chuck Bohr. "Archangel's here. Verified that he's in the Starbucks, and I think he's planning something violent. Where's your plainclothes guy?"

"You have him identified?"

"Not physically, just digitally. But —"

"I need more. I can't have a police officer charge into Starbucks and demand to see everybody's e-mails. I have no probable cause."

Frustrated, she tried Tang again. This time she got hold of her. "Amy, I need help."

"I'm in the middle of a situation. This isn't a good time," Tang said.

Jo explained what was happening. There was a lengthy, strained silence on Tang's end. "Okay. I'll get there. Keep him online."

Tang hung up before Jo could reiterate that they'd just kicked Archangel X offline and made that tactic impossible.

Jo scrolled through Archangel's blog comments. *Sure, everybody idolizes the dead. But face facts, she used men and ruined them for everybody else.*

Fear? Fear of women? Of sex?

And at the end it wasn't enough for her to have the president of the united states she had to have the number 1 billboard country singer too.

Jealousy?

She had to have Searle Lecroix. Didn't she know that mere mortals were waiting? That what she was doing ruined it for us?

Vast, egomaniacal presumption.

We wait, still, but she made it all impossible. NMP.

Jo stared at the message. "When he's been in touch with you, has he ever signed a message NMP?"

Ferd nodded. "The first couple of times."

She handed him back his phone. "Search for those initials in connection with Tasia McFarland, with the president, and with Searle Lecroix."

She got up and walked to the counter and poured milk into her lukewarm coffee. *Archangel X, who are you?* And what was so out of kilter about the messages?

Behind her, the baby screeched. Two men scraped their chairs back and stood up. At the counter the woman in the green hat complained that her coffee was the wrong blend. Jo walked back to the table.

Ferd said, "Got it. Jo, look at this." He showed her the tiny screen. A comment thread on a political message board, right after Tasia's death.

She took them all. All the men in the west. And look where it got her. Dead.

The comment was signed. The name jumped out at Jo.

Her vision pinged. "Got you."

There was no way to see if the commenter was writing from the Archangel X e-mail address, but from the structure and tone and vocabulary of his messages, this was NMP. And NMP was Archangel X.

She called Tang back.

Tang answered. "I'll be there in fifteen minutes. Hold your horses."

"Noel Michael Petty," Jo said.

CHAPTER
THIRTY-FOUR

Jo gazed around the Starbucks. At a table near the door, a chunky man with deep acne scars frowned at his cell phone. He lumbered to his feet and turned to go.

"Is it him?" Ferd said.

"Maybe." For a second, she held back. "Come on."

Hoisting her satchel, she strolled toward the door. She scrounged in the satchel and brought out a crumpled piece of notepaper.

"Sir? Excuse me, I think you dropped this."

The man turned. Jo held out the crumpled paper, her pulse ticking like rats' feet running across a wooden floor. His cigarettes were in his hand, one protruding, ready for insertion once he stepped onto the sidewalk.

He said indistinctly, "Sorry, could you repeat?"

He had two hearing aids. He'd also clearly had a stroke at some point. He was wall-eyed and his mouth drooped on one side. He wasn't the attacker who had so nimbly raced away from Tasia's house.

"Sorry, my mistake," she said.

He turned and left. She went to the counter. In a strident voice, she said, "I'm having trouble staying online. Is something wrong with your Wi-Fi today?"

Ferd looked around, waiting to see who looked up. Nobody did.

And Jo smelled Right Guard deodorant.

She stilled. Right Guard and perfumed fabric softener — the same sharp odors she had smelled when the intruder fell on top of her. Her skin prickled.

"He's close," she said.

She scanned the crowded room. The scents lingered but were quickly swallowed up by others — coffee, sugar, sour baby spit-up.

"He's here. No question."

Her palms itched. Bohr's plainclothes officer and Tang were still miles away.

How could she narrow it down? "May I see your phone again?"

Ferd handed it over, and she scrolled back through the e-mails and messages left by her quarry — as Archangel, as NMP, and as Noel Michael Petty.

His descriptions of Tasia. *Greedy for men . . . voracious . . . selfish . . . Queen bee, hoarding all for herself . . .*

All the talk was of possession, consumption, ownership, and entitlement. It pulsed with jealousy. And yet it did not sound possessive of Tasia. Not in the way violent stalkers often talked.

And Jo realized what had sounded wrong to her about Archangel's messages. The subtext didn't lie in Archangel's words, but in what was missing from them.

Archangel never talked about Tasia being his, of her belonging to him. He talked about her taking others away, of hoarding men and locking him out.

"Oh, man," she whispered.

Archangel was enraged at Tasia, but not because she had spurned him. He didn't think she belonged to him. He never spoke about her as though they had a relationship.

He spoke about all the men she took and kept for herself.

Archangel hadn't wanted Tasia for himself. He resented her for taking another man away from him. *We wait, still, but she made it all impossible.*

In the crowded coffee bar, the mother with the stroller nudged past. The baby was howling. The stroller bumped Jo's shins. The woman mumbled, "Excuse me."

Jo reset her thoughts. She'd been looking at everything from the wrong angle. Archangel was obsessed, and blamed Tasia for ruining his life. But he never expressed fantasies or delusions that they had a relationship. She saw that now.

Was he gay, and obsessed with another man?

Her palms began to sweat. The mom struggled to open the door. Another woman, the one in the green beanie, squeezed through it ahead of her.

"Well, it's not like I have anything else to do," the mom said, snark breaking through her composure. The woman in the beanie flipped her the bird and walked off.

Jo smelled it again, the scent of Right Guard men's deodorant.

"Oh no."

She redialed Tang as she hurried for the door.

Ferd trailed behind her. "What?"

She looked out through the plate-glass windows. The women had disappeared from sight.

"It's Archangel." She rushed toward the door. "It's not a man. It's a woman."

It was the woman in the beanie. And she was gone.

CHAPTER
THIRTY-FIVE

Noel Michael Petty stormed up Kearny Street. Head down, lips tight, shoes slapping the sidewalk. Anger jangled in the air, sharp as shards of red glass.

Who was after Archangel? It was not coincidence that wireless access had been cut off at the Starbucks. Somebody had done it deliberately. Tasia's people? Robert McFarland? The police?

They'd silenced Archangel. Halfway through the grand finale, the ultimate truth telling, Archangel's digital throat had been cut.

They were on to Archangel. That meant they were on to NMP. The disguise hadn't held up.

Petty pulled off the beanie and threw it in the gutter. Kept walking. Took off the jean jacket and stuck it under a parked car. Pulled hard at the buttons on the man's denim shirt, trying to rip them off. Big Bad Bastard hadn't worked. Thinking of NMP as the meanest man in the Tenderloin, so nobody would see little Noel inside the coat and hat and attitude, hadn't worked. Somebody must have told on her.

She knew who.

She tore at the denim shirt, popped a button, pulled it off and stuffed it in a trash can. Her T-shirt was thin and the misty breeze curled around her, cooling her to sheer, reflective rage. She squinted through the cloudy lenses of her glasses. She had only minutes to get out of sight before the rest of the world found her. She had to get out of the Financial District. She had to become somebody else, fast. She broke into a run, cut across Kearny and headed west on Sutter. She knew who to blame. She knew who to punish.

Jo burst through the door of the Starbucks onto the sidewalk. Ferd stumbled out behind her.

"What do you mean, a woman?" he said.

"Where'd she go?"

Jo looked up and down Kearny. The mother with the iPhone baby was halfway up the block, fumbling with her purse and her to-go cup.

Jo put a hand on her head. "Archangel's a woman. I should have seen it before."

Ferd's mouth slowly opened. "That big woman in the beanie?"

"We have to find her." She pointed north on Kearny. "You go that way."

Ferd took off, lumbering up the street.

"Don't approach her," Jo called. "If you see her, phone me and we'll tell the cops."

She ran the other way, redialing Tang as she went.

"I'm coming, Beckett."

"It's a woman. Noel Michael Petty. We missed it."

"Are you kidding me?"

"No."

She jogged down Kearny past her truck. At the corner with Sutter she stopped and looked around. Old brick buildings, wild with fire escapes. Overhead electrical wires for the Muni buses. Down Sutter, sleek glass and granite skyscrapers. Chic retail stores.

No sign. Then she spied, in the gutter, the green beanie.

"She's dumping the clothes she had on. She knows something's wrong."

"Are you sure about this?" Tang said.

"As positive as I can be without seeing her in a line-up and reading her driver's license. Same deodorant, same fabric softener. Same *size* as the guy who tackled me at Tasia's. Amy, we presumed it was a man because of the intruder's size and because all Archangel's e-mails to Tasia sounded so jealous and possessive. And the overwhelming majority of stalkers are heterosexual. My mistake."

"No, not a mistake. You've caught it. If this is for real, Petty was disguising herself. She wanted everybody to think she was a man."

"She's wearing a jean jacket and green combats. But if she's dumping the disguise, she's trying to get away. I think she's gone out to do something bad."

"What kind of bad?"

"I think Tasia isn't her only target."

Scanning the street, she caught a flash of green. Up a block on Sutter, a person in combats was running away. A bus passed in front of Jo. When it went by, the figure was gone.

254

"She's heading west. Can you get a patrol unit to look for her?" she said.

"On it."

Jo took a step back in the direction of her truck, and hesitated. Kearny was a one-way street, and by the time she could drive around the block and turn around to head in the direction Archangel had gone, the woman could take a dozen different paths.

"I'm going to follow her on foot," Jo said.

"Don't get near her," Tang said sharply.

Jo darted across the street and headed up Sutter.

"Tang, I'm worried. I saw a message she was writing before she took off. It was an obituary."

CHAPTER
THIRTY-SIX

The stores on Union Square were bright and flashy, huge boxes where advertising posters in the front windows showed perfect young people airbrushed and half undressed. Noel Michael Petty hustled through the doors at Gap and grabbed the first shirt off the rack that was extra large. She grabbed a pair of tan slacks from a pile. Wiping her brow, she stormed to a dressing room. She changed and ripped the tags off.

At the cash register, the sales girl, a twig with breath like spearmint gum, looked at her funny.

"What?" Petty said.

"Nothing, ma'am. That's eighty-nine fifty."

She shoved a hundred-dollar bill at the twig. "It's important to look well-groomed. You should think about that."

Petty smoothed down her hair. Pushed her glasses up her nose. *Stop looking at me*, she thought. Everybody wanted to look at her, and that wasn't good.

She got her change and hurried outside into the chilly sunlight.

By the time Jo had gone two blocks uphill, she was breathing hard and beginning to lose hope. Archangel had vanished into the teeming downtown streets.

"I've lost her," she said to Tang.

"I've given her description to all units. They're issuing a BOLO." Be on the lookout.

Jo slowed at a corner. Which way to go?

"What's she going to do?" Tang said.

"End a life."

"Her own?"

"I don't know. Maybe. Maybe somebody else's life as well."

"I'm on Market, driving north."

Jo had a flash. "Can you head for Union Square?"

"Sure. Why?"

Jo broke into a run again. "I think she's after —"

"Jesus Christ, the president isn't here, is he?"

Jo held tight to her satchel and aimed through the canyon of skyscrapers for the St. Francis Hotel.

"No. I think she's stalking Searle Lecroix."

At the television studio, Edie Wilson picked through a salad, flicking black olives and carrot shavings aside with the tines of her fork. A plastic fork — she wasn't a snob, could get down in the trenches with the best of them. Even though she constantly had to prove it to people like that skinny young producer, Tranh. Just because she had gotten her break on a natural disaster, some folks thought she was lucky. That her career was a fluke, that she'd taken advantage of human suffering to put a shiny star around her name at the network.

Damn straight, and she wasn't about to apologize. Twenty Hours of Terror in Topeka had been her story from start to finish — because she was the only reporter brave and lucky enough to have been on the ground near the massive super cell that day. She'd been following a team of storm chasers from Oklahoma University. Yeah, she'd gotten lost, and yeah, she ended up hiding from a tornado in a trash can. She wasn't ashamed of that. Hell, she talked about the trash can in the network promo for her show. She'd had the guts to drive through a swarm of twisters and report the news. Ninety-six dead, and she'd told the nation. She'd held on to the shoulder of that old woman while firefighters searched for her husband in the wreckage of their mobile home. Top that, Brian Williams.

Edie Wilson, The Bravest Woman in Television News, apologized to nobody.

When her phone rang, she asked the intern to answer it. She ran her tongue over her teeth, making sure her smile was white.

Finally she took the call. "Tell me you have information."

"The SUV is registered to a Gabriel Quintana."

She wrote down the address. "Find me everything you can on this guy. Especially any connection with Dr. Jo Beckett."

She shut the phone off. Handed the salad plate to the intern. "Where's Andy?"

If her cameraman was eating lunch, he could leave it. They had investigative reporting to do.

Jo dodged pedestrians, working her way through busy streets toward Union Square. She pressed her phone to her ear.

"In some of Archangel's e-mails to Tasia, she referred to Tasia taking all the men. But she particularly mentioned Searle Lecroix."

"You think he's in danger?"

"Call the Saint Francis. Tell him to watch out."

At the corner with Grant she stepped onto the crosswalk and heard a horn blare. She jumped back and a yellow cab roared past.

"I'll call you back," Tang said.

Jo waited for a break in traffic. The wind coiled her hair around her face. Did she think Lecroix was in danger? She couldn't afford not to think so.

The doorman at the St. Francis touched his hat and opened the door. Petty squinted and scratched her armpit and avoided his gaze.

Tasia McFarland had been bad enough on her own. A drain, a sinkhole, a human latrine. Stealing Searle, manipulating him, when Petty had been waiting — it had been hell.

The sight of the lobby stopped her. It was luxurious beyond anything she'd ever seen. She smoothed down the new shirt and tried to finger-comb her frizzy hair into the pink scrunchy that held her ponytail. How was she going to do this? How could she? This was a world where she didn't belong.

And that made her chest burn. She had tried to protect Searle from Tasia. She had sent him warnings — always gentle, because she had thought he was a gentle soul. But it had always been about protecting him. He needed help. He had warned her through his songs and messages. *Shh. Tell nobody, my eternal love. Tasia's dangerous.*

That's why she had focused her e-mail campaign on Tasia. Get rid of the bitch, save Searle the pain of having to see the truth. The truth was too bright, too terrifying, too holy for most people. She was saving him from himself. Why else had she used Archangel as her online identity? She'd been named Michael after Michal in the Bible, King Saul's daughter, but she felt closer to the archangel Michael, protector of the innocent.

She had thought that with Tasia gone, Searle would see. His lyrics spoke to her. His messages spoke with such purity and understanding, such piercing insight into her secret, innermost truths, that they could be meant for nobody but her. Their beauty and power, and Searle's passion when he sang, convinced her of it. She knew them by heart. *Be quiet and careful.* She heard the special messages embedded in them. *Don't mention me, don't say a word.* Special messages, sung to the angel whose heart he had touched. *Tell nobody about our love.*

She knew why he sang those words to her. He didn't need to say the real message: *Because Tasia will get between us and spoil it all.*

And on the day of triumph when Tasia lay lifeless with a bloody gunshot wound, Petty had been sure Searle would turn to her. She thought he would thank her for the kind condolences she sent to his Web site. But he had not replied to her. Not once. Instead, he had written a song to sing at Tasia's memorial service.

260

Angel, Flown. Heat spiraled around Petty like the flame of an acetylene torch. Searle had let the whole world know how he felt. He had named Tasia as his angel. He had explicitly, personally, humiliatingly, spurned Noel Michael Petty. It was a deliberate, permanent slap in the face.

She blew breath from her nostrils, fighting down the stinging rage that threatened to turn to tears. No, she didn't belong here. The world had conspired to make sure of that. Except that she did. Because otherwise, why would it have gotten out that Searle was staying here?

She walked across the lobby, past tourists with maps and businessmen who sipped from tiny coffee cups and women wearing diamonds, to the front desk.

"I need to call a guest," she said.

Jo ducked around a tourist family that was posing for a photo, and emerged onto Union Square. Under bright sunlight, the trees in the square shivered in the breeze.

Her phone rang. "Called the Saint Francis and left a message for Lecroix," Tang said. "Do you have a personal number for him?"

"Just his cell. He's not answering?"

"Hence my haste to get there."

Jo ran along the sidewalk. The St. Francis was at the west end of the square, dominating the street.

"I'll be there in sixty seconds," she said.

"If you spot Petty, don't approach her. Alert hotel security. I'll be there in five."

Jo didn't know long those five minutes would feel.

The stereo in the suite was turned all the way up. The walls in the St. Francis were thick, and Lecroix had some hearing damage at the high end. He turned off the shower and heard the room phone ringing.

Wrapping a towel around his waist, he came out of the bathroom, steam swirling in his wake, and picked it up from the nightstand in the bedroom. It was the front desk.

"Mr. Lecroix, you have a visitor asking permission to come up. Vienna Hicks."

Lecroix wiped water from his eyes with the back of his wrist. "Substantial-sized lady, with probably a sad look on her face?"

"That would be accurate, sir."

In the background, he heard a woman say, "I've got some things Tasia wanted him to have."

"Mr. Lecroix, she —"

"I heard. It's fine. She can come up."

He hung up, unwrapped the towel from around his waist, and dried off. On the phone he saw the red message light blinking. He left it and began to dress.

The woman behind the front desk set down the phone and tilted her head with corporate unctuousness. "Mr. Lecroix says you can go up to his suite."

"Where is it?" Petty said.

"Sixth floor."

The hotel woman took out a hotel map and drew a circle around a room. She handed it to Petty. The circle looked like a bull's-eye. Petty headed for the elevators.

CHAPTER
THIRTY-SEVEN

Jo jogged across the lobby of the St. Francis. She swept the space with her gaze, as she'd seen Gabe do when hunting for threats. She didn't see Noel Michael Petty.

At the front desk, people were lined up to check in. Jo turned in a slow circle, scanning the opulent lobby. Nothing. She picked up a house phone and asked for Lecroix's room. It rang but nobody answered. She left a message.

"Searle, the stalker who was after Tasia is in San Francisco. It's a woman. I think she's dangerous, and that she's after you. I'm at the St. Francis and the police are on their way. If you get this message, contact hotel security, and please phone me back."

At the front desk the staff was still busy. She headed to the concierge's desk. The concierge was speaking to a tourist, circling landmarks on a San Francisco map. Jo interrupted him.

"Sorry, but it's urgent I speak to the head of security."

The concierge flicked her a glance. Smiling imperturbably at the tourist, he said, "Excuse me."

"Now, please," Jo said.

★ ★ ★

The knock sounded on the door of the suite. Lecroix buckled his silver rodeo-style belt buckle and jammed his feet into his cowboy boots. He caught a glimpse of himself in the bedroom mirror. He smoothed down his wet hair. The cowboy hat?

No, that would be impolite. He needed to look respectful in front of Tasia's sister, so no hats indoors. He stood up straight. He'd never met Vienna Hicks and wished he didn't have to introduce himself under such circumstances.

He attempted a smile in the mirror. "Tasia spoke so often about you."

He heard another knock on the door. With a quick, whispered *please* to Jesus and whichever saint kept bereaved sisters from blaming country singers for talking their little sis into performing a fatal stunt, he crossed the suite to the door.

The concierge calmly beckoned a colleague to the desk and asked him to assist the well-dressed tourist, who wanted to visit Alcatraz. Then he phoned Security. Jo clenched and unclenched her fists.

When he hung up the phone the concierge came around the desk and ushered Jo out of the tourist's earshot. "Is there a problem?"

"Assume so." She gave him the gist. "The police are on their way, but I can't reach Mr. Lecroix. He doesn't have personal security. What can your people do?"

A few feet away, a sleek young woman behind the front desk said, "Excuse me. Mr. Lecroix was in his room a minute ago. Do you want me to try him again?"

264

"Please," Jo said.

The young woman phoned Lecroix's suite. She looked bright-eyed and imperturbable. Her name tag said KARA. "Ringing."

Jo stepped to the desk. "How do you know Mr. Lecroix was in his room a minute ago?"

"I spoke to him."

"Any reason?" Jo said.

"I told him he had a visitor."

"Who?"

"A lady — her name was . . ." Kara put down the phone and shook her head. "No answer. The woman's name was Vienna."

"Vienna Hicks?"

"That's it."

Jo's nerves fired. "What did Mr. Lecroix say?"

"For her to come on up."

"Six feet tall, big red hair —"

Kara shook her head. "Short, wide, dirty brown ponytail."

"Try Lecroix again. Tell him not to open the door," Jo nearly shouted. To the concierge she said, "Get security up there, *now*."

She ran toward the stairs, phoning 911.

Lecroix opened the door. "Miz Hicks. Come in."

The gal stood in the hallway, seemingly frozen.

"Vienna?" he said.

Good Lord, grief had done terrible things to her. He didn't recognize her at all from the photo on Tasia's kitchen counter. Of course, that snapshot had been taken decades ago. But God in heaven, the years had been cruel to Vienna Hicks.

She looked petrified and near collapse, as though a twister was on the loose inside her. For a second, he thought she was going to faint, or turn tail and bolt.

"Are you all right?" he said. "Please, come in."

He put a hand on her elbow. She looked like she dearly needed a glass of water. When he touched her, she almost sagged to the floor.

Then her face lit with a fierce determination. Bless her, she was barely holding it together, but still trying.

"Yes, I'll come in," she said.

Pinning her eyes on his, she let him lead her into the living room. The door shut with a heavy clack.

"It's so nice to finally meet you," he said.

She turned, slowly, and stared at him like he was on fire. "Yes. Finally."

Under the power of her gaze, he felt a strange worry. "Miz Hicks?"

"Shh, Searle." She stepped toward him. "Searle, my precious love. It could have been so different."

CHAPTER
THIRTY-EIGHT

Halfway up the stairs, Jo's phone rang in her hand. "I'm in the lobby," Tang said.

"Sixth floor," Jo wheezed. "Petty went up to Lecroix's suite."

"Where are you?"

"Fourth-floor stairwell. Concierge wanted me to wait in the lobby for security and then take the elevator. I couldn't."

Tang's voice sharpened. "Beckett, do not approach Petty. Do not knock on Lecroix's door. Do not wander the sixth-floor hallway. Wait inside the stairwell for me."

"If —"

"You're unarmed. If Petty is as dangerous as you think she is, that puts you in danger in addition to Lecroix."

At the fifth-floor landing, the stairs turned. Jo kept running, under bluish fluorescent lighting. "Petty claimed she was Vienna Hicks. He's waiting for her. And now he's not answering."

"I'm coming, Beckett. Stay put."

Tang sounded out of breath. Below Jo in the stairwell a door slammed and feet scuffed on the concrete stairs. Tang was running up.

Blowing hard, Jo reached the sixth-floor landing. She was glad she didn't have to run higher. Tang's footsteps drew closer, and more ragged. Jo edged to the fire door and quietly eased it open an inch.

She saw a sliver of the hallway, plush and hushed. Heard nothing. Saw nobody, just a used room service tray on the floor outside a room. She could see the door to Lecroix's suite at the end of the hall.

Footsteps closer, and harsh breathing. Jo closed the door and stepped back. Tang appeared, hand white on the stairway railing, practically pulling herself up. Her face was set, flat and intense.

"Nobody in sight in the hallway," Jo said.

Angrily Tang shook her head. "I told you." Then, brushing Jo's incursion aside, she unsnapped the holster of her service weapon. She silently turned the door handle and cracked open the fire door. Checked the hallway.

"Stay inside the stairwell," she said.

Tang stepped into the hallway just as the elevator dinged and the doors opened. She walked toward Lecroix's suite, her head swiveling to look at the elevator. Out stepped the concierge and three security men in suits. They all had earpieces and walkie-talkies.

Tang showed her badge. "Behind me."

The men fell in and followed her to Lecroix's door. She knocked, hard.

"Mr. Lecroix? Police."

The security men nearly pawed the carpet behind her, shoulders shifting inside their suit jackets.

Tang knocked again. "Police, Mr. Lecroix. Open up."

268

Jo held poised in the stairwell doorway, her foot propping the door open a few inches. Tang pounded on Lecroix's door again. Then she nodded to one of the security men.

"Unlock it." She raised a hand. "I'll go in first. All of you step back."

The security man nodded. The concierge and two of the suits stepped away from the door and stood against the wall outside the suite. Tang drew her weapon. Nodded to the security man. He slid a master key card into the lock.

His walkie-talkie hissed, and a voice said, "SFPD just walked into the lobby."

Tang said, "Tell them to send one officer up, and have the second stay in the lobby. But I'm not waiting."

Jo kept her foot in the door. She had a clear view. She hated hanging back, but knew that if she joined Tang she'd only be in the way. And she hated that thought too. Her palms were hot. She imagined she could smell Right Guard wafting in the hallway.

Tang shoved open the door of Lecroix's suite and went in, weapon raised in a two-handed combat grip. She swept the pistol left and disappeared from view.

The concierge and security men held back against the wall. Jo pulled the fire door open another inch. She realized she was gripping the door handle as hard as a hand jam on a pitch hundreds of feet off the ground. The silence from Lecroix's suite was like a cold bitter wind.

On the fire door, a blemish of color caught her eye.

Red. Smeared on the side of the door facing the hallway was a crescent patch of deep red.

It was a bloody partial handprint.

From Lecroix's suite, Tang shouted, "Clear. Stay out."

The handprint was so fresh that it glistened.

It hadn't been visible to Tang when she walked out of the stairwell to Lecroix's suite. Jo held on to the door. Every hair on her neck was standing straight up.

She looked over her shoulder. In the stairwell, on the railing, about six feet up the stairs on the way to the next floor, was another handprint.

Tang's voice echoed up the hall. "Call an ambulance, *now*. Beckett, get in here."

Petty had gone up the stairs because Jo and Tang had been below her in the stairwell, charging toward the sixth floor, and if she'd tried to run down she would have collided with them.

And Jo smelled it again, Right Guard deodorant, and knew it wasn't her imagination. Jesus on a pony, was Petty hiding right above her?

"*Tang.*"

"Beckett, hurry," Tang yelled back.

"She's in the stairwell above us," Jo yelled.

She threw open the door, skin crawling, and tore down the hall to Lecroix's suite. The concierge and security men were huddled in the doorway, jabbering into their walkie-talkies. Jo pushed past them.

In the living room, on the floor, Tang knelt over Searle Lecroix. His feet were splayed, cowboy boots motionless. The blood was everywhere.

270

Tang looked at Jo, her eyes liquid with desperation. She was pressing on Lecroix's chest, hands spread. Lecroix was looking up at Tang, his eyes dark with a fear that went beyond pain, beyond shock, to clarity. Death was near. Death was closer than Tang's frantic attempt to stanch the bleeding from multiple stab wounds.

CHAPTER
THIRTY-NINE

Shock poured down on Jo like water from a broken dam. For a second she couldn't move. *Don't put this on me, God.* Then she forcibly pushed herself past it and went to Lecroix's side.

She knelt down beside him. Tang looked at her, helpless and hopeful.

The blood chugging from his abdomen through the sticky slices in his shirt was dark, almost brown. He'd been stabbed in the liver, more than once, with what had to have been a sharp knife.

"Get the security men in here to help," Jo said. "I've got him."

Tang didn't seem to hear her.

"Go," Jo said. "Petty was hiding in the stairwell above this floor. But I left the landing. She's bound to be running down the stairs to the lobby."

Tang blinked and snapped out of it. She stood, jumped over Lecroix, and charged out of the suite, shouting instructions at the security guards. If she could raise the cop in the lobby on the radio, they could cut Petty off.

Jo ripped open Lecroix's shirt and pressed a hand hard against the gushing wound in his side. "Paramedics are on their way."

His face was a mess of stark colors. White skin, bright blood running from his mouth and nose across both sides of his face, a Japanese imperial flag of disaster. His teeth chattered. He tried to speak but nothing came out.

The second set of stab wounds had gone straight between his ribs into his right lung. When he inhaled Jo heard a sucking sound. Air bubbles formed in the pink blood along the violent gash in his chest.

"Hold on. Look at me," she said.

His eyes moved. He looked at her.

"Don't look away."

He was terribly short of breath. She needed to put an occlusive dressing on the sucking chest wound and seal it.

The security men appeared.

"Bring everything you can find in the bathroom. Ransack it," she said. "Cellophane, aluminum foil, shower cap, a candy wrapper, anything. And Vaseline. Lubricant." She continued to press her hand to his chest. "Check the old room service tray down the hall. If there's cling wrap, grab it. Hurry."

Lecroix's lips moved. "Pain."

"I know. Keep looking at me. Hang on."

A uniformed police officer appeared in the doorway. "EMTs are downstairs."

Jo looked up. "Assist Lieutenant Tang. She ran to the stairwell. Attacker is armed with a knife and extremely dangerous."

Drawing his weapon, the cop spun and disappeared.

Lecroix spat something that sounded like a word. Jo leaned close to his face.

"What?"

"Gun . . ."

She looked at him, shocked. "Gun?"

"Her."

"Who — Petty? The woman who stabbed you?" Jo said.

His words weren't even air, just clicks. "Took mine."

"She took your gun? You had a gun?"

He blinked. Jo recalled him telling her, *I carry all kinds of protection*.

"Officer," Jo yelled. "Hey — the perpetrator has a gun."

The security suit in the doorway looked frozen. Then he put a hand to his ear and ran from the room, walkie-talkie to his face.

"Tell the cops," Jo yelled. But she was shouting at an empty doorway.

Beneath her, Lecroix shivered. She kept the pressure on his wounds, and still felt his life seeping between her fingers.

Two security guards ran up and dumped supplies from the bathroom and room service tray on the carpet. With one hand Jo uncrumpled a ball of cling wrap, smeared it with K-Y, and pressed it against Lecroix's chest wound to stop air leaking out of his lung.

The security man said, "Steak dinner was on the room service tray, but no steak knife."

She glanced at the door. Had anybody managed to warn Tang that Petty was armed with a gun? The scene

274

was so confused, the message might not have reached her. Jo needed to be sure Tang knew.

She kept pressure on Lecroix's wounds. She could do nothing except try to slow the bleeding.

Blood foamed from his mouth. "Scared."

In his eyes she saw the depths of his confrontation with the irrevocable. He knew. He was hovering on the threshold. He was a soft breath away from stepping through.

Lecroix, she feared, wasn't going to survive. When she'd been a resident, she had moonlighted in emergency medicine. Wounds this severe taxed a fully equipped ER. The paramedics were going to have an almost insurmountable fight to get him into the ambulance alive.

He put his hand on hers. It was cold. It was slick with blood. His eyes begged her to tell him what he wished to hear. Begged her to say the word *live*.

She couldn't. She couldn't do a goddamned thing.

No, that was wrong. She could. She tried to swallow and her throat caught. "If I say the words to "Amazing Grace," can you sing them in your head?"

He blinked.

"Four verses," she said. "Paramedics will be here by then."

Lecroix, she feared, wouldn't.

"'Amazing grace,'" she said unsteadily. "'How sweet the sound.'" With an effort of will that nearly crushed her heart, she pressed her hands against his wounds. And she forced her lips to speak words of life, hoping they were true.

"'I once was lost, but now am found,'" she said, barely above a whisper.

He blinked, and a tear formed at the corner of his eye.

"'Was blind, but now I see,'" Jo said.

She heard the elevator ding. The paramedics were coming. Had to be. Please, hurry. She couldn't leave Lecroix by himself, wouldn't. *Come on, come on.*

His hand shook. She didn't look up, wouldn't look away. She leaned closer to his face. Second verse — what were the words? Any verse.

"'Through many dangers, toils and snares, I have already come,'" she said. Lecroix's lips moved. What was next — Christ, what? The paramedics came through the door, accompanied by a cop. They hurried to Lecroix's side.

"Multiple stab wounds," Jo said. "Five minutes ago. Apparent liver wound, probably to the hepatic vein. Pneumothorax and sucking chest wound. He's not getting oxygen. Pulse one seventy and thready. He's been conscious the whole time."

A male paramedic knelt at Lecroix's side. "Got it."

Jo lifted her hand from the abdominal wound and moved back. She turned to get to her feet. She had to find Tang and warn her.

Lecroix squeezed her hand. His lips formed the word *Stay.*

Jo's breath snagged. The depths of pain from which he was staring up at her were so monstrously apparent that she nearly bent double.

The paramedic said, "Doc?"

Lecroix held on to her. She was all he had to hold on to.

Jo knelt back down. She put a hand on Lecroix's head and stroked his hair. Leaning near his ear, she said, "'Tis grace . . .'" — she cleared her throat — "'. . . that brought me safe thus far.'"

He closed his eyes slowly and opened them. His gaze defocused.

"'And grace will lead me home,'" Jo said.

His chest stilled and his grip on her hand released. His eyes stopped staring and became blue stones, glossy, reflecting her face but beyond sight.

"Losing him," the paramedic said. "Doc, we gotta bag him."

Jo stumbled back. She sat down hard on her ass and watched the paramedics intubate Lecroix so they could pump air into his quiet lungs. They pulled out the paddles and powered up the defibrillator.

He wasn't coming back.

She hung her arms on her knees. She couldn't speak. She couldn't tell the EMTs to call it. They had to try. She looked at her hands. They were slick to the wrists with Lecroix's blood.

"Clear," the male paramedic said.

A lump lodged in Jo's throat. She climbed to her feet and rushed from the room to warn Tang.

CHAPTER
FORTY

A security suit stood outside the closed door to the sixth-floor stairwell. He turned in alarm when he heard Jo running toward him. He seemed loath to touch the door, with its bloody handprint.

"Did you tell the cops the suspect has a gun?" she yelled.

He waved his walkie-talkie at her. "Tried — called downstairs and told them to alert the cops in the lobby."

She ran to the door. "So you don't know if Lieutenant Tang got the message?"

"We shut down the elevators. The suspect hasn't emerged in the lobby and won't be able to exit except through this stairwell."

"She's still in there?" Jo said.

He nodded. "Has to be. All the elevators are locked out, and we have security people on all floors between here and the lobby, monitoring the fire doors, so if the suspect exits we'll spot her."

"You haven't yet?"

He didn't answer.

"She already got out of the stairwell," Jo said. "Otherwise they'd have boxed her in."

She reached for the door. The security man put an arm out to stop her.

"She could be right on the other side," he said.

"And she could be coming up behind several police officers who don't know she's armed with a gun."

Behind her Jo heard footsteps and equipment jostling. A cop was jogging toward her from Lecroix's suite. His radio buzzed with voices. He waved Jo and the suit away from the fire door.

"Back."

On the radio, a voice said, "She ran back into the stairwell. Third floor. She's heading up."

Jo heard footsteps inside the stairwell, fast and light. Heading down.

"I'm at six, heading toward her," Tang called.

Jo bulled past the security guard and pushed the door open. Tang sped past her, weapon drawn, and flew down the stairs.

"Amy, Petty has a gun," Jo called.

Tang's head swiveled. She caught Jo's eye, just for a second, then pummeled down the stairs out of sight.

The security man grabbed Jo's arm and pulled her back. The door shut with a heavy click.

In the stairwell a woman shrieked. The noise echoed through the fire door, a high, sustained scream. And then came the crack of gunfire.

The security guard jumped clear of the doorway and threw himself to the floor by an elegant table. He rolled and hit it and knocked an expensive lamp to the floor. The cop pulled Jo clear of the door and pushed her against the wall.

A second shot echoed from the stairwell, deeper. Then a crack, the sound of the first gun.

More gunfire, dulled by the door frame and walls, pinging with ricochets. No more screams.

The cop drew his weapon. "Stay here."

Jo didn't move. The air in her lungs felt heavy. The cop threw open the door and charged into the stairwell.

Footsteps. Echoes. A second passed, and more.

"Clear. Stand down."

Jo bolted into the stairwell. Two floors down she stopped. Below her, the cop stood holstering his weapon. Down the twisting stairs, Jo heard metal skitter across concrete. She inched down the stairs until she got a view.

Noel Petty sat sprawled in a corner of the stairwell, imposing, implacable, and completely dead. Blood was pouring from a gunshot wound in her forehead, over her eyeglasses and down her chin. Three feet away, weapon still aimed at her center of mass, stood Tang.

Jo put a hand against the wall.

Tang uncocked her weapon and holstered it. She told everybody to clear out. Asked one officer to secure the scene.

She stepped back. Her shoulders were heaving. She looked like a bird, tiny compared to the beast it had just fought off, half-crazed with adrenaline and unable to calm down. She looked up and saw Jo.

"Lecroix?" she said.

Jo shook her head.

For a moment Tang simply stared. Then she turned, pushed past the other cops in the stairwell, and fled through the fire door.

CHAPTER
FORTY-ONE

Jo found Tang at the end of the third-floor hallway. She was leaning, arms stiff, against the wall. She looked like she was trying to keep it from collapsing on top of her.

"They'll put me on desk duty for ten days," she said. "Protocol for an officer-involved shooting."

"You hanging in?" Jo said.

"The main attraction will be here in a few minutes. Homicide Detail — they'll take my weapon, drive me someplace quiet and official to find out whether I shot Petty in self-defense, or lost it and went *Dirty Harry* on her."

"I heard multiple gunshots."

Tang turned and leaned over a potted palm. Hands on her knees, she fought down a dry heave.

"Got any gum?" she said.

"In my front pocket. You don't want me to reach for it."

Tang noticed the blood, tacky and smeared, on Jo's hands. Jo turned her hip and Tang dug the pack of gum from her jeans.

"They won't want me to confer with anybody. So I have about two minutes to tell you what just happened." Without touching the gum itself, she popped a piece from the package into her mouth. "It was suicide by cop."

"Petty fired on you?"

"Realized she was cornered. Uniforms were running up the stairs from the lobby. I was running down from above. All the elevators were locked. She stopped on the landing, screamed, and began firing. I returned fire."

"Then you're going to be exonerated," Jo said.

"Yes. And I'm so far off this case that I'll never see its backside disappearing over the horizon."

"What do you mean?"

"I was already under orders to pull you back. To figure out how to wind it down quietly."

"You just killed a homicidal stalker. There's no way this case can be wound down quietly."

"I came over here at your request. I was . . . acting independently of my superiors' guidance. They won't be happy. When my desk duty ends, I'll be assigned to other cases."

"Chuck Bohr won't —"

"Chuck Bohr won't care. He's got his own problems."

"What?"

"IRS audit." Tang waved dismissively, as if to swat away an irrelevance.

"No, Amy. You just ended this."

"Not fast enough."

And the tough, predatory bird faltered. Tang's head dropped and she crumpled against the wall.

Jo put an arm around her. Instantly Tang stiffened and shook Jo off. She spun and punched a framed oil painting. Her fist drove the canvas into the wall.

She grabbed her hand. "Crap. Jesus, that hurts."

She shook her fist. Blinked as though her eyes stung. Jo was sure they did. Her own eyes certainly did.

"You weren't late getting here. I was," Jo said.

"Lecroix didn't answer the phone. He let Petty in. Not your fault."

"Did the press know Lecroix was staying at this hotel? Because if they didn't, how did Petty find out?"

The elevator dinged. Two men in blue suits stepped out and glanced around.

"Here we go," Tang said.

The departmental suits looked as grim and gray as dead fish. "Lieutenant Amy Tang?"

She unholstered her pistol and handed it to them, butt first. "I fired the fatal round, with this weapon. Once I determined that the scene was secure and everybody was safe, I holstered the weapon. Nobody else has handled it."

They nodded. They mentioned that the Crisis Incident Response Team was being assembled to debrief her. "Come this way, Lieutenant."

She followed them. Halfway down the hall, she looked back at Jo. "You okay?"

"Yeah," Jo said.

Lie of the afternoon. The first of many.

Tang shook her head. "And to think — on the drive here, I thought my day couldn't get any worse."

Jo gave her a funny look. "What?"

"My parents have been raided by the ATF."

★ ★ ★

284

The rented silver Volvo SUV crept up the street through Noe Valley. The neighborhood was tidy, slightly ramshackle — a comfortable place for striving families, Edie Wilson guessed. Small houses stacked one right next to the other on hilly streets. Bright colors. People in San Francisco had a thing for homes painted like M&M'S.

"Quirky place," she said.

Tranh, behind the wheel, gave her a distinctly unpleasant look. Just a fraction of a second, but she saw it. She was highly attuned to other people's vibrations. And she was from suburban Dallas, so she had a far better sense of what was normal and what was quirky than did a Californian like Tranh.

From the backseat, Andy said, "That's it."

Tranh slowed. They all looked at the compact Craftsman house with the green-painted trim, shaded by a live oak.

"His SUV's not in the driveway," Andy said.

"But somebody's home." Edie pointed at a Honda Accord. "Pull over."

Tranh parked. Edie got out. "Andy, follow me."

She hiked to the door, taking in the ambience. An American flag flew from the porch. A child's tennis shoes sat by the welcome mat. She knocked.

When the little girl opened the door, Edie tipped her head to one side and smiled. She was good with children, even quirky children from San Francisco.

"Hello, young lady. Is your daddy home?"

The child had alert brown eyes and a long, shining braid. She was television-cute. Edie had a knack for knowing who looked good onscreen.

"Well?" Edie said. "Hello?"

"Excuse me, he can't come to the door right now." The child turned and called, "Aunt Regina, somebody's here." She turned back. "May I ask who's calling?"

"So serious," Edie said. She saw the child's eyes glance past her to Andy and his gear. She smiled. "Have you ever seen a TV camera before?"

A woman stepped into the doorway. Mid-thirties, solid, Latina, looked like she had played water polo in school. Like she could throw an elbow. She patted the child on the shoulder.

"Thanks. I'll take care of it." Her expression was veiled. "May I help you?"

"Edie Wilson. Is Gabriel Quintana in?" She raised an eyebrow. "Mrs. Quintana?"

"He's not. And I'm not Mrs. Quintana. But I'll tell him you stopped by." The woman, Aunt Regina, glanced over Edie's shoulder, calmly but with a deathly coldness, at Andy. Making sure the camera wasn't rolling.

Always a good sign. These people had something to hide.

Edie handed the woman her card. "Have him call me. We'd like to talk to him."

"What about?"

"Tell him it's a good idea to phone. He will really appreciate the chance to tell us his side of the story."

The woman shut the door on them.

Edie turned. "Get that, Andy? Did you get the door slam?"

"Got it."

Edie practically skipped down the steps to the sidewalk. "They never learn, do they?"

They were back in the rented SUV and halfway up the block, headed for the studio, when a rattletrap VW Bug squealed past and pulled to the curb in front of the Craftsman house. A woman popped out.

"Wait," Edie said.

Tranh pulled over. They peered out the tailgate window.

The woman from the VW looked like she had fallen through a time portal from the summer of love. And, it appeared to Edie, on the way down she'd bounced off some goths, from Bollywood. And maybe landed in a pile of vodka bottles.

She knocked on Quintana's front door. After a minute the Latina tank opened it. They spoke. The VW woman didn't go in. The door shut again.

"My, Aunt Regina does like her door slams," Edie said.

The VW woman stood in front of the closed door. She gave Aunt Regina the finger, vehemently, with both hands.

"Turn around," Edie said to Tranh.

They drove back up the street and Edie hopped out. The VW woman paused next to her car, hand on the driver's door handle.

She raised her chin at Edie. "What's going on here?"

Quirky didn't begin to cover this gal. No, what covered this gal looked like pure gold.

"Edie Wilson, *News Slam*. I'm looking for Gabriel Quintana. Can you tell me anything about him?"

The woman barked a laugh. She scratched her arms, and tucked her velvet-black hair behind an ear pierced with a dozen silver studs. The magenta streak continued to fall in her eyes.

"You're not the only one looking for him," she said.

On her arm, in uneven Gothic letters, the word SOPHIE was tattooed. Edie said, "You're Sophie . . ."

"She's my kid. What's Gabe done?"

Edie tried not to look too excited. "Mrs. Quintana?"

Another bark. "He never went as far as actually marrying me."

Edie heard Andy behind her, hoisting the camera to his shoulder. "I'd like to talk about that."

"No kidding? About Gabe?" The woman shifted her weight and tilted her head, curious. "What do you want to know?"

"The truth," Edie said.

Dawn nodded at the television camera. "That thing working?"

288

CHAPTER
FORTY-TWO

"It wasn't a hotel employee. No way."

In the lobby of the St. Francis, a hotel manager insisted that the hotel had not leaked word that Searle Lecroix was staying there. Not to the media, not to family or friends, not to anybody.

Jo turned to the detective from Homicide Detail who was interviewing her about Lecroix's death and the shooting of Noel Michael Petty.

"He may be right. Lecroix could have mentioned it, or his management, anybody. Word was out. Earlier today I saw a photographer across the street in Union Square."

The cop wrote it down. He underlined it casually. He was done debriefing her.

"Thanks, Doctor."

Outside the front doors, the doorman was flanked by uniformed SFPD officers. The press and paparazzi had been moved across the street into Union Square. The scene was a scrum of people, cameras, lights, microphones, TV vans, and microwave antennas.

Jo gave the detective her card. "If you need anything else."

He put it in his jacket pocket. "Sounds like you couldn't have done anything more for Lecroix."

Jo tried not to frown. The man was trying awfully hard to put her mind at ease. "Thanks. I wish it had ended differently."

She stood to go. Across the lobby she spied two men headed in her direction — the SFPD's mismatched departmental twins, Donald Dart, the media spokesman, and Chuck Bohr, Tang's bald and burly superior.

Bohr's jaw was working a piece of gum. It looked as though his jaw had been working at something for years. His neck was so thick that his white dress shirt was about to rip at the collar.

"Dr. Beckett. Don't go anywhere," he said.

Dart's mustache had been brushed to a silvery sheen, maybe with a Brillo pad. His aviator shades were tucked in his jacket pocket. He nodded at the press mosh pit outside.

"We need to make a statement to the media."

Jo felt drained. She wanted out of this hotel. She wanted to go home and clean off under a shower with the water pounding so loud that nobody could hear her cry, not even herself.

"You need sound bites from me?" she said.

Bohr's jaw worked the gum. "Don't look so down. You were right. You've been vindicated."

"Excuse me?"

"And it's over. You can write your report and sign off on the case."

"A stalker," Dart said. "You spotted it."

290

"You called the whole thing," Bohr said. "Don't look so surprised. Credit where due."

Jo's shoulders ached. Her hands, though she'd scrubbed them with soap and near-scalding water, nevertheless still felt bathed in Searle Lecroix's blood.

"Excuse me if I don't feel like bragging," she said.

Dart said, "You don't have to. Just stand beside Captain Bohr while I make a statement to the press. You're part of the team."

"And then you can sign off on the McFarland case," Bohr said.

Jo felt a headache coming on. "I need to complete my interviews and review Ms. McFarland's medical records before I can finish my report."

Dart looked at her, either incredulous or anxiety-ridden. "But we got her. Petty. We got her, in the act."

The headache crawled up Jo's scalp. "Maybe."

Bohr took Jo's elbow and led her toward the front doors. "This case has been unpleasant and difficult. And you don't want any more unpleasantness and difficulty dumped on you. Make it simple. Stand beside me while Dart gives them the news."

"But —"

"You're a hero, Doctor. You figured it out. You warned the police about Petty being armed. You tried to save Lecroix." He glanced at her. "I'm not bullshitting you. I'm serious." He reached the door. "Take a bow. Then bow out gracefully."

Dart swept past them. He straightened his tie and smoothed down his Ronald Reagan hair. Bohr urged Jo out the door.

When they stepped onto the sidewalk, the media swarmed across the street, dodging traffic, swerving around a cable car, pouring toward them like a sandstorm. Dart raised a hand. Bohr positioned himself and Jo a few feet behind. A crowd had gathered in Union Square. Overhead, three helicopters hovered. The noise, the painful *whup* of their rotors, battered the walls of buildings all around. The sun was still bright, the sky an innocent blue. Jo's head pounded.

Had Noel Michael Petty killed Tasia McFarland?

Dart and Bohr wanted to think so. They wanted Jo to think so, and say so in her psychological autopsy report. Jo couldn't. Not yet. She didn't know whether Petty had killed Tasia. She had a strong feeling that the scenario was wrong.

She leaned toward Bohr. "Have you been encouraged to tell me to wrap up my report?"

The gum worked in his jaw. His eyes, watchful and cautious, held on to her gaze for a second too long.

The hovering helicopters thundered overhead. The headache crawled across her skull. The media pressed forward. Dart raised both hands, gesturing for quiet.

"Ladies and gentlemen," he began. "At 3.45p.m. this afternoon, a nine-one-one call was received requesting police and an emergency medical response at the St. Francis Hotel."

Jo wanted to sink into the pavement. She saw Lecroix's eyes, begging her to tell him he was going to live.

292

"When officers arrived, they found a white male suffering multiple stab wounds. At 4p.m. today, Searle Lecroix was pronounced dead of those wounds."

Noise erupted. Reporters shouted. Shutters clicked. People in the square screamed. A young woman fell to the sidewalk in tears. Cameras and lights seemed to bleach the view white.

Over? Jo thought. Not even close. And the media rodeo was just getting started.

The president was coming to town.

"Replay that." Edie Wilson was in the backseat of the Volvo SUV, leaning toward Andy, the cameraman. "Pure gold. We're going to eat this story alive."

Tranh's phone rang. Five seconds after saying hello, he braked and pulled a wild U-turn in the middle of Castro Street, phone to his ear, steering with one hand.

Edie grabbed the door handle for balance. "What's going on?"

Tranh put his foot down. "Stabbing at the Saint Francis. Searle Lecroix's dead."

"Are you shitting me?"

"Suspect was shot and killed by the cops. Police are giving a news conference."

He sped up Castro, aiming for Market Street.

Edie grabbed the driver's seat. "Now? Right now?"

"Right freaking now."

"I'm missing it? Goddamn it." She punched the back of Tranh's seat. "God-shitting-damn it."

She hauled out her phone and called the network. By the time they got to Union Square, she was still yelling at her network producer. She hung up.

"Local affiliate got the news conference. But I wasn't there. Tranh, why didn't you know about this?"

"Maybe because they didn't announce it until the police spokesman walked out the door of the hotel?" he said.

Ahead, Edie saw the side entrance to the St. Francis. "Pull in. If anybody's still around, they won't be leaving through the front door. We'll catch them coming out the back."

Jo crossed the echoing lobby of the St. Francis and headed toward the back exit, away from the click of camera shutters and the jostling press horde and the sobbing fans and Lieutenant Dart's smooth patter. She called and left Ferd a message, thanking him for all he'd done. She said she'd tell him the whole story when she got home. She headed through the door and turned toward the street. She didn't think she could walk another step.

She raised her hand to flag a yellow cab. And on the sidewalk she saw Edie Wilson, her big blonde hair, and her raptor's smile.

"Doctor Beckett."

Wilson didn't seem to walk toward her. Perhaps it was an optical illusion caused by the monstrous headache, but Wilson seemed to glide instantly in front of her, like a demon-possessed mannequin. She raised a microphone.

294

"Why didn't the police get to the hotel in time to save Searle Lecroix?" she said.

Jo fought every instinct for fight and flight. She had no reserves left. She told herself: *Don't crack.*

"I'm not going to talk about it," she said.

"Why were the police so slow to react to the threat?" The microphone jabbed nearer to her face.

"Really, I can't talk right now. Please excuse me."

She tried to walk away. Wilson and her cameraman blocked her path.

"Why won't you talk to us? What about Searle Lecroix? Doesn't he deserve an answer?"

"Please, don't."

"Who's going to speak for Searle? Why didn't the police get there in time? What did you do?"

The yellow cab stopped at the curb. The driver gaped at the scene outside his window, as if Godzilla had just appeared to snack on the cars and trucks and shrinks of San Francisco.

"Did you tell the cops to back off?" Wilson said. "Did you lead them astray?"

"Sorry, but I have to go."

Jo blinked back tears. If she got angry, she'd blow it. She climbed in the cab and slammed the door. The cabbie peered at her in the rear-view mirror, perplexed.

"Kearny and Sutter. Go," she said.

"Is that —"

"Yeah. Let's roll."

The cab pulled out. Wilson shouted, "How about Gabe Quintana?"

Jo whirled to look out the back window.

Wilson's eyes were bright. "Quintana, Doctor Beckett."

Shit. Jo knew she'd just made a big mistake. The cab accelerated toward Union Square, taking her out of Wilson's range. But she knew more shots would be arriving soon.

CHAPTER
FORTY-THREE

Jo locked the front door behind her and sat down on the stairs. The light in the hall seemed green and cracked, as if the horrors of the afternoon had dropped her inside a funhouse tiled with broken bottles. "Amazing Grace" played endlessly in her head.

And she could no longer persuade herself that she was being paranoid. Tang and Captain Bohr had convinced her otherwise. Bohr, because he had tax problems. Tang, because her parents' business had been raided. And it was all federal. Internal Revenue Service. ATF — the Bureau of Alcohol, Tobacco, Firearms and Explosives.

Air National Guard.

Gabe's orders had been changed as a message to her. He was being ripped from his little girl and dropped into a hot war to pressure her to drop her investigation into Tasia McFarland's death.

She took her phone from her pocket and punched a number. "Beer. I'm buying."

"I'm not in the mood," Tang said.

"You know Mijita, outside the ballpark? I'll meet you there."

The Giants were on the road, a three-game stand against the Cubs. In the plaza outside the ballpark, the bronze statue of Willie Mays shone in the sun. The sky, blue and crisp, seemed sterile. When Jo walked into Mijita, Tang was sitting against the wall, holding a Corona. Jo got a Sam Adams and joined her.

"Don't ask me how I feel," Tang said.

"Not planning to."

"Because the Homicide Detail has my service weapon. To keep you from shrinking me, I'd have to beat you to death with a Mexican beer bottle, which would be messy and tiring. Besides, we're heroes. That's how we feel. Heroic."

Tang tried to live inside a spiny shell, where none of her vulnerabilities could be seen, much less attacked. But the shell had fractured, and she looked ashamed.

Jo thought it was because Tang had been so quick to leave Lecroix's side, and so relieved. She hadn't been able to deal with a dying man. She'd tossed the responsibility in Jo's lap, and she knew it.

Tang slid a sheaf of photos across the table. "Even though I'm on desk duty, they slipped these to me. Detectives found a key in Noel Petty's pocket. Cheap residence hotel in the Tenderloin."

As Jo examined the photos, a creepy chill infused her. Petty's room was wallpapered with photos of Searle Lecroix and Tasia McFarland. The Lecroix walls featured full-color pictures torn from glossy magazines. The wall of Tasia consisted of photos with eyes scratched out, horns drawn on, or other faces pasted

298

over hers. Miss Piggy, Margaret Thatcher, and, most commonly, a mad cow.

"These were beside the bed," Tang said.

They were photos from *Bad Dogs and Bullets* concerts: Searle, center stage, guitar in his hands. In the front row, nearly crushed against the barrier separating the crowd from the stage, Petty's frowning face was clearly visible.

"Seattle and Tucson," Tang said. "She was following him."

"Ace Chennault mentioned an incident at the concert in Tucson."

"Petty had a bit of money from a slip-and-fall settlement against an employer. Apparently she used the settlement to support herself as Searle's number one groupie and stalker."

"Did he know her? Had he met her?" Jo said.

"That's the next phase of the investigation. We haven't even begun to crack open her computer and phone records."

"Was she at the concert here when Tasia died?" Jo said.

"Found a ticket on her desk. So, yes." Tang leaned back. "But you don't consider that dispositive, do you?"

"No. The idea that Noel Michael Petty shot Tasia is implausible."

Tang pushed a photo toward Jo: Tasia, with her face replaced by a wild-eyed Guernsey heifer.

"She loathed Tasia," Jo said. "But unless your colleagues uncover proof that Petty got within kissing distance of Tasia in the seconds before her death, I don't buy it. Hatred isn't action."

"No. It's motive."

"Yes, Petty was obsessed with Lecroix. She might have had a delusional belief that she and Lecroix had a relationship. She almost certainly believed that her 'love' entitled her to claim him as her soul mate. But I don't buy her as Tasia's killer."

"Why not?" Tang said.

"Tasia's death is different from his." The memory swelled in her vision. "Petty attacked him directly, and with a knife. You know full well that knife attacks are more intimate than gun attacks. She used subterfuge to get into his suite, but once he opened the door her assault was immediate and full frontal. She stabbed him repeatedly, while he stared her in the eye."

Tang didn't disagree.

"But Tasia's death is equivocal. That's the entire reason you drew me into the investigation. If it had been straightforward, Petty would have been seen and arrested at the ballpark," Jo said. "But *if* Tasia's death was murder, it was accomplished by stealth and guile. A killer had to gain access either to Tasia's weapon or to areas of the ballpark that required an invitation or an access-all-areas pass. Petty had neither. And nobody who was within a hundred yards of Tasia that night saw anyone remotely like Petty, because if they had, you would have been hunting her from the get-go."

Tang grunted. "Absolutely right."

"The fatal shot was a contact wound, fired from the Colt forty-five Tasia had in her grip when she stepped

300

onto the balcony. But Petty wasn't in the stunt team's hospitality suite. She wasn't in the surrounding suites, which were holding private parties. She wasn't visible on nearby balconies in any of the concert footage. The chance that Petty murdered Tasia is minuscule."

Tang stared at her, long and hard. "You can bet that all Petty's venomous e-mails will be released by the department."

"You're saying she's going to be named as Tasia's killer." Jo held on to her beer bottle. "Somebody's pressuring Bohr to close the investigation."

Tang's eyes went hot. "I told you that from the beginning."

"And somebody's pressuring you. Through your parents."

"Beckett, that's —"

"Crazy? It's not. Tell me what happened."

Tang's mouth hung half-open for a second. "The feds got a tip that my mom and dad were smuggling illegal weapons. Came into their import-export business with the bomb-sniffing dogs, put everybody on the floor with their hands behind their heads. My mom and pop."

"That's awful."

"Jo, they sell fireworks — they're Chinese. Of course the bomb dogs found evidence of explosives. Gunpowder. Pyrotechnics. Christ." She pressed her fingertips to her temples. "Anonymous tip."

"Are your parents okay?"

"Tough as barnacles. Those ATF agents can probably still hear Mom swearing at them." She rubbed her temples. "Mistake, the feds say."

"And they're pressuring me." Jo's face felt cold. "Gabe's orders have been changed. He's being deployed to Afghanistan."

Tang's mouth slowly opened. "You okay?"

Jo laughed uncontrollably. "No. I'm not within sight of okay, not even with a telescopic night scope. It's all federal, Amy. It's all too close and too scary to be coincidence. And I don't know what to do, or whether to tell Gabe."

Tang seemed frozen. "We'll never find proof."

"I know." Jo's eyes began to sting. "So I'll file my report, saying I quit."

Tang leaned back.

"Without further evidence, I can't determine Tasia's state of mind. And I'm not going to get it. No psychiatric records. No interview with the man who owns the weapon that killed her. I'm stymied." The stinging in her eyes increased. "And Gabe's going to pay the price."

Tang's shoulders slumped. "I don't blame you. I'm sorry, Beckett."

"Checkmate," Jo said. "The bastards win."

Tang didn't argue. And with her silence, so died Jo's last scintilla of hope. There was no way to right this sinking ship. She wanted to hurl her beer bottle across the room.

"Before I drove over here, I phoned the office of the White House chief of staff. I left a message asking K. T.

Lewicki to phone me. Now I know for certain what I'll tell him. We're done."

At the bar, a group of men broke into friendly laughter. Tang glanced at them.

"I'll tell Vienna Hicks I'm wrapping things up," Jo said. "I hate to let her down, but . . . what?"

Tang looked like she'd just swallowed a glass of straight pins. "The news."

On the television above the bar, the bloodbath at the St. Francis dominated the headlines. Helicopter shots of Union Square. Manic speculation about Noel Michael Petty. Lecroix's last music video played repeatedly. But this was a break from the Cirque du Searle.

Edie Wilson was on-screen, her expression jubilant. "Startling new information has come to light regarding psychiatrist Dr. Johanna Beckett."

The shot switched to news footage: Jo in Gabe's 4Runner, driving away from the news scrum outside her house.

"I've learned that Dr. Beckett has some unsavory connections. This police psychiatrist has a boyfriend with a dicey past."

Jo stood up. "Jesus Christ."

Flash to a grainy shot of Gabe's face, captured through the window of the 4Runner. His black eye was visible.

"Sources tell me Gabriel Miguel Quintana, currently a civilian employee of the California Air National Guard, has a history of violent assault."

Jo kicked her chair into the next table as she walked toward the television.

"Quintana's criminal record, I'm told, includes assault with a deadly weapon," Wilson said.

Dawn Parnell appeared on-screen. Jo thought her hair was going to ignite.

"Maybe the record is officially sealed for some reason," Dawn said. "Maybe the military decided it could use somebody with his tendencies. I can't explain it. But all I care about is protecting my daughter."

Tang caught Jo. "Forget it."

"I'm climbing up on the bar and I'm ripping that TV off its mount," Jo said.

On a split screen, an anchor appeared. His supercilious expression suggested that his biggest investigation had been whether the Easter Bunny left hard-boiled eggs in the basket, or just the chocolate bunnies. "What are the security implications, Edie?"

Edie nodded. "That's the real question. Rumors persist that the police were not informed that Searle Lecroix was in danger until it was too late to warn him."

"Rumors . . ." Jo stepped toward the bar. Tang pulled her back.

"The question people seem afraid to ask is whether this psychiatrist led the police to think the threat was lower than it actually was. And is the military lax about monitoring its civilian employees? Quintana works at Moffett Federal Airfield, which puts him in close proximity to a number of Special Forces units."

"Scary stuff, Edie."

The channel went to commercial. Jo rushed outside and called Gabe.

"Did Sophie see that?" she said.

"Can't talk now. I'll call you back."

"I'm sorry."

"I know."

He hung up. Jo lowered her hand and the phone rang again.

"K. T. Lewicki." The White House chief of staff sounded energized. "You called?"

CHAPTER
FORTY-FOUR

The doors were locked. The windows were bolted, shutting out the run-down Daly City neighborhood outside. Yellow light soaked through the blinds into the living room. Keyes stood in front of the television, mesmerized by Edie Wilson's report. Ivory paced back and forth. A cigarette dangled between her fingers, ash grown an inch long.

"They shot her," she said. "They killed Searle and then they shot her. They shot her dead, Keyes."

"I know. It's on."

Ivory's swan-white hair, tangled and dirty, stuck up like torn feathers. It had been in a mess since she heard the news and pulled on it and started screaming. Her white nail polish looked tarnished in the light. She was barefoot, her tattoos blue like ice, her underwear revealing the scorpion tattoo at the base of her back.

"Searle knew too much about Tasia. He was bound to talk. So they killed him. The cops" — she pointed at the television screen — "they killed him and then they shot her fucking dead and blamed it on her."

Keyes stared at the television. "Oswald. She'll go down as a scapegoat, just like Lee Harvey." He shook his head. "And McFarland has operatives in the

National Guard — this greaser Quintana, working at Moffett. Mexican name, what a coincidence."

Ivory's mascara had run across her cheeks. Her white lipstick was smeared. The cigarette burned down to her skin, and she jerked. Dropped it, ground it out with her heel, and sucked on her fingers.

"They shot her. What are we gonna do?" she said.

"You know what we're gonna do."

On the kitchen table were the Desert Eagle pistol he'd bought at a gun fair in Yuma, and the MAC-10 machine pistol and Glock he and Ivory had taken off a drug dealer's wife when they robbed her house outside El Paso. All reliable weapons, all untraceable, all ready and waiting.

Ivory went to the window, stuck her finger through the blinds, and squinted out. She saw broken concrete and a dead yucca tree and the chain-link fence. How long until the cops showed up?

"They shot her, Keyes."

"Stop saying that."

"Shot her in the head. And I'm next."

Keyes crossed the room and grabbed her arm. "Shut up. You're hysterical."

She tore his hand from her arm. "Of course I am. She was my sister."

She shoved him aside, raked her fingers into her hair again, and stalked across the room. "What am I gonna do? All my ID has her name on it. Driver's license, employee ID, the damned TV cable bill, they all say 'Noel Michael Petty.'"

She turned. Keyes's eyes were flat. He knew they were cornered. He couldn't deny it.

"Blue Eagle's gonna hear her name on the news and wonder why the hell it's the same as one of their drivers, and they're gonna call to ask me and when I don't answer, they're gonna call the police."

Everybody at work thought Ivory was just a nickname. They didn't know their snow-white driver had taken the identity of Noel Michael Petty from her crackpot sister. Her sister who only cared about country music, her sister with the money from her slip-and-fall settlement, who wouldn't share a cent with Ivory, even when Ivory got out of prison and needed cash. Her sister, Noel, who didn't deserve a breath of mercy.

"Jesus, they shot her. In the head."

"And she was a night crawler. A creep."

"Who cares now? She was my sister." Ivory looked at him. "Contact Paine."

They stared at each other. This was the moment Keyes could bolt if he wanted.

"'We must hang together, or we'll hang separately.' Thomas Paine. You buying it?" she said.

He didn't move, for a long, cool moment. Then he brushed past her and got on the computer. He logged in to the Webmail site Paine had set up for him, and drafted a new message. She watched him type.

"You using that quote?" she said.

"No. Somebody else who meant what he said."

Ivory leaned over his shoulder. He wrote, "*Isn't it kind of scary that one man could wreak this kind of hell?*"

Timothy McVeigh. She slid to her knees, sank her fingers into Keyes's shirt, and kissed the back of his neck with gratitude. Her heart filled with brilliant intent.

CHAPTER
FORTY-FIVE

Jo paced the lobby of Waymire & Fong LLP. The workday was nearing an end, and the reception area was empty. She stared at the Wyeth prints on the wall. Two attorneys came through, chatting amiably. They didn't give her a second glance.

They couldn't tell. Jo guessed that being slapped around over the phone by the White House chief of staff didn't leave visible marks.

She turned and paced along the windows. She tried to work out what she was going to tell Vienna Hicks. On the windowsill outside, a sparrow landed and sheathed its wings.

The door behind the receptionist's desk blew open and Vienna swept through. Her face was flushed. The gold and black scarf that flew around her neck gave her the look of a giant, ferocious monarch butterfly.

She crushed Jo in a hug. "Bless you. Poor girl, bless you."

Jo resisted, stunned, as she was gathered to a giant, neon-bright bosom.

"God love you, it must have been horrible." Vienna squeezed her tight. "You tried, honey. You tried to save him."

Jo gulped. For a second, she nearly surrendered to Vienna's outpouring of compassion. But she couldn't let Lecroix's death puncture her defenses and lay her flat. She couldn't lower the walls. To do so would be unprofessional and self-destructive. She screwed down the font of sadness that was welling.

Vienna exhaled. "I'm *verklempt*, excuse me. This has been a hell of a day." She took Jo's elbow and led her down the hall. "Who would have believed — a stalker. Poor Searle." She swept into her office and sat down with a thump. "The conspiracy theorists had it half right."

Jo put on her look of studied neutrality. It didn't stick.

"The police have told me they expect to close their investigation into my sister's death. They're with the wackos — they think Tasia was murdered. And they don't expect to look in any other direction for her killer. They got Petty."

"They're satisfied that your sister's case can be closed. That's why I came by. I want to talk to you about the psychological autopsy."

Vienna's brows drew down. "Let me guess. The police department sees no need to pay you for your services any longer. They want you to shelve your report."

"The police would like me to summarize the information I've gathered, but don't want me to pursue it any further."

"You're dropping it?"

Jo didn't answer.

Vienna shifted in her chair. "So what does your report say?"

"If I submitted it tonight? It would be inconclusive. I haven't had the opportunity to review your sister's medical and psychiatric records, or to interview everybody on my list." She held her voice steady. "Right now I cannot draw any conclusion about the cause of Tasia's death. And I regret that."

"You didn't answer my question. Were the conspiracy theorists right?"

"Meaning, did Noel Petty shoot your sister —"

"Or are the police closing the case because of political pressure?"

"I don't know."

Vienna leaned forward. "Rob lied about meeting with Tasia a few days before she died. She wrote a goddamned song about being assassinated. I don't want the police to close the case until they investigate that angle. I don't think you want them to close it, either."

"What I want the police to do won't have much effect at this point," Jo said.

"What's bugging you?" Vienna spread her hands. "Same thing that's bugging me. Right? Petty killed Searle. But I have a sick feeling in the pit of my stomach that the cops are rushing to close the case and shout *booya!* Claim the win and tell everybody to move along, there's nothing more to see." She drummed her fingers on the desk. "What do you really think?"

"First, a comment. Then a question," Jo said. "Don't over-rely on my ability to lay your questions to rest. Sometimes the best I can do is to offer an opinion as to the likely mental state of the victim before death. I don't have a crystal ball."

"Damn it. Are you quitting?"

Jo raised a hand. "Now, my question. Tasia's ghostwriter claims that her autobiography will feature explosive revelations about her marriage. Does that sound like marketing hype, or does it ring true to you?"

Vienna's eyes widened with alarm. "What revelations?"

"He refuses to say."

Vienna tamped down her emotions and shook her head. "The only explosive thing in that marriage was Tasia. She blew up all the time. She was impossible to live with. You want the sad reality? She swept Rob away. He thought she was wild about him — because she was so *up,* so vital, so thrilled whenever she saw him. But she was just manic. What she loved was being the center of attention. It wasn't him. It was all about her." Vienna quieted. "She broke his heart."

Jo nodded. Bipolar people, while often charismatic and winning, sometimes engaged others only on a superficial level.

Vienna crossed his arms. "Your turn. Are you punting on your investigation?"

"To the contrary," Jo said. "I came to tell you about the talk I just had with your ex-brother-in-law's right-hand man."

K. T. Lewicki's voice, with its clipped and nasal, go-for-the-viscera tone, had carried a different tenor this time. Jo hadn't been able to pin it down.

"I heard what happened at the Saint Francis," he said. "Are you all right? You weren't harmed?"

Standing outside Mijita, shivering in the breeze, she told him, "I'm all right. The police officers involved are all right."

"I've seen some information about the suspect. It sounds as though Petty was a classic model of the obsessed celebrity stalker."

"No such thing as a classic, but I'll go out on a limb and say she was obsessed with Searle Lecroix and stabbed him to death in a homicidal rage. It was an ugly scene, Mr. Lewicki."

"As I said, I'm relieved to hear you and the officers involved are unharmed."

The breeze, rushing toward the bay, chilled her face. She held her tongue. Everything she wanted to scream, she clamped down. She wanted to play this, to hear what he had to say.

It wasn't good.

"I appreciate your taking the time to phone me earlier. In a way, it must seem a relief," he said.

"How's that?"

"That the suspect's actions were so overt. Counterintuitive though it may seem, it's lifted a burden from your shoulders."

She kept quiet.

"There's no need for you to continue your probe now, is there?"

And Jo recognized the new top note in his voice. Knew how he sounded.

Exultant.

"I don't consider it a relief," she said.

"You're the one who figured out that a stalker was to blame. You're to be congratulated."

She thought she'd put out the embers that threatened to set her hair on fire. She thought she was under control. She realized she wasn't.

"Congratulated?"

"You contacted the Secret Service, and my office. It turns out there was no need to worry about the president's safety, but your concern that a dangerous stalker might be at large was certainly warranted — if belatedly heeded. You should be applauded."

"Searle Lecroix is dead. He was stabbed multiple times with a steak knife. I held his hand while he bled profusely onto his hotel room carpet. I watched his lips turn blue and air bubble out of a knife wound that sliced halfway through his lung. Don't applaud me."

Lewicki was silent.

"I know you've gotten the SFPD to shut down the investigation into Tasia's death. I don't know what kind of pressure has been applied to the top brass. I doubt I'll ever find out. I can only extrapolate from the kind of pressure that's been applied to me and others. And it stinks."

She knew at that moment she'd let loose a snarling pit bull, and that if she didn't fling the phone into the bay and dunk her head in a tub of ice, she would not be able to rein it in.

"Message received, Mr. Lewicki. The political lesson has been absorbed. I concede. But honestly, sending the ATF to raid an elderly couple's mom-and-pop business? The IRS audit of Captain Bohr, that's a cliché. It shows lack of imagination. The ATF raid may have been an attempt at freshness and flair, but it's so damned crude, I can't believe it's something the people pulling the strings will get high marks for."

"Doctor, watch your words."

"As for changing Gabe Quintana's orders — that's a trick. That's the golden ticket. Sly. An oblique attack. Probably half a dozen intermediaries between the idea and the execution."

The pit bull was barking, snapping, lunging. She surrendered to the rage.

"And, ultimately, it's unnecessary. Sending a man to war, leaving his child bereft — slick. And I'll probably never be able to prove it. But who knows, maybe I'll walk onstage when the *Bad Dogs and Bullets* tour holds its requiem for fallen performers, and take the mike to tell everybody how *efficiently* the elected government of our country encourages citizens to take a clear look at their civic duty."

She took a breath. Her heart was pounding hard, and she thought maybe the spot where she was standing had started to melt. Lewicki didn't come back right away.

Then he said, "Do I need to use the term *projection*, Doctor? I saw Edie Wilson's segment a few minutes ago, as I'm assuming you did. Speaking with Mr. Quintana's ex . . . girlfriend, is it? Is that accurate?"

This time it was Jo's turn to stay silent.

"Effective reportage, I'd say, gauging from your reaction. Though there isn't a sealed criminal record. Just an arrest, eleven years ago. Quintana beat a man to within an inch of his life with a silver belt buckle in a bar fight. I don't know why he escaped prosecution — perhaps because he agreed to report for duty in the air force immediately thereafter."

Jo shut her eyes.

"I don't know all the circumstances, but having been in the military myself, I'd guess it's lucky Mr. Quintana is being permitted to serve as a pararescueman, instead of serving a prison sentence."

Jo didn't open her eyes. She couldn't.

"It's a shame his daughter will probably hear all of this for the first time while he's preparing to deploy. Of course, it's still possible that the military, or the California court system, could be in possession of further documents that find their way into the public eye. Or not."

Jo clenched her teeth. She wanted to speak, but knew if she moved her lips she'd simply scream, into the phone, the air, at God.

Lewicki's voice returned to its sprightly initial tone. "But as I said to begin with, there's no need to further embroil yourself in any of these issues. And since you can put your report to bed, the media attention should abate as well."

Tightly, with the scene pulsing before her eyes, she said, "Got it. Loud and clear."

"Excellent. It's been illuminating to speak with you. Good evening, Doctor."

He hung up, leaving her to stare at traffic and gulls hovering overhead like scavengers, waiting to pick her bones.

Vienna leaned forward. "That high-handed son of a bitch."

"An hour ago I had decided to fold my tent. Crawl home and shut up, to keep from making things worse. Then Lewicki phoned," Jo said.

"That pissant ball-licker. I danced with him at Rob and Tasia's wedding. I drank tequila shots with him until we saw double. I really *like* the little cocksucker. Puke-ass weenie." Vienna crossed her arms. "If you can't find out the truth, I will. I'll hire a private investigator. I'll hire my own forensic psychiatrist. You have colleagues, right? There's a professional organization, bowling league, something?"

"You'd take it all the way?"

"We're talking about my sister. Hell yes, I would."

"It won't be pleasant."

"Do I look like unpleasant scares me?"

"Good. Because I'm in."

"Really?"

"Yeah. If I run away, Lewicki won't relent. He'll try to finish me off. Am I right?"

Vienna nodded slowly. "You are. He doesn't let up — he doubles down. Kel wants you to quit before you uncover information that could damage the president. That's all that matters. He's a steamroller in support of the public good. It's not personal, it's instinctual. It's his mission." She frowned. "Retreat, and he'd see you as wounded prey. He might try to discredit you professionally. Something long-term. So that later, if you found more evidence, you'd have no credibility."

"The only way to protect myself and my loved ones from getting hammered like that is to beat Lewicki to the punch. To find evidence that definitively explains your sister's death. I have to fight back." She stood up. "Game on."

Vienna inhaled. It was an impressive sight. "If Noel Petty didn't kill Tasia, did somebody else?"

"If so, it was an audacious and desperate murder. It would mean she was killed by somebody who took a huge risk, perhaps because there were huge stakes."

"You're worried about a conspiracy. You goddamned are."

"I'm worried that if the White House crushes the investigation, we may overlook a serious threat. I'm worried that something's brewing, and it's dangerous."

"What's your plan?"

"Air Force One is flying in around noon tomorrow. Can you persuade Lewicki to stop by here and see you before the memorial service?"

Paine rocked back and forth in the desk chair, thinking. The message from Keyes was blinking on his computer screen. *Isn't it kind of scary that one man could wreak this kind of hell?* But that wasn't what interested him at the moment. He focused on the news clip from Edie Wilson's latest report. Hit *Replay*.

Her overheated, shouty take on the story didn't excite him. She was a carnival sideshow, the

319

two-headed Pekinese dog who'd made it to the big top and could only stay in the center ring by barking ever louder. Innuendo, gossip, anonymous sources — and who was this outrageous hippie playing he-said, she-said about her ex? Save it for *I'm an Attention Junkie, Look at Me!*

The video clip played. He muted Edie Wilson's mad seal voice. Hit *Pause*.

He leaned toward the screen. "Interesting."

The screen shot showed Dr. Jo Beckett driving away from Wilson and her press colleagues. Beckett was in a vehicle owned by the object of the hippie woman's scorn and Wilson's current hysteria, this man, Gabriel Quintana. Paine zoomed in. Saved the screen shot, fiddled with the photo and enhanced the picture for clarity.

He smiled.

Edie Wilson's sideshow was nothing but distraction, a discoball refraction of the real truth. But sideshows provided cover, and cover provided insurance. Misdirection and disinformation could be allies on the battlefield. Beckett and Quintana were shiny tiles on the twirling ball. Paine could use that. Rumor, fear, hints of violence in the heart of the Tasia McFarland investigation — those things could turn his enemies against each other.

He saved the screen shot and printed it.

Then he wrote to Keyes. *You understand, I know, that what is wrong with the world is the continuation of the jackal's life. Anything is justified to stop Robert*

McFarland. And we are uniquely able and willing to do that.

Tyrannicide is not murder. It is liberation.

The screen shot printed. When Paine examined it again, he felt reassured. The license number for Gabriel Quintana's SUV was plainly visible.

CHAPTER
FORTY-SIX

Noe Valley lay in dusk. Lights were coming on in houses along the block. In the street, kids practiced skateboard tricks, laughing as night came toward them. Jo knocked.

When Gabe opened the front door, she held still. His eyes were weary. His gaze shifted from her face to the driveway and the street beyond.

"I parked two blocks away. Nobody's going to spot my truck," she said.

He nodded her in and closed the door. The blinds were closed. A Hannah Montana album was playing on the stereo. In the living room Sophie sat cross-legged on the floor, coloring. She looked up. Her eyes were weary too.

Jo raised a hand. "Hey, kiddo."

"Hey."

Jo followed Gabe into the kitchen. He poured her a mug of coffee and headed out the door to the backyard. Jo followed and sat down at the patio table. The lawn was covered with fallen oak leaves, like a messy wind had blown through.

Gabe stood by the table and stared at the western horizon. It was soaked with crimson light. Overhead, where it hushed to blue, stars salted the sky.

"We're on communications lockdown. No TV, no computer, I answer the phone. I don't want Sophie to hear anything except from my lips."

"I'm sorry," Jo said.

He finally looked at her. "You have nothing to apologize for. You're doing your job. I jumped into the middle of it. I got splashed with mud."

Except that it wasn't that simple, and they both knew it. He had warned her that the job would get nasty. She'd taken it anyway, without fully considering what that nastiness might involve. His instincts to protect her, his altruism and righteous machismo, had led him to leap in with her. And now they were swimming in a fast-flowing stream, barely keeping their heads above water.

And that wasn't the half of it. Her hurt and her anger were as great as her regret. She felt excluded. She felt blindsided.

"Please tell me what's going on," she said.

"Dawn found out about my deployment from her lawyer. She came tearing over here. Showed up as Edie Wilson was pulling out. Decided to go for broke."

"Does she want custody?"

"She says yes. Which means she wants to play games in court, using Sophie as a bargaining chip. She couldn't manage full-time custody and she knows it." He turned. "You want the story?"

Her chest tightened. She wanted him to shrug and say, *nothing to tell*. But he didn't.

"Please," she said.

He nodded, and settled his stance, as if getting ready for battle. "Dawn was my sophomore year college girlfriend. She wasn't always like she is now. She was sweet. She had a great laugh."

"Everybody has people in their past. You don't need to apologize for your relationship."

"Summer after that year, I was miserable. Hated school. Couldn't stand the thought of going back to San Francisco State in the fall. I enlisted. And that's when Dawn told me she was pregnant."

Under the endless arch of the twilight sky, Jo felt a weight descend on her.

"I offered to marry her. Told her we'd have an adventure, and with me in the air force we'd have housing, a support system, medical care. But she didn't want to be a military wife," he said. "She wanted me to get out of my commitment."

"She wanted you — how?" Jo said.

"Tell the air force I'd changed my mind. Thanks, but no thanks."

"She thought you could really . . ." Jo stopped. There was no point.

"I told her if I didn't report, the military would throw me in jail. She got furious. She said she'd stay with me if I told the air force to screw off. It was her or the military. She didn't — I couldn't get her to believe that . . ." He spread his hands. "I said I had to go but I'd marry her and she could stay with her folks, I'd come home when I could. She didn't want that. Wanted me to stay in San Francisco."

"What happened?"

"The weekend before I was supposed to report for basic training, we met friends for a farewell night out. I was mixed up. No clue how to solve things. Feeling relieved, if I'm honest, that I had an out — the air force was going to take me away from the whole problem." He made a face. "For nine months, anyway. I couldn't picture being a dad. All I knew was that I'd screwed up, big-time. I was scared, and I was secretly glad that Dawn didn't want to accept my noble Mexican Catholic idea of solving the problem with a ring and a priest."

He put his hands in his back pockets. "The evening was a nightmare. Dawn spent it sulking and in tears. Until finally she ran outside to the car. When she didn't come back, I went to find her. I got to the parking lot and heard her yelling my name." He turned around and looked at Jo. "She screamed for help. I saw a guy dragging her around the back of the restaurant."

"God."

"Guy was hauling her toward the bushes. I went nuts. I charged him."

"Oh, Gabe."

"I tackled him and yelled at Dawn to run. Call the cops. That's when the guy's friends jumped me," he said. "Three against one, I knew if they put me on the ground I wouldn't get up. I chose the guy who looked like he most wanted to fight. Figured if I could hurt him, the other two might not want any of it, and they'd split." He paused. "I kicked the shit out of him."

Jo waited. Seconds passed. "Gabe?"

"I should have stopped sooner, but I thought if I let him up, Dawn was cooked. Thing is, I didn't see one of the other guys grab a bottle out of the Dumpster. He smashed it and stabbed me. Twice."

His calm seemed like the peace that comes when all the blood has poured from a body, when nothing is left to pump through the heart. Jo's gaze sank from his face to his hip, where the jagged scars lived beneath his shirt and jeans.

"After that, the two guys split. Ran and left me on the ground bleeding beside their buddy."

Jo reached out and took his hand. He let her take it, but didn't squeeze back.

"I thought — shit, the dude actually shanked me. Never saw *that* coming." He wet his lips. "I wondered, is this where I float overhead and watch the scene from above? Where's the light?"

Jo held on.

"I started crawling toward the restaurant. The cops came, and an ambulance. They took me to surgery and patched me up."

Jo's throat was dry. She knew "patched up" was a euphemism.

He went quiet. She thought: Was that it? Horrible as the attack was, where was the problem for Gabe? He was the hero. He saved his pregnant girlfriend from a gang of rapists.

"But?" she said.

"Nobody saw the fight. Dawn had split. There was just me and the guy I kicked the shit out of, and he was spitting teeth and telling everybody I tried to kill him.

Nothing about the other two guys. Nothing about how he grabbed Dawn." He shrugged. "So, yeah, the cops put me under arrest in the hospital. Said they were going to prosecute me for assault, maybe attempted murder."

Jo leaned forward. "But they didn't."

"They found the broken bottle. The fingerprints on it didn't match the guy I took down. They matched his buddy, who had a record."

"And?" She was confused. "And that was the end of it?"

He stared at the ground. A feeling of dread settled on Jo's shoulders.

"Dawn's parents made her come forward," he said. "She said it was a prank that got out of hand."

"Dear God."

"She wanted to scare me into staying in town. To protect her. She knew all three guys. It was a setup."

Rage, a bright spike of steel, seemed to cut through the dusk. Jo stood and walked to the center of the lawn, trying to get a grip on herself. After a minute she walked back and put her hands on Gabe's shoulders.

"I know why you didn't tell me. I'm not going to explode, or spend the next year constantly harping on what a bitch Dawn is, or staring at you funny." She made sure he was looking at her. "But don't ever hold back again."

His lips parted. Not a smile, not a frown. An expression, maybe, of surprise. "You sure about that?"

"Yes."

"Really sure?"

They were talking about the war now. She nodded. "Trust me."

It was a plea, and a pledge, and an expression of her hurt. He took her hands from his shoulders, covered them with his, and put his lips against her knuckles.

"Can you see why I didn't want this story to come out? How the hell is Sophie going to take it when she finds out what her mother did?" he said.

"I know."

"Thank God for Dawn's parents. They suffered more than anybody. I mean, I healed. The cops got footage from a CCTV camera behind the restaurant, and once they saw it, they uncuffed me and never mentioned the possibility of rearrest or prosecution."

"But you don't want me to talk about this to anybody, do you?" Jo said.

"No. The guy I put in the hospital, he left with his jaw wired shut and his knee pinned together. I don't think he'll ever walk without a limp."

Jo held on to his hands. His shadows took on texture.

"You didn't need to keep this from me," she said.

"Talking doesn't come easy to everybody. And it doesn't always help a situation," he said. "I have to handle things like this. And I don't want people to worry about stuff it's my responsibility to deal with."

"I understand. But keeping secrets isn't the only way to keep control."

"Really? If I tell you things, you won't judge me and try to influence my decisions?"

Jo's throat tightened again. He'd told her something beyond painful and difficult. But she couldn't shut down her anger completely: He'd kept something so fundamental from her for so long, despite her open desire to know.

But he'd also just promised her that he would not keep secrets in the future. And she hadn't told him her own fear, her own dark knowledge: that his call-up was a message to her. She screwed up her courage.

In the kitchen the phone rang. Gabe squeezed her hand and jogged inside to pick it up. Jo tilted her head back and stared at the stars. After a minute she headed in. Gabe was still on the phone. She went to the living room and sat down on the floor beside Sophie.

The little girl was leaning close to the construction paper on which she was drawing with colored pencils, her face intent.

"I like the Appaloosa," Jo said.

"Thanks."

"Are the horses fighting the vampires?"

"Just the evil vampires. And the werewolves are on the horses' side." Sophie picked up a crimson pencil and colored a wound on the flank of a wolf. "Dad doesn't think I know that stuff is going on."

"He knows you know." Jo picked up a pencil and a sheet of paper. "You mind?"

Sophie shook her head.

Jo began to draw. "What has he talked to you about?"

Sophie stopped coloring. Her eyes were anxious. "He's going overseas on Friday." Her lips fought a quiver. "But not to Africa. To Afghanistan."

She stared at Jo with a gaze like flame, challenging Jo to say otherwise. Then she blinked and inhaled in jerking breaths.

"I want him to stay here," she whispered. "I wish they would call up somebody else. Don't tell him."

Gabe's footsteps creaked on the hardwood floor. Sophie turned her face to hide her tears, but he walked in and saw her. Looking stricken, he crouched at her side and hugged her. Slowly, like a cramped muscle, she shuddered and turned to him.

Jo sat, hands loose on her knees. Her phone rang. She saw *Tang* on the display. "Excuse me." She stood and stepped away to answer. "Amy?"

"And by the way, Tasia's medical records from the time she was married to Robert McFarland are missing."

"No kidding."

"I'm not talking 'unavailable.' I mean they should be accessible from the army, but they've gone poof. Imagine my surprise."

Jo thought about it. "Thanks."

"That's the kind of information that would create a ruckus if it became public."

"It's not quite time for that. But it could be useful."

"Let me know if you need an assist."

"Will do." Jo hung up.

A moment later the phone rang again. It was Vienna. "Lewicki said yes."

Jo's ears pricked up. "When and where?"

"My office, 1p.m. tomorrow. He's coming straight here from the plane. I still seem to have powers of

330

persuasion. Or maybe the shrimp is just afraid of big women."

Jo felt a buzz of hope. "I'll be there. Thanks."

Gabe approached, holding Sophie's hand. She was wiping her eyes.

"We have to go. I'm meeting with my lawyer. I'll take Sophie to Regina's."

Jo nodded. She opened her mouth to tell him her fears, but closed it again. Wrong time, wrong place.

"What?" he said.

"It'll keep."

As if that would make it any better.

CHAPTER
FORTY-SEVEN

Jo walked barefoot into the kitchen at 6:30a.m. Sharp sunlight angled across the house. Tucking messy curls behind her ear, she turned on the coffee maker. The air was cool, the sky cobalt. Three thousand miles east, she calculated, Air Force One was taxiing into takeoff position at Andrews Air Force Base.

While the coffee brewed, she laid out her notes on the kitchen table: the information she knew, and needed, and planned to cajole and berate out of White House Chief of Staff Kelvin T. Lewicki.

Three issues touched her like a burning brand. First was her apprehension that Tasia McFarland's death might not be an isolated event. Second was her fear that the president's imminent arrival might put more people in danger. She kept hearing Tasia's recorded warning: *Things have gone haywire . . . If I die, it means the countdown's on.*

Third was her conviction that Lewicki, or the president's political machine, had managed to change Gabe's military orders.

She needed to find out whether Tasia McFarland had been murdered. And she wanted to put Lewicki on his knees, moaning like a sick baboon.

She reread her notes, trying to untangle the final days of Tasia's life like a skein of string. Tasia had stopped taking the medication that controlled her moods. Longing for a manic high, during the spring she instead suffered a major depressive episode. She then got a prescription for Prozac, which probably sent her into a mixed state. Several days before her death, she rendezvoused with Robert McFarland at a hotel in Virginia. She returned to San Francisco agitated, wild, and frightened. The night before the concert at the Giants' ballpark, she wrote two songs to be played if she was assassinated. The next evening, she was shot to death with McFarland's Colt .45.

"The Liar's Lullaby" and "After Me" were never meant to be hits. They were weird and moody, ambiguous and elliptical. But effective: songs that burrowed under the skin. At Tasia's house Jo had snapped photos of the sheet music. She printed them and spread the music on the kitchen table.

You say you love our land, you liar
Who dreams its end in blood and fire
Said you wanted me to be your choir
Help you build the funeral pyre.

Along with the ominous lyrics, the music featured dissonant arrangements and compulsive melodic motifs.

But Robby T is not the One
All that's needed is the gun

Load the weapon, call his name
Unlock the door, he dies in shame.

Repetitive melodic progressions and chord arrangements that, put together with the lyrics, seemed puzzling.

Almost literally puzzling.

Jo thought back to the med school lecture series on the mind and music. She went to her office and dug through the file cabinet. After fifteen minutes she came up with some notes she'd sketched. She read them and her pulse quickened.

People with bipolar disorder could, when manic, play elaborate word games and become obsessed with puns. And bipolar musicians could turn their compositions into puzzles.

They did so by sampling famous melodies, secretly referencing the work of other composers. Or by hiding codes in their own melodies and orchestration.

Jo picked up Tasia's sheet music. She realized how a composer could embed a code in a song: with the notes of the scale. C, D, E, F, F-sharp, and so on.

Tasia's music was written in both the treble and bass clefs. No sharps or flats. The notes on the staff clustered around middle C. At the top, Tasia had scrawled *Counterpoint/Round*.

Jo tapped her foot. According to Tasia's stunt coordinator, Rez Shirazi, Tasia had steamrollered him with talk of martyrdom and conspiracy — and music. She insisted that her music could protect her, and that it held the truth. Melody, harmony, counterpoint, lyrics. She threaded her manic monologue with musical references. Round, round, get around. *Do, re, mi, fa, so long, suckers.*

The doorbell rang.

Jo went to her office window and peeked through the shutters. The street was quiet. She saw no reporters — just Ahnuld the robot racing along the sidewalk. Behind Ahnuld came Mr. Peebles, teeth bared. Then Ferd, chasing them both. She went to the front door and squinted through the peephole.

Outside, her sister, Tina, stood on tiptoe, waving a sack of muffins. Jo opened the door and yanked her inside.

Tina was dressed for work at the coffeehouse in a black Java Jones blouse and jeans. Her hair was piled in a ponytail on top of her head, spilling brown curls. The silver ring in her nose flashed in the sun as she jerked through the door.

"Your caffeine problem is much worse than I thought," she said.

"The media's been hounding me."

"We know. The whole family's talking about how you looked on TV."

Jo led her to the kitchen. "What do they think?"

"Aunt Lolo says that running from the press makes your butt look big."

Jo spun on her, eyes bugging.

Tina handed her the muffins. "Take the edge off."

Jo tilted her head back and groaned.

"Seriously, sit down and eat, before you burn your little wings off like a moth flying through a candle," Tina said.

Jo scooped up her notes, dropped onto a chair, and opened the sack. "Thanks."

"Were you really at the Saint Francis yesterday when —"

"Yes. It was a nightmare. But I'll deal with it emotionally later."

Tina sat down across from her. "What do you call that? Displacement? Denial?"

"Suppression." Jo leaned her eyes on the heels of her hands. "If I keep moving, I won't feel the arrows when they hit me."

Tina said nothing. Jo looked up. Her sister's sunny face had clouded.

"Been a heavy twenty-four hours." Jo tried to keep her voice even, but heard a hitch creeping into it. "Gabe's shipping out in two days."

"Oh my God." Tina put a hand on her arm. "Tell me everything."

Jo explained. "Hence my desire to deflect all those arrows."

"Cut yourself some freakin' slack. This is major."

She rubbed her eyes. "I'm just . . . at sea."

Tina's head tilted. She looked acerbically thoughtful. "Are you in love with Gabe?"

Jo looked up. "Yes."

Slowly, completely, Tina's face split into a smile. "Hot shit. That's awesome."

Jo's face warmed, and she smiled too. "It is, isn't it?"

Tina shot both her fists straight overhead and threw her head back. "She shoots, she scores. *Woo.*"

Jo laughed.

Tina brought an arm down and pointed a finger at Jo, like the wrath of God. "And it's inevitable."

"Meaning what?"

"Don't act like Gabe's a bolt from the blue. You're an adrenaline junkie."

"This again?"

"You're a thrill seeker."

"I listen to people talk all day."

"You stare in their faces nine-to-five. And climb mountains for relaxation."

"Rocks: faces that don't talk back."

"They just pitch you off if you do something they don't like. One mistake, the smallest annoyance, and *boom*, it's nothing but air all the way to the ground. Climbing is unforgiving. And you relish it. Tackling faces that will never yield."

"Wrong. The rocks present a problem to solve. That's even the lingo climbers use."

"Jo, give it up."

"No, seriously — climbing is about finding the hidden truths in the rock *and* yourself. Exploring until it reveals its secrets and lets you reach the summit."

"You really don't know?" Tina said.

"It's a rush, absolutely. And plenty of climbers take too many risks. I'm not one of them. You know the saying —"

"There are old climbers, and there are bold climbers. But there are no old, bold climbers." Tina gazed at her as if staring at a dumb stone. "It's not all about problem-solving."

"Of course not. I get a huge buzz from climbing."

"You get a buzz from taking risks in your personal life."

"That's an exaggeration."

"With men."

Jo went still. "That's outrageous. That's — Tina, that's ridiculous, and a slur on . . . what men? Gabe? *Daniel?*"

Tina waved her hands to ward off Jo's pique. "You like excitement. You're a thinker who doesn't seek tranquility, that's for sure."

"Will you please make your point, before I dunk your head in the sink?"

"After you lost Daniel, you got back into the game. You didn't pull the covers over your head." Tina took a breath. "Gabe's an awesome guy. But do you realize you actually sought out the person most likely to die the same way Daniel did?"

The light in the kitchen seemed to twist.

"You lost your husband in a helicopter crash. Now you're in a relationship where the risk of that being repeated couldn't be higher. You're seeing a man who flies in a chopper for work — and deliberately flies into terrible conditions."

Jo tried to breathe. She tried to quiet the snapping noise in her head, the sound of insight smacking her between the eyes. *Stick another bullet in the revolver, Jo. Spin the chamber, pull the trigger, one more time.*

"You better believe I actually said it," Tina said. "Don't kill me."

Jo stood and walked to the French doors and looked out at the magnolia, vivid green in the morning sun.

She had long sensed something wounded in Gabe. Buried deep, scarred over, but working away, still cutting. She now knew that he had fought off three attackers, survived a stabbing, and in the process damaged a man permanently.

Was he seeking redemption for that? Was that why he'd become a PJ?

When he was asked about search and rescue, his job, he said, "I find people and get them back."

It was what he was doing for himself as well.

Her breath caught. He just had to do it without dying in the process.

God, they were a pair.

Tina said, "Need to breathe into a paper bag? Dump the muffins."

She came over and put a hand on Jo's shoulder. "Don't look so shocked. My sister, in most areas of existence you are large and in charge, but when it comes to your love life, you're as clueless as the rest of us."

Jo tipped her head back. She tried to stay serious, but laughed.

"Our time is up. My office will send you a bill," Tina said.

Jo caught her halfway to the front door. "Don't open it until I check for locusts."

When she peeked through her office shutters, her blood pressure jumped. Across the street, Edie Wilson was stepping out of a Volvo SUV.

Tina joined her at the window. "She doesn't look so heroic in person."

"Heroic?" Jo said.

"On her show, the intro shows her in tornado wreckage, and wearing a flak jacket riding around with the Green Berets, like she's the Statue of Liberty." Tina peered at her. "With gigantic hair."

Edie Wilson sipped from a Starbucks cup and pointed around the street, telling the producer and cameraman where to set up. She gave Jo's house a leisurely, contemplative look. *The better to eat you with, my dear.*

Jo marched to the kitchen and turned on the television. On Edie's network, the morning news was talking about a Lhasa apso caught in a washing machine. Edie's show, *News Slam,* was scheduled to start in five minutes, at the top of the hour.

"Can you wait five minutes to go to work?" Jo said.

"Whatever you're planning, I want in. What are you thinking?"

"Whether I dare."

Tina put a hand on her hip. "What were we discussing a minute ago?"

Thrill seeking. Right. Her penchant for death-defying stunts.

"Come on."

She pulled Tina out the back door. They ran across the lawn to the fence. Jo boosted Tina up, clambered over herself, and they hurried to Ferd's kitchen door.

"How good an actor are you?" Jo said.

"I'm auditioning for the national tour of *Spamalot*."

Jo did a double take, wondering if she was serious.

Inside Ferd's kitchen, Mr. Peebles was crouched on top of Ahnuld, drinking from an espresso cup. As if he needed that. When Ferd spotted Jo he nearly skipped with glee. He bustled to the door, slicking his hair down with the flats of both hands.

Behind his glasses, his eyes were electric. "It's Edie Wilson, isn't it?"

"It's war." Jo pointed at Ahnuld. "And he's going in."

CHAPTER
FORTY-EIGHT

Edie Wilson ran over her notes one more time. As she read, she finished her coffee and held out the empty cup. When nobody took it, she looked up.

"Andy."

The cameraman was adjusting the television camera. "Recycle it."

She exhaled with annoyance. Through her earpiece she heard the voice of the director at the network in New York.

"We're going to you in two."

"Got it." She checked the radio mike clipped to her blouse, and refreshed her lipstick in the SUV's wing mirror. Behind her reflection she saw a van coming.

"Damn it."

Some other network was pulling up the hill. They wanted to step on her scoop and catch the "hero" doctor on her way out. But Edie was going to play the story with her own spin.

She ran down her list of talking points. Snapped her fingers at Tranh. "Moffett Field, this National Guard base — they work with the NASA people there? Spy satellites, terror tracking? They're what, on call if there's a bomb threat or attack on Air Force One?"

Tranh took out his BlackBerry. "I don't think so."

"Find out."

In her ear, the network said, "Going live to you in one."

The rival news van parked and people climbed out. This neighborhood was even more quirky than most — the joggers going past, giving her looks, weren't the usual admirers. A few dog walkers had paused to watch, and a bunch of people had wandered over from the cable car stop to pose in the background, hoping to mouth *Hi, Mom*. As the other news crew — what were they, European? Russian? — ran a sound check, a dozen lookie-lous congregated on the sidewalk behind Tranh and Andy. Several snapped photos of Edie on their cell phones.

One man was speaking in a stressed-out murmur to a neighbor. "Police have been to Jo's house twice. With dogs."

Edie glanced at him. He had greasy hair and glasses and wore a computer store T-shirt. He looked seriously alarmed.

"Sniffer dogs. I know it sounds crazy, but . . ."

In her ear, the network said, "Thirty seconds, Edie."

She tossed her hair back. Glanced again at Computer Man.

He was shaking his head. "No, if there's an undercover operation you'd never spot the cops." Peering at the rooftops, he lowered his voice. "I think those were explosive sniffer dogs."

She heard the studio feed. The morning show host said, "Edie Wilson has a live update on the situation in San Francisco."

Andy had the camera on his shoulder. She rolled out the news voice.

"As the president flies toward this city to attend the memorial service for Tasia Hicks McFarland, questions persist about the attack that took the life of Searle Lecroix — and particularly about the police response to that attack. I'm outside the home of Doctor Jo Beckett, the psychiatrist who yesterday failed to resuscitate Lecroix as he lay dying from multiple stab wounds."

She waved her notes at the house. "Serious concerns have also been raised about Doctor Beckett's relationship with an Air National Guard employee who has a criminal record. With the nation on edge after the deaths of two beloved singers and a president who won't put rumors to rest about his role in this, the question is —"

Someone in the crowd said, "What's that?"

"— the question is . . ." Crap, what was her point? *Don't freeze. Talk. Talk big.* "With blatant gaps in the police and security cordon around the president's first wife, why did the police permit a consultant with criminal connections to have intimate access to their investigation? Her boyfriend" — she glanced at her notes — "Gabriel Quintana, is employed at Moffett Field south of San Francisco. He has access to the National Guard's armory and possibly even NASA's satellite and air traffic control monitoring

344

systems. The security implications are mind-boggling."

Tranh stared at her, his face waxen. Well, sure, she'd deviated from her script. But this was *news*. A fresh take.

"Some people claim that the administration was behind Tasia's death. Presumably, Doctor Beckett was hired to put those rumors to bed. Instead, the flames have been fanned. And whether Tasia was silenced, or attempts to silence those of us in the media who insist on bringing the issue into the clear light of day —"

The crowd stirred. People murmured. A woman's voice rose above the crowd. "It's coming this way."

Andy kept the camera on Edie, but pulled back on the focus. She saw his hand adjust it. Moving away from close-up — she wanted to slug him.

In her ear, the network said, "Keep talking, Edie."

"It's . . ."

"What *is* that? It came from the psychiatrist's house."

A young woman in the crowd pointed. Her hair was in a curly ponytail piled high on her head. She was wearing black jeans and a black blouse with some restaurant's logo on it.

"It's coming this way," she said.

Edie turned her head. "Something's going on."

She saw, motoring across the street toward her, the strangest sight of her life. A little . . . what the hell was that, an eight-wheeled toy car?

"Edie, keep talking," the network said.

"It's some kind of — little mechanized *tank*, it looks like, and . . ."

It was covered with radiation hazard symbols and explosives logos.

"It's got bomb symbols on it," Edie said. "It's a bomb sniffer robot."

From the studio, the morning news host said, "What's riding it? Is that a monkey?"

The European news crew aimed their camera at it and babbled in Greek, or French. Ponytail Girl backed up.

"That monkey doesn't look right." Inching away, the girl said, "I don't like this."

A dog walker said, "Oh no." He swept his terrier into his arms and took off as the dog howled. Ponytail Girl put a hand to her mouth. A jogger said, "This ain't good," turned, and jumped a hedge into the park. More spectators bolted.

Bolted? What was going on?

Ponytail Girl pointed. "Oh my God, what's wrong with it?"

The little tank accelerated at Edie from across the street. The monkey straddled its back like Slim Pickens riding the H-bomb in *Dr. Strangelove*, shrieking and biting and seemingly trying to pull it apart. A car came around the corner, saw the tank zooming across the road, and braked sharply. The little tank veered around it.

"Jesus Christ, it can steer," Edie said.

The car honked and swerved toward the curb. The crowd scattered. Somebody screamed. Tires squealed. Coffee flew.

Edie threw down her notes and ran.

346

She charged into Andy, knocking her face against the lens of his camera. In her ear, network shouted, "What are you doing?"

"Run!" she screamed. "Out of my way. Move!"

She knocked Tranh over and ran down the sidewalk, shoving spectators aside. The little deathtrap followed her.

She swerved into the road. A truck honked and slammed on its brakes to avoid her. Ahead, Ponytail Girl sprinted across the street with people behind her. Edie charged past a woman running with grocery bags. Ponytail Girl cut along a path between houses, waving and shouting, "This way."

Behind her Edie heard tiny wheels and a whirring motor and ticky little monkey sounds. She followed.

"Where the hell did that monkey come from?" she yelled.

Ponytail Girl ran down a narrow sidewalk between two houses, toward a gate. "I don't know — maybe Jo was keeping it for psych research."

"How'd it get control of a bomb disposal robot?"

"Bomb disposal? Oh Jesus, it's a suicide monkey. She must have trained it. God, what's it doing?"

Edie turned. The robot was pelting along the narrow sidewalk toward them.

"It's coming. Run faster."

Ponytail Girl reached the gate and yanked on it. "Locked," she cried. "We're trapped."

Here it came. Death on tiny wheels, rattling at them down the path. The monkey's eyes were frantic. Why, Edie thought, was he glaring at her?

Ponytail Girl pressed her back against the gate. "If that thing's packed with plastique, we won't stand a chance." She turned to the homeowners' trash can. "Hide."

She pulled off the lid and began throwing things out. Edie shoved her aside, upended the trash can, and dumped the contents. She dropped it and crawled inside. Scrabbled around for the lid. She couldn't reach it.

Crouched in the stinking garbage can, she heard an electric motor whir. She looked up. The little tank was outside. The monkey perched on top of it, teeth bared.

"What the hell?"

The monkey leaped at her.

The view from across the street was good. It was pretty damned fine. Ferd stood beside Jo, making excited squeaking sounds. Jo held the remote control by her side. Ahnuld didn't need to go anyplace else at the moment.

Down the path beside Ferd's house, the trash can bucked and rolled. The screaming was high-pitched.

Ferd murmured, "Oh, I hope he's okay."

"That's not Mr. Peebles, it's Edie," Jo said.

Tina crouched near the trash can, peering in. She caught Jo's eye. Jo shrugged.

Tina stood, put her foot against the trash can and gave it a hard shove. It rolled along the sidewalk, slowly turning to display its contents.

The cameraman from Edie Wilson's crew was still filming. The Asian American producer was standing openmouthed in shock. A second film crew, shouting in German, ran across the street to get a closer look.

The producer said, "Shut it down, Andy."

Andy kept filming.

"Cut. *Cut*." The producer took off toward the trash can. Jo strolled over to Andy.

He kept filming. Gave her a quick glance. "You drove that thing out here?"

"It's a prototype for a robotic vehicle competition. Nifty, huh?"

The producer reached the trash can and dragged Edie out.

"Ultrasonic navigation system," Jo said. "Drives animals insane."

"That explains why he went for her. Her radio mike probably picked up the sound and fed it back through her earpiece," Andy said.

Edie lay on the ground, kicking her feet in the air and flapping at Mr. Peebles. He was hanging on to her hair, tiny hands gripping her blond tresses, shaking her head like a crazed hairdresser in the Monkeyhouse salon.

"Are you live?" Jo said.

"Oh yeah."

Across the street, the producer turned to Andy and made a slashing motion across his throat. "*Cut*."

Andy lowered his camera. The producer waved his arms at the German crew, shooing them away.

"YouTube?" Jo said.

"Of course."

Jo leaned back against the fender of the Volvo SUV. Andy joined her. He lit a cigarette and watched the free-for-all with a smile as bright as neon.

In the break room at the SFPD Homicide Detail in the Hall of Justice, two detectives broke into laughter. Amy Tang walked through the door. A uniformed officer was staring at the television, shaking his head. One of the detectives was shaking spilled coffee from his hand. He grabbed a napkin and wiped his tie. Tang looked at the screen.

She saw a trash can, Jo's sister, Tina, and a frantic Asian American man trying to pull a monkey out of Edie Wilson's hair.

"Well, now I'm awake," she said.

Gabe pulled a T-shirt over his head, put on his diver's watch, and opened the blinds. Downstairs in the kitchen, the television came on.

"Sophie," he called.

He loped barefoot down the stairs. He heard a news-caster's rapid-fire narration, and high-pitched shrieking.

He walked into the kitchen. "What'd I say? No TV without asking first."

Sophie was dressed in her school uniform, holding a bowl of Cheerios, gaping at the morning news. He reached to turn off the television, and stopped.

They watched Mr. Peebles ride Edie Wilson's head like a tiny camel jockey.

Sophie turned to him. "I *knew* there was gorilla warfare."

CHAPTER
FORTY-NINE

Amy Tang pushed through the door into the cramped deli. Jo stood at the counter. Through the plate-glass windows, the Hall of Justice shone like alabaster, looming over the street's bail bondsmen and auto body shops.

Tang took off her sunglasses and looked Jo over. "You testifying to Congress?"

"Ambushing the White House chief of staff."

"Aren't you the scalp taker?" She suppressed a smile. "I suppose you're entitled to dress like a dominatrix."

Jo considered her black suit conservative, though the slacks did fit like a surgical glove. And her heels were sharp.

She got her bagel and they found a table. "I haven't signed off on my report," she said. "I've had a change of heart."

Tang drummed her fingers on the table. "You ate the whole box of Wheaties this morning, didn't you?"

"Call it professional responsibility."

Tang feigned cool, but again Jo saw her secret smile.

"Very well," Tang said. "Unofficially, here's what we've learned about Noel Michael Petty. She had a record of small-time thefts, mostly related to musicians and movie stars she was infatuated with. Posters, DVDs, T-shirts. She contributed to a number of online forums about Tasia McFarland and Searle Lecroix. Her computer search history lists Lecroix-related searches as the top thousand things she hunted for online."

"But? There's a but, I can tell."

"She's not on any footage from the concert where Tasia died. None."

Jo nodded, not in agreement but excitement. "And?"

"She didn't vandalize Tasia's rented SUV at the ballpark. CCTV caught somebody keying the vehicle, and it wasn't Petty. The vandal wore sunglasses, gloves, and a hoodie, but had a dramatically slimmer silhouette."

"Who was it?"

"Good question. Here's something that doesn't fit. We found matchbooks at both Petty's hotel room and in Tasia's kitchen."

"What makes that unusual?"

"Same design. From Smiley's Gas 'n' Go in Hoback, Wyoming. Near Grand Teton National Park."

"Let me guess — there's no record of either woman ever being in Hoback?"

"Petty had never even visited Wyoming."

"It's not much."

Tang leaned forward. "The matchbook in Tasia's kitchen was set next to an envelope. Self-sealing, so no DNA. Mailed from Herndon, Virginia — down the road from the hotel where Tasia met the president. Postmarked the day after their meeting."

"And the matchbook in Petty's possession?"

"We have a request in for a search of her premises in Tucson."

"I have a question. Petty sent more than fourteen hundred messages to an e-mail address Tasia hadn't publicized. How did she get the address?"

"We're working on it."

"Thanks, Amy." Jo stood up. "Wish me luck. Will you be at the Hall of Justice?"

"No, I'm taking the afternoon off. Going to help my parents put their store back together." She made sparkle fingers. "We're ordering fireworks. It should be a hell of a day."

Ivory sat in a booth at the Hi-Way coffee shop, a mile south of San Francisco International Airport. Her steak sandwich was half-eaten. The waitress came by again with the coffeepot.

"Warm you up, hon?"

Ivory had already drunk four cups of the disgusting coffee, but she held up her mug. She couldn't let the waitress think she was loitering. She opened the newspaper. Nothing but the ROW blowing things up, eating weird shit, planning ways to destroy the U.S.A. The waitress went away. Ivory glanced out the big windows that overlooked the bay. Any time now.

At San Francisco International, planes approached over the water. Normally, flights passed overhead every two minutes. But not a single plane had flown past for fifteen. The skies were being cleared.

Ivory forced a sloppy bite of the steak sandwich. She needed the red meat. But all she could think about was blood pouring out of her sister Noel's head.

She hadn't clocked in today. Blue Eagle Security could shove their job, and their confiscatory illegal taxes, up their ass. After today, she and Keyes weren't coming back. They were going to take the day's cash haul with them when they hit the highway. Sixteen hours hard driving, she figured, and they'd get into the mountains up in Washington, near the Canadian border. Some sovereign citizens had a compound in the back country. She and Keyes planned on joining them.

After today, it would be time to get out of San Fran-sewer. Run for it before the bridges were blockaded or blown. Hunker down and wait while the fires raged.

She drew a hard breath. This was actually it.

In a booth by the window, a kid pressed his face to the glass. "It's Air Force One."

His mother glanced up idly. "It's just a seven forty-seven."

"It says 'United States of America' on the side. Mom, *look*."

His mom looked again, along with everybody in the restaurant. Ivory froze, eyes pinned on the sky.

In the distance, gear down like an evil bird, the blue-and-white 747 floated toward the runway. People scurried to the windows. Several pulled out cameras and phones and snapped photos.

"That is so cool," the boy said.

The sandwich fell from Ivory's hand. The roar of the engines, the shriek of death, passed outside, not close enough to touch. Not yet.

She called Keyes as she headed out the door. "Wheels down in thirty seconds. I'm moving and will report when the motorcade is sighted."

Paine picked up his mail from the post office box. The envelope was slim, the handwriting crabbed. No return address. Keyes had got that right. So far so good.

Paine tore open the envelope and shook out a claim check ticket from the Hilton near Union Square. One of the busiest hotels in the city — two points for Keyes. Twenty minutes later he handed over the ticket at the bell stand in the Hilton. The bellman retrieved a gray sports bag and said, "Need help loading your car?"

"No." Paine took it from him. "It's no trouble."

He set the bag down and dug two bucks from his pocket. The bellman already found him distinctive; fail to tip, and he'd become *that asshole*. Tips were insurance against standing out. He hoisted the sports bag over his shoulder and left.

Three blocks uphill, he walked into another chain hotel. It was bustling and upscale, but not so ritzy that the staff were all over people who walked through the doors or — as Paine did — into the men's room. Good: no attendant. Nobody would see and remember him.

He locked himself in a stall and opened the sports bag. Maneuvering awkwardly in the tight quarters, he changed into the Blue Eagle Security uniform Keyes had left for him. He could barely zip the navy blue pants. He fumbled with the buttons of the shirt, sucking in his gut. The short jacket was roomier. He zipped it halfway.

Today was shaping up. Today was going to be the pinnacle.

Today, the fire would be lit.

To have a task before him that so united all his goals — a task that aligned with his beliefs, and promised riches — filled him with awe. It was righteous and beautiful.

And it chilled him. If he failed, he'd die.

He would be hunted, relentlessly, and there wouldn't be arrest and trial. Federal agents might try to capture him. But his paymaster would expend huge resources to ensure that he was never taken alive. His paymaster would break the bank to kill him before he could talk. Fail this time, and he had no out. He couldn't turn back. He had to succeed.

So he would.

Today the message would be delivered. He would, as usual, come at the task obliquely. But today the message wouldn't be oblique. Today, he would drive home the point in blood and fire.

Tasia McFarland had been a message too. Her death was collateral damage. Today's damage would strike harder, spread deeper. Today's damage would not be merely collateral, or family-oriented, though that was his specialty. And really, "family" could not truly describe the relationship of the Usurper and the new succubus who shared his bed. Today's damage would be direct and irrevocable. It would light the fire, the big one, the one that would cleanse and purge the nation.

Stuffing his own clothes in the sports bag, he walked out of the men's room, staring straight ahead. Man in a company uniform, quiet, bland — he would blend with the furniture, the background, and a crowd. He would become invisible.

So when he struck, it would seem to come straight out of nowhere.

CHAPTER
FIFTY

Jo paused outside Waymire & Fong's Art Deco office building. She kicked off one of her heels to get rid of a pebble. She braced a hand against the wall of the building and, for a moment, wished this weren't a city street but a mountainside, that this wind was funneling between spires in the high country, beckoning her to climb.

All the mountains could do was kill her. They wouldn't laugh over her grave and toast their success at dragging her name through the mud. They wouldn't punish her lover. They wouldn't shoulder her aside when she tried to warn people of danger.

She put her shoe back on, smoothed her hair, and entered the building to face K. T. Lewicki.

Parked beneath a freeway interchange outside San Francisco airport, Ivory held a map and talked into her phone, though nobody was on the other end. Overhead, foreign jumbo jets lugged themselves into the air, engines annoying the hell out of her already ragged nerves.

Half a mile away, a gate in the airport fence rolled open. On the tarmac Ivory saw seagulls, coast guard planes, private jets, and in the distance, the white-and-blue paint on the 747 with the lettering on the side that said UNITED STATES OF AMERICA.

Through the gate came a parade of police motorcycles and black Chevy Suburbans. They accelerated and roared past, three vehicles, four — how did you know which one the bastard was riding in? — and zoomed onto the freeway.

She dropped the map, started the car, and pulled out to follow them.

The receptionist at Waymire & Fong, Dana Jean, invited Jo to take a seat, but Jo couldn't sit still. She paced in front of the windows. Below on Sacramento Street, traffic burbled in the gleaming day.

A constant stream of people headed for the elevators. The office was emptying out. Everybody was heading for the memorial service.

Her phone rang. She saw *Gabe* on the display and her nerves sparked, hotter. "Hey."

"Jo Beckett, Harpy Slayer. I don't know how you did it, but I want to hear. In lingering, sarcastic detail."

She grinned. "I'm at a meeting downtown, can I —"

"I'll pick you up. I've got forty-five minutes free today, and I want to spend them carrying you around on my shoulders. You can howl like a warrior queen. Change your name to Boudicca. Where are you?"

Still grinning, she gave him the address. "See you soon," she said, and hung up, feeling better than she had in days.

"Jo."

Vienna strode into the lobby. She was wearing a black suit with a jacket that swept below her knees like a duster, and a red silk blouse with ruffles like exploding roses. In black patent leather boots, she was six foot two. She looked like the new sheriff from the land of the Amazons, riding into town to clear out the outlaws.

Her smile was rueful. "Tasia wouldn't want me to dress like a mouse. We are going to celebrate her in style."

She locked her elbow around Jo's and swept her down the hall to her office. "It's going to be beautiful. Music, flowers — the concert promoter paid for the sound system, and bless dumb old Ace Chennault, he spent an hour at the funeral home helping with the floral arrangements." She smiled. "Ready for Kelvin?"

"You bet."

"Sure you are. Want a Zoloft or something?" She laughed. "Kidding. You should see your face."

She cleared a pile of papers from a chair for Jo. "Lewicki's a pussycat. And by that, I mean he's a blood letter. But he'll listen, as a favor to me. For ten seconds. After that, you'd better hold his attention."

Jo wiped her palms on her slacks. "I'm ready."

Two hundred yards behind the Presidential motorcade in downtown San Francisco, Ivory was stuck at a stoplight. The armada of SUVs and police motorcycles had raced up the freeway and along the waterfront — grandstanding, sirens blaring, *El Presidente* telling the peons to get the fuck out of his way. Ivory stuck her head out the window of her car to see past traffic, and spotted the motorcade pulling into the Hyatt Regency at the Embarcadero Center. So that's where Legion was going to stay until the memorial service. The lap of luxury.

She called Keyes. "Hyatt Regency. They just drove into the garage."

"On my way," he said.

The light turned green. She veered across lanes and raced ahead of traffic. But when she reached the turn-in to the hotel, the cops had blocked it off. She braked, swearing.

And she saw that one of the SUVs hadn't driven into the hotel's underground garage. It was idling at the curb. Its doors opened and two young suits hopped out and bustled toward the hotel. Then the SUV pulled out behind a police motorcycle and headed toward the heart of the Financial District.

"One of the Suburbans just drove off. What if it's him?" Ivory said.

"Just one?"

"With an escort."

Keyes was quiet a second. "Follow it."

"What if it's not? Doesn't he ride in a special car — the Beast?"

"That's Secret Service disinformation. Nobody actually knows which vehicle he's in. The point is, he's either in the Suburban that just pulled out . . ."

"Or he's at the Hyatt. But if he did just drive away —"

"Then we'll get the jump on him."

She sped up and cut around the Hyatt toward the Financial District. When she turned the corner, the black Suburban was fifty yards ahead.

Vienna brought Jo a cup of scorched instant coffee. "What's this?"

Jo had spread copies of Tasia's last songs on Vienna's desk. "Your sister wrote puzzles into these songs. Can you help me decipher them?"

Vienna bent over the music. Just as she did, Jo's phone rang. *Ferd Bismuth.*

"Excuse me." She answered. "Has Mr. Peebles recovered from playing Mad Max?"

"Mr. P saw a replay of the incident on television and threw a bowl of oatmeal at the screen. I fear that now he has a complex about blondes. My heavens, the way that woman screamed."

Yes, it was Mr. Peebles who had the complex.

"I've been digging around online, tracing Archangel X," he said.

"Why?" she said. "What have you found?"

"Strange connections. Archangel commented on political forums that discussed Tasia's link with the president. To be precise, rightwing forums that talked down Searle Lecroix as a 'betrayer of the cause' because he was sleeping with 'the enemy.' You know, because Tasia was once married —"

"Got it. Archangel was trawling for mentions of Searle online, defending him in cyberspace."

"Basically. And she got some push-back. A character named Paine."

362

"As in infliction of?"

"As in Thomas. Jo, this guy isn't just any Internet troll. He has a following. And he's extreme. He runs a site called Tree of Liberty."

"I know that site — Tasia visited it. It's ugly."

"It's given me indigestion and a definite shortness of breath. This guy, I'm not exaggerating, he's a guru to some of the extreme antigovernment people out there. And he was slapping Archangel around, brutally, in the forums. There's also an e-mail reply from her to him. They were sending each other personal messages."

Vienna glanced at Jo and frowned. "What?"

Ferd said, "I'll forward the e-mails to you. But there's more. Archangel thought she was having an e-mail correspondence with Searle Lecroix."

Jo stood up as straight as a stick. "What?"

"I . . . oh gosh, I managed to get a peek into her Hotmail account. Don't ask me how, because I'll break out in a rash. But she was e-mailing somebody she thought was Lecroix. Somebody who wrote her love notes and told her to keep quiet about it all."

"Ferd, the police need to see those."

"I know. I'm going to call them, right away. But here's the thing. I think the 'Lecroix' e-mails came from an address associated with Tom Paine."

Jo went quiet. Ferd talked about IP addresses and traceroutes and X-Originating e-mails. Her head was ringing.

"And one other thing. Petty made a reference that just seems . . . spooky. Archangel wrote to Paine and said something about a matchbook."

Jo stilled. "What about it?"

"She said, 'You sent it, didn't you? Are you trying to burn me?'"

Jo tried to slot the information into the missing pieces of the puzzle. "Thanks, Ferd. Call Captain Bohr, right away."

Vienna eyed her. "Good news?"

"Maybe major." Tom Paine, goading Noel Petty with fake love letters? What was going on?

Vienna picked up Tasia's sheet music. "We only have a minute. What did you want to know?"

Jo focused. "Tasia told both Lecroix and the stuntman that the truth was in her music. There has to be meaning in here."

They leaned over the pages and read the lyrics. *After me, what'll you do?* The song was written in 4/4 time. No sharps or flats. The chords were too dense for Jo to decipher by sight. She picked up a pencil, found a piece of scratch paper, and wrote down the chord progression. C-E-A-C . . . D-E . . .

It was all of a piece. Independently, the words and music each made partial sense. But the composition only truly held together as a whole: lyrics, melody, harmony, arrangement.

After me . . .

The refrain began on the downbeat. The melodic line hovered around C while a riff went on below it in the accompaniment.

He wants me . . .

She tried to decipher the chord. "Vienna?"

"It's a D, just voiced differently."

It still didn't make sense. Then Tasia's manic soliloquy popped back into her head. Not just A, B, C, but Do, Re, Mi.

"When you play Do-Re-Mi it starts on what?" she said. "Middle C?"

"No. Depends on the key. It starts on the first note of the scale. D, if it's in the key of D. G, if it's in G."

"And this song is in C, right? No sharps or flats."

Vienna shook her head. "A minor." Her phone rang. She answered, listened, and said, "Thanks."

Jo scribbled:

Do = A
Re = B
Mi = C
Fa = D
Sol = E
La = F
Ti = G
Do = A

Vienna hung up. "Time's up, puzzle girl. Lewicki's here."

Ivory watched the black Suburban pull up outside a sleek office building in the Financial District. She was eighty yards behind it in heavy traffic on a one-way street. A Muni bus partially blocked her view. The Suburban stopped and somebody climbed out. But she couldn't see who.

She called Keyes. "Sacramento Street. Big gray stone building. The Gub SUV stopped out in front."

"You sure?" Keyes said.

"Positive. I can't see what's happening because a bus is in my way, but —"

The brief whoop of a siren jolted her. She looked in the rear-view mirror. A motorcycle cop was behind her, face hidden behind mirrored sunglasses. His lights were flashing.

"Porky pig. Oh God," she said.

"Be cool. Get off the phone. Maybe he's after somebody else."

The cop pointed at her.

"He wants me. Keyes, he's onto me. I don't know how, but —"

"Don't panic. Ivory, be a law-abiding citizen and go with traffic when the light changes. I'm on my way. Just drive. See if he's after somebody else."

"No, he wants me. If he stops me and sees my driver's license, he'll know for sure. I can't let him. Keyes, this is it. This is fucking *it*."

"Ivory, no —"

She dropped the phone. The light changed. She screeched away from the intersection, zooming past the Muni bus. She grabbed a glance at the black Suburban. It had its flashers on. It was definitely planning to stay outside the office building.

Behind her, the cop burst from traffic in pursuit. His lights were hysterical in her mirror, blue and red. His face was a shiny mask.

They knew. They'd found her out, and they were hunting her down, the cops who had murdered Noel, shot Noel in the head. The Gub and its machinery were going to take her off the board.

The cop hit his siren again, a bright yelp. Ahead the traffic light turned yellow. She gunned it through the intersection and headed up the hill toward Chinatown. But after a hundred yards, traffic snarled. Damn, damn, damn.

She had no choice, and no time. She had to act. She braked and pulled to the curb. She clenched her fists so they wouldn't shake. The cop parked his bike behind her. In the mirror, she watched him approach.

She felt under the driver's seat for the Glock.

CHAPTER
FIFTY-ONE

Vienna beckoned Jo. "Remember, Lewicki will go for your knees. Get him around the throat first."

Jo grabbed the sheet music from the desk. Vienna led her to a conference room at the end of the hall, where sunlight fell through tall windows onto a burnished teak table. On a credenza, beneath a plasma-screen television, coffee was set out on a silver tray.

"I'll get Kel," Vienna said. "Shake out your nerves before we get back."

Jo spread the music on the table. "After Me." The lyrics read, *What's next? Who's next?* On her scratch paper, she wrote down the notes in the melody. B. G. C. D. F. A.

Do-re-mi. On her cheat sheet — the decoder pad — she translated. Re-Ti-Mi-Fa-La-Do.

Did it mean anything? She mouthed it, separating the mini musical words. Re. Ti.

The door opened and Vienna swirled through. She stepped aside to reveal the man who'd been eclipsed behind her Shootout-at-the-OK-Corral suit.

K. T. Lewicki's small, bull terrier eyes zeroed on Jo. He looked like he could barely keep his teeth sheathed.

For a second Jo thought he was going to throw a chair through the windows.

Vienna hadn't told him Jo was going to be there. She shot Vienna a look. Vienna merely inhaled and said, "Kel, this is Doctor Beckett."

Jo extended her hand. "Thanks for taking the time, Mr. Lewicki."

Brusquely, he shook. "Vi has powers of persuasion."

"Tell me about it."

His little eyes blinked in his bullet head. For a moment, he seemed disarmed. Then he checked his watch. "I have ten minutes."

"I won't waste them. The single point I must emphasize is that I believe there's a threat to the president's safety."

"The Secret Service is here in force."

"The night Tasia died she was fearful. She was possibly homicidal. That should concern you."

"The president can't shed any light on that." Lewicki stuck his hands in his pockets and walked to the windows.

"I can't take your word for that. Tasia and Searle Lecroix are dead. And the president can certainly shed light on why Tasia showed up at the concert armed with his Colt forty-five."

"The media has made hay over that, but reasonable people understand that the president hadn't seen that weapon in twenty years."

"The president hadn't seen Tasia in almost twenty years, either, yet last week he secretly met with her in Virginia. Three days later, she left Searle Lecroix a message saying things had gone haywire, that her life was in danger, and that if she died, quote, 'It means the countdown's on.' "

Lewicki paced in front of the windows as if positioning himself. As if other people were opponents. Or lunch. Pausing, he opened a window and drew a breath of fresh air. The sounds of city traffic floated in. He stared down at the street.

"Prove that's a threat to the president. Give me one good reason," he said.

In the wing mirror, Ivory watched the motorcycle cop approach her car. That helmet and mirrored sunglasses, the tight uniform, like the Gestapo.

They knew she was using her sister's ID. Her driver's license had Noel's name on it. Her lousy sister, Noel, fat crazy Noel who only loved music and singers and for that got shot in the head by the same SFPD that was now storming toward her car.

She set the Glock on her lap. She looked out the windshield at the street. Crowded, packed with cars and trucks parked for delivery, pedestrians, skyscrapers. Nowhere to run. The cop swelled in the mirror, his badge filling it.

He tapped on the window.

She raised the gun, put it to the glass, and pulled the trigger.

CHAPTER
FIFTY-TWO

Jo's temper ignited. "One good reason? You don't want a good reason. You want any excuse to knock me down."

Turning from the window, Lewicki stepped toward her, eyes sharp. "Tasia played games. Love, life, war, it didn't matter. She played people against each other like they were toys in her playhouse of mania. So I want one single shred of evidence that the night she died, she wasn't playing one last game, killing herself with Rob's forty-five to ruin his reputation."

"Toys in her playhouse? What —"

Vienna stepped between them like a referee. "Cut this out."

Jo pointed at him. "Please clarify what you meant by —"

"Stop it." Vienna put up a hand. "Now."

Jo closed her mouth, but wondered what had inspired Lewicki's remark. Vienna turned to him.

"Look who's talking — the champion of gamesmanship. Don't deny it, darlin'. I remember your toast at Rob and Tasia's wedding. But there aren't any prizewinners here. Tasia's dead."

Lewicki stepped back. The breeze carried street sounds through the open window. Abruptly he turned and leaned an ear toward the glass.

Vienna softened her glare. "Kel, if you won't do this for Tasia, do it for me."

He had gone as silent as a gargoyle. He held up a hand to quiet her.

"What?" she said.

He took out his phone. Before he could push any buttons, it rang. He turned his back on Jo and Vienna. "Lewicki."

Vienna put her hands on her hips, annoyed. Jo, feeling confused and curious, tried to catch her eye, but Vienna waved her off.

"Yeah, Bill. I'll have them take me straight to Grace Cathedral . . . what? No, just . . ." He looked out the window again. "Thought I heard something. Popping sound. But everything's all right?"

He listened, and snorted. "Call her Senate office. We'll go to the Hill ourselves when I get back." He beckoned Vienna. "I may need videoconferencing capability. Does that TV have a cable hookup for telepresence?"

He pointed at the plasma screen above the credenza. Vienna looked ready to slap his butt clean through the wall.

With a sharp knock, the receptionist opened the door. Dana Jean's easily surprised face looked unusually subdued. "Sorry to disturb you. Vienna, the car's here to take you to the service."

"All right."

Dana Jean left. Vienna crossed to the window and stared at Lewicki until he lowered the phone.

"I'm leaving you and Jo to your argument. I have my sister's funeral to attend." Her expression was piquant. "I'll be waiting at the church, with your boss, when you finish hashing this out. And you will." She stepped closer. "I'm short a pallbearer. I know you cared for Tasia. I need to find a man who can carry something heavy."

Vienna let her stare linger on Lewicki. He actually blanched. She turned and swept out the door, trailing the scent of roses.

Abashed, Lewicki glanced at Jo. He raised a finger, mouthed, *One minute*, and spoke into the phone. "Bill?"

He turned back to the window, speaking rapid-fire.

Steamed, Jo looked at the music on the conference table. She was close, she felt it, almost like she could touch the meaning with her fingertips. And Lewicki was close to walking out.

After me . . .

Chord progression. A minor. C major. A third chord, she couldn't decipher by sight. She put her fingers on the notes.

E major.

She stopped. "Oh Jesus."

She looked at the next line. The melody echoed the chord progression. The lyrics read, *He wants me . . .*

Beneath it was a D chord, followed by an E.

"Dead," Jo said.

Lewicki glanced at her, eyes guarded.

She picked up the sheet music. "I've solved the puzzle."

"What are you talking about?"

"Tasia wrote a code into these songs. The words are the setup, the question. The notes are the answers, the payoff." She put her index finger on the staff. "'After Me.' The chord progression. Look."

Lewicki did. "A minor, C, E." He looked up sharply. "What?"

"Ace." Jo scanned the next words. "'He wants me.'"

"Ace? What are you saying? Ace Chennault? Tasia's ghostwriter?"

"Yes. Look." Jo punched the sheet music. "The repetitive chord progression. It's not random. A-C-E, and then, every fourth measure, A-C-E . . ."

"With a rest, followed by another C."

"Ace C. Ace Chennault."

"He wants her? He was in love with her?" Lewicki said.

"No. Look at the chords." Jo's pulse was jumping in her veins. "D major, E major, A minor, D," Jo said. *He wants me . . .* "D-E-A-D."

Lewicki looked at her, perplexed. "This is the music Tasia left, with her 'If you read this, I've been assassinated' recording?"

"Yes."

Jo read further through the lyrics. *What's next? Who's next?*

The air seemed to brighten. She reread the notes she'd translated from A-B-C to Do-Re-Mi.

Re-Ti-Mi-Fa-La-Do.

374

Re. Ti. "R.T."

Mi. Fa. La. Do. Unfocus a bit, play loose with the spelling, and it became: M'Fa'la'd.

"R. T. McFarland," she said. "Robert Titus McFarland." She grabbed the music. "One thing? One reason — I got it. Tasia says in here that Ace Chennault wants her dead, and the president is next."

Lewicki looked at Jo like her hair had just sprouted snakes. Into the phone he said, "Hold on." He covered the receiver with his hand. "This is not a joke?"

She held up the music. He saw that she was not joking. Still, he looked skeptical. She grabbed the music for "Liar's Lullaby."

You say you love our land, you liar
Who dreams its end in blood and fire
Said you wanted me to be your choir
Help you build the funeral pyre.

But Robby T is not the One
All that's needed is the gun
Load the weapon, call his name
Unlock the door, he dies in shame.

This was a puzzle too. What was the key?

Jo looked at the top of the first measure, where Tasia had written "Counterpoint/Round." *Round, round, get around*. Melody, harmony, counterpoint, lyrics. *The truth is in my music.*

Counterpoint meant two contrasting melodies, combined. That much Jo remembered from Sister Dominica's music class. And round —

"Damn." Could it be as simple as that? As simple as "Frère Jacques" or "Row, Row, Row Your Boat"?

She scrawled the first verse on her scratch paper, triple-spacing. Then she wrote the second verse, interspersing its lines between those of the first. The alternating lines intertwined, and a new composition appeared: the lyrics as they'd be sung in a round.

> You say you love our land, you liar
> But Robby T is not the One
> Who dreams its end in blood and fire
> All that's needed is the gun
> Said you wanted me to be your choir
> Load the weapon, call his name
> Help you build the funeral pyre.
> Unlock the door, he dies in shame.

Jo looked at Lewicki. "It was an assassination plot. Tasia was supposed to set the president up to be killed."

Lewicki shook his head. "That's ridiculous."

"Read the goddamned words. 'You wanted me to be your choir, load the weapon, call his name, help *you* build the funeral pyre.' Jesus Christ, 'Unlock the door, he dies in shame' — she got McFarland alone in a hotel room in Virginia. That was supposed to be an opportunity for somebody to shoot the president. And she's saying the man who lured her into setting up the meeting is still out there."

Lewicki shook his head, but with less vehemence. "I think you're seeing what you want to see."

"No." She stepped toward him. "Vienna Hicks is a formidable woman. You know that full well. Her sister was equally formidable. Her bipolar disorder didn't make her any less intelligent or driven. And on the last night of her life, it came out in a flood of creativity." She spread her hands. "If she wasn't a powerhouse, do you think Robert McFarland would ever have married her?"

"Good point."

He took the music and the scratch paper from her. Slowly, as he read over it, he inhaled. "Why would she write it out in code?"

" 'Load the weapon' may refer to the Colt forty-five. Do you think she wanted to confess to being under the sway of some Rasputin who persuaded her to take a loaded gun to a meeting with the president?"

"What's the refrain mean?" he said. "It's got to mean something, right?"

She took the sheet music. She was so focused on reading the lyrics, it took a second before she realized: *He believes me.*

Look and see the way it ends
Who's the liar, where's the game
Love and death, it's all the same
Liar's words all end in pain

She focused. *Look and see the way it ends.* Ends . . .
She skipped to the final verse.

> I fell into your embrace
> Felt tears streaming down my face
> Fought the fight, ran the race
> Faltered, finally fell from grace.

She whispered the words. Fell into your embrace . . .
ran the race . . . face . . . grace . . .

All the same . . . "All the words end in 'ace,'" she
said. "Ace Chennault."

"Are you sure?"

Liar's words all end in pain.

"Pain," Jo said. "Christ. It's a reference to the guy
online who calls himself Tom Paine." She explained.
"He's a screed-master, whips extremists into a lather.
Tasia's saying that he's actually Ace Chennault."

Jo remembered Chennault in the hospital after Noel
Petty had brained him with a rock. "He has a tattoo
around his ankle. *Semper T* . . . 'Always —'"

"Fuck," Lewicki said. "Fuck me to shitting hell and
back. *Sic semper tyrannis?*"

"What's wrong?"

He pulled out his phone. "It's what John Wilkes
Booth shouted after he shot Abraham Lincoln."

378

CHAPTER
FIFTY-THREE

Ivory sideswiped a parked Toyota, bounced off with a screech, and rebounded into a mailbox. She could barely see for the screaming in her head.

Porky Pig was down. She'd shot him. Shot the bastard in the face.

Leaving the sideswiped Toyota and the mailbox behind, she gunned the car into a parking garage. Ninety seconds, and she'd taken out a rice burner and a Gub symbol. Score three. She was on a roll.

She jammed the car into a disabled space, grabbed her bag, and jumped out. She ran into the building, some kind of office, and into the women's room.

She stripped off her glass-spattered sweater and stuffed it into the trash. She put on her Blue Eagle Security uniform shirt. Trying to button it, she felt like an old woman playing a washboard in a jug band, her hands were shaking so hard.

Shot Porky. Shot him *down*.

She brushed safety-glass chips from her glorious white hair. No turning back now. She pulled on the helmet and shades, and slammed through the women's room door. She stormed out of the office building and headed downhill, back to the skyscraper on Sacramento where the Gub Suburban was waiting.

She sent Keyes a text. *Go.*

The new world was about to come into being.

The text message arrived while Ace Chennault was in line at a busy Hertz office near Union Square. His windbreaker covered the Blue Eagle Security shirt. To the other people in the queue, he looked like a guy with a sports bag, shuffling up to the counter. He didn't look like a man loitering in public, waiting for instructions. He didn't look like a suspicious character, the kind the Secret Service would zero in on.

He read Keyes's message. *It's go.*

The address was beneath that. Chennault felt his world expand.

Tasia had received letters from the law firm at that address, Waymire & Fong. Her sister worked there. He'd rifled through those letters, early on, hoping to unearth scraps of usable intelligence.

He stepped out of line and casually walked out. If anybody noticed him, if they caught a glimpse of his face, clothing, anything, they quickly forgot, excited by the chance to move forward an extra two feet in the line. Sheeple. Nobody had commented on the blue cast that covered his left wrist. With his baggy windbreaker, it was virtually unnoticeable.

He strode toward Sacramento Street. The wind felt bracing. With his good hand, he texted Ivory. *Waymire & Fong. Vienna Hicks.*

He signed it, *Paine*. Ace Chennault was a ghostwriter, and a ghost. Paine was Revolution, its spirit and its fuse.

He picked up his pace. This day hadn't been in his original outline. But he'd had to work around the failure of Plan A.

Tasia had been Plan A. And her death had to be seen as a sacrifice. The sheeple who listened to talk radio and watched Edie Wilson and swallowed the hyperbolic nectar written at Tree of Liberty believed Tasia's death to be a political murder.

And, in a perverse way, it was. The faithful saw Tasia's death as a crucifixion. To them she was a martyr. But Tasia hadn't been Christ. She'd been Judas.

The conspiracy theorists believed Tasia had died because she knew too much about the McFarland administration. In fact, she had died because she knew too much about the plans of people scheming to bring down the McFarland administration.

And today the hardest of the hard-core True Americans were ready to storm the Gub, on Paine's orders. He inhaled. God almighty, power felt good.

He leaned into the wind and set his face in the buffoonishly pleasant mask that defined Ace Chennault. It was the face that had gotten people to sign up for his services as an insurance agent. It was the affable look that won him freelance gigs for current affairs and music magazines. It was the happy fanboy face that had persuaded Tasia to accept him as a music journalist and eventually her ghostwriter.

And he was a hell of a writer. He had a legitimate career, with years of publication credits. But words could never surpass his political performance art. His most recent jobs had been quiet masterpieces. Hacking into a federal appeals court justice's cell phone to plant texts and photos from underage hookers. That got international weapons smuggling charges against a military contractor dismissed. Sending newspaper cuttings to an investigative journalist whose little boy was undergoing treatment for leukemia — stories about tragic cases in which the wrong medications had been administered and killed fragile hospital patients. That persuaded the journo to quash his investigation into links between a fundamentalist megachurch and private paramilitaries in Central America.

Subtlety had its uses.

But subtlety was mainly useful for putting money in the bank. Political violence was poetry, and Chennault was possibly the richest poet in America because his work paid big cash. That cash would finance his escape to the sunny climes where, after today, he would need to hide out for a decade or so.

Fear trilled through his stomach. He would go abroad, as Thomas Paine had done. He would take refuge while True America's patriots fought to cleanse and restore the nation.

But he wouldn't be a coward. Today, subtlety had run out of uses. He'd tried that with Tasia, had worked on it for fourteen long goddamned months, only to see her crumble in the face of the Usurper's hypnotic power.

Plan A had failed. And if Plan B failed today, none of his precautions or insurance policies could save him. He had records of the meeting at which the mission's parameters and his fee had been arranged. He had photos and credit card records from his trip, and a password-protected recording of the meeting stashed on his computer and in a safe deposit box. He had matchbooks from that truck stop in Hoback, Wyoming. But none of that could protect him now. He'd taken half his fee up front. He'd put the plan into motion. Keyes and Ivory were involved. And, above all, he knew everything. Fail, and he'd be silenced for good. Mercs, a hit man, government agents acting under official orders — somebody would kill him.

Through rising anxiety, Chennault maintained the cheery buffoon mask and walked toward Sacramento Street. An open-air, double-decker tour bus gargled past. The driver was droning an amplified travelogue to a mob of Chinese tourists. *That* was soon going to stop.

Fourteen months he'd worked with Tasia. When he had been hired for this assignment, he at first thought it would be impossible. The mission parameters were strict: Robert McFarland must exit the White House. He must leave in such a way that he could never return. His legacy must be tainted forever. This must be accomplished by embroiling him in a major scandal involving his ex-wife.

Chennault had not been instructed on how to accomplish these goals. But he had been told that Fawn Tasia McFarland was bipolar with paranoid tendencies, sometimes hypersexual, sometimes suicidal, and in possession of a handgun legally registered to the president. The poetic details had been left up to him, though the phrase "murder-suicide" was mentioned more than once.

So for fourteen months, Chennault had worked on Tasia. And she had been so intense, so eager to listen to him, that he had come to think she was the real thing: a renegade, a Madonna who had lived inside the jackal's tent and escaped to tell the truth.

Fourteen months. He had convinced her of Big Pharma's mission to tranquilize the populace on behalf of the Gub, and so she'd quit taking her medication. Once she did, her creativity and huge animal energy had roared to the fore. So too had her paranoia. As in earlier times when her mania was uncontrolled, she was easily convinced that Robert McFarland had destroyed her health and happiness — and had never apologized for it. And then, when she inevitably crashed into depression, Chennault had given Tasia a doctor's name. *Forget about the mood stabilizer — ask him for Prozac. Live with passion and commitment, but not the blues.*

Send her into orbit, that had been Chennault's goal. Agitate her. Agitation was a risk factor for suicide. Turn her into the energizer bunny of mania. In that condition, Tasia had been ready to help bring down the false god that was devouring Washington.

Chennault convinced her that McFarland needed to own up to the terrible choices he had forced her to make during their marriage. Contact him, he told her. Tell him you're writing an autobiography. He'll meet with you — he'll be desperate to know what you're

384

writing. And when you get him alone, force him to beg forgiveness for leaving you lonely and depressed while he was deployed overseas.

Oh . . . and reserve connecting hotel rooms. That way, Chennault said, he could record everything McFarland admitted to, in crisp stereo sound, through the connecting door.

Tasia had asked: *And if he refuses to talk?*

You know how to make him speak honestly, Chennault answered. *Bring the gun. McFarland won't possibly balk if you threaten suicide.*

You're an artist, he told her. *And the Colt .45 is a showstopper. He'll talk.*

So Tasia reserved connecting rooms at the Reston Hyatt. Chennault hid in the second room. He told her to wait until the Secret Service left the room before unlocking the connecting door, so he could "protect" her if McFarland called the agents back in.

That was the key to everything: the unlocked door. It was the only way he could gain access, shoot McFarland and Tasia, and escape out the window.

She was the perfect scapegoat. But she'd betrayed him.

"Bitch," he said.

Tasia had been a vector, a subtlety, beyond all dreaming. She had become gloriously enraged at McFarland. She had been wild with pain and eager to force him to apologize for their marriage.

But she didn't carry through. At the last minute, when McFarland arrived, she kept the connecting door locked. Chennault had been helpless. Then she left the

Hyatt and returned to her D.C. hotel. The next morning she climbed aboard the tour bus and continued on the *Bad Dogs and Bullets* tour. And the jackal had gone back to the White House and continued subverting the country.

McFarland had mesmerized Tasia, and reclaimed her. He had probably taken her sexually, too. Chennault swallowed, nauseated at the image.

And then Tasia had shut him out. She had refused to see him. She had ignored his calls. When he went to her house the night before the San Francisco concert, she'd had the gall to send her pussy-whipped dog, Searle Lecroix, to shoo him away.

Noel Michael Petty, at least, had seen to Lecroix. Things were not totally out of balance.

Tasia had obviously realized that he had intended harm to the president. She had become a loose, loud, unmedicated cannon. He could not have let her live.

But no evidence existed that he had gone to Reston, Virginia. All his discussions with Tasia had been one-on-one, and the only recording devices present had been the ones he had secretly planted. And he'd always used a jammer to detect bugs and wreck cell phone reception. He was in the clear.

And that left him an open field on which to run today. He had two loyal soldiers in Ivory and Keyes. They would do what he asked. He had no doubts — he'd been given dossiers on them, as potential recruits, before he put this project into action.

And didn't he have a perfect stage today.

386

He turned the corner onto Sacramento. Granite and glass skyscrapers lined the street. He had a clear view downhill to the office tower beyond the corner with Montgomery. He slowed. Despite pedestrians and heavy cross traffic, he could see a black Suburban parked outside at the curb. Sunlight kicked off its windshield.

Chennault sent Keyes a text. *Now.*

He inhaled the diesel fumes of the nation's decay. *Steady*, he told himself. He kept his eyes on the vehicle parked outside the office building.

Wait. One black Suburban.

He picked up his pace. Elbowed a man in the side as he strode past. Cross traffic blocked his view, red Muni buses, yellow cabs, pedestrians in kaleidoscope colors.

Just one Suburban. Not a fleet. And no police motorcycle escort loitering around, either. The sound of sirens bounced off the buildings in the wind. He hurried down the street.

Don't run, Ivory told herself. She was breathless, had tunnel vision. The office building was dead ahead.

Parked across the street from it, directly opposite the black Gub Suburban, was a Blue Eagle Security armored car. Keyes climbed out from behind the wheel.

He was wearing his helmet, company issue, which looked like a motorcycle helmet with a clear faceplate. He frowned at her.

"Have you been running?" He turned his head. "What's with the sirens?"

She pushed past him and climbed into the cab. "I kicked it off. We can't wait."

"What did you do?"

She pulled the secure aluminum carry-case from the front seat.

Keyes grabbed her arm. "Ivory."

"One less porker to get in our way."

She handed him the secure case. With it, they'd look exactly like security company guards making a cash delivery. Keyes stared at her with shock.

Then he buckled down. "Send any messages now, because the jammer will freak out both text and voice calls."

"I've said all I need to say. Leave the keys in the ignition for Paine. He'll be here, ready to drive when we come out."

Keyes glanced across the street. "Just one Suburban."

"This is where Tasia's sister works. The president's here. He's visiting family. Who else could it be?"

They crossed the street to the building. Waymire & Fong was on the fifth floor.

CHAPTER
FIFTY-FOUR

Lewicki punched a number on his phone. He threw a fierce gaze at Jo.

"*Sic semper tyrannis*. Booth shouted it after he jumped from the president's box to the stage at Ford's Theatre. This guy Chennault is an assassination groupie."

He spoke into the phone. "Bill, we have a problem. It . . ." He pulled the phone from his ear. "Dammit. Cut me off. What —" He punched the number again.

The screams came from the lobby.

Keyes was first out of the elevator but Ivory raced past him across the law firm lobby, straight at the receptionist sitting behind the desk.

The woman was on the phone. She looked up. Her eyes registered confusion. She was seeing a man and a woman from Blue Eagle Security, dressed in their armored-car driver uniforms, wearing the regulation motorcycle helmets with clear faceplates. Carrying the silver case they always did whenever they went into a bank or brokerage to pick up cash.

But Blue Eagle Security drivers didn't usually open the secure case and pull out weapons. And they never aimed those weapons at wide-eyed receptionists whose mouths were hanging open.

Keyes extended the stock on the MAC-10 machine pistol. Ivory shoved the Desert Eagle into her waistband and picked up the Glock.

Before the receptionist could rise halfway out of her seat, Ivory charged the desk and raised the butt of the gun like a club. The receptionist shrieked like a fool. Ivory leaped over the desk and battered the girl from her chair with the Glock. Then she lifted the receiver on the phone bank and activated all the lights, jamming the system.

The receptionist crawled away screaming, crabbed to her feet, and ran down the hall.

"Lock the elevators," Ivory told Keyes. "Is the cell phone jammer working?"

She felt unleashed, fully human for the first time in years, ready to wreak scary hell on all these sheeple.

She racked the slide on the Glock. "Let's find him."

Jo turned toward the open conference room door. Lewicki paused, gripping his phone like a grenade.

More screams, a woman's voice. Distant, muffled by walls and carpet, a man shouted, "On the floor."

Jo rushed to the door. In the hall people were running. Lewicki came up beside her and slammed the door.

From the lobby the man shouted, "This is the New American Revolution. We are watering the tree of liberty."

The gunfire was loud and sudden. Jo jumped. Screams furrowed the air. Footsteps pounded in the hall.

Jo reached into her pocket for her phone. It wasn't there.

She'd left it in her purse in Vienna's office. She ran to the credenza and grabbed the office phone. She got a circuits-busy sound.

Lewicki eased the door open an inch. Jo saw lawyers and assistants rushing into offices, crashing into walls and potted plants and each other. More shots, deeper and closer. The screaming was intense. Lewicki shut the door and grabbed a chair. Before he could jam it under the knob, the door burst open.

He swung a fist, hard. He hit Dana Jean in the nose. She bounced against the wall. Lewicki cocked his arm again, but Dana Jean covered her nose with one hand and slugged him back with the other. "Son of a bitch."

Jo jumped between them. "She works here."

Behind her came a portly attorney, glasses askew on his face. He barreled through the door. Lewicki slammed it and jammed the chair under the handle.

"They're shooting at people." The man was in his late fifties, an African American who looked like he was ten seconds from a heart attack. And five seconds from running back into the hall to grab his colleagues.

Lewicki pushed him away from the door. "How many?"

Another shot. Dana Jean squealed.

Lewicki pointed at Jo. "Shut her up."

The attorney put his arm around Dana Jean. "Who the hell —"

"All of you, be quiet," Lewicki said.

The attorney straightened his glasses. "I'm Howell Waymire. This is my firm." He pointed at the door. "Those are my friends out there, and they're being shot at like dogs."

"How many shooters?" Lewicki said.

Dana Jean fought not to sob. "A man and a woman with crazy white hair."

Lewicki blinked. "White?"

"As soap. They're wearing Blue Eagle Security uniforms. Armored car drivers. They pulled guns out of their briefcase." She stuck her fingers in her mouth. She was shaking like a loose wheel.

Down the hall a door was kicked open. "Where's the president?"

Lewicki looked confounded by Dana Jean's description of the attackers. He tried his phone again. Hung up. "Nothing. They're jamming the cell phones."

"*Where is he?*"

A woman screamed, "Who?"

The shot was deep and carried the sound of finality. Dana Jean jumped and cringed against Waymire's lapels.

"Why do they think the president is here?" she said.

Waymire looked at Lewicki. "I know who you are."

Another door was kicked open, closer. Jo's throat constricted. The walls themselves seemed to constrict. Claustrophobia crawled over her skin.

"Where's the president?" the man bellowed. "Take me to him or I'll shoot you."

His voice was deep and backwoodsy. It was not Ace Chennault.

Waymire stepped toward the door. "We have to get out of here."

Dana Jean grabbed his sleeve. "No. They jammed the elevator doors open and put chains on the fire stairs. The woman's guarding the lobby."

Sweat beaded Waymire's forehead. "We don't have phones, we can't call for help. We have to do something."

In response, Lewicki picked up the phone on the credenza, though Jo had already tried it. He seemed to believe things only when he did them himself.

Dana Jean said, "They don't know we're in here. We'll hide."

Jo no longer heard fleeing footsteps or screams outside. Nobody from the firm was left in the hall. The conference room felt like a shrinking cardboard box. And the shooters were working their way toward it.

The chair jammed under the doorknob wouldn't stop them. "They'll shoot through the door," she said.

Lewicki turned to the conference table. "Barricade. Come on."

He picked up one end of the conference table, his neck and shoulders bulging with the strain. Jo and the others added their muscle and they dragged the table to the door. Waymire shoved it hard against the wood.

He winced. His face had gone gray and sweaty. He put a hand to his chest, swiped at the table for support, and sank to his knees. Jo's throat turned papery. He actually had been ten seconds from a heart attack. And now he was having it.

Ivory marched down the hall, blood ringing in her ears. She hadn't shot these law firm fools in the head because she needed them to talk. But if they didn't stop screaming, she was going to open up on them.

Where the hell was McFarland?

She reached the end of the hall and turned the corner, ran to the far side of the building, saw Keyes coming toward her. He booted open an office door and fired a volley inside. Glass shattered and a man begged for his life.

"Where is he?" Keyes bellowed.

Ivory turned in a circle. At the end of the hall was a closed door. CONFERENCE ROOM.

"This way," she said.

Waymire slumped to the floor. Dana Jean grabbed his arm. "What's wrong?"

"Pain." He gasped for breath. The beds of his fingernails were blue.

Jo knelt beside him. "Hold on." She loosened his tie. "Anybody have an aspirin?" No one replied. She helped him to lie down beneath the conference table. She could do little else. He needed an ambulance.

The whole place did.

Lewicki ducked beneath the table. "Come on. Everybody under."

Dana Jean scooted beneath it.

Jo caught Lewicki's eye. "The table won't stop rounds from automatic weapons, will it?"

He hesitated. "Maybe the first couple."

In the hall, a man shouted, "Surrender the president or be executed for treason."

Jo eyed the door. Certainty pealed through her. The attackers would blow off the lock, then keep shooting. And if they could kick open the door even two inches, they'd have an angle to fire into the room. It would be open season.

Dana Jean clutched her knees. "We're trapped. There's no way out."

Jo turned to the windows. "Yes, there is."

CHAPTER
FIFTY-FIVE

Gabe drove through heavy traffic on Sansome, inching past smoked-glass skyscrapers and neoclassical bank buildings toward Sacramento Street. The stereo was blasting Elvis Costello, "Complicated Shadows." For the first time in twenty-four hours, he felt that his head was above water. It was raging white water, to be sure, but he could breathe, and was swimming for shore.

He'd reach it. Jo was there.

At the corner, traffic clogged completely. Down Sacramento he saw trucks, a police car, buses. He cruised past the corner. Of course traffic was a mess — the White House chief of staff was at Waymire & Fong. He circled the block. Halfway around, he spotted an alley. He cut through and came out not far from the Waymire building.

When he stopped, he heard sirens.

Jo's heart jumped high and hard into her throat. She ran to the window and muscled it farther open. The noise of the city flowed in. Distantly she heard sirens.

Lewicki sounded incredulous. "Are you going to throw paper airplanes with *Help* written on them? Get down. Stand there and your head might as well be a watermelon on a pike."

Outside the barricaded door, a woman cried, "Keyes, over here."

The doorknob turned and the door jiggled. Dana Jean squealed. Crouching low, Jo hurried to the conference table. Beneath it, Waymire put a hand to his chest.

"Pain . . . crushing," he said.

"Hang in."

The attackers thumped against the door.

Lewicki gave Jo a pitiless bull terrier stare. "Get your ass under the table and brace it."

"No. We'll never hold them off. We have to escape."

Lewicki opened his mouth to bark at her but Jo grabbed him by the necktie. "We can climb down to the floor below."

"What if there are more of them outside?"

Jo got right in his face. "There are more. Ace Chennault is not here with them. He's someplace else."

"I —"

"And he's going to try to kill the president."

Lewicki flinched, but briefly, as if she'd poked him in the eye. He had bigger worries than the president. Namely, his own ass.

With thunder and splinters, the doorknob blew off. It clattered across the tabletop. The blast created a ragged hole in the door. Cordite stank in the air.

Jo held tight to Lewicki's tie. "We have to get out. Waymire's going to die otherwise. Nobody but you and I know that Chennault's gunning for President

McFarland. And the shooters are going to bust the door down in a matter of minutes."

Lewicki looked angrier, and more disbelieving, than any man she'd ever seen.

Her skittering heart beat in her ears. "We have to escape — to save ourselves, and the president. I have to climb down to the floor below."

They heard a hand working to pull apart the broken doorknob assembly. Then grunts and a shoulder slamming into the door.

The shooter yelled, "We know you're in there, McFarland. Surrender or everybody dies."

They heard metal ratchet against metal, then a slap. Somebody had inserted a full magazine of ammunition into a big weapon. Jo's nerves tried to jump out of her pores. The urge to flee felt so powerful, she could barely hold herself to the floor.

She clutched Lewicki's shoulder. "Help me."

Lewicki looked like a dog with a bone in his teeth. He was fighting to hold on to the notion that he was in control, that things would be determined by his command.

Then he said, "I'll hold them off."

Jo squeezed his shoulder. Staying low, she ran to the window, leaned out, and looked down. The view was nauseating: a five-story vertical drop to concrete.

Behind her, she heard a sawing sound. The barrel of an automatic weapon was being wedged into the door frame as leverage.

The window ledge was eight inches wide. The building's Art Deco design offered her corners and cracks and juts, but the fourth-floor window was ten feet down, recessed in solid stone casements. And the wall directly below her was a flat, virtually featureless surface.

She took a breath. Free climb it? *Holy shit.*

She had to find a rope. Then she could get down to the fourth floor. After that Lewicki could lower Dana Jean and Waymire, one at a time, and she could pull them in. Hook their belts to the rope, or use nylons as a swami belt, something.

She scurried to the credenza. Inside — thank you, god of chaos — was the cable for the audio-visual system. It was heavy black television cable, wound around a wooden spool.

She yanked the spool out. She needed maybe ninety feet of cable. If she couldn't get inside the fourth-floor window she'd have to keep going down the side of the building, so she wanted plenty of extra rope. Cable. Life.

The long barrel of an automatic weapon squirmed through the slit in the door, working up and down like an obscene appendage.

The credenza was a single piece of ornately carved wood, undoubtedly from some endangered old-growth forest. Its feet were three inches thick. The whole thing probably weighed two hundred pounds. Jo tied off the cable on the credenza's feet and threw the spool out the window. It unfurled and disappeared over the ledge, the cable hitting the side of the building with a sound like a dull whip.

She waved to Lewicki. "Come here."

He crawled over. She whipped the cable around his back. Then she had him spread his hands and grab the cable at two points.

"Put your feet against the wall under the window. Lean back and anchor the cable."

If the feet of the credenza ripped off under the strain of carrying her weight and the cable came free, he would have to stop her from plummeting.

"What are you going to do?" he said.

She tested the flexibility of the cable. She hoped she was right about it.

"Body rappel."

She said it without any spit in her mouth. She'd never body rappelled on a real pitch. She'd done it at the climbing gym, a few meters off the mats. Almost nobody did it anymore, because they now used what she would have given her front teeth for, a harness, a belay device, and a 'biner. And nobody, even in the days of classic Alpinism, had rappelled with CATV cable.

"It'll go. I think." She breathed. "I can climb it. If I get over the ledge and rappel about six feet, I can chimney down the window casement below."

Lewicki inched over to the window. "You'll fall."

"No, I won't."

Her guardian angel shot her a salute and said, *Good luck with that, honey. You're on your own.*

Behind her at the door came kicking, grunting, boots hitting the wood. "Give him to us, fuckers, or you're the first to face the patriots' firing squad."

Jo eyed Lewicki. "You ever body rappel in the army?"

"It's been twenty years, but yeah."

"Good." She squeezed his arm. "Please don't let go."

"I won't." He looked dead serious.

The gunshot echoed through the room. It pounded the conference table and wood flew everywhere. Lewicki flinched.

"Hurry," he said.

Jo took off her shoes and scrambled onto the windowsill. The wind caught her. The blue sky and shining canyon walls of the city should have exhilarated her. This should have been a safe climber's naughty dream: the chance to scale an urban monolith. But she'd never felt so vulnerable. Inside the conference room, Lewicki braced his legs against the wall beneath the window and leaned back, ready to take her weight.

Jo called to Dana Jean. "Watch what I do. You're next."

"Okay." Dana Jean's face crumpled. "No."

Jo's stomach cramped, but Dana Jean didn't know how to rappel and this was no time to learn. "Buckle your belt around your waist *and* the cable. We'll figure a way to lower you while you hold on." To Lewicki, she said, "Don't put her on the cable until I tell you I'm safe and can anchor her."

Jo wriggled under the open sash window and stood up on the narrow ledge. Delicately she turned to face the window and conference room. She slid her feet apart and jammed them against either side of the window casement to brace herself.

She was straddling the cable where it hung out the window. She picked it up and held it so it ran between her legs. She reached behind her, grabbed the cable, slung it around her right hip, brought it up across her chest diagonally, and tossed it over her left shoulder. It draped over her back. She reached behind her with her right hand — now her brake hand — and grabbed the dangling part. She held it near her hip.

The friction created by the S-shaped rappel configuration would allow her to control the pace of her descent with one hand. She'd done it before. She'd do it now.

She inched back. Inside, Waymire and Lewicki stared at her. Her palms were sweaty.

"Now," she said.

Lewicki braced.

She leaned back, putting her weight on the cable. It tightened and held. She leaned back farther, and farther, and inched her feet back and over the edge.

Holy living Christ.

She'd never felt heights, and the smooth blankness of a stone face, as pure vacancy before. Her legs locked and wouldn't move. She shut her eyes.

I have to do this. If I go back in there, I'll die from a gunshot blast to the head. And so will all of them.

Her right hand squeaked against the black rubberized casing of the cable. She began inching her feet down the wall. Leaned back farther. Bent her legs a little from the hips. The cable bit into her butt, her chest, her shoulder. Her palm.

"Hold me."

"I got you," Lewicki said. His voice was breathless with effort.

Trust, she said. If the cable failed, or Lewicki failed, she'd only experience a single second of fear. And a single second to repent her sins before she hit the concrete.

The window ledge was hard. Her feet scraped on the stone. She leaned back, beyond forty-five degrees, and lowered herself completely over the edge.

She was hanging off the side of the building.

Just breathe. She pushed off and let the cable slide through her palm. Slipped down. Her feet swung back against the building. She pushed off again and let out more cable. Bounced down six inches. A foot. Two feet.

The stone was polished granite and too smooth against her feet. Above her the cable squeezed tight against the window ledge, as if pressed against the blade of a knife. Overhead, clouds fled across the blue sky, almost screaming in the wind. Her hair whipped into her eyes and mouth.

Dana Jean yelled, "Jo, they're coming. *Go*."

The cable was stretched so tight that it looked attenuated. She pointed her toes down, seeking. Seeking — and found the top of the window casement below her.

From above, the cable went slack. She dropped abruptly, loose in the air. Two feet, three . . . Oh God, had the cable come loose? *Christ* —

She jerked to a stop. The cable bit into her flesh. Her feet lost their purchase on the wall and she slapped against the building.

"Jesus," she gasped.

She scrambled to get her feet flat against the wall again. "Hang on to the cable. Please." *Please God Jesus Mother Mary please.*

Above, a blast echoed. Dana Jean screamed and began sobbing. Jo looked up. Lewicki was leaning out the window, staring down at her.

Behind her, a window in a building across the street screeched open. "Christ, lady, what are you doing?"

On Sacramento Street, Chennault approached the Blue Eagle Security armored car. He opened the door. The keys were in the ignition.

The Doppler pounding of sirens grew higher pitched. Down at the corner, two black-and-white SFPD units swerved into sight, lights booming.

Above him, a man shouted what sounded like a warning. Chennault looked up.

"Lady, what the hell?"

Five stories up, a man was leaning out a window, waving and pointing across the street. Chennault turned toward the Waymire & Fong building.

A grunt escaped him. High up the Waymire building, rappelling down the side like a crazy spider on a piece of string, was Jo Beckett.

He might have been punched in the diaphragm. She was clearly in desperate straits. But just as clearly, Keyes and Ivory had not finished things inside. The situation was out of control.

Chennault scanned the scene on the street. A black Suburban was parked at the curb, but without police escort. No, the police were all screaming this way, right now.

The president wasn't here. If he was, the street would have been crawling with men wearing earpieces and dark glasses, carrying shotguns.

Keyes and Ivory had attacked somebody else.

For a second, Chennault felt his plan dissolving into sand. Then he thought: No. This was an opportunity. It was risky, but he was past the point of caution now.

The police cars pulled up. He walked toward them.

The cable stretched with a rubbery sound. Jo's sticky palm stuck to it. She gaped at Lewicki. Why had he let go of the cable?

Across the street, the man shouted, "Holy crap, haul her back in!"

Lewicki's eyes were wide. "I thought you'd fallen."

Speechless, near panic, she sped up her descent. Her knees cleared the top of the fourth-floor window casement. Then her hips, her waist, her chest. She inched down, hearing the cable begin to whine. What was she trusting her life to, coaxial cable, or fiber? Glass? *Sand?* She pushed off with her feet once again and let the cable slide through her hand, humming and squeaking. She slid down far enough to get her entire body inside the window casement.

She wedged herself into the casement and turned sideways. Feet against one side, back against the other. Now that she was so close to safety, she began to hyperventilate. She held her breath. She chimneyed down, inch by inch, and set her feet on the narrow fourth-floor windowsill.

"I'm on the sill," she yelled. "But I'm not inside yet."

The window was locked. Inside was an open-plan office. Desks, potted ferns. In the distance, people huddled around a copier.

She pounded on the glass. "Help. Let me in."

Looking up in surprise, two men rushed to the window and opened it. "What the hell?"

Jo climbed in and hopped down from the sill. "Call the police."

They simply gaped. She realized nobody was panicking. People were at their desks. The air-conditioning was on and the ceiling was solid concrete. They couldn't hear anything from upstairs.

"Gun attack at Waymire and Fong," she said.

A man said, "You're serious?"

"No, I always rappel down the sides of buildings in a black suit for the freaking hell of it. Call the goddamned cops."

The men flinched. Then they all heard, through the open window, the wail of sirens.

"People are trapped upstairs. We have to help them get down like I did."

Jo still had the cable wound around her body in the rappelling configuration. Her shaking right hand had cramped around it. She couldn't let go.

From above came Dana Jean's voice, on the edge of frenzy. "I'm coming, Jo, hang on to the rope. Oh God. Hang on to it."

406

Jo turned. Outside the window the cable swung against the glass.

"No, don't — wait!" Jo shouted. "Lewicki, no, the cable's not anchored."

An instant later Dana Jean plummeted past the window, buckled to the cable by her belt, hanging on like Tarzan.

Oh, shit.

The cable went rigid. The tension caught Jo, with the cable still wrapped around her, and jerked her toward the window. Automatically, out of reflex, she held tight.

She slammed against the window. Dana Jean jerked to a halt in midair, screaming like a factory whistle.

Twelve feet below the window, Dana Jean hung like a banana. Only her belt was holding her up on the cable. What the hell had she tried to do, cinch the belt over the cable and Batman down the side of the building, hand over fist? With one end of the cable secured to the credenza in the conference room above and the other end wrapped around Jo, Dana Jean had fallen like a sack of beans and wrenched to a stop. Spinning, she flailed, her face red and suffused with terror.

Her weight pinned Jo against the window. And if Jo undid the body rappel and let go, the cable would fly out the window and dump Dana Jean loose. She'd fall.

Breathlessly, Jo called to the men in the office. "Help me."

CHAPTER
FIFTY-SIX

On Sacramento Street, cops pulled up in black-and-whites. Several rushed into the Waymire building. One blocked traffic. Another began clearing people from the street. He waved at Chennault and pointed at the Blue Eagle Security armored car.

"Move your vehicle, sir."

Chennault pointed at the Waymire offices. "Officer, look."

Between the third and fourth floor, a young woman hung like a rag doll tied with the pull cord for a window shade.

"It's a terror attack," Chennault said. "She's trying to escape."

The cop reached for his radio.

Chennault pointed emphatically. "There's one of the terrorists."

Clearly visible at the fourth-floor window was Jo Beckett. Her dark hair flew around her head in the wind. She was hauling on the rope that held the young woman.

"She's trying to kill her," Chennault said. "Do something."

The cop spoke urgently into his radio. Then he turned again to Chennault. "Have you seen anything else?"

He pointed at Beckett. "Saw that woman waiting for the elevator when I was coming out of the building. She had an accomplice. A man. Tall guy, Latino."

The cop stared up at Beckett. "Thanks. Now get out of here. It isn't safe."

Chennault nodded. As the cop jogged across the street, he climbed into the cab of the armored car. Of course they'd believed him. He was inherently credible — a member of the security community. He started the big engine and pulled out.

Pinned against the fourth-floor window by Dana Jean's hanging weight, Jo gripped the cable with all her might.

"Jesus, help," she yelled. "Pull her up."

The men from the office reached around Jo, leaned out the window, and grabbed the cable. They pulled. Dana Jean hit the building, still screaming. She scrabbled like a rat, grabbed the ledge of the third-floor windowsill below them, and pulled herself onto it.

"Take the back end of the cable and anchor it," Jo said. "Let me get loose."

That had been a freaking close call. Dana Jean should never have jumped. Lewicki should have stopped her. Angry words rolled toward Jo's lips, but before she could speak, a gunshot overhead shattered the conference room window. One of the men in the office with her turned and ran.

The cable outside thrashed — somebody was rappelling down. Jo couldn't see who, but Dana Jean could, and her face was tense but hopeful. It was Lewicki. Jo held on to the cable to anchor him.

She heard Lewicki's shoes hit the wall of the building, heard him puff with effort. The cable flailed. His feet came into view.

Gunfire erupted again, this time in the clear air outside. Dana Jean cringed on the sill. One of the attackers was leaning out the conference room window to fire down at Lewicki.

The attacker yelled, "Where's McFarland?"

It was the man. Jo could barely breathe — Lewicki was absolutely exposed, with no chance to reach the fourth-floor window before being shot.

But in a remarkably steady voice he cried, "Stop shooting and I'll tell you."

For a moment the air seemed to still. The attacker had paused to consider Lewicki's words.

Then voices shouted, desperate. The cable whipped back and forth. Lewicki's legs scissored and he hit the building. The attacker screamed. A gun dropped past the window.

And both men swung into view.

Lewicki had come unwound from the body rappel but was gripping the cable like a bell ringer. The attacker, a muscular man with a flat, terrified face, was hanging by his fingers from Lewicki's belt.

Lewicki had pulled the man out the window. He'd tried to pitch him to the ground, but the attacker had managed to claw his hands under Lewicki's belt. They spun, entwined. Lewicki's face was desperate. Struggling under the burden of the attacker's weight, he was slowly sliding down the cable. He fought to get his feet onto the windowsill.

He locked eyes with Jo. For an instant, the look on his face was shock. Then he seemed to realize that she, and she alone, could pull him onto the sill. Beneath fear and eagerness, unreadable emotion swam in his eyes.

The attacker was trying to crawl up Lewicki's back. He looked like a drowning man who pulls the lifeguard under. Jo reached out the window. But before she could grab Lewicki, the attacker's ferocious momentum swung the cable against the building. Lewicki's hands cracked against granite.

The attacker grabbed Lewicki's left arm. The sudden addition of weight pulled Lewicki's left hand off the cable. Lewicki scrambled, but certainty flashed in his eyes. His right hand lost its grip.

They fell, arms windmilling.

Dana Jean screamed, "*No.*"

Jo's breath left her like she'd been punched. She squeezed her eyes shut.

Dana Jean shrieked again. The cable vibrated. Jo opened her eyes.

A woman stood outside the window on the sill in front of her.

She was pale, with a smoker's worn skin. Her lipstick was the color of ice. In the wind her white hair flew around her head like an electrical storm. She hadn't rappelled but had simply slid down the cable. She wore a blue uniform shirt and had two guns jammed in her belt. Stenciled on the big one, in front of Jo's face, were the words DESERT EAGLE.

"Holy fuck."

Jo scrambled free of the body rappel. The woman ducked under the window and jumped off the sill into the office. She drew the Desert Eagle from her belt.

Jo, the men, even the air in the room, fled.

Heedless, running like panicked deer, they careered across the office. Two men, acting out of habit, aimed for the elevator. Jo heard the metallic *shrick* of a slide being racked on a pistol.

All the hairs on her head jumped to attention. She pinned her eyes on the big red EXIT sign over the fire door. She crashed through it just as she heard a deep gunshot behind her.

The men screamed. She bolted down the stairs. She didn't think she could take any more of this. But her legs didn't pay attention, and kept going.

The cops were outside. That meant the cops might be in the lobby too. They were four flights down. With every raggedy step she took, they came closer.

The stairwell door above her slammed open. Her world seemed to flare white. She heard footsteps and phlegmy breathing. She passed the third floor, and the second, heard metal scrape concrete as the shooter knocked the gun against the wall. She thought she was going to pee herself.

She reached the ground floor, threw open the fire door, and sprinted barefoot along a forty-yard-long hall toward the marble lobby. She heard a police voice shouting information to his colleagues. *Thank God, oh thank God.*

"Multiple shots fired. Suspect is a white woman with long brown hair, wearing a black suit. Armed and extremely dangerous."

What?

"I repeat, the suspect has fired indiscriminately at civilians."

Behind her, the stairwell door flew open. She heard breathing. She ran into the lobby. It was full of cops.

"Hey!" she yelled.

Before the officers could turn, before Jo could raise her hands in surrender, the Desert Eagle fired with a bass-clef roar.

CHAPTER
FIFTY-SEVEN

The lobby spread out to Jo's right, gleaming and full of echoes. And full of cops. They had guns. When they heard the blast of the Desert Eagle pistol, they crouched and threw themselves against the marble walls.

Drew their weapons, aimed them at Jo, and shouted, "Freeze."

"No. *No.*"

She heard the slide rack again on the giant pistol. The white-haired woman was in the hall behind her, coming, and the cops couldn't see her.

"On the ground," the cops yelled. "Now, do it. Do it."

If she stopped, she'd die. "The shooter's in the hall behind me!" Jo screamed.

Ahead was a side door, an emergency exit. The giant pistol fired.

The cops fired. Jo crashed through the door into the sunshine and kept running.

Holy shit. The cops thought she was a bad guy. A bad guy, her, how the hell?

She ran, hearing more gunfire inside. She didn't dare look back. Look back and they'd shoot her, and this was how it happened — how undercover cops got shot by DEA agents, how Army Rangers ambushed their comrades by mistake and we brought home soldiers in caskets and called it friendly fire. She would explain later. She ran.

She heard the emergency exit blow open behind her. She didn't look back.

Gabe scanned the street. He saw too many cops. Up the block, a black-and-white was stopped sideways in the street. A uniform was waving traffic toward a detour. Vehicles and pedestrians were being ushered away from Waymire & Fong's building.

He kept his right hand on the gearshift. This was pit-of-the-stomach bad. He looked at the building. The side doors. The emergency exit.

And he saw Jo. She was running straight toward him. And she was being chased, only this time it wasn't by a news team. There were cops behind her. Were they running from the building too? It didn't make . . .

"Oh, crap."

"Gabe, unlock the doors," she yelled.

He did. She leaped in.

"Go," she yelled.

Chennault was a hundred yards up the street, behind the wheel of the armored car, when he saw the cops storm the building. There must have been shooting. And then he saw a 4Runner pull out from a side alley and accelerate toward him up Sacramento.

Black 4Runner. "I'll be damned."

It was Beckett's boyfriend, driving the SUV he'd seen on TV — the SUV whose license number he'd written down, for a time such as right damned now. He was a certified genius.

The 4Runner raced past him. The boyfriend, the National Guard prick, was driving. Beckett was in the passenger seat, more or less, fighting to close the door, turned around backward, staring at the scene behind them.

Chennault phoned 911.

"I'm on Sacramento Street near the terrorist attack." His voice quivered, panicky. "One of the terrorists jumped in an SUV and drove away — a woman with long brown hair, dressed in black. It's a Toyota FourRunner with a Hispanic guy driving. Or maybe Middle Eastern." He grinned. "Oh my God — they just hit a woman in the crosswalk. Ran her down . . . Jesus, she's just lying there. And the woman is shooting at people."

The dispatcher asked him a question. He smiled like the god he was.

"Yes, I got the license number."

He gave it to the dispatcher. Hung up and put the armored car in gear.

The 4Runner drummed through traffic, swerving around cars and delivery trucks on the one-way street. Jo knelt backward on the front passenger seat. Through the rear window Waymire & Fong's office building receded. She felt like she'd grabbed a lightning rod just before a bolt cracked from the clouds.

416

Gabe kept the pedal down. "Any time."

Back at the Waymire building cops poured into the street. Cars started and their light bars lit up.

"Get out of sight so I can phone the police," she said.

He cast a look in the mirror. The view was full of uniforms. "You seem to be missing an opportunity here."

"Head for Grace Cathedral."

"Jo."

"And give me your phone."

Grimly he slapped the phone into her hand. They barreled across an intersection. Sacramento steepened, traffic thinned, and the signs changed from English to Chinese. Jo turned and sat down.

"Vienna's law firm was attacked." Her voice began a slide toward a cliff. She clenched her teeth to keep it from tumbling off. "There's going to be an assassination attempt on the president."

Gabe hit the brakes, as hard as a wrecking ball. He spun the wheel and swerved left to the tree-lined curb.

He turned and took Jo's face in his hands. "Are you hurt?"

"No."

"What do we need to do?"

A revving engine drowned out his voice. Jo glanced in the wing mirror. An armored car loomed and filled it and kept coming.

"Gabe —"

The armored car sideswiped them, hard. It shoved the 4Runner into a row of bollards, crushing Jo's door.

The noise was horrendous. Glass shattered. Jo was flung against the dashboard.

She bounced back against the passenger seat, stunned.

Through the buckled windshield, she saw the armored car stopped in the street fifty yards ahead. Its backup lights came on, its wheels spun, and it reversed toward them.

"Out," Gabe shouted.

He grabbed her arm, threw open his door, and pulled her across the gearshift to safety. Jo jumped out as the armored car screeched into the 4Runner and sliced off the wing mirror. It braked. Beneath a helmet and dark glasses, the driver's boyish face looked mean. His left hand, encased in a blue cast, could barely grip the wheel.

At the bottom of the hill, sirens and lights filled the road. For a moment Chennault glared at Jo. Then he put the armored car in gear and floored it up Sacramento. Jo glanced back at the orchestra of police sirens.

"Run," she told Gabe.

They sprinted into the warren of streets that made up Chinatown.

Accelerating, Chennault watched Beckett and Quintana vanish down an alley. He urged the Blue Eagle Security armored car up the street.

Grace Cathedral sat on top of Nob Hill, across a park from the Fairmont Hotel. The view from its steps coasted over the Financial District, the deep waters of

418

the bay, and the distant hills of the People's Republic of Berkeley — which would soon be laid to waste. Who was going to defend Berkeley, the homeless and old hippies?

Two blocks from the cathedral, police cars barricaded the intersection. A Filipino cop approached Chennault's window.

"Street's closed."

"I'm late for a pick-up at the Wells Fargo on Fillmore."

"You'll have to find another route."

"Come on, man. Ten seconds and I'm straight across."

"Sorry. You can get through on Washington."

Chennault's nerves flared. That was exactly the information he needed. And this little dandy dog ROW cop would soon regret his arrogance.

He detoured toward Washington Street. He skirted the edges of the no-go zone, angling around the cathedral, until he found a parking spot. His chest swelled. Half a block away from Sacramento on a cross street, he had a beautiful view of the cathedral. He parked the rear end of the armored car facing the church.

In the back of the truck, he changed from the Blue Eagle uniform into a dress shirt, jacket, and tie. He tucked his broken arm back in the sling, and his invitation to the memorial service in his pocket. He was, after all, closer than family. He was Tasia's ghost.

Jo and Gabe ran down a narrow street between red brick buildings on one side, a chain-link fence and playground on the other. The concrete stung Jo's bare feet.

"Nobody knows Chennault's behind this," she said, "except me and K. T. Lewicki. And Lewicki . . ."

Her voice caught. Again she saw him and the attacker plummet to their deaths.

"Call nine-one-one," Gabe said.

"They won't believe me." She still had his phone. "Tang."

She slowed and stared at the phone, trying to remember the number. It wouldn't come. Gabe took the phone from her shaky fingers. He scrolled through his phone book. Punched a number and handed the phone back.

"Tang gave me her cell number a few months back. And I never delete a cop from my contacts."

Jo put the phone to her ear. *Pick up.* After four rings, she heard, "Tang."

"Amy, I need your help and I need it now."

She explained. She felt like a climber sliding down a rock face toward the fatal drop into a chasm. She was digging her fingers in, trying to arrest the fall.

"Where are you?" Tang said.

"Hang Ah Alley, near Sacramento." She glanced back across at the steep hillside and saw an ornate, red-tiled Chinese gate. "Near the YMCA."

"I'll find out what's going on and call you back," Tang said.

"Amy, I ran from the cops. They think I'm one of the bad guys. They drew on me. I made tracks like hell."

"I'll call them off."

"This attack isn't a surgical strike. These people think they're the vanguard of a revolution. They want to spill blood. They want major damage."

"What are you suggesting?" Tang said.

"Don't look for a highly disciplined sniper. I think Chennault is more likely to launch a brute force assault. And he won't care who gets killed, as long as it includes the president."

"I'll meet you outside the cathedral," Tang said. "I'm in Chinatown. I'll be right there."

Jo said goodbye, and kept running. They passed bright awnings, tight Chinese script, and stores where silk dresses lent an aura of glory, of past empires. They ran by elderly Chinese San Franciscans in Reeboks, chinos, and Giants sweatshirts. When they came out on Clay Street, pedestrians eyed them with more-than-idle curiosity. Jo's suit was filthy, covered with dust and teak splinters. Her hair was snarled. Her bare feet slapped the hot sidewalk. She winced against grit on the concrete.

Without warning, Gabe veered into a corner shop. "Keep going. I'll catch up."

Winded, Jo ran. Two minutes later, he caught up and shoved a cheap pair of ballet shoes into her hands. They were lime green with orange plastic daisies, ugly-ass, and brilliant. She jammed her feet into them.

"Thank you."

A police car roared over the lip of Nob Hill toward them, lights whirling. They ducked into an alley. Jo leaned back against a brick wall. The car raced past.

She tried to catch her breath. "They think I'm a killer. A president-hunting killer. And now they think you're in it with me. Jesus God." Her voice skipped. "If they take us down, they'll never believe my story in time."

"Then let's hope Tang can call off the hounds. She's the only one who can protect us."

The street was clear. They ran uphill, breathing hard.

"Jo, we're running *toward* the president. How's that going to look?"

She didn't answer. They reached the top of the hill and saw the Gothic towers and rose window of Grace Cathedral.

CHAPTER
FIFTY-EIGHT

In front of Grace Cathedral, Huntington Park was blocked off by police. Barricades were set up around the gray stone, fake-Notre Dame façade of the church. Police were checking everybody who sought to get inside the cordon. Chennault adopted a pleasant face, laced with sadness, and walked toward the entry checkpoint.

A mob had gathered, thousands of sheeple. Ahead, he saw tables set up where guests going into the church were placing their purses and coats for search. At the top of the cathedral steps, near the doors, the Secret Service was checking invitations.

Distrustful black shirts, turning the nation into a police state. His blood frothed.

He had to decide where to make his stand. He had little time. News of the attack on Waymire & Fong was bound to reach the Secret Service, and when they learned that a White House apparatchik had been there, they would yank the president out of the church behind a bristle of automatic weapons.

Reverent and eager, he pushed through the crowd toward the barricade.

★ ★ ★

Jo and Gabe emerged onto the plaza in front of the Fairmont. Behind barricades, a thick crowd had gathered around the perimeter of Huntington Park. On the far side of the park, across Taylor Street, the cathedral doors stood open. People in sober clothing climbed the stairs toward the entrance.

Jo and Gabe jogged toward the park, past the chocolate brownstone building that housed the Pacific-Union Club. Television news vans were lined up in front of it on Sproule Lane. Cameras on platforms pointed over the tops of bonsai-styled trees and playground equipment, toward the steps of the cathedral.

The skies overhead were empty. The airspace above San Francisco was closed.

She couldn't see snipers on the rooftops, but knew they were there. She was sure explosive sniffer dogs had combed the park and church earlier. But the security presence was meant to be discreet. This was not a state occasion. The president and First Lady were mourners at a private funeral.

She glanced around. Thousands of people. "How are we going to find Chennault?"

The phone rang. It was Tang. "I sent a warning up the chain of command but it'll take a couple of minutes to reach the Secret Service. I'm a block from —"

The call cut out. Jo tried to redial but could get no reception.

Her skin prickled. "Does the Secret Service screw with cell phone reception when the president's near?"

"They monitor all calls within a sixty-mile radius," Gabe said.

"But they don't shut down cell towers?"

"Not that I know of. Why?"

Her skin goose-bumped. "Right before the attack at the law firm, cell phones went out. And yours just did."

They looked at each other. Jo said, "He's here."

"Come on." Gabe grabbed her hand and pulled her through the crowd toward the barricades.

The cop appeared in front of them with the suddenness of a falling hammer. His weapon was gripped in both hands, aimed at Jo's chest.

"Freeze, right there," he said.

The checkpoint where invited guests were vetted by the cops, and let through the barricades, was set up near the cathedral steps. Chennault worked his way toward it. Getting inside the church before the service started was vital. The heavy crowd jostled his broken arm as he struggled past. He pressed the cast against his chest, protecting the sling.

The cop's hands were steady, the gun aimed solidly at Jo's center of mass. Behind his freckles, his eyes looked dead certain. Jo and Gabe raised their hands.

"On the ground, facedown. Now. Do it."

Jo and Gabe dropped immediately to the asphalt. The crowd shied back and a bubble of silence enveloped them.

"Lace your hands behind your head."

Jo did it, keeping the cop in the corner of her eye. He leaned into the radio clipped to his navy blue shirt and called for backup. His weapon never deviated from Jo's body. He was a gap-toothed redhead, a virtual Cub Scout with his finger on the trigger.

"Officer, listen to me," Jo said.

"Shut up."

Another cop jogged through the crowd. "McNamara?"

The Cub Scout looked up. "Report over the radio — gun attack on a law firm in the Financial District. These two match the description of suspects seen fleeing the scene."

The second cop, a trim Filipino, reached for his handcuffs. Then he stopped, and stared hard at Jo. "I saw you on the news this morning."

"With Edie Wilson," Jo said.

He pointed, and smiled. "You guys got her to climb in a trash can."

"That was me."

His smile expanded in Gabe's direction. "You're the Air National Guard guy."

"Yeah," Gabe said.

Full-fledged grin. "She got a monkey to ride Edie Wilson's head like a rodeo cowboy. She's a department consultant — friend of the lieutenant's. They're on our side."

McNamara waited a long second, then lowered and holstered his weapon. Jo and Gabe stood up, nerves chiming.

The Filipino cop, Dandoy, said, "What's going on?"

Jo pointed at the cathedral. "A man named Ace Chennault is planning to attack the president. He has an invitation to the memorial. Lieutenant Tang's on her way. She and I can identify him."

A buzz went through the crowd. Television cameras swiveled in unison. Through the throng Jo saw a motorcade draw up in front of the cathedral.

The bishop, attired in embroidered vestments, wearing a miter and carrying his shepherd's staff, came out the cathedral doors. From an armored vehicle, a man and woman dressed in black emerged and climbed the steps. Secret Service agents followed a step behind, looking exceptionally alert.

"Get the president out of here," Jo said.

"You got it," said the Cub Scout cop.

Jo heard her voice being called. She turned and saw Tang burrow through the crowd toward them.

"Chennault's here," Jo said. "Gabe's phone won't work. I think Chennault's got a jamming device."

Tang stretched on tiptoe, attempting to see the church over the heads of the crowd.

Gabe said, "President and First Lady are walking up the steps. They're surrounded by Secret Service. Bishop just came out the doors to greet them."

Tang snapped her fingers at McNamara and Dandoy. "White man, blond hair, blue eyes, five-nine. Beer belly. Arm in a blue cast." She nodded toward the church steps. "I'll go that way. Officer McNamara, come with me." To Dandoy, she said, "Doctor Beckett knows what he looks like. Stay with her."

"I saw him too," Gabe said.

"Let's go."

Tang flashed her badge and got inside the barricades. She, Gabe, and the Cub Scout worked their way toward the church. Jo eyed the park and packed plaza. High-rise apartments and the Mark Hopkins Hotel bordered the square. An assassin could hide in any of a hundred windows with a shot at the church steps. How was she going to spot Chennault?

McNamara's patrol car was parked nearby. She climbed onto the hood and scrambled atop its roof.

She turned three-hundred-sixty degrees. Tang, Gabe, and McNamara were walking across the park toward the cathedral, scanning the crowd. Outside the cathedral doors, President Robert McFarland and his wife, Sandy, stood speaking to the bishop. The Secret Service faced the park, silent and watchful.

Another murmur swept the throng. A black limousine pulled up in front of the cathedral. Television cameras swiveled. The limo driver opened the back door for Vienna Hicks. She climbed the cathedral steps, her duster swirling in the wind, dignified and solitary. The bishop excused himself from the president and descended the steps to greet her.

Behind the limo came the hearse. Stately, gleaming, it stopped directly in front of the cathedral. Vienna paused in the middle of the steps, with the bishop at her side.

And, from the crowd, near the checkpoint, Jo saw movement. A blue rectangle.

"Is that . . ."

It was a blue swatch of fabric, a semaphore flag in a sea of colors against the barricades near the church steps. It swam in and out of sight. Tang and McNamara walked right past it.

Was it Chennault? A gust of wind swirled around Jo. Her hair lifted from her neck. Music carried on the breeze, a melody flowing from the cathedral's pipe organ.

Chennault was blocked. Twenty feet from the checkpoint that would allow him access to the church, the crowd crammed against the barricades. He couldn't get past. Plan B was turning to dust in front of his eyes.

And on the steps of the church, he saw him. Legion. Surrounded by his goons, right there in front of him.

He reached into the sling.

The funeral director walked solemnly to the back of the hearse and opened the door.

Outside the cathedral doors stood five somber men. Jo realized that they were the pallbearers. She thought briefly of K. T. Lewicki, and her throat caught. Then she saw Vienna speak to the bishop. In the church doorway, the president had lingered to greet her. Vienna moved toward him.

Christ, was she going to ask him to be the sixth pallbearer?

Again Jo saw a flash of blue. She tented a hand over her eyes to block the sun, like Sacajawea scanning the horizon. A burst of light caught her peripheral vision.

Beyond the cathedral, beyond the crowd, sunlight reflected off a silver surface.

Parked on a side street was the Blue Eagle Security armored car.

Nearer, pressed against the barricades, the blue rectangle flashed again. And stayed visible. It was a sling on the arm of a man struggling to reach the checkpoint.

"It's him," Jo said.

"Where?" said Dandoy.

She pointed. "By the barrier. Ten feet this side of Lieutenant Tang."

The Filipino cop ducked under the barricade, face to his radio.

Jesus. Jo put her hands to her face like a megaphone. "*Tang.*"

Tang, the Cub Scout cop, and Gabe had spread out. They didn't hear her. Vienna and the bishop kept walking down the steps.

Jo heard a beep. She looked down. Gabe's phone had just activated.

Did that mean Chennault had just moved beyond the range to jam it?

No. Chennault hadn't moved. It meant something else.

The wind whispered again. The sounds of the church organ swirled over Jo. The melody was "Amazing Grace."

Chennault was staring across the plaza. Was he looking at the armored car?

He was a hundred yards away from her. She'd never get through the thick crowd to him. She'd never even get close enough to shout to Tang in time.

"*Gabe,*" she screamed.

He turned.

Behind him, against the barricade in the crowd, Chennault was staring across the plaza. But he wasn't staring at the armored car. He was staring at the hearse. The funeral director was arranging a huge floral display on top of Tasia's casket — white roses and lilies piled two feet high. It looked like a wedding dress of flowers heaped on the coffin.

Chennault had gone to the mortuary to pay Tasia his respects. Vienna had said, *Bless dumb old Ace Chennault, he spent an hour at the funeral home helping with the floral arrangements.*

"Oh my God," Jo said.

The armored car was a decoy.

Vienna was descending the steps with the bishop and five pallbearers. Ten feet behind, surrounded by Secret Service agents, came Robert McFarland.

Halfway across the park, Gabe was looking at her.

She could tell him to come back. She could wave him in this direction.

Chennault was beyond him in the crowd. Tang and Officer McNamara were beyond Chennault. Amy had missed Chennault. She was walking with the young cop toward the steps of the church. Toward the hearse.

Gabe looked at Jo. Tang was too far away to hear her. So were Vienna, the bishop and pallbearers, the Secret Service, and the president.

Jo's lips parted. She could tell Gabe, *Come back. Run this way.*

Her heart paused, pleading with her. Then she cupped her hands to her face and shouted, "Gabe — Chennault's behind you. Warn the president."

She pointed.

Gabe turned toward the church. He saw McFarland, Tang, everybody near the hearse. A Secret Service agent touched his ear. Gabe ran toward the president, shouting, "*Move*. Take cover."

Chennault reached into the sling. He pulled out a cell phone.

Gabe threw himself up the steps. Chennault pressed a number. He dropped the phone, reached into the sling again, and drew a gun.

And the bomb in the flowers exploded.

CHAPTER
FIFTY-NINE

The hearse caught the blast. It blew high into the air and flipped. The gas tank exploded. Orange fire swarmed across the view.

Standing on top of the police car, Jo felt the blast wave like a wall of pressure. The air shoved her back. Her ears popped.

Then noise came, and heat. She threw herself to the roof of the cruiser.

People screamed. They fled. The scene turned to a lather of shrieks and gunshots.

Jo rolled off the roof of the cruiser and ran in the direction of the explosion.

The Secret Service charged down the cathedral steps, weapons drawn. Television crews ran in all directions — some for cover, some filming as people careened past them for safety. Jo ran through the crowd as people poured toward her in waves, like banshees, parents hoisting children into their arms and sprinting away from the gunfire.

The heat from the fire reached her face. The hearse lay upside down on the cathedral steps, burning like a rocket.

In the distance, beyond the cathedral, sunlight flashed off the windows of two Suburbans as they roared from the scene. The president was out of there.

The first person Jo saw was Vienna. She was facedown in the street, covered in blood. Her clothes were smoking. The bishop was nearby, crawling toward her. He pulled his vestments over his head. He tried to throw the vestments over Vienna as a blanket but collapsed six feet from her.

Jo grabbed them and threw them on top of Vienna. Vienna's coat was toasted, her boots scorched, her red hair blackened. She moved her fingers.

The screams continued. People were clearing the square. Vaguely, yet sharply, Jo saw the Secret Service and SFPD converge on the spot near the barricades where Chennault had been standing. Jo saw feet splayed, legs crooked, a hand covered in blood. She didn't look at the rest. The agents approached Chennault and kicked his gun away.

Vienna moaned.

"Hold still," Jo said.

Vienna coughed. "God."

Jo's hands were trembling. Vienna rolled over and sat up. She stared weirdly at Jo, reached out, and patted Jo's arm. Jo looked. All Vienna's fingers were broken.

"Everybody okay?" Vienna said.

Carefully, Jo pulled off Vienna's smoldering coat. "Hold still."

"Fine, hon." Vienna blinked. "Holy cow."

Jo took her pulse. It was going like a runaway train, but felt strong. She was breathing well. Her eyes were clear.

"Wings . . . ," she said. "Ringing. I can't hear you."

Paramedics descended on the plaza. Of course they'd been on alert — the president had been here. Jo called to them.

Again she saw the Secret Service agents surrounding Chennault. This time she couldn't help seeing his upper body. It looked like a doll that had been filled with meat and blood and cloth, and then ripped open with a crochet hook.

A paramedic ran up to her.

"Help Ms. Hicks," she said.

The paramedic set down her equipment case and got to work. Jo looked around the plaza. Beyond Chennault's body, against the barrier, she saw Gabe. He was on his hands and knees, head down, leaning over Tang.

Jo was squeezing Vienna's shoulder. Vienna said, "What's wrong?"

Jo's vision constricted and began to gray at the edges. Tang was nearly flat on the ground, scrunched against the barricade, looking up at Gabe with horror.

Vienna saw. With her broken fingers she touched Jo's hand. "Go."

Jo held on, eyeing her injuries.

"Don't you dare sing to me," Vienna said. "I ain't about to die. Get going to your friends."

The paramedic looked up at Jo. Nodded.

Jo stumbled to her feet and ran toward Tang. Amy was hanging on to Gabe's shirt. Blood soaked her chest and neck. It wrapped her arms like long gloves.

Jo leaped over a piece of the hearse. An axle, with a burning tire attached. Tang was holding tight to Gabe's shirt. She said something inaudible to him. Her face was broken with pain.

"Amy." Jo fell to her knees at Tang's side.

Clinging to Gabe's shirt, clinging like Gabe's shirt was life itself, Tang looked at her. "Help."

Jo turned and shouted, "Medic!"

Tang grabbed her arm. Her hand was warm and wet and gripped like a vise.

"Where are you hit?" Jo said.

Tang opened her mouth and shook her head. Jo ran her hands across Tang's chest, searching for the wound.

Tang squeezed Jo's hand. "Not me."

Jo ripped Tang's shirt open. "Hold on, Amy."

Tang looked at Gabe. Jo stopped, still.

Tang was gripping Gabe's shirt, but not in pain. She was holding him up. She was pressing her palm against his chest. Jo turned to him. He was shaking. As she watched, he collapsed at Tang's side. When he fell over, Jo saw the wound. He was the one who had been shot.

CHAPTER
SIXTY

The Klaxon in Jo's head drowned out all other sounds. She waved her arms overhead at the EMTs and screamed, "*Medic!*" The Klaxon swallowed the word, she didn't hear it, but the paramedics looked up. Tang got to her knees. She pushed her hands against Gabe's ribs. She was glued to him. She wouldn't let go.

Jo kept waving. "Gunshot wound to the chest."

The EMTs grabbed their equipment case and hustled toward them through greasy black smoke and gun barrels and police lights.

Tang leaned close to Gabe's face. Her lips worked. She seemed to be trying to press her own life force into him.

Gabe watched her lips. Then his gaze slid to Jo.

Her ears cleared. She heard Tang, saying over and over, "You saved me."

Jo tried to get a look at the wound. All she could see was blood, and the rough dimensions of the exit. The noise returned to her head, a high, solid droning squeal.

Gabe blinked. He seemed to look at her from the far end of a periscope. His fingers crept across the dirty asphalt to touch her arm. Though he was flat on his back, it seemed to Jo that he was examining her from a great height.

"Saved me, Quintana," Tang said.

The EMTs rushed up. Tang was shaking but wouldn't stop reciting her mantra.

Jo touched her shoulder. "Let go."

Tang pressed her hand to Gabe's chest. "Saved me."

"Amy, let go," Jo said.

"Ma'am, let us get to work," said the EMT.

Tang looked up. She stared at her arms as if they belonged to somebody else. Finally, she lifted her hands from Gabe's chest. The EMTs cut away his shirt and began to work on him.

He seemed to unthread, as if a seam were being pulled loose. He'd been holding on, or Tang had been holding him here, until the EMTs arrived. The pain in his eyes was deep but didn't seem to surprise him. He closed his eyes.

Jo put her hands on either side of his face. "No."

He opened his eyes.

"You're here," she said. "No place else. Listen to me."

He blinked and tried to focus.

"Be here," she said. "Sophie's here. You have to stay." The high-pitched drone increased in intensity. "I'm here."

His lips moved but nothing came out. The paramedics scrambled, pulling equipment from their case. One of them called on her radio for a medevac helicopter.

Jo leaned down, pressing her hands against Gabe's face, trying by the force of her stare to keep him from closing his eyes.

"Turn away from the light, Quintana, and look at me. It's not time yet. I love you."

She never knew whether he heard her.

The bodies of the dead lay on the street and cathedral steps for hours, while the authorities took photos and forensics teams walked among them in white bodysuits, ghostly and dedicated. The news helicopters were kept at bay like circling barracudas, but low-angle camera shots captured footage clear enough to show the world Chennault's handiwork. His coda.

In the waiting area at San Francisco General Hospital, Jo watched the news coverage. Vienna Hicks was in surgery. She had shrapnel embedded in her back, plus second-degree burns, but her condition was stable.

Tang found Jo near the television and handed her a cup of coffee. "Who's with Sophie?"

"Gabe's mom and dad," Jo said.

Tang looked at the TV screen, only briefly, and turned her back on it. She hugged herself. "Gabe shouted to take cover."

"I know."

"Did you see Chennault first?"

"Yes. The sling."

"And you tried to warn us?"

Jo nodded. "You didn't hear. Gabe did."

"Secret Service heard him and grabbed McFarland. Gabe knocked me and Officer McNamara to the ground. Threw himself on top of me. And he took the round."

Jo didn't respond. What could she say?

"They found Chennault's lair. He planned this spectacle from his computer. He worked with the man and woman who attacked the law firm," Tang said. "Both of whom are dead. Officers killed the woman when she fired on them in the lobby."

Jo had a sense that the currents in the case ran to deep and powerful depths. She needed to piece together disturbing scraps of information, once she could rouse herself to focus. She needed to understand what had happened during the attack on the law firm.

She rubbed her forehead. "Howell Waymire, the head of the firm — I spoke to him in the ER after he was stabilized. He told me something that . . . bothers me."

"What?"

Jo shook her head. "Later."

Tang put up her hands, indicating *okay*. "Chennault had a number of careers. He was briefly in the army, and then an insurance agent before he became a journalist. His specialty was arson. And I don't just mean arson investigations. He was adept at setting fires himself."

"Is that how he learned about explosives?"

Jo's voice was flat. She couldn't put any inflection into it. She didn't care.

440

"I'd wager a year's salary he got the bomb from his accomplice. Keyes — guy was ex-army, ex-merc. We're investigating how, exactly, they found each other."

Tang hugged herself tighter. She looked like she was wearing her own invisible straitjacket. "Chennault was a professional political extortionist. He liked to threaten people by burning down their families' schools and workplaces. Then he'd send them a calling card — a matchbook."

"He sent the matchbooks to Tasia and Noel Michael Petty?"

"Yes."

Jo nodded. "Check CCTV from the ballpark. You'll spot Chennault outside the corporate hospitality suite. I'm sure," she said.

"You're convinced he killed Tasia?"

At the end of the hall, double doors opened. A surgeon walked out, wearing scrubs and a cap.

He looked around. "Mr. Quintana's sister?"

Jo's system cascaded into overdrive. Sparks poured down her arms like water. "Went to get coffee."

"Gabe's in recovery," the surgeon said. "He's stable. He'll be in intensive care tonight, but what we need to do is let his body rest and marshal its resources." He rubbed the back of his neck and stretched. "He's young, he's strong, and he held on right until we put him under. He has a lot of fight in him, and a lot to fight with."

The entire hospital seemed to light up. Electric, like a Disneyland parade.

The surgeon turned to Tang. "You kept pressure on the wound, I hear, even though there was gunfire and an explosion."

Tang shrugged.

"Good job. You ever want to go into emergency medicine, let me know."

"I'm squeamish," she said. "I'd rather get shot out of a cannon."

He laughed, clapped her on the shoulder, and left.

Jo saw it through a tunnel. No longer gray at the edges but throbbing with color. She tried to let out the breath she'd been holding. Couldn't.

The door hadn't blown shut. The tide hadn't taken him. Gabe was on this side of daylight.

She didn't believe that prayers worked as magic, or as a tether to keep people from sinking into the realm of the dead, so she hadn't said any prayers. But right then she leaned her forehead against the wall, felt the cool plaster, and shut her eyes.

Slam that door, she said to the universe. *Lock it, throw the key away, and keep it sealed until Sophie has grandchildren. Until Gabe knocks and says it's time.*

Tang stood in the center of the waiting area, small and isolated. Without a word, she turned and left. After a moment Jo went to find her. She rounded the corner and nearly tripped.

Tang was crouched against the wall, hands over her face. Jo held back. Tang inhaled.

Jo sat down beside her. Amy Tang, who tried to let nobody see past the briars, who wanted the world to think she was nothing but nails and tar, wouldn't look up. For her, the only thing worse than feeling pain was showing it. And letting anybody soothe her was anathema.

"I'm upset about the ATF raid on my parents," she said.

"I'm upset about the Giants losing to the Cubs," Jo said. "I don't think I can be alone right now."

Tang lowered her head. Jo leaned close to her.

"You did good, Amy. You're my hero."

For a long moment Tang held herself motionless. Then her shoulders shook. She pressed her fists to her eyes and let out a heaving sob.

"If you tell anybody, I'll tear out your tongue with needle-nosed pliers."

Jo put an arm around her shoulder. "Wouldn't have it any other way."

CHAPTER
SIXTY-ONE

The next morning, Jo walked down the hospital hallway toward Gabe's room. The corridor was hushed and bright with sunlight. As she approached the door, the SFPD's mutant twins, Bohr and Dart, came out.

Dart's hand went to his chest to smooth his tie, even though he wasn't wearing one. Bohr smiled.

It humanized him. "Doctor."

"Gentlemen."

"The department wanted to express its gratitude to Sergeant Quintana for his actions yesterday." He tipped his shaven head. "And to you."

"Thank you."

Dart said, "Have you submitted your psychological autopsy report?"

"Monday."

"I presume you'll conclude that Tasia McFarland was the victim of homicide."

"Judging from the evidence I've seen, I conclude that at the time of her death Ms. McFarland was in fear for her life, and had an overwhelming desire to preserve it. She was not suicidal. And she had legitimate reason to believe that Ace Chennault wanted her dead."

"Chennault killed her," Bohr said.

She gave him a thoughtful look. "You found him on CCTV footage from the ballpark, didn't you?"

"Wearing a hoodie and sunglasses, but we think it's him. The hallway outside the stunt team's hospitality suite is full of people, but he crosses in and out of view four times. Then the stunt coordinator runs out and tells security to go through the adjoining suite to reach Tasia on the balcony. The guards race next door and in the confusion, Chennault ducks in behind them."

"He followed them straight onto the balcony and grabbed Tasia in the chaos. He twisted the gun against her neck and squeezed the trigger," Jo said.

Bohr nodded.

"It was an opportunistic attack," she said. "Which still doesn't answer the question of whether Tasia knew the Colt forty-five was loaded."

Bohr couldn't stifle a satisfied smile. "Remember the guy who grabbed the gun when it fell into the crowd? We had another talk with him. And surprise, surprise, he changed his story," he said. "Turns out he had a drawer of cartridges at home. He'd unloaded them from the weapon before he handed it in to us. When her death proved to be part of a conspiracy to assassinate the President, keeping them as souvenirs suddenly seemed too risky to him."

"Tasia loaded the weapon to protect herself," Jo said. "And it backfired on her."

They were all quiet a moment.

"Last night a long screed by Tom Paine was posted online," Bohr said. "It had been written ahead of time and set up to post automatically. Paine says Tasia betrayed the cause, and met the fate of collaborators worldwide."

Dart said, "He claims responsibility for the attack on the memorial service. He's vague, because he couldn't count on killing the president. But he clearly intended to do so. It's a declaration of war."

"Amazing," Jo said. "Keep digging. I think you'll find that he believed he was destined to reshape the country's political landscape through violent spectacle."

"Modest guy," Dart said.

The phrase that came to Jo's mind was *paranoid narcissist with delusions of grandeur.*

"We're still going through his computer files. He had dossiers on his accomplices, Keyes and Ivory Petty. He knew that Ivory was using her sister's identity."

"So he learned what he did about Noel Michael Petty through Ivory," Jo said.

Bohr nodded. "Knew Noel was nuts, an obsessed fan of Searle Lecroix. He wrote the e-mails to her pretending to be Lecroix. We think he sent Noel travel money and concert tickets, too."

"He set her up. She was a scapegoat, just waiting in the wings," Jo said.

"Amy Tang says you're the one who discovered that Chennault used Tasia to gain access to the president."

Jo nodded. "The clues were in her music. Chennault groomed her. He wormed his way into her entourage and got her to hire him as her ghostwriter. He persuaded her to set up the secret meeting with McFarland." She paused. "Maybe you can answer this question. There's a line in 'The Liar's Lullaby' —

446

'unlock the door, he dies in shame.' Do you know what that could refer to?"

Bohr looked thoughtful. "Tasia's credit card records show that she reserved connecting rooms that night at the Reston Hyatt."

"Chennault was hiding in the second room," Jo said. "She was supposed to unlock the door so he could get in. Did she know what he intended to do?"

Dart grunted. "Not beforehand. But she must have figured it out that night. Something tipped her off that Chennault was up to no good, and she locked him out."

Jo said, "Chennault thought he could kill them both that night, lay it at Tasia's feet, and stay in the shadows."

Both men eyed her. It fit, but they all sensed that something was missing.

"But when she got cold feet, why didn't Tasia warn McFarland?" Jo glanced back and forth between Dart and Bohr. "Did Chennault have something on her?"

Bohr raised an eyebrow. *Yes.* "He secretly recorded his conversations with Tasia."

"I'm not surprised. He recorded everything," Jo said. "He recorded *me.*"

"He caught her saying, out loud, that she would take the Colt forty-five to the meeting to be sure McFarland talked to her. If McFarland held back, she was going to threaten suicide. She was going to "make him talk" for the record, and for 'closure.'"

"Closure. Right. Permanent, for both Tasia and the president."

"Chennault convinced her that if she ever breathed a word about the gun, or him being next door, she would be arrested for conspiracy and imprisoned for life — either in a federal prison or a psychiatric hospital for the criminally insane."

"And she probably would have been. Christ." Jo ran a hand through her hair. "Tasia was terrified, so she kept quiet. But she knew Chennault considered her a loose end. So she wrote songs and recorded her 'If you get this, I'm dead' message."

"Makes sense," Dart said.

"Not completely." A thread of uncertainty crept across her. "Chennault was an extremist, but he was also a pro. He intimidated people for money. It's hard to see him coming up with something like this on his own, and sacrificing his life for it."

Dart and Bohr both stayed quiet.

"Have you checked to see why Chennault might have been in Hoback, Wyoming? What's near there?" she said.

They said nothing.

"And Chennault had dossiers on right-wing extremists, including an ex-mercenary for a government contractor. He apparently sent airfare and concert tickets to Noel Petty. Where'd he get the information? And the funds?"

Neither man answered.

"He had too much official information on Keyes and Ivory. I think he'd been fed government intelligence from an inside source."

They continued to stare silently at her.

448

"Who hired him?" Jo said.

Dart again smoothed his nonexistent tie. "That question, Dr. Beckett, belongs in the realm of conspiracy theory."

Jo's smile was sour and hot. "In other words, you'll never answer it."

Dart shrugged, and shifted gears. "Edie Wilson contacted my office. She wants an interview."

Jo blinked. "With me?" She giggled. Covered her mouth with the back of her hand. Snorted. "No." She burst into laughter and couldn't stop, until the nurses at the desk shushed her and she had to wipe her eyes with the heels of her palms. "Thanks. I haven't felt so good all week."

Bohr extended his hand. "We'll let you know if we find anything else."

They walked away, looking like men who'd plugged the hole in a dike.

Jo called after Bohr. "And good luck with that IRS audit."

He shot her a wary look over his shoulder.

CHAPTER
SIXTY-TWO

Jo watched Bohr and Dart turn the corner. When she was sure they were gone, she opened the door.

"No way. You may not play Halo Three."

Gabe was on the phone, his voice a rasp. To her utter surprise he was sitting on the edge of the bed, pale, with ash-gray smudges under his eyes. He was wearing jeans, half-zipped, a swath of white gauze around his chest, an IV line, and nothing else.

"Because I say so, cricket," he wheezed.

He looked exhausted, and Jo guessed it wasn't simply from having had a bullet tear through him, but from putting his jeans on. His old scars were visible near his hip. Cuts and stitches stippled his right side up into his hairline; more spots for the leopard.

"Aunt Regina's going to bring you over after lunch. I'll see you then, *mija*." He smiled, weakly but warmly, and said goodbye.

Jo crossed her arms. "What are you doing out of bed?"

"I couldn't get dressed lying down. And no way am I walking into Dave Rabin's room with my ass catching a breeze in a hospital gown."

With a finger, Jo gestured for him to stand up. He did, barely. Pain striped his face, but he swallowed it.

He wouldn't be able to take two steps on his own. And he'd never admit it.

But she didn't call him on it, not then. "Hold your breath." She took hold of the zipper. "This is going to hurt."

He didn't inhale, which would have been excruciating. Jo caught his eye, silently asking, *You sure?*

He put his hands on her shoulders. She pulled the zipper up.

Under his breath, he said, "*Dios.*"

Jo touched his chest. Could they get anywhere with their eyes closed and histories buried, or were they headed for a cliff?

Gingerly, he sat back down. "Bohr and Dart seemed genuinely pleased that I'm alive."

"They should be. You took a bullet for the president. Probably saved their jobs."

He looked pensive. "Do you think we know the whole story?"

"No, I don't. The official story is not the whole story, and all kinds of people will be happy if it stays that way."

"You going to let it lay?"

"Possibly," she said. "But not yet."

He eyed her for a long moment. She took his hand.

"I've been told you're like crack and I'm an addict," she said.

"I think of myself more as eye candy."

"That I seek out dangerous situations and throw myself into them."

"And I jumped this time without a chute?" he said.

She shook her head. *Spin the barrel. Pull the trigger, one more time.* She had urged him to risk his life. How lucky had they been?

"You're redeemed, Gabe. You don't have to put yourself in hock for me."

"Johanna Renee." He said it softly. "I may be a slow learner, but I get there in the end. And I do what I want. You don't push me."

"I —" Her voice cracked.

"I'm sorry I worried you." He cleared his throat, but his voice remained a rasp. "The look on your face, when you got to me outside the cathedral, it was . . . it told me there were depths of loss I had never touched." Sorrow crossed his face like a breaking wave. "I'd seen it once before. I saw it on your face the day Daniel died."

Jo went cold. She tried to speak. Gabe put a finger to her lips.

"You don't always have to say something."

"It's what I do. I talk to people for a living."

"No, you listen to them. So listen to me." He leaned close and whispered in her ear. "We're going to be okay."

She held him, her heart beating with fear and love, and prayed, *please*.

CHAPTER
SIXTY-THREE

The sun hung gold in the western sky when Jo heard music float on the air outside her house. She was cross-legged on the sofa holding a plate heaped with tempura and sashimi from the sushi bar down the hill. *The Sopranos* was cued up on the TV. Tina was on her way over with popcorn and a five-pound box of Ghirardelli chocolate.

She pushed *Play*, but again heard a melody thread the air. It sounded ancient and Asian. She carried her plate to the bay window. And she froze, chopsticks halfway to her mouth. In the park, a portable stereo was playing traditional Japanese Shakuhachi bamboo flute music. Ferd, dressed in basketball shorts and a headband, was practicing — kickboxing? The hustle? — against Ahnuld the robot. He spun, saw her, and erupted in a grin.

"Hi, partner!" He gave her two vigorous thumbs up.

"Oh dear God."

She was still standing there, horrified, when two black Suburbans pulled up at the curb. The knock on her door a moment later was sharp and imperative.

When she answered it, the man in the dark suit stared as though seeing through her with an X-ray scanner. His black jacket fit well, but didn't disguise the holster beneath his left arm. The earpiece and sunglasses completed the look.

"Doctor Beckett?" he said.

His companion stood three feet behind him so she had his back and a clear view of the street. She was the same model, decked out in smaller sizes.

"Can I help you?" Jo said.

Inside, music pulsed from the television. *Woke up this morning, got yourself a gun . . .*

"Could you come with us?"

"What's going on?" Jo said.

The woman suspended her surveillance of the street and looked Jo up and down. "You'll probably want to change out of sweatpants."

Jo held on to the doorknob.

"Maybe brush your hair," the woman said.

"You can wait out here, or you can watch *The Sopranos* while I change."

"Season Six?" the woman said.

Forty-five minutes later, the Suburbans swung off the Bayshore Freeway near San Francisco International Airport. Through smoked glass, Jo watched the road race by. A gate rolled open, granting them access to a remote operations area of the airport.

Jo held her phone to her ear. "Thanks, Vienna."

She said goodbye and put the phone away. What Vienna had just told her finally clarified things. It focused all the bizarre and disturbing moments of the past few days into a coherent picture, even as it burned

454

Jo's nerves like lye. She inhaled, her mind racing, and pondered what to do.

The Suburbans rushed past parked corporate jets and coast guard aircraft and JAL cargo 747s, toward the bay. Parked on the tarmac beyond the runways was Air Force One.

They parked at the foot of the stairs outside the 747. Mr. Special Agent Dark Suit opened Jo's door. She got out and smoothed down her skirt.

"You look fine," said Ms. Special Agent Dark Suit.

Jo climbed the stairs between the agents. A salt breeze blew off the bay. In the cockpit two pilots were going over checklists.

She stepped through the jet's forward door. The dark suits led her through the aircraft, past uniformed airmen and women, past wonkish types slouched in first-class seats, sleeves rolled up, reading fivethirtyeight.com. The carpet was plush. They stopped outside a door, and knocked.

"Come."

Mr. Dark Suit opened the door. "Doctor Beckett, sir."

The agent stepped aside and let Jo enter. He closed the door and left her standing on even plusher carpet that bore the presidential seal.

Robert McFarland stood up from behind a desk and came around with his hand out. "Doctor Beckett. A pleasure."

Jo shook his hand as if in a trance, taking in his cassock-black hair, his runner's ease, and his cool, cowboy stare. "Mr. President."

"Thanks for coming."

"Of course." *Because I missed you at the cathedral yesterday*, she nearly blurted.

He gestured to a sofa and chairs. "Please."

She sat down. He walked to a sideboard where liquors glittered inside crystal decanters. "Drink? The Secret Service is your designated driver tonight."

He was taller than she'd imagined, and slighter. And far more intense. He radiated . . . mastery. If Air Force One ran out of fuel over South Dakota, she thought, it would continue flying to Washington under the power of McFarland's self-confidence and energy. He poured himself a Jameson, and glanced at her.

"Scotch," she said.

He poured her a finger of Glenmorangie. Brought the glass.

"Thanks," she said. "*Sláinte*."

He raised his glass, and sat down across from her. "Thank you for what you did yesterday. That comes from me, personally, on behalf of myself and my wife."

"You're welcome."

"I owe my thanks to Sergeant Quintana as well, and to Lieutenant Tang. Their bravery was exemplary."

"It certainly was."

His eyes flashed. She hadn't meant for her voice to carry undertones. She was trying not to shake, or go crazy klepto and steal an ashtray. He stared at her. She thought she'd never felt such a deliberative, concentrated gaze.

"I want to talk about Tasia. In confidence," he said.

"Of course, Mr. President."

Please tell me about Tasia, and more, she thought. Would he say it, or would she have to ask? "Why did she come to see you in Virginia?"

"I think you know."

"Ace Chennault sent her."

"Yes."

"She was off baseline," Jo said. "Manic and poorly medicated."

"That was painfully obvious." He leaned on his knees and examined his Waterford tumbler. "We married too young, but I loved her. She was a meteor. Neither of us knew about bipolar disorder. I don't need to tell you that those years were a particular kind of hell for both of us. Her mood disturbances, my deployments . . . and we wanted to start a family. She miscarried five times." He looked at her. "It was crushing."

Jo nodded.

"She became suicidal. An army physician put her on antidepressants. MAOIs."

Monoamine oxidase inhibitors. They could cause birth defects.

"And then she got pregnant again. Not planned. We were scared. We both knew that in her state she couldn't possibly handle having a child." His gaze held hers. "You understand?"

"I do."

"She terminated the pregnancy."

Jo said nothing. McFarland assessed her.

"I've always been pro-choice. Never run as anything but. However, Tasia begged me never to reveal the truth

457

to the world. And I told her I never would. I mean to keep that promise."

"Tasia's medical records have been removed from military files," Jo said.

"Making those records public would serve no purpose. And they'd kindle a political free-for-all."

No shit. "Undoubtedly."

"I'm keeping my promise to Tasia."

"I see."

His eyes flashed. He did hear her undertone. *How fortunate that your political aspirations align with keeping Tasia's abortion secret. How lucky you're in a position to make military records disappear.*

She turned her glass. The crystal refracted the light. "Did Tasia persuade you to meet with her in Virginia by saying she wanted to talk about her autobiography?"

Jo gauged his face. It had turned hard, and crafty. "She told you she was going to spill everything, didn't she? You met with her to find out if she was going to reveal the truth about the pregnancy. You wanted to talk her out of it."

"That's a good-percentage guess."

"Chennault wanted access to you. Tasia needed a compelling reason to persuade you to meet secretly with her. It's the logical conclusion."

He leaned back. His eyes never left her.

"On the way over here, I talked to Vienna," Jo said.

McFarland took a breath. He seemed to take half the oxygen in the cabin. And that reaction corroborated everything Vienna had told her on the phone, and explained the things she had seen during the attack on

458

the law firm, and had heard from Searle Lecroix, Ace Chennault, Howell Waymire, and K. T. Lewicki.

She leaped into it, all the way.

"Lewicki was in love with Tasia," she said.

McFarland didn't move.

"He was your best man, but Vienna told me the two of them got stinking drunk at your wedding reception. He was drowning his sorrows," she said.

McFarland hadn't let out the breath.

"At Vienna's office, before the attack, Lewicki said something strange. He said Tasia played games. 'Love, life, war, it didn't matter.' He was angry and passionate. He said she played people against each other like they were toys in her playhouse of mania."

McFarland looked like he was going to crush his tumbler.

"I didn't understand the remark, or his vehemence. And I didn't understand how Vienna shut him up with a crack about his wedding toast. But she just told me what Lewicki said to you that day. 'I guess you win.'"

He let silence roll for a moment. "That was Kel."

Jo shook her head. "It's a hell of a toast."

She took a photo from her purse: McFarland and Lewicki in army fatigues, hoisting Tasia between them on their shoulders.

"He loved her from the start and he never quit, even after you married. She got under Lewicki's skin and he could never shake it."

McFarland stared at the photo. Though he had taken only two sips of his Jameson, he got up for a refill. His reaction substantiated Jo's suspicions. Her qualms faded. She braced herself.

"And it wasn't an unrequited love, was it?" she said.

"What's your point?"

"Vienna told me that when Tasia was manic, she jumped into bed with every man in arm's reach. She also said that Lewicki had a soft spot for Tasia, and understood her mental health issues before you did. Vienna was also alarmed when Chennault said Tasia's autobiography would feature 'explosive' revelations about your marriage."

McFarland poured himself a measure of whiskey and began to pace.

"Searle Lecroix told me that Tasia identified with Jackie Kennedy's lost babies. More than that, mentioning pregnancy made Tasia angry," Jo said.

"Yes. Miscarriage and abortion can have that effect."

"Lecroix also said Tasia would never be satisfied with a mere entertainer when she'd had more powerful men in love with her. Men, plural."

He paused. "Kel was my friend."

"And rival," Jo said. "He lost Tasia as well as his own hope for political supremacy. It motivated him to ruin you, and eventually to want to kill you."

McFarland turned and stared at her.

"The press called him the Guard Dog, but he felt like a lap dog. He thought he deserved the presidency himself. He decided to get rid of you and position himself as your successor."

She held tight to her glass. "Lewicki hired Chennault to get rid of you. And he told him to use Tasia as his scapegoat. If it looked like murder-suicide, and that crazy Tasia was the killer, there would be no hint that it was a political assassination; no congressional hearings, no special prosecutors looking into it. Just a sordid mess."

His gaze nearly knocked her over. He was daring her to back up her accusation.

"Chennault had partners — a former mercenary and a white supremacist. He had extensive dossiers on both of them. He got the information from a government source."

"You have to do better than that."

"In the first moments of the attack on the law firm, Lewicki did things that seemed strange, but I had no time to stop and examine them. The receptionist described Ivory as having hair 'as white as soap.' It was a distinctive feature — I mean wild. Lewicki seemed shocked. But now I think he wasn't surprised by the description — he was shocked because he knew who she was."

McFarland sipped his whiskey, eyeing her as he drank.

"Then, twice — not once, but twice — when I was on rappel, Lewicki did things that might have killed me. First, he let go of the cable. It nearly knocked me loose. He leaned out the window and believe me, his shock at seeing me was huge. He even said, 'I thought you fell.' Second, he sent Dana Jean out the window even though I'd yelled more than once that I wasn't ready, that it was dangerous."

"Panic."

"That's what I thought, until I spoke to Howell Waymire." Jo took a breath. "When I saw him in the ER, he took my hand and said, 'I just wanted to see with my own eyes that you're alive.' I said I was lucky. He said, 'No, that bastard dropped you.'"

Jo leaned forward. "Lewicki tried to kill me. I was the only person who knew about Chennault and the plan to assassinate you. He let me go out the window first, to see if the cable would hold. Then he tried to force me to fall." She paused. "When he saw I'd made it to safety, he looked . . . irate. And a second later, he realized that he needed me to pull him inside the window. But it was too late. He and Keyes fell."

McFarland sat down. He stared at his hands. When he looked up, he seemed unconvinced.

Jo said, "Have you ever been to Hoback, Wyoming?"

He went as still as a sniper.

"Chennault sent both Tasia and Noel Michael Petty matchbooks from a truck stop in Hoback."

He waited a long moment. "Kel had a lodge in the mountains not far from there."

Jo let the silence settle. When she spoke again, McFarland didn't interrupt or contradict her.

"Lewicki wanted to destroy you. And he hated Tasia because she left him for you." She leaned forward. "And Lewicki's involvement explains why the government tried to suppress the investigation into Tasia's death by intimidating those of us looking into it. He was behind that."

McFarland sat unmoving in the hushed light. "What else did Vienna tell you?"

Jo paused. She downed the rest of her scotch for courage. "Tasia became pregnant while you were deployed overseas. The baby couldn't have been yours." Outside, a jet took off.

"The child was Lewicki's," she said.

In the cabin, the suffocating silence was an admission, without doubt the only one she was going to get.

"That was why you hid Tasia's medical records," she said.

He must have wondered who Tasia had cheated with, and dreaded the possibility that she was about to reveal it in her autobiography. Jo recalled Vienna saying, *She broke his heart.*

"Lewicki's animus wasn't just political. It was deeply personal," she said.

It was the deepest possible animosity. McFarland had persuaded Tasia to abort Lewicki's child.

Jo needed more scotch. She needed the entire bottle.

McFarland sat silent for a full minute. Then he set down his glass.

"I'll lie through my teeth and deny this conversation ever took place. Don't doubt that."

"I believe you." She quieted. "I won't put any of this in my report."

Then, rising to the occasion, rising beyond anything Jo could have predicted, he said, "But thank you for digging so hard to understand Tasia's death. She deserved that."

"I appreciate your saying so, Mr. President."

He looked at her, long, slow, carefully. "Rough week. Anything else I can do before you head home?"

"Actually, now that I'm getting a chance to see Air Force One, I have a question about military procedure."

He spread his hands expansively. "I was in the army. Ask away."

She opened her purse and took out a copy of Gabe's military orders.

She handed them to McFarland. He leaned back. Slowly, his face neutral, the president read through them. The cabin was silent.

"Does Quintana know his orders might have been changed because of political —"

"No. And he doesn't know I'm showing them to you. He would never request deferment or redeployment." Her voice caught. "And I'm not requesting it. He's ready to go."

She steadied herself. "But I wanted you to know."

He looked Jo straight in the eye. "I'm going to check this out."

He stood up. Jo did too. They shook hands.

There was a knock on the door. An aide stuck her head in. "We're ready for the broadcast, Mr. President."

The dark suits were waiting for Jo by the open door of the jet. Behind her, television sets broadcast McFarland's voice as he addressed the nation.

"My fellow Americans, tonight I want to speak about the courage of those people who yesterday, in the face of grave danger, saved my life. Sergeant Gabriel

Quintana of the California Air National Guard, Lieutenant Amy Tang of the San Francisco Police Department, Officer Declan McNamara of the SFPD . . ."

Jo wondered what would happen next — Congressional hearings? A commission to investigate the assassination plot? Would Lewicki's role be explained as a quest for power?

She paused at the door of the jet.

". . . and especially my lifelong friend, K. T. Lewicki, who gave his own life not only to rescue others from the siege at Waymire and Fong, but to protect and defend the office of the president. There is no greater act of public service than to sacrifice oneself for his country."

The wind buffeted Jo through the open door. She gazed across the tarmac. The evening sun shone gold in her eyes, failing and constant. She put on her sunglasses and turned to the Secret Service.

"Let's get out of here."

Acknowledgments

For their superb advice and tireless support, my thanks go to my editors, Ben Sevier at Dutton and Patrick Janson-Smith at Blue Door; my literary agents, Sheila Crowley and Deborah Schneider; and a host of others who have helped make this novel the best it could be: Paul Shreve, Sara Gardiner, M.D., John Plombon, Ph.D., Lloyd Wood, Mary Albanese, Suzanne Davidovac, Adrienne Dines, Kelly Gerrard, Susan Graunke, and Kathy Montgomery.